The Traveler's Magic

The Traveler's Magic

BOOK 2 OF BEADS OF BONE

C.J. Hosack

Space Wizard Science Fantasy
Raleigh, NC
www.spacewizardsciencefantasy.com

Publisher's Note: This is a work of fiction. Names, characters, places, and incidents are a product of the author's imagination. Locales and public names are sometimes used for atmospheric purposes. Any resemblance to actual people, living or dead, or to businesses, companies, events, institutions, or locales is completely coincidental.

Cover art by Katie Cordy
Editing by Courtney Brooks
Book Layout © 2015 BookDesignTemplates.com
"Gesta Praediana" by Lehonti A. Pérez Ovalle
Luc's Poem by Praedo's Scribe by Emily Gearheart Lim

The Traveler's Magic/C.J. Hosack.— 1st ed.
ISBN 978-1-960247-37-7

Author's website: https://cjhosack.com/

For Noreen and John
Thank you for making me your pumpkin and your
princess.

CONTENTS

Chapter One

Dearest Ryette,

Everything is fine here in the Library. Ryn seems to be settling into her job as researcher nicely. I have to warn you she's found an orphanage book in the Restoration department. I don't think she's discovered anything else. I will keep my eye on the situation. Have you found Jett yet? It's been a couple moons and I could use you here. Jaris and the rest of the Board of Regents are up to something. They've been holding secret meetings and shutting me out. I could really use your support. Please come home as soon as possible.

Clayr, Madame Curator of the Library

PS—please tell Lar Zo has been doing a fine job, even if he does still try to skirt authority. Sometimes I worry about the trouble that boy tends to find.

The Library felt chillier and darker than normal, even though Ryn knew Zo worked hard to keep the temperature even. Something about the change of seasons made it feel cold, or maybe it was the pile of books on the table in front of her.

Ryn closed the cover on the orphanage record in front of her, her fingers caressing the soft leather. Another dead end.

She had searched every orphanage book she could find in the Library. None of them matched her mystery book she found in the Repairs and Restorations Department almost exactly a moon ago. The one ledger that so clearly showed her being left on the steps by a whitehaired young man. The book her father showed her in a dream. A dream she couldn't believe had some grounding in reality.

A cold draft wrapped around her feet and drifted up to make the lantern on her table flicker. Alone in her dark corner, she shivered. All these books around her and she couldn't find one drop of evidence about where she came from. She knew she couldn't ask her mother. Considering all the stories her mother told, about how she feared someone would take Ryn away from her, Ryn knew her mother wouldn't approve of her search. The last thing Ryn wanted was to hurt her mother, but now Ryn had begun to search for her birth parents, it taunted her—pulled at her need to know. Ryn had no magic, but she had the ability to find information in the Library. Except, the Library seemed to be thwarting her efforts on the topic of her ancestry.

A sharp snap of static on her shoulder made her jump.

"So sorry!" A docent stood over Ryn, one hand quickly withdrawing to her mouth in surprise.

Ryn covered her heart to calm it. "No worries, it's blustery out there today, small shocks are to be expected."

The docent gently laid her hand on the books. Ryn's hiding place today was a dark corner of the reference section. She wasn't supposed to be searching orphanage books, she was supposed to be cataloging. Her manager Sandy wouldn't approve. Of course, Sandy didn't approve of anything Ryn did.

"Do you want me to reshelve these for you?" The docent asked.

Ryn couldn't quite remember the docent's name. There were so many Library workers and Ryn was barely getting to know them.

"No, that's alright. I'll reshelve them." Ryn's gaze shifted back to the stack of leather-bound books.

The docent put a warm hand on Ryn's shoulder, no shock this time, and gave her a friendly smile. She moved on, her blue dress and white pinafore almost glowing in the gloom. Ryn gave her retreating back a sad smile. It was nice to know someone had stopped to help. If only helping her was that simple.

She stood and piled all the books into a neat stack. They were all another failure. She was ready to admit defeat. No matter how many books she pulled, none of them had the same binding, nor did they have a similar paleography. It was like her book came from nowhere. Just like her.

She lifted all of them and found her way toward where she'd pulled the first book. At least she had the Library to research where she came from, there were still thousands of more sources to look through. As long as she had access to the Library there was still hope. She glanced at the directions she had in her hand, then counted shelves and books to the correct shelf mark. She reached up on tip toe to place it back on the shelf, using the covers to wiggle the book back into its spot.

A blood curdling scream reverberated down the aisle and echoed off the ceiling in the silence of the Library.

The book slipped from her hand, banging her head, and knocking the other books from her arms to crash to the floor. People ran past the end of the row of shelves. Library guards Fergus and Norm flashed by running upstream against the tide of docents and researchers. Ryn started after them.

She sprinted down the aisle, almost colliding with a researcher, then dodged more docents till she skidded to a stop in the Grand Foyer.

More Library guards were scattered throughout the hall holding brooms and buckets. One of them, Ed, was fanning a researcher who looked like she had passed out.

Ryn caught up to Fergus, the youngest of the Library guards. Only a couple years older than Ryn, he was the most approachable.

"What happened?" she asked.

Fergus grimaced down at her. "Someone screamed 'mouse'," he said.

"Just a mouse? That's ridiculous," Ryn replied. "Everyone looks like they've lost their..."

Through the archway into the foyer Ryn saw the front door open. Regg, her stepbrother to be, walked through the door, his hairs standing on end as he crossed the magic barrier that kept pests out of the Library.

Pests.

Library.

Magic barrier.

A mouse!

How was there a mouse in the Library?

Then she saw it, a small tuft of fur almost blending into the mosaic representation of the island of Viatoro.

Ryn's jaw started working without sound.

"How?" she finally croaked out the question.

Fergus didn't answer as he joined the rest of the guards fanning out to surround the mouse.

Yll, her best friend since she was two, slid to a stop behind Ryn. "What..." she stared.

The mouse made a dash for it, coming straight at them and the Library proper. Yll let out a squeak. Errol, the captain of the Library guard, used a broom to knock it tumbling back across the foyer. It slid to a stop, then was off again toward the registration desk. One of the docent girls behind the desk screamed and jumped up to sit on the desk, tucking up her feet.

A guard with a bucket rushed the mouse, diving to pounce on it before it could get away from him, but he missed and the bucket rolled away.

The mouse did an about face and ran toward the front doors.

Regg scooped up the rolling bucket, flipped it over and slammed it down right on top of the mouse.

The girls behind the registration desk started clapping.

Regg put one foot on the bucket and gave a bow.

Norm pushed his way into the foyer, took a folder from the registration desk, and crossed to Regg.

"Yeah, yeah, yeah," he said, moving Regg off so he could shove the folder underneath the bucket. Flipping the bucket over with the mouse trapped inside, he was ushered quickly out the front doors.

Yll rushed to Regg's arms, squealing about him being a hero and planting a kiss on his lips.

"My office! Now!" Madame Curator's voice boomed through the foyer.

Ryn startled, she hadn't seen Clayr approach.

"Ed, fetch Nix for me," Clayr said. "Errol, Fergus, come with me." She seemed to suddenly notice her daughter there.

"Yll, bring Regg." She turned and almost bumped into Ryn. "And Ryn-everyone who saw what happened, report to my office."

Ryn stood, still staring at the spot in the mosaic where the mouse had been captured. She couldn't quite process it. She thought about the books she'd left scattered in the middle of the aisle and knew she would get into trouble for leaving books that way, but she turned and followed Fergus back into the dark, toward Clayr's office.

Fergus shut the office door behind them as Clayr paced behind her desk, fingertips on her lips. Ryn couldn't bring herself to sit in the chairs facing Clayr's desk. She flashed back to that day when she had stolen Luc's journal for Master Wes and had almost gotten herself banned from the Library. The memory of being in trouble with Clayr and the Library was still too fresh, so she leaned against the windowsill, watching as Norm crossed the yard to bring the bucket into the guardhouse.

"Why didn't they just kill the mouse?" Ryn asked.

"They have to check to see if it's a shapeshifter before they dispatch it," Fergus answered.

Ryn stiffened. "But you can't do magic in the Library."

Silence reigned in the office except the click, click, click of Clayr's shoes on the stone floors.

The door opened.

"Oh thank goodness, Nix," Clayr started, turning from the window, and froze.

Nix, the Master of the Boiler Room, didn't enter. Instead, Zo, Regg's brother and Ryn's other stepbrother to be, walked in the door. He took in all tense faces, then strolled over and sat in one of the empty chairs.

"Don't look so excited to see me," he said.

"Where's Master Nix?" Clayr asked.

"He got called away, and put me in charge." Zo smiled his big toothy grin.

"There's no way he put an apprentice in charge of the Library regulatory systems. Hal's next in command. Where's Hal?" Clayr started.

Zo shrugged. "Hal's not back from his cousin's wedding, I'm all you've got."

Clayr's face got all puffy and red like she was about to have a tirade, but she cut it off with a frustrated squeak. She closed her eyes and took a deep breath.

Zo pounded his knuckles against his leg.

Clayr opened her eyes. "Fine. I've gathered you all here because I need to know what happened and we need to do damage control." She turned. "Errol, report."

"Just before lunch bell as everyone was crowding the halls, a researcher screamed in the foyer and fainted. Ed rushed to her side." Errol turned to Ed who had entered the room after Zo.

Ed shifted from one foot to another. "I was standing guard at the front door, when I heard Maybel scream and I saw her go down. I was halfway across the floor when I saw the thing scurry out from under the Registration desk. At first I was frustrated with Maybel, since there's plenty of mice in the carriage house, then it hit me where we were. I immediately raised the alarm."

"Fergus, Yll, Ryn, what did you see?"

"We got there while the mouse chase was on," Fergus said.

Yll looked at Regg with those doe eyes she had for him these days. "Regg came in to pick me up for lunch and he saved the day by catching the mouse."

Zo rolled his eyes at his brother's admirer.

Ryn's mind flipped back to that moment Regg walked in the door. "Madame Curator, Regg's hair stood on end as it should when he passed through the protective barrier. If the barrier is working then..."

"Where did the mouse come from, and where has it been? For all we know it's been here long enough to make a nest. The Library needs to be sealed immediately. I need an all-hands meeting in the Meeting Hall at the end of lunch bell to contain the spread of rumors. Not a word of this leaves Library grounds." Clayr put her hands on her desk and leaned forward.

Ed nodded and left.

"Mother," Yll started, "how did a mouse get in? I thought the magic repelled pests from the portal."

"It does," Errol grunted.

Clayr fixed her eyes on Zo. He cracked his knuckles against his thigh.

"That's why I summoned Nix, but I believe you've also met the Protector of the Library?"

Zo glanced over at Ryn. "Briefly, once."

Ryn was confused. Why was he looking at her? Then a cold shiver ran up her spine as she remembered running through the tunnels beneath the Library, away from something dark, cold and menacing chasing them.

"I need Nix to contact the Protector, not his subordinates. It will know what's wrong," Clayr said, rubbing her hands up and down her arms.

It did seem like the temperature had dropped.

Zo nodded slowly.

"What's wrong, Mama?" Yll went to her mother's side.

Clayr stood silent.

"The only way a pest could get into the Library is..." Regg started.

"If the magic is failing," Zo finished.

Clayr's eyes raised from her desk to Zo. "We can't know that for sure. That's why we need to communicate with the Protector." Clayr's gaze shifted to Ryn and Regg. "The rest of you, I need you to keep what you saw today quiet. I don't want panic to spread. We'll have half of Waatch on our doorstep demanding answers I don't have. I need you to be my ears. Listen to the other workers, and report to me anything that sounds suspicious, or like they might know how this happened. At this point I'm open to any possibility as to how the Library's barrier was penetrated, and everyone is a potential suspect."

Ryn's eyes darted to each person in the room. She couldn't imagine anyone in the room being responsible for the breach. Her eyes found Fergus. He was leaning against the door, arms folded. His eyes met hers in a penetrating gaze. She knew in that moment that even she was under suspicion.

"Yet I have to trust someone," Clayr continued. "So I am trusting you all. Keep your eyes and ears open and report to me personally anything you hear. Dismissed."

Zo stood and stretched. Ryn made a beeline to his side.

"Do you think something is wrong with the Library?" Ryn asked in a hushed whisper. "How could anyone tell if it was?" She looked up into his closed expression as they passed through the doorway and out into the hall. "Can a Healer heal a building?" It was a weird thought that just popped into her head.

"Nah, buildings aren't alive," he said.

"But the Library is," Ryn whispered to herself.

Her gaze drifted up to where the bookshelves met the ceiling. Zo's long strides took him quickly away.

"Frater," she called to him in the language of the Ancestors.

Zo paused and turned back to her. "Parva soror." They were both learning the Ancestor language, and had taken to using the words for brother and sister, like a code between themselves.

She swallowed hard. "You're not going to seek out that monster under the Library are you? We barely escaped it." She shuddered. "I can still feel the cold reaching for me."

Zo shrugged. "Truth is Nix and Wilmar have gone for a bit. I'm balancing the Boiler Room and the physician's office while they are gone."

Ryn knew Zo was currently the only Library temperature monitor. There were supposed to be two people, but Master Nix was struggling to get anyone else to stay in the position. Everyone else who tried it ended up begging Master Nix to put them on the midnight boiler heater shift, anything to get out of crawling around the underbelly of the Library. Zo just rolled his eyes at them.

"You should wait for Master Nix," Ryn said.

"Naw, I'll be fine. Let me know if anything else happens." And with that he turned and disappeared into the gloom of the Library.

Chapter Two

Master Paxon Headmaster of Waatch Healing House,

I have received your letter about Zo of Ingis, son of Fyri de Sano. Although I agree the boy is talented and should study his Healing magic, it's not for the reasons you would wish. I would like to see him become the first Waatch physician who can Heal as well. I know that is against your archaic Ancestor sentiments, but as magic is free to you, so should Healing be free to those you serve. Regardless, Zo has deep wounds regarding his Healing magic that will take time to heal. I suggest you let the boy come to you when he's ready. Pushing him will yield bad results.

Wilmar, physician for Waatch

As Zo's feet crunched on the gravel walkway to the Boiler Room, the bell tower began to peal the signal for the all-hands meeting. With an exasperated sigh, he spun on his heel and headed for the meeting hall. He should have known Clayr wouldn't wait until after lunch hour to call the meeting, nor did she give him time to try and find the Library Protector. He would just have to go to the meeting without any new information for Clayr. That was on her. It also meant he wouldn't have time to find the Protector during daylight. Zo was already due at the physician's office to see patients. With Wilmar and Nix away, he was juggling both jobs, and both were suffering. If this meeting took too much time, the line outside Wilmar's office would get long. Zo tried to take a deep breath, but just ended up expelling the air in frustration.

Inside the meeting hall, he spied a bright spot leaning against a windowsill. He quickly bent his course in that direction.

"Well, there's a face I didn't expect to see," Iden greeted him.

Zo raised an eyebrow. "It's an all-hands meeting."

"Yes, but you always avoid me at these things." Iden had a teasing smile on his lips, but his gaze was penetrating.

"Maybe you're a welcome sight today." Zo stood a respectable distance from Iden, but his body yearned to be closer. Just being in his smiling presence was uplifting.

"So what happened?" Iden asked. "I've heard all kinds of salacious rumors."

"What makes you think I know? I work in the Boiler Room," Zo said.

Iden put his hand on Zo's shoulder. Zo stiffened as his stomach twisted. He resisted the urge to look around the room to see who might be watching them. It was a perfectly normal gesture, but Zo couldn't stop his concern that someone might find out they were dating. On the streets of Waatch, no one cared. Here at the Library, in Ancestor territory, it was dangerous.

Iden gave his shoulder a gentle shake. It was his way of telling Zo to relax.

"Come now, the rumors say you were summoned to Madame Curator's office." He gave Zo his most mischievous smile as he whispered, "I know you know."

Just then the side door opened, and a hush fell over the hall as Clayr and two Library Regents entered. Clayr mounted the stage, with Jeris. He was that utterly loathsome Regent, the father of Prym—Iden's ex and tormentor of Ryn. Prym delighted in bullying Ryn, and Jeris was no better. Zo bristled at the sight of him, and Iden's hand fell away. Clayr took position behind the podium. The crowd became silent enough to hear a pin drop.

"Good afternoon. I have called this all-hands meeting, because just before lunch bell this morning we had an incident in the Library."

"It was a breach, Clayr, call it what it is," Regent Jeris said from behind her.

Clayr squeezed her eyes shut, visibly took a deep breath, then opened her eyes, fixing her gaze on everyone in attendance.

"As of this time, the circumstances surrounding the incident are still under investigation. I would appreciate everyone keeping speculation to a minimum." She glanced back at Jeris. The message to him was clear. "Because we don't have any solid information as to the cause, I must ask every one of you to report to your areas and do a thorough inspection. If anything is amiss, report it immediately." Her lips turned up into a weary smile. "I'm also asking for your complete discretion at this point. Until we know the true nature of this incident, I would ask you to not discuss this with anyone outside Library staff. That includes spouses and other family members. Thank you so much for your cooperation. We will keep you posted as our investigation develops."

Clayr stepped back from the podium and the hall erupted into murmuring discussions.

"Well, that was fun," Iden said. "Let's go get lunch."

"Lunch hour is almost over, and I'm due at Wilmar's."

Iden pushed away from the windowsill. "I'll go with you."

"Don't you have a job to do?" Zo asked.

Iden waved a dismissive hand. "It'll wait for me."

"It's a good thing your mother is Assistant Curator over legal documents."

Iden flashed his easy grin. The one that made all the ladies swoon and Zo's insides turn to a bubbly mush, making him feel light and worry free. He grinned back.

After pressing through the crowd leaving the meeting hall, they walked side by side across the Library grounds. Neither of them said a word, but the air between them crackled with anticipatory energy. Zo couldn't wait for them to be far enough away from the Library. Even still, when Iden put his arm around Zo one block out from the Library grounds, Zo stiffened and searched the faces on the street, checking for people he might know. After a few more blocks Zo relaxed, snaking his arm around Iden's waist.

"So a mouse, huh?" Iden asked.

"Who told you that? You're not going to give it up, are you?"

"No way! This is the most exciting thing that's happened in the Library since…"

"Since two moons ago when Master Wes tried to steal from the Library, kidnap my sister, and stab my brother?"

"Technically it wasn't Master Wes who stabbed Regg." Iden's mouth did a grim twist.

"Whatever, fine. Yes, there was a mouse in the Library this morning. No one knows how it got in."

Iden gave a whistle that started high then drifted downward. "That's not good."

"Well, duh—of course it's not."

"You sure it was just a mouse, not a shapeshifter?" Iden asked.

"The mouse checked out as normal. A shapeshifter would be worse. A pest getting past the protective barrier is bad, someone doing magic in the Library is worse."

"What's the plan?" Iden asked.

"Keep it under wraps. Don't tell anyone I told you, and I need to talk to the Protector of the Library. The Protector could know why the magic let the mouse in."

At that, Iden stopped dead in the street. He was pale when he turned to Zo.

"You can't do this. Let Nix do it, he's got more years and experience."

Zo frowned. "What are you talking about? I spend more time under the Library than he does. I've seen the Protector before, or at least felt its presence. I'm pretty sure I can find it again."

"I'm not worried about you finding it, I'm worried about what it will do to you. I've heard stories…"

Iden's grip on Zo's shoulder became tight and protective. Zo would have been flattered, but he didn't want to be told what to do.

"It's fine. Clayr wouldn't have me do something she thought was dangerous." Zo's hand pressed against Iden's back to get him walking again. He could only imagine the line outside Wilmar's getting longer and longer.

Iden's walk was frustratingly slow, as slow as Ryn with her short legs.

"Let me know when you plan on finding the Protector and I'll go with you," Iden said.

"Sure." Taking Iden with him was the last thing Zo planned to do, but in the interest of time, he chose not to argue.

When they were one block away from the street to Wilmar's place and the Healing House, Iden pulled Zo into an arched doorway, deep in shadow. Zo's pulse quickened as he found himself pushed up against the wall with Iden's mouth on his, a warm reminder of how passionately he cared for Zo. Iden's lips were soft, even in the harsh cold, his tongue was like fire in Zo's mouth. Mice, protectors, and patients were wiped from Zo's mind in an instant. All there was in that moment was Iden, and the sudden urge to follow Wilmar and Nix's example in finding a nice quiet corner they could call their own. Zo's hands ached as they slid inside Iden's coat and across his far too-covered chest. Iden chuckled, then brought the kiss to a slow, lingering end, right before Zo could decide he didn't care about privacy and did something inappropriate for a doorway. Zo groaned and buried his face in Iden's neck.

"It's a date then," Iden whispered, sliding his hand down Zo's back, eliciting tingles as it went. "Wildfire." Zo's stomach pulled with pleasure Iden's nickname for him.

He shivered. He hated how Iden made it hard to deny him.

Back on the street they turned the corner to a much smaller crowd than Zo had anticipated, which was good, but also a person leaning against the door to Wilmar's with blood-soaked hands and shirt, swaying like he was barely staying on his feet. Zo rushed forward, pulling Wilmar's keys from his pocket. Despite the blood, Iden dove in and supported the man, as Zo fumbled to unlock the door. When it opened, they almost tumbled inside onto the floor, but Iden managed to keep the man upright long enough till Zo could help move him onto the exam room table.

"What's your name?" Zo asked as he tried to pull the man's hands away from where he was holding his gut.

The man moaned.

"What happened?" Iden tried to get the man to focus on him so Zo could work.

The man raised his head, eyes wide he stared at Zo. "Kill the roots, take the fruits."

Iden tried to turn the man to focus on him, but the man pulled away, curling around his wound, still intent on Zo.

"The Library! Kill the roots, take the fruits!" The man collapsed back onto the table, his breathing turned into gasps.

Zo's hands itched to go to the man's neck. Healing magic worked best from the neck. He was having flashbacks of Regg stabbed and dying beneath his hands. He was in the physician's office though, and although he had fully committed to studying the art of healing, he wasn't anxious to use his Healing magic. His lingering doubts made it elusive.

"Grab that bottle." Zo pointed with his chin, still working to pry away the man's hands. "The last one on the shelf, and the mask next to it. We'll have to put him out so I can see what to do."

Iden passed them to Zo, who let him take over holding the man's arms while Zo poured a few drops of the liquid from the bottle into the mask. He had never done this without Wilmar, but he had assisted a couple times. He held the mask to the man's face. After a few cycles of breath, the man relaxed into a sleep.

"Hold this, will you?" Zo said, switching places with Iden.

Upon opening the man's shirt, Zo felt his own insides turn to liquid ice. The man had been stabbed—or possibly impaled—and the wound had a strange four-point star shape.

"Gross, are those mouse droppings on his chest?" Iden asked.

Zo realized he'd made a beginner's mistake in triage and hadn't assessed the whole patient. He took in the small, black, oval shaped droppings all over the man's chest.

His insides squirmed, and he made a beeline to wash his hands in the basin.

"Do you think he could have had something to do with the Library mouse?"

Zo frowned. That seemed a bit too coincidental. Once his hands were clean, he examined the wound more closely. It was deep, and looked as if the intestines had been compromised.

Zo stepped back, closing his eyes and taking a deep breath.

"What's wrong?" Iden asked.

"I've only been a physician's assistant for a few moons. This wound is beyond me."

Iden paled. "What do we do?"

Zo paced for a moment, then he turned and thrust his bloodied hand onto the man's neck. His anxiety rose. His insides quivered, and his breathing quickened. He tried to think of the childhood song his father had hummed to calm him so he could use his magic on Regg. It didn't help. All he could think about was his mother reaching for his fire bead, ready to rip his fire away in the name of making him a great Healer. He tried to empty his mind of the image. Slowed his breathing, tried to count his breaths.

The man's pulse began to fade beneath his fingers.

Zo swore. "Not on my watch!"

With two long strides he threw open the office door and raced across the street. There was a Healing magic student mounting the stairs to the Waatch Healing House. Zo ran up to him, grabbed him by the arm, and dragged him across the street. The student almost tripped; Zo didn't care.

"What in the name of the Ancestors do you think you are doing?" the student protested.

A carriage hurrying down the street to the Healing House almost ran them over.

"Are you trying to get us killed? Let go!" The student pulled at Zo, but Zo tightened his grip.

Zo pulled the student into Wilmar's office.

"Heal him!" Zo demanded.

"I can't heal a physician's patient, it's forbidden!" The student protested.

"I'll pay for it, just do it!" Zo didn't know where he'd find the money, but he would find it.

The student glared, his face red with anger, but he put his hand on the stabbing victim's neck. With a jolt Zo remembered a similar hand, one with a ring on every finger. Zo took a closer look at the student's face. Even with his eyes closed in concentration Zo recognized him as the healing student who had come to fetch him that day in Regg's room. He was still just as attractive. All of the redness fled the student's face, and it faded to white. His eyes opened in alarm.

"This patient is dead," the student said.

"What?" Zo's eyes darted to the man on the table. "No, he can't be. He can't *be*."

Zo grabbed the man's neck. He shifted his hand, he pressed, he searched, but he couldn't find a pulse. He withdrew his hand in shock.

"No. No, no, no, no, no. He can't. I'm in charge. Wilmar's gone. He can't..."

Iden stepped around the table and put his arm around Zo. "I'm sorry, Wildfire."

Zo started at Iden's intimacy in front of a stranger. He shifted to find the Healing student's eyes wide and staring at him. It was too much. The walls were closing in on him. He couldn't breathe.

"I have to get out."

"What about the rest of the patients?" Iden asked. "And him?" He gestured to the body on the table.

Zo's mouth worked silently for a moment, then, "I can't..."

"I'll do it. I'll take care of..." the Healing student was talking, but Zo's ears were rushing with the sound of water.

Iden turned on the student sharply. "But that's illegal."

Zo didn't care. He threw open the door and fled onto the streets of Waatch.

Chapter Three

Clayr,

I've looked everywhere for Jett. I highly suspect my mother is keeping him well hidden within the manor house on Viatoro. Too much time has passed. I'm certain by now she has taken him to the Origin. Why she thinks that forsaken place with Praedo's sword driven into its center can give her what she wants is beyond me. Every person she has taken there in an attempt to add more magic to themselves has come home broken in their mind. The power that sword gives off is wild and untamable. I can't stop thinking she's broken my son for her own gain. I will never forgive her. I heard what happened at the Library. I'm heading home tonight.

Ryette

Ryn checked her desk, the books, and everything on it several times. Each time she thought she had finished, someone else mentioned another potentially nasty pest that would be disastrous for the Library and its contents, and she had to search again. This last time she had pulled everything out of her drawers, and wiped the insides down with polish before putting her papers, ink, and pencils back. She kept waiting for someone to assign her to examine a series of shelves, or boxes of documents, but her only instructions from her supervisor was to secure her area. Given that she was responsible for referencing and shelving new materials, her only official area was her desk.

Ryn returned her last stack of papers to her drawer, snapped it shut, and began to pace. Yll had scoured her desk, then had gone off in hopes that acquisitions would let her help. Despite having been in the meeting with Clayr this morning, both of them felt helpless. Listen to people gossip and chatter, fine, but having a mouse in the Library was troubling. If the Library's magic was coming undone, what would happen to the Library and its contents? A shiver ran up Ryn's spine as she thought of the Library falling apart, or worse, closing. They needed to figure out how that mouse got in through the magical barrier.

Yll came around the endcap of a bookshelf looking more petulant than Ryn had seen her since she was a little girl throwing a fit about her mother not letting her swim in Crystal Lake on her own.

"They wouldn't let you help." It was a statement, Ryn didn't even need to ask.

"No, and if I clean my desk one more time I'm going to scream."

Ryn's hand went to the orphanage book at the center of her desk. The soft leather was familiar beneath her fingers. "I have an appointment with Master Maurice, the Waatch book binder, but I'm not up to it right now. We can't leave the Library. What if they need us? What if something else happens?"

Yll stepped around Ryn's chair and picked up the orphanage book. Ryn tensed. The move brought bad memories of Yll's betrayal by giving the book about Luc to Prym. Yll had apologized several times, and Ryn felt like she'd forgiven her, but she still found herself not quite trusting Yll.

"This place is like an angry hive of bees and if I don't stop buzzing around with the tension I'm going to end up flying away and never come back. Literally." Yll picked at a spot in her hair where normally she had a leftover feather from her shapeshifting back from a bird. "Let's get out and go to your appointment. It will be good to get some fresh air."

Ryn clasped her hands together, resisting the urge to rip the orphanage book from Yll's arms. "Alright, but after we see him, we need to come back. I'm worried about being gone too long."

"Oh fine, it's not like we missed lunch or anything like that," Yll rolled her eyes.

Ryn got out the waterproof satchel she had borrowed from Walt the Master Restorer to put the orphanage book in when it left the Library. He had given her permission to take the book from the Library for the purpose of finding its providence. She tried not to seem so eager to have it back in her hands, but one sidelong glance at Yll's frown said she wasn't fooling her.

They collected their cloaks from the cloakroom, and headed out into the sunny, but blustery day.

As they passed the Boiler Room, Ryn wondered if Zo was somewhere deep beneath the Library, searching for the Protector. She shivered.

The main streets of Waatch were laid out like the spokes of a wheel. The cross streets were concentric rings moving out from the Library, growing larger the closer they got to the walls of Waatch. Some blocks were cramped with narrow alleyways between buildings. Within the first two rings were shops, and businesses associated with Library business. Ryn and Yll headed up the west spoke and two street rings out, then turned right. Master Walt had said the bookbinder they were looking for was an out of the way shop down an alley, just after a shop with crystals in the window and advertisements for maps of Library hidden passageways. Ryn wondered if this was where Master Wes had gotten the book about Clayr's office. She pushed the memory of his manipulation away.

"This place is awfully far out of the way for being the only bookbinder in Waatch," Ryn said.

Yll looked up to the blue sky peeking in between the alley rooftops. "Bookbinders are odd. If you find you're in need of one, you'll go out of your way to find them."

The buildings overhung the alley, making it more like a dark tunnel. Halfway down the alley was a white, now grayish, plastered building with dark timbers atop it. The overhanging sign read "Master Maurice, Bookbinder." They peeked into the window. Books lined the shelves, but no one seemed to be about.

When Ryn pointed this out, Yll rolled her eyes. "We have an appointment, just go in."

The latch lifted and Ryn pushed the door open to the sound of creaking hinges that needed oiling.

"Hello?" Ryn called.

An orange tabby cat jumped onto the counter and stared at them.

"We have an appointment," Yll said to the cat.

The cat glared at them, then gave a very human-like sigh before morphing from a cat into a man.

Despite growing up in a village full of people who did magic, Ryn startled and jumped back, heart pounding.

When the cat had fully taken on the form of a middle-aged man, Yll put forth her hand. "I'm Yll de Muto."

Ryn could see by the way their eyes held each other, that an understanding passed between Yll and Master Maurice. Ryn fought back her jealousy. He better have answers to where her and the orphanage book belonged. She hated the fact that other people could shapeshift, and all she could do was stand and watch.

Master Maurice hopped off the counter without taking Yll's hand. "And a good day to you. I must tell you I'm not normally in the business of finding the providence of books."

Ryn found her voice. "We appreciate you taking the time to look at my book. I wouldn't have bothered you, but I'm adopted and I'm searching for my ancestry. This book is the only clue I have. Master Walt in Library Restorations felt you were the one person in Waatch who could help me."

Maurice sniffed and took the orphanage book Ryn held out to him. Placing it on the counter he began to examine it.

"Tree calf binding, takes an expert, of which I am." He examined the spine. "Looks like double needle coptic stitch." He opened the cover and gasped. "There are pages torn from this book."

"That's why I need help." Ryn fought to stay patient. "There's no indication beyond the entries as to where this book came from."

Maurice flipped through the pages and entries in the book. "So, you believe one of these urchins to be you." It wasn't a question.

Ryn didn't know what to say to that. She shrank back.

"Yes, Ryn here is a valuable researcher in the Library. She helped capture Master Wes and his thieves a couple moons back." Yll's face was red hot. "My mother is the curator, and Ryn's adopted mother is Matriarch in Waiting for House Viator. Any clues you could give would be appreciated and helpful."

Master Maurice eyed Yll as if he was trying to decide if she was telling the truth. He examined the back boards and finished corners, then sniffed.

"This is fine workmanship. The kind you don't find in orphanages, and although inferior to my work, it still requires skill. The only book binder I know who does tree calf and uses a double coptic stitch is Master Clark out on Viatoro. Don't know why his work would be here on the mainland, or how a mainland orphanage could afford such an item, and if they could, why they wouldn't just buy it from me."

Master Maurice handed the book back to Ryn.

"You're sure? I mean, how do you know it's a mainland orphanage?" she asked.

Maurice gave her a glare that made her shrink back further.

"Look." Yll menaced toward Maurice. "We really need to find this orphanage, and my mother could make you..."

Ryn grabbed her by the sleeve and started pulling her toward the door.

"Thank you so much for your help," Ryn called above Yll's tirade. "We really appreciate it."

With that, she pulled Yll out the door and shut it with a squeaky groan and a snap.

"You should have let me peck that guy's eyes out!" Yll protested.

"He would have turned into a cat and eaten you!"

Yll deflated. "Fine. Can we at least go get some salmon salad sandwiches at the tea shop? We did miss lunch."

Ryn rolled her eyes, stashed the orphanage book back in her satchel, and headed for the street.

"Oh come on, I'm starving, especially after dealing with that jerk."

Ryn stopped so abruptly Yll bumped into her.

"Brynd!" Ryn called to her roommate across the street.

Brynd was chatting with a girl as she carried a basket down the street. She looked up and nodded her head toward Ryn and Yll. Ryn dragged Yll across the street.

"How come..." Ryn started.

"You're not at the Library," Brynd finished.

Yll giggled. "You two are spending too much time together."

Brynd smiled. "Well, we are roommates. To answer your questions, I'm not on duty today."

"Oh, yeah." In all the excitement Ryn had forgotten Brynd had the day off and wasn't there for everything. Having just turned sixteen meant Ryn would officially live and work at the Library. She loved having Brynd as a roommate. She was quickly becoming like an older sister. She'd worked for the Library a year before Ryn started, but she was only a couple years older than Ryn.

"Why aren't *you* in the Library?" Brynd asked.

Ryn patted her satchel. "I had that appointment with the book binder."

"I remember," Brynd said. "But I heard they had everyone scouring the Library after whatever it was that happened this morning."

"There's only so many times we can search our desks," Yll piped in.

Brynd frowned. "I'm so mad I wasn't there. I was on my way to see Tory here to help me mend some of my clothes when I heard the bells for the all-hands. They didn't say what happened. What happened?"

Ryn eyed the girl who must be Tory. "We aren't supposed to say."

Yll's head swiveled around them, probably looking to see who might have overheard them.

"Look." Brynd leaned in. "Tory has connections in Waatch. From the rumors I've heard, I think maybe she can help."

Ryn took a harder look at Tory. She had dark black hair which suggested some sort of Ancestral House lineage, like house Ignis. There were a few houses that tended toward black hair. She was slightly taller than Brynd, and though she looked to be around Brynd's age, had an air about her that said she'd experienced a lot more in her life than any of them combined. It made her seem street wise, and maybe a bit mysterious at the same time.

"You can trust me," Tory said.

Ryn wasn't entirely sure she believed that, but she did trust Brynd implicitly.

"Alright, but not here."

"Sandwiches, sandwiches!" Yll whispered.

"Right. There's a tea house not far from here, let's go chat there." Brynd suggested.

* * *

The server sat them in a corner of the tea shop mostly away from the other customers, which was difficult, given everyone was out to chat and gossip with their friends about what happened in the Library that morning. Tory went straight to the chair with its back to the wall. Ryn took a seat in the sunshine next to the window.

After they ordered two tea sandwich trays and a pot of chamomile tea, Brynd leaned in.

"So spill it, I'm dying. The one day I take off to run errands and get my torn hem fixed, the Library falls apart without me," Brynd said.

Ryn's gaze wandered around the room, trying to discern if anyone was listening to them while pondering if this was going to get her into trouble.

"It was a mouse," Yll leaned in and whispered.

Brynd gasped, but Tory frowned, brow furrowing.

"But how?" Brynd's hands went to her mouth as she noticed the people closest to them glancing at them.

"It can't happen." Tory leaned back. "It's impossible."

"Unless..." Brynd's eyes got wide.

"Unless something is wrong with the Library," Yll finished.

At that point the tea, sandwiches and pastries arrived. The girls stopped talking till the server left. As soon as she left, Yll set about devouring sandwiches while everyone else stared thoughtfully into their teacups.

"I don't really understand," Ryn said. "I mean, I know the Library is built on a magical foundation that keeps the pests out, but how could that be damaged? It's stood for thousands of years and has never failed before."

"That we know of," Brynd added.

"Um, I suppose that is a point. What do we really know about the Library and its magic? I guess we take it for granted." Ryn took a cookie and dunked it in her tea.

"Research!" Yll piped up around her salmon salad sandwich.

"Except everyone and their cat is now going to be doing research on the Library's history. How will we get our hands on the materials?" Brynd asked.

Ryn looked over at Tory, who was staring out into the tea house, but not saying anything. "Well, what do you think? Brynd says you have connections."

Tory's eyes focused on Ryn. "There is an old legend, allegedly written by someone who *is* a legend."

"Don't tell me," Yll said.

"Luc." Ryn frowned. Everything always seemed to lead back to Praedo's scribe and his "missing" journals which Ryn had found hiding in the Library.

Tory's eyes got wide. "You've heard of him. Not many Library types heard of Luc or believed he existed. Not enough documented evidence for you scholarly types. His stories are told by our grammas and aunties around the fire."

"We've seen the documentation." Ryn shifted. "What's this legend?"

"Legend says there was once a tree on sacred Wild magic grounds where the Library was eventually built."

"Yeah, we've heard this. It's part of every docent's orientation. It's why there is the magic barrier," Brynd said.

Tory rolled her eyes. "Yes, but word on the street passed down through generations of Mainlanders is that the tree wasn't cut down to make way for the Library—it grows inside."

"Preposterous, I've worked in the Library for a couple years and I've never seen a tree." Brynd took a sip of tea.

"And I've been down crawling around in the underbelly of the Library and I didn't see any evidence of a tree growing there," Ryn added.

"How could a tree grow inside a building?" Yll asked around bites of sandwich. Ryn could see why her and Regg got along so well.

Tory shrugged while lifting her cup to her lips. "I'm just telling you what has been rumored around town for centuries, maybe longer."

Tory took a sip. They all sat around the table with their thoughts.

"So, besides this tidbit of Waatch lore, is there more you can do to help us?" Ryn asked Tory.

Tory nodded. "Ghost festival is coming at New Moon in less than a fortnight. I'll have a booth selling ladies bags I make from Thax's tailor scraps. Buy one and I'll see what information I can dig up for you."

Ryn looked at Yll, whose eyes were bright with excitement. Yll always loved the Ghost Festival.

"Done!" Yll said.

* * *

Tory left them to head back to the Tailor's shop where she worked, as Ryn, Brynd and Yll headed back to the Library. While crossing the street, Ryn noticed a tall figure with a familiar gait walking up the street.

"Go on, I'll catch up with you later." Ryn said.

Yll gave her a dubious look that Ryn knew meant she was nervous they would get in trouble for being out on their errand for so long, but it was Yll's fault for dragging her to the tea shop.

"Hey," Ryn said when she reached Zo.

He glanced at her but kept walking.

Ryn looked back down the street but couldn't determine exactly where he had come from. Something was bothering him. She hurried to catch up with him.

"Did you find the Protector?" Ryn asked. "It didn't hurt you, did it?" Ryn shivered. "I can still feel its claws just missing my back."

"No, I haven't been into the tunnels yet," Zo said.

"Oh." Ryn took in the twitch of the muscle on his jaw, the tightness in his shoulders, and the determined nature of his stride. "Something is wrong? What happened?"

Zo stopped and faced her, there was something dark in his eyes. "A man is dead because of me."

Then he turned and was running up the street so fast, dodging around the foot traffic on the street, Ryn could hardly keep track of him.

Ryn glanced for a second at the Library towering over the rest of the buildings on the street. She was overdue to be back at her station. It was not a good time to have the managers upset with her.

She took a deep breath, set her jaw, turned away from the Library, and ran after Zo.

Chapter Four

Journal entry ???

I can't even tell what date it is anymore. Me—the once great mind of Viator. My brain and my body don't connect anymore. I can't speak the words I need to say. People fear me. What price power, right? Even now, I write this and it looks like chicken scratch on the paper, but I must try to regain my sanity. It can't be permanent. It just can't. I saw her today. She's afraid of me. Who wouldn't be? How am I supposed to take care of her? He asks too much, but what else can I do? He's still my best friend.

— From the Journals of Schiz

Zo strode out the north gates of Waatch struggling to contain the torrent of anger that rose inside him like the tide of the sea. He had come so far. From finally being able to touch his healing magic again to studying with the physician, healing had become something he was letting back into his life. He thought he was finally overcoming the blocks his mother gave him from forcing him to make Healing magic his life's focus. He thought of Wilmar's love of being a physician and helping people, and how infectious it was. He had tentatively taken Wilmar's offer to teach him.

Now a man died because of him. Because he didn't do something—anything.

Dead. Gone.

Someone who was alive this morning was now gone forever.

He couldn't even comprehend what just happened. Death was not something he had experienced. Once a wildfire had overrun some fire fighters, but Zo was nowhere near the front line, and none of the fighters had been anyone he knew. All of his grandparents were still alive, though he hadn't seen much of them in recent years. He hadn't worked with Wilmar long enough to see any patients die. Almost losing Regg a couple moons back had been as close as he'd ever been to death. The memory of that day caused him to walk faster, just to escape it.

The water. The sea. That was his escape. That's what he needed.

He followed the path across the rough, green seagrass till it dropped off into sand. He picked up some rounded flat stones and threw them at the placid waves gently lapping on the harbor's shore. One of the rocks went over a small wave and into the cold, dark water, sinking instead of skipping, never to rise again.

It was the end of everything he'd been working for these past few moons. He didn't mind crawling around the depths of the Library taking its temperature, but it wasn't something he wanted to do for the rest of his life. He wasn't sure healing was what he wanted to do either, but up until today he had enjoyed it. And now...

Neither Healing magic nor his physician skills had been enough.

Zo wanted to crawl out of his skin. Be somebody else. At that moment he wished he was a shapeshifter like Yll. Maybe transforming into a bird and flying away would get him out of all of this.

The sound of someone out of breath behind him made him turn. All of the feelings inside he couldn't contain threatened to unleash.

"I told you to go back to the Library," Zo snapped.

Still breathing hard, and holding her side, Ryn crossed the sand to join him by the water. "I..." was all she could get out. She'd clearly been working hard to catch up to him.

"I really want to be alone right now. Leave." He closed his eyes against the hurt look on her face. "Please," he managed to choke out.

She looked back toward Waatch, but didn't move.

Zo growled in frustration and headed for the trail through the woods. It led to a smaller, rockier beach. It was a quiet place to think. Iden had shown it to him on one of their first dates. The water there made a funny bubbling noise as the waves rolled out, tossing around the pebbles.

The walk through the woods was cold and damp, being out of the sun beneath the canopy of pine trees, maples, and alders. Leaves on the underbrush and brambles were reds and browns, or green but dormant looking. The brush that had once been lively and green was now bare twigs and branches. It smelled of wet damp earth instead of warm summer cedar. Fall was ending and winter was on the doorstep.

At the end of the trail, he crunched his way across the rocky beach to his favorite driftwood log and sat down just staring out across the water. He couldn't quite see the Ancestral islands out there across the water, but he could feel their presence.

Feet crunched on the rocks behind him.

He heaved a sigh, then scooted over to make room on the log.

Ryn sat next to him. She didn't say anything, just sat there.

He didn't know what to say. Words could not express what he felt inside. He had done all he could, but it hadn't been enough. He was not good enough to save someone's life.

Ryn didn't ask him anything. She just sat with him while they watched the water and listened to the pebbles ever tumbling in the waves, becoming smoother and smoother.

Ryn picked up a rock beneath their feet and threw it toward the water. It fell short. She tried again. The second time it fell into the waves. She stood up and threw them harder, and with more determination, or maybe frustration.

Zo threw a rock that landed in the water at the same time as Ryn's. She looked over at him, then scooped up a bunch more rocks.

It became a steady hail of stones thrown by them, hitting the water. Ryn picked up a larger stone, yelling as she threw it. It fell short of the water, but Ryn's yell grew and swelled, a guttural sound coming from deep inside her. Zo searched the ground till he found a rock bigger than his hand. With a mighty heave, he chucked it toward the water, letting out his own howl of frustration. As his yell crescendoed, Ryn took a deep breath and cried out again. Their voices swallowed by the rhythm of the waves and the pebbles.

Once his throat was raw and there was nothing left to scream, his legs gave out, plopping him back onto the driftwood log. Ryn sat beside him. There were tears running down her cheeks. He was tempted to ask why, but he was wiping his own eye. No explanations were needed.

The sun dropped below the treeline and Ryn shivered.

"We should..." Zo started, but his voice was almost gone from shouting. He cleared his throat and tried again. "We should get back."

Ryn nodded, but continued to stare out at the water, unmoving.

When she shivered again, Zo took her hand and gently pulled her to her feet. They made their way back across the pebbled beach toward the trail through the woods. Once they were halfway down the trail, a growl made the hairs on the back of Zo's neck stand up. He wanted to snap his fingers and make a flame for light, but he knew it would only make seeing into the twilight woods harder. Ryn pressed closer to him.

The snap of a tree branch made Zo spin on his heel, igniting his fingers to bring the flames up right beneath the face of a disheveled, wild man who looked like he was living in the woods. Ryn let out a squeak of fear.

"Are you alright, Lady Ryn?" Wild Man asked, trying to peer around Zo at Ryn behind him.

Zo reached behind, and pressed Ryn in closer to him with his free hand.

"Who are you?" Zo asked.

"I have met him before," Ryn said.

Zo turned his head enough so he could see Ryn, but also keep his eye on Wild Man.

Wild Man began tapping his fingers to his temple in a compulsive way. Most people shied away from or bullied people with a tic like that.

"I am Schiz, sworn protector of Lady Ryn." Wild Man gave a slight bow, which made a twig fall out of his untamed hair.

"I've never seen you before." Zo moved himself and Ryn back a step.

With a twinkle in his eye, the man held Zo's gaze. "Oh, but you have."

Zo searched his brain for a time that could have been true, but then the angles of the man's posture struck him. Zo searched Schiz's collar bones. There were bead scars for Travel magic and Water magic.

Zo's eyes got wide. "You! You're the one who almost drowned us at the lake!"

Schiz tapped his temple again. "Save the forest, save the children."

"I had it under control," Zo said.

Schiz gave him an uneasy lopsided grin, that was somehow condescending.

The man moved fast; before Zo could turn and shift Ryn to keep her behind him, Schiz was down on one knee in front of her.

"My lady, I heard you scream." At that Schiz's eyes shifted suspiciously to Zo and back. "Are you alright?"

"Oh." Ryn glanced at Zo with a nervous laugh. "We're fine, we were just letting out some frustration."

Schiz heaved a great sigh and relaxed, almost crumpling to the ground.

"I was so worried." He tapped at his temple again.

"You said you wanted to see me again? You said my father asked you to protect me. Who is he?" Ryn asked.

Zo startled, shifting his attention solely to Ryn.

"Yes..." Schiz's gaze drifted out into the darkened forest. Something rustled in the bushes. Zo searched, but couldn't see anything out there.

"Yes, that is my duty to him," Schiz said, tapping his temple again.

Zo was tired. Sustaining the flame in his hand to see was starting to make him thirsty. He wanted out of the woods and back into Waatch, but the firelight reflecting a tear on Schiz's cheek made Zo pause.

"So who is he?" Ryn asked again.

Schiz paced back and forth. His hands holding his head. "Can't. Can't tell. Not now. Not ready."

"We need to go," Zo said.

"No! Wait!" Schiz reached out and took her hand. "I know I'm not the protector I should be. I am broken and not whole, but I have to...have to tell you. Please."

Ryn nodded her consent.

Schiz sighed. "You must be away. Your grandmother has been informed of your whereabouts, and will come for you."

"My grandmother?" Ryn asked.

"Yes, it's Them. House Viator. She is the head. They want you, like me...and the Library. You mustn't let them." He turned to Zo. "You have to keep her safe. I can't be there. You are there, you must watch. They will try to take her."

There was a growling noise and a rustle in the bushes, a flash of white in the corner of Zo's eye. He'd seen that flash before in the woods by their cabin in Sooke.

Ryn pulled her hand back. "I'll be fine. They want my mother, not me. I'm adopted, I can't do anything for them."

"No, they don't know that." Schiz's eyes were wide and wild. "Please listen, please." His eyes darted to the bush where the growl had come from. "At all costs, stay away from your grandmother." He choked on his words as tears flowed down his face.

Zo was done with this conversation. It was too much on top of everything that had happened that day.

"We'll take your words under advisement," Zo said, as he moved Ryn away down the trail.

Schiz buried his face in his hands, and let them go.

Zo hurried Ryn along down the path till they broke through the woods onto the sandy beach. He shook the flame in his hand out.

"Weirdo," Zo said.

Ryn only nodded, her eyes still looking back into the woods.

* * *

They walked back to the Library in silence. Zo was wrapped up in too many emotions he didn't want to deal with. He was anxious to get back to the Library and confront the monster beneath it. At least he was either going to help the Library or meet his end, which sounded like just the thing to take his mind off of the day.

"Let me go with you," Ryn said as they crossed the street to the Library grounds.

Zo remembered how he had to carry Ryn through the tunnels as cold shadowy claws raked down his back, running for their lives beneath the Library. If they hadn't hit the magic barrier at the edge of the Library foundation, he was sure the thing would have had him. He said nothing, but gave Ryn his best "What do *you* think" look.

"Please? I don't want you to go alone, especially when you're feeling so out of sorts."

He looked toward the Library. The lamplighters were lighting the grounds, as the lights in Library windows were slowly being extinguished. He took a deep breath, then turned back to Ryn.

"Screaming into the waves felt pretty good today." He ticked the corners of his mouth up a bit, even though his heart was still too heavy.

"It did, didn't it?" She took a tentative step forward and hugged him around the middle, burying her face into his chest.

He relented and put his arms around her.

"Be safe," she said, her voice breaking to betray her emotion.

"I'll be fine," he said, even though he wasn't feeling sure of that.

"I'll wait for you," she said.

"Go get dinner, and get some sleep."

She rolled her eyes, then walked off down the path toward the kitchens.

"I saw that!" he called after her.

For a moment he watched her go, and knew he'd been too hard on her. Guilt kicked at his heart and he turned toward the boiler room, noticing for the first time that he still had dried blood on the backs of his hands and bloodstains on his clothes. He thought for a minute about going back to his new dorm room and getting cleaned up, but he figured if this Library Protector was going to mess with him, why bother?

Fergus was on guard at the Boiler Room door, and he reached out and grabbed Zo's arm as he passed.

"You alright man?" he asked.

Zo forced a half smile. "Fine."

"You look pale as an Ancestor apparition."

Zo gave Fergus his toothiest grin. "*Oh well.*"

He wrenched the Boiler Room door open and disappeared into its boiling hot interior.

* * *

When Zo got to Hal's desk and saw who was sitting at it, he groaned and sped past it as fast as he could.

Despite having shorter legs, Wilmar was around the desk and pulling Zo to a stop before Zo even set foot into the tunnel under Library. The one person Zo's raging heart of guilt didn't want to see was the physician.

Refusing to look at Wilmar, he tried to wrench his arm away.

"We need to talk," Wilmar said.

"I have an assignment from the curator I need to complete."

Nix appeared from around the tangle of piping and ductwork, like the great wall of a man that he was, to stand in front of Zo, arms folded.

"I'm back, I'll handle it. Do as your master says," Nix rumbled.

"I was committed to the Library first," Zo tried.

Nix's face and stance said he wasn't going to budge.

Zo just wanted to be away, lost in the tunnels of the under Library. He had sought solitude at the beach and hadn't got it. The anxious hurt of having lost a patient weighed on him. He feared being alone with his dark thoughts, but he needed to be gone. Talking with Wilmar was the last thing he wanted.

Nix was immovable. In the end, Zo had no choice but to let Wilmar drag him into Nix's office, closing the door quietly behind him. Zo went straight around the desk and sat in Nix's chair, just to throw the whole interview off.

Wilmar slumped into the chair in front of the desk, looking for all the world like *he* was in the hot seat and in trouble.

Zo leaned onto the desk, putting his chin on his knuckles.

Wilmar examined his fingers, running his thumb over the back of his hand. The sounds of the Boiler Room—steam, fire, yelling—came muffled through the door.

"I failed you," Wilmar started. "I was too eager for some time alone with Nix, and I did something I should have never done—left a new apprentice alone with my patients. Anything could have happened."

"And it did," Zo choked, despite his want to sound hard.

"And it did," Wilmar echoed. Then he looked up into Zo's eyes. "Will you forgive me?"

Zo rocked back. He wanted to be yelled at, to be reprimanded for causing a patient to die. It's what he deserved, but of course gentle Wilmar apologized. It was somehow worse. Zo took slow, deep breaths, guilt and shame bubbling up to the surface.

Wilmar reached out and covered Zo's hand with his. The gesture completely undid Zo, who quickly turned away so Wilmar couldn't see the tear that escaped out of the corner of his eye.

"I'm sorry," Wilmar said again. "This should have been my burden to bear, I'm more experienced bearing it. You were not ready."

Zo rubbed at the corner of his eye as if it itched, then turned back to Wilmar.

"What do you mean, it should have been your burden to bear, if you had been there the man would have lived."

Wilmar shook his head. "That wound was beyond my skill. It's possible the Healers could have saved him if they acted quickly, but the man was at my door for a reason—either he couldn't pay or he wasn't a member of "polite" society."

Wilmar squeezed Zo's hand. "You did your best, but the man was doomed."

Zo stood and paced behind Nix's desk.

"No," he said. "No, if I had the skill, he could have been helped. I've seen you deal with worse, this one was not beyond your skill."

"Perhaps if he had gotten to me sooner, but there was more than one wound, and more than one organ had been pierced. I've seen worse, but I've seen better. The man was going to die in my office even if both of us were there working together."

Wilmar leaned forward. "It's not your fault."

Zo stopped. He put his hands in his hair and pulled. There was more than one wound? How did he miss that?

"A man is dead on my watch," he said.

"A man is dead in a physician's office. We did the best we could for him. That is all," Wilmar said.

Before Zo's eyes, the whole incident ran through his brain. There was only one thing he could have done differently, but in that moment his Healing failed him. He couldn't find the calm he needed.

"Do you ever stop feeling so helpless?" Zo asked.

"No."

"How do I get past this?" The thought slipped out before Zo could check it.

"You will carry it forever."

Startled, Zo's eyes found Wilmar's. His heart hammered. He felt trapped. He couldn't live with this forever.

"But"—Wilmar gave a slight smile—"so will every time you help someone. Every time you mend a wound that will heal, and send them back to their families."

Zo thought of the smile on the face of the little girl whose broken leg he helped mend a couple moons back. One corner of his mouth ticked up.

"Now, I'm off to clean up the mess that Healer boy you recruited made out of my office."

The squeak of chair legs across the stone floor said Wilmar had stood. Zo turned back to him.

"There's somebody outside the Boiler Room waiting for you." Wilmar smiled.

"But..."

"Your errand for Madame Curator can wait."

Wilmar came around the desk and pulled Zo toward the office door, dragged him through the Boiler Room, and shoved him out the door past a surprised Fergus. He stumbled into Iden, who, for once, looked around at the people heading for the mess hall, then pulled Zo around the corner and into some bushes before enveloping him in a tight hug. Being in Iden's arms and the wet trickle of tears on his neck finally released the torrent of emotion inside.

Zo wept. "I hate you."

"I know."

Chapter Five

Ryette,

I know it's been a while since I sent a message. Our connection via Mind magic is growing weak. I realize this is my fault. I shouldn't have made Praedo's beads such an obsession, but I feel I am getting close and you know very well what a disaster it would be if any of the other powers that be get to them before I do. I think I finally know what these verses of Luc's poem mean: "Till under the echoes of earth's arcane, A deep song of bones calls my heart to play." I'm planning to test my theory. If you don't hear from me in a moon I probably failed.

By the way, I think it's time I told Ryn where I found her. She's old enough to know.

Yours, Moult

The stack of books teetering in Ryn's arms almost toppled to the ground. Ryn and Yll's workload had increased since the "incident" as everyone was now calling it. Ryn really wasn't sure increasing the rate of books entering the Library was the wisest choice, but everything in the Library seemed to be operating at a frantic pace, as if working faster and harder could move the Library to a safer space than where it was at the moment. Ryn and Yll had barely kept up with the load they had before. Now there was certainly no time to do any side research. Not with the near glee Sandy, their supervisor, enjoyed making their job as impossible as she could. It was an overt effort to get them to quit, or look so incompetent they would be released from Library service. Sandy was on the side of only Ancestor descendants working in the Library, and even though Yll had one magic, it wasn't enough for Sandy.

As Ryn passed the foyer on her way to her desk, Yll popped out from behind a bookshelf, grabbed her by the arm, and dragged her into the shadows of the archway.

Ryn opened her mouth to ask what Yll was doing, but Yll put her finger to her lips to keep Ryn quiet, then pointed to the foyer, then her ears.

"Of course Master Ubert, we would be happy to comply with your inspection as the Library Board of Regents has directed." Clayr's voice bounced off the ceiling of the foyer and out into the Library proper where other workers, besides Ryn and Yll, stopped to listen.

Ryn peeked around the corner in time to see Clayr curtsy to a man who was taller than Clayr, but not as tall as Prym's father who was standing next to him. The man wore embroidered robes that were so tight around his middle Ryn thought the stitching might pop out. His face was rather pinched, and his eyes were beady and small. One of the boys in the village had kept a rat as a pet. He'd fed it so much it became quite round. Master Ubert reminded Ryn of that rat.

Prym's father, Jeris, gestured to someone behind him.

"The Board of Regents has assigned Prym to take notes on the inspector's findings and make a final report to the Board. We trust that as a servant of the Library her report will be balanced and fair."

Ryn and Yll both choked as Prym came to stand next to the Master with a large notebook in hand. She was wearing a stole about her shoulders decorated in the same embroidery and colors as adorned the Master's robes.

"We look forward to a full report of Master Ubert's findings." Clayr curtseyed again, but not as deeply.

"See that you comply with all their wishes and needs," Jeris said.

Ryn started at that, to make Prym, of all people, his scribe. Prym's face was exceedingly smug at being included by her father.

Her father smiled like a cat who was up to no good. "This inspection will play a pivotal role in the Board's decision on whether or not to take House Viator's offering of a brand new facility they have built on Viatoro for the Library." The look on his face suggested that decision was already made, at least for him.

"I understand what is at stake." Clayr dipped her head. This time it didn't seem to be out of formality, but sadness.

"Good." Jeris smiled, turning toward Master Ubert. "Shall we begin with a tour?"

"Certainly." Clayr pulled her keyring out of her pocket.

Ryn knew it well, as she had stolen it just a couple moons back.

Master Ubert wiped his brow with a handkerchief. "Madame Curator, if you please, it's been a long journey. If we could begin the inspection sometime tomorrow?"

Clayr made a show of placing the heavy ring back into her pocket. "Of course."

She made eye contact with Fergus, on guard at the door, who came directly to stand next to Clayr.

"Fergus will see you to the guest quarters. I will send someone round bright and early tomorrow so we can begin." Clayr sounded all business.

Master Ubert grimaced at the words bright and early, but gave a slight nod, as Fergus took him by the arm to lead him out.

Prym stood for a long moment, her face flushed red. She was staring at her father the way she always did when she wasn't getting what she wanted, when she wanted it. Ryn caught his curt dismissive gesture to her, at which she turned and stomped off after Master Ubert.

Clayr stood unmoving till Master Ubert and Prym were out the door, then she spun on her heel toward the Library proper.

"A word, Madame Curator," Jeris said.

"In my office." Clayr's voice was curt, the way it was when she wasn't going to take any excuses from the girls when they had gotten into something they shouldn't have.

Ryn pulled Yll behind a bookshelf as Clayr led Jeris toward her office. When her sharp steps on the stone floor had receded, Ryn and Yll emerged from behind the shelf. Yll's hands covered her mouth.

"What are they talking about? They can't move the Library." Ryn's eyes rolled over the hundreds of books, just within her sight. That didn't include the rest of that floor, nor the other two floors of books, documents, and objects.

"It's worse than that." Brynd startled Ryn, appearing around the archway from the foyer.

Yll's hands moved to cover her face.

"What?" Ryn asked.

Brynd watched to see if Yll would say something, but when she didn't, she took up the answer. "I've heard whispers among the managers that if the inspector's report is bad enough there could be a vote of no confidence by the Board."

"I don't understand," Ryn said.

Yll wiped her hands down her face. "The position of curator is for life. It keeps the leadership of the Library out of the politics the Board of Regents likes to play. Except..."

"Except if there's a vote of no confidence by the Board," Ryn guessed.

Brynd put an arm around Yll. "It has to be unanimous though. Your mother has powerful friends on the Board."

Yll gave a slow nod, but Ryn could tell she wasn't comforted. Ryn didn't blame her. The tales in the village of Regent politics were legendary, and Clayr was at a disadvantage being an Ordinary who came up through the ranks. Clayr had told them stories of the battles she fought to be allowed to become a researcher, and then how she made her way through the ranks. They were thrilling, even for a ten-year-old. Clayr was tough. She had a reputation of being an unrivaled researcher, an ability to lead with firm kindness, a deep respect for everyone she worked with, and a passion for the Library. She was by all accounts the most beloved Curator to come along in many generations, but the mouse scare, and an inspection like this, could easily turn Library workers against her in an effort to save their own jobs. Finding neglect somewhere could carry heavy penalties, and Clayr was the type to go down with the ship if that meant saving the Library.

"There's got to be something we can do besides cataloging new acquisitions," Ryn said.

Yll straightened, her mouth going flat for a moment. "There is, but we're going to have to work long hours."

Ryn nodded.

"I'm in," Brynd said. "I can't stand the look of that weaselly Master."

"I rather thought he looked more like a rat," Yll said.

"That rat Dar used to have," Ryn agreed.

Yll leaned in, lowering her voice. "I think we should start with finding every book we can on the Library's history, plus anything about the magic that protects the Library."

"I doubt there's books solely about the Library's magic, but we can look," Ryn said.

"Right, then maybe some books on the history of Waatch? Perhaps there's something there about these legends Tory mentioned," Brynd added.

"Good thought." Yll nodded. "We need to figure out how the Library works. We can't figure out what's broken if we don't even know what kind of magic protects the Library."

"Agreed," Ryn said.

"Let's get started! I'm off to the reference section." With that, Brynd set off into the dark of the Library.

"I want to get my notepad and pencil," Ryn said, heading off toward her desk.

"I need to check with acquisitions and make sure they don't have a pile of work for us before we go too far," Yll said, following Ryn.

"Good plan."

Yll's idea was going to be tricky. They already had a heavy workload, and trying to do research on top of that wasn't going to be easy, but if they could find the references to history books about the Library, and those materials weren't already in use, they could figure out what was happening to the Library.

After some searching, they found the references indicated the Library history books were on the third floor in the restricted section. Luckily, Ryn happened to have a stack of new books that needed to be shelved in that area. She was allowed to shelve materials in the restricted section, but she wasn't supposed to remove materials. After shelving her new acquisitions, she scanned the area to see if anyone was watching before sneaking over to the aisle where the history books were shelved. Shelf marks twenty and thirty-two were the books they hoped had useful information on the Library's origins. Ryn pulled them down, then slipped around the wall of bookcases to where she knew there was a hidden doorway that led to a secret stairway. She still remembered which book it was that Brynd showed her to pull on for the bookcase to swing open. Checking to make sure no one was looking, she slipped inside, closing the bookcase behind her. True to Library form, there was a lantern already burning low. Of course a secret passage in the Library was well used enough that the lanterns remained lit.

Ryn raised the wick to shine brighter and took the lantern with her down the stairs. In the dark stairwell, pressed against the Library walls to keep her balance, she felt the cold of the Library. There was something distinctly sad about that cold and its touch. Thoughts of an abandoned Library, of its shelves emptied of its treasures, overwhelmed Ryn. In her mind's eye she could see books crated and torn away. The walls seemed to crumble as they left. Ryn shuddered as she reached the bottom of the stairs and moved away from the walls. It was a horrific vision she needed to prevent at all costs.

* * *

"Same stuff, over and over again. The site of the Wild magic taken to build the Library, blah, blah, blah. There's nothing new here," Ryn said.

The Library closing bell had rung long ago, and the only light was the lantern which sat in the middle of Ryn and Yll's desks. The Library was always quiet, but at night it was oppressively so.

"Some of them reference a tree that once grew here, but none of them mention what happened to it," Yll said.

Ryn pushed the book she'd been reading aside and rubbed her eyes. "They cut it down, of course. What else would they do with it?"

"But don't you think it's strange that those original inhabitants of Waatch, who were followers of the Wild magic, would have just let them take over their sacred site to build a Library dedicated to Ancestry magic?"

Ryn shrugged.

Brynd came hurrying up with a book open. "Look at this!"

She showed it to Yll first, who immediately sat forward. "Ryn!"

She spun the book and pushed it across their desks.

It was a picture of Luc, the Dragon Slayer's chronicler, and the only member of his company who didn't take on the Slayer's magic. Luc stood next to a tree, with bright shining fruit. He was talking to a group of people while pointing at a mound of rocks. The picture was captioned, *Luc at the Founding*.

"You read Luc's journal," Yll said. "Did it say anything about the founding of the Library?"

"No." Ryn ran her fingers over the brightly painted picture. "But the reference book for it did mention he had more than one journal."

"We've got to find the others! If the stories are true, he chronicled everything that happened after the fall of the dragon. Maybe he wrote about the founding of the Library." Yll said.

Ryn groaned. "Do you know what I went through to find that one journal? And then it was cursed to make whoever possessed it obsessed with setting it free."

"Where did you find the reference for it?" Brynd asked.

Ryn looked at Yll. "Your mother's office."

"Let's have a look." Yll stood.

"We don't have a key," Ryn pointed out.

Yll shrugged. "She's probably working late, but maybe she went to dinner. Let's check."

Ryn closed the book on Luc's picture and took the lantern. They moved as silently as they could toward the curator's office. Any sound at night seemed to be magnified tenfold.

At Clayr's office hallway there was a light shining in front of her office. The girls ducked behind a row of shelving. Ryn shuttered their lantern light.

A voice drifted down the hallway to them. Ryn couldn't tell if it was male or female, but it had a slightly unhinged quality to it.

"Kill the roots, take the fruits," the voice laughed.

"Shhhh. Be quiet, idiot," another voice said. This voice was distinctly male.

The other voice giggled.

"Will you stop? I'm almost done here," the second voice said.

Ryn peeked around the corner, but all she saw was a roundish green shadow and a skinny red shadow on the hallway wall.

"Water, water, this will kill everything," the first voice said.

Yll gasped.

"What was that?" the second voice said.

Bryn grabbed Ryn and Yll's arms and dragged them down the aisle.

They ran for the foyer in search of a Library guard.

* * *

They found Norm pacing the mosaic floor, idly examining each statue of the Ancestors as he passed them. As if he hadn't seen them hundreds of times before while he stood guard.

"Come quick!" Ryn called to him as they tumbled into the foyer out of breath.

Norm was next to them in two strides.

"What's happened?"

"We heard strange voices outside Madame Curator's office," Brynd said.

Norm raised an eyebrow at that. Apparently strange voices in the Library wasn't that unusual, but it was certainly a sign of how the Library was taking every report seriously that he didn't hesitate to follow them back to the spot in the hallway outside the curator's door. Now all was still and dark. Ryn lifted her lantern, shining it down the adjacent aisle.

"There was someone here, I promise," Yll said. "We came to find my mother, but we heard two people talking."

Norm scratched his head. "Probably just some late working researchers."

"No, what they said was odd," Brynd said. "Something about water, and killing roots."

Norm shrugged. "Nobody here now, and nothing looks amiss."

Ryn was still moving up and down the hall shining the lantern down rows of books. It didn't feel right. Something was off about those two voices. She was certain they were up to no good, but with no proof there was nothing they could do. Something bad would come of it, she could feel it in her gut.

"Brynd, do you think Tory's friends she talked about might have connections to find out who could be sneaking around the Library?" Ryn asked.

Brynd shrugged. "Maybe?"

Ryn massaged her temples. Her brain hurt from thinking.

"We should get back to our research. We'll have to get mama to let us into her office some other time," Yll said.

Ryn let out a long breath. "No, it's late. Regg's probably looking for you. We'll drop you off at the Curator's cottage, then we need to head back to our dorm room. I have a date with my brother tonight, and I need time to change."

Yll's eyes lingered on her mother's office door. "But maybe there's another book somewhere we missed."

Norm returned from the sweep he had been doing of the surrounding area. "Nothing out of the ordinary, time for you ladies to go on back to your dorms."

"But..." Yll started.

"Don't worry, I will make a report, and the guard will keep an eye out. Go get some rest." Norm spread his arms to shoo them toward the back entrance.

Ryn took Yll's hand. "I promise we're going to figure this out. One way or another."

Yll let out a long breath. "Right."

Chapter Six

Madame Curator,

I don't know what the girls saw last night, but it's not the first time someone has broken into the Library. I'm afraid we've relied a bit too much on the protective magic of the Library to keep it safe and are a bit understaffed for a situation where we need to be vigilant on every entry point. I've doubled the guard, but quite frankly, they are tired. The initial shock of the breach has worn off, and now they grow restless. I will do my best, but I fear we need more help. I know the Library is opposed to looking outside its walls, but maybe we could hire some of the Waatch guard? At least temporarily? Consider this my official request for assistance.

Regards, Errol

Zo stood outside the dorm room door and took a deep breath. He did not want to do this, but he was running out of options. His knuckles rapped on the solid wood door. It opened to Brynd with her white-blond hair and soft smile.

"Come in." She stepped back to admit him.

He ducked inside the doorway. The lower ceiling would never bother Ryn. She had moved in with Brynd shortly after Ryn's Debut party. The attic rooms were the least desirable given the number of stairs to climb and the pitched roof, so Brynd had been alone in her room and eagerly welcomed Ryn as a roommate.

Abby, Ryn's cat, ran across the room to rub against Zo's legs.

Zo bent to pet Abby and gave her chin scratches. "I've missed you too."

Ryn was dressed in some of Regg's old clothes that Zo was surprised were still around. She was twisting her warm brown hair into a low bun to put a messenger boy style cap over it. What they were planning tonight didn't require sneaking around, not like when they had used the underground to sneak into the Library, but Ryn had insisted trousers were easier to run in than a skirt. Which was good, because he was taking Ryn with him to find the Protector.

A spike of fear settled in his stomach as he looked at her.

"I don't know, Ryn. I think this is a bad idea," he said.

She glanced over at him as she picked up Regg's old coat from her bed. "Well, security has been tightened around Clayr's office because of the strangers we found outside her door...What else can we do? You and Nix have tried to find this Library Protector. Neither one of you have been successful."

"I felt a cold presence last night. Maybe I'll find them tonight," Zo said.

Ryn shook her head. "The last time we saw the Protector, I was with you."

The memory of cold claws raked down his back.

"I don't know why, but maybe it was because I was an outsider." She held her palms up.

"You work for the Library now. You're not an outsider anymore." They'd already had this argument, but he was trying one more time to dissuade her.

"It's worth a try," Brynd piped up from her chair at the table. "You've tried everything else you could think of to contact the Protector—if it even exists."

Zo and Ryn exchanged a long, knowing look.

"It exists," Ryn said.

"Let's get this over with." Zo's voice edged toward snapping.

"Right." Ryn pulled on the coat and started out the door, then turned to Brynd. "If we don't come back..."

"Oh, get going. Master Nix is around, you'll be fine." Brynd shooed them out the door.

As she was closing it, Zo heard Brynd muttering, "And I'm going to have a gloriously quiet evening to read."

The comment made Zo smile. Brynd's casual calm about Ryn going into the underground of the Library eased his worry a bit.

They walked the Library gardens on their way to the Boiler Room in silence. His anxiousness made his chest tight.

"I'm sorry I've been moody lately," he said.

"It's alright. I can tell something bad happened."

Zo let out a long exhale.

"I lost a patient."

"Lost? They wandered away?"

"As in, they died."

Ryn's eyes searched his face, her mouth opened like she wanted to say something, but nothing came out.

"I couldn't save him. He came to Wilmar's with a knife wound to the gut, and I didn't know what to do. I had assisted Wilmar with wounds before, but nothing like that, and I tried to use my healing magic like I did with Regg, but nothing came. It was different, he was a stranger. Wilmar says there's nothing I could have done, but I think there was, if I only knew how."

Ryn gave a slow nod, just listening to him.

He went on. "I don't know if I should really be apprenticed to the physician. I like helping people, but I don't like feeling helpless. When I work with Wilmar there's only so much we can do: patch them up, give them the concoctions Wimar mixes up from his garden, and send them on their way. I never know if not seeing them again means they got better, or they died."

He gulped, but then the words kept tumbling out. "I know. I know if I became a Healer I could save them. Well, most of them, but—I can't. Whenever I try to use my magic, my anger bubbles out, and I just see red, which is not any kind of state that you can heal someone in...And then there's Madame Sano, the Ancestor hag teacher, who hates me, which doesn't help at all."

His gaze darted all over the grounds as he tried to ease the tension in his chest. They eventually found Ryn's eyes, brimming with tears, but not spilling over. It almost undid him completely.

"I wish I could do something for you," she said. "I know, despite everything, that healing is always with you. There's something about it that makes you peaceful, but your mother has hurt that. I think you need to look inside your heart and figure out what you really want. Forget about what everyone else wants. Focus on where your heart takes you, and push everything else away."

He took a deep breath. She was right.

The knot inside his chest eased a bit, but didn't leave.

They crossed Library garden with Ryn speculating on what she'd heard outside Clayr's office.

"One of them said, 'Kill the roots, take the fruits.' Isn't that weird?"

Zo sucked in his breath. "But Ryn...That's what the man who had been stabbed said before he died. 'Kill the roots, take the fruits.'"

"What?" Ryn stopped.

"Somehow your Library prowlers are connected with the man I couldn't save, who died on Wilmar's exam table." Zo shook his head.

Ryn reached out to him, her hand covering her mouth.

"Come on, this is bigger than a mouse." Zo resumed their walk toward the Boiler Room, his anxiousness causing him to pick up the pace.

He could hear Ryn's feet on the pavers hurrying after him, till they reached the door to the Boiler Room.

Ed was standing guard and let them in. They found Nix pacing beside Hal's desk. He took two steps to stand directly in front of Zo as soon as he saw them, moving faster than his bulk would suggest.

"Are you sure this is wise?" Master Nix asked.

"No," Zo frowned.

"Yes," Ryn piped up.

Nix and Zo both turned to stare at her. She seemed unusually confident under their combined gaze.

"I should go with you," Nix said. He seemed to grow a few inches to tower over them.

Ryn bowed her head a bit to him. "Master Nix, the last time we saw the Protector was when Zo and I were in the tunnels together."

Nix grunted. "Apparently without my permission. When was that exactly?"

"Uhhhh—doesn't matter. The point is we'll be fine." Ryn's grin was a huge cheesy exaggeration.

Master Nix sighed. Head bowed for a moment, then, "I'm worried about Zo's description of your last encounter with the Protector, but I guess it's worth a shot. The Protector only seems to show up when it feels needed, and I certainly haven't been able to make it appear."

"We'll do our best!" Ryn gave a jaunty wave and started off toward the tunnel under the Library.

"She's entirely too cheery for someone who's had a run-in with the Protector," Nix whispered under his breath.

"Don't I know it." Zo followed after her. It didn't take much for his long strides to catch up to her short ones.

At the junction of cold and hot water piping, Ryn grabbed a lantern and stared off into the dark. As always, the tunnels were warm despite being underground. It was a genius way to heat the Library, but required enormous amounts of magic work, from fire magic to heat the water, to water magic to send it under the flooring. Usually, Ancestor descendants disdained such practical use of magic, but not for the Library. Working for the Library was the ultimate honor among those who held Ancestor magic. Zo felt the sentiment was terribly hypocritical.

As usual, as soon as Zo passed the border that marked where the Library's walls began, he felt his magic cut off. As much as he worked here every day, it was still disconcerting.

Ryn's face in the lantern light had a faraway listening look as they traversed the tunnel to the first ladder where Zo took temperature readings for the Library. Beyond the ladder they passed a small side tunnel, and Ryn shined the lantern down it.

"Where does this go?" she asked.

"Leads outside to the water intake for the heating system."

Ryn held the lantern up peering into the gloom of the side tunnel like she was expecting the Protector to emerge from it, then she moved on.

The only noise was the scraping of their feet on the stone tunnel, and the strange thumping of the pipes expanding and contracting warm and cold water flowing through them. The sudden clanging would make Ryn jump every time it happened. Otherwise, there was only the oppressive silence the Library always exuded.

"Are you and Iden going to the Ghost Festival tomorrow night?"

Zo started at the sudden break in the quiet. He wasn't used to having anyone with him in the tunnels under the Library.

"I guess, if we make contact with the Protector tonight. If not, maybe the night the Ancestors walk among the living will lure out our illusive friend."

Ryn nodded like she was listening, but her eyes were far away.

"So where do you think this Protector hangs out?" she asked.

"Well, it was chasing us down this tunnel the last time we saw it."

The lantern dimmed and the air was suddenly crisp and cold, like a clear snowbound day. Shadowy claws swiped at him from the wall next to his head, and he swept up Ryn and started running.

The thing chased them down the tunnel. It was right on their heels, and Zo could feel its cold breath on his neck. He ran faster.

"Wait!" Ryn cried. "This is what we came for."

"It's going to tear us apart!" Zo shouted.

"But we have to try."

At the next ladder Zo threw Ryn so she could grab on, clinging to a rung almost above the tunnel ceiling, then he spun to face the Protector.

Ryn held up the lantern to reveal a shadowy form made of what looked like black smoke.

Zo put his hands up in surrender.

"Protector, we need your help," he said.

The shadow moved in an inky way, first smoke, then liquid, then solid razor-sharp claws.

"The curator sent us," Ryn said, hanging from the ladder.

The Protector coalesced into an almost solid human form, one arm-like tendril questing out toward Ryn's face. Zo's stomach dropped. He couldn't get between them. A bladelike hand hung in front of Ryn for a long moment, while Zo's gut twisted.

"Something is wrong." Zo kept his hands up. "A mouse was found in the foyer. Pests shouldn't be able to get into the Library. We came to ask, is there something wrong with the Library?"

"Please. We are only trying to help," Ryn said, eyes wide and fixed on the smokey blade in front of her nose.

The Protector's body language was startled. Its head looked up, then it turned to smoke and shot through the ceiling so fast, it was gone before Zo could do anything to stop it.

Zo swore.

"Welp. There goes our chance," Ryn said.

Zo let out a sigh of frustration before turning to Ryn.

"Oh well."

* * *

Despite not gaining any new information, Nix was encouraged that they had found the specter. Zo didn't share his enthusiasm, especially when Nix told him he'd just have to try again. Zo really didn't want to tell Nix how much the Protector terrified him, and he especially didn't like any suggestions that he bring Ryn with him again. This was the second close call that almost ended badly. Ryn tried to argue that the Protector seemed friendly, but Zo completely disagreed. For sure next time he was going alone. Hopefully now that he'd made contact, he'd be able to do so without Ryn.

"So I'll see you tomorrow for the Ghost Festival?" Ryn asked as he dropped her off at her dorm room. "Mother sent word, she and your father are going to be there with us."

"Sure. What time are we supposed to meet them?"

"Just before noon at the dock," she said.

"Alright, I'll grab Iden and pick you up before then."

Ryn turned to the door.

"Thank you, parva soror," he said, quiet, but inflicted with meaning.

"Of course!" She hugged him around the middle, then disappeared through the door.

He watched until the door clicked shut, then he turned around to face whatever life was going to throw at him next.

Chapter Seven

The one day Ryn could actually sleep in, she was up and getting ready early. Abby was dancing around her feet meowing for food and attention, while Ryn was digging through her trunk trying to find a dress that wasn't Library Researcher black. Finally, she fished out an old blue dress she hoped still fit. Abby jumped on the bed and stared Ryn down until she caved.

"Alright, alright, your crock of fish is empty, but as soon as I'm dressed I'll go see if Norm has some for you," she said.

As Ryn finished dressing, the door opened and Brynd came in with a full basket in her arms. Abby jumped down and rushed to intertwine herself between Brynd's legs.

"My family is in town for the festival, and they brought us a bushel of apples," she said.

Brynd pulled a crock out of the basket. "And I ran into Norm who gave me a treat for you," she said to Abby.

"Perfect, now I'll have time to make something warm to eat instead of just grabbing a piece of bread," Ryn said.

"I'll see you at the festival," Ryn called to Brynd as she ducked out of the room.

On her way across the grounds she met Fergus, hurrying across the gardens toward her.

"Hey, you want to grab breakfast?" he asked.

"Sure," she said.

Fergus had been upset with her after her last unauthorized trip into the locked restricted section. There had been little time since then to repair the damage from that night. Breakfast seemed like it might help.

Fergus held out a uniformed arm for her. She took it, allowing him to lead her through the garden path full of dormant hedges and bushes, waiting for the oncoming winter. Even though he was only a couple years older than her, his seriousness about his job as Library guard always made him seem older.

"So, I heard you saw the Protector," he said.

And there it was.

"That's curator's ears only, how did you hear?"

Fergus shrugged. "There's few secrets between the curator and the Library guard. Clayr has always had an open policy. Easier to keep the Library safe if we know all the intrigue."

"Yeah well, I went with Zo last night and the Protector came. Didn't get to say much. It darted away when we mentioned the mouse. We didn't even get to ask our questions."

Fergus was quiet. Ryn glanced up to see his frown and furrowed brow. Something was troubling him.

"What is it?" She asked. "It used to seem like you were always around, but you've seemed distant lately."

He started from whatever thoughts he was having and looked down into her eyes.

"I didn't know you noticed," he said.

"Of course I noticed, you're one of the few Library people who has welcomed me in. Most others think I'm too young, or I'm just here as Clayr's pet project."

Fergus pursed his lips. "I'm a guard. My family has sworn for decades to protect the Library. I wasn't happy with how you broke a whole host of Library rules. You also have an instinctive connection with the Library I've never seen with anyone else. I guess I've been a bit frustrated, and a whole lot of jealous."

"Sorry." Ryn bowed her head. One of the worst things that came out of the whole escapade with Master Wes was the mistrust she had garnered in some people. She really liked

Fergus. He had always been kind to her, and she didn't want to lose him as a friend.

"Ryn!"

At the sound of her name, she looked up to see Yll jogging across the grounds from the Library.

Ryn looked up at Fergus. "Why don't you come with us to the Ghost Festival?"

He looked down at her and smiled. "As much as I would love to worship Ancestors I don't have, I am on duty today. You wouldn't believe how many people think the short staff day is a good opportunity to sneak into restricted sections."

Ryn tried not to blush. She and Yll had actually been considering doing that this morning. Ryn had wanted to see if Luc's journal was still where she found it for Master Wes, or at least maybe find a clue to where it might have been taken. In the end they had decided against it. She could see now that that was a good thing.

"Let's hurry and eat, I'm starved. It's going to be a long shift, and I want to hear every detail about your encounter with the Protector," Fergus said, picking up the pace with his stride.

Ryn had to almost run to keep up.

After breakfast, Ryn and Yll bid Fergus goodbye. Ryn hoped she could find more time to spend healing her friendship with Fergus. She hated how she had hurt him and betrayed his trust. For now, they hurried to Ryn's dorm room to pick up Ryn's heavy winter cloak. The day was mild, but Ryn knew being outside all day would eventually make her cold. When she opened the door, she found Zo and Iden sitting at the table chatting with Brynd.

"I thought you decided to meet me at the festival," Ryn said.

Iden stood, bowing to kiss her hand. "We thought we should escort you, my lady."

"In other words, Zo is feeling overprotective this morning," Yll said.

Ryn blushed. Iden was about Zo's age, who would be two years older than Ryn on his birthday at the end of winter.

When they were growing up in the village, Ryn had always looked up to Iden, and had a huge crush on him, but he hadn't paid much attention to her. He was always surrounded by a gaggle of girls following him everywhere. Ryn wasn't the "follow boys around" type. Besides, no Ancestor magic boy would ever look twice at Ryn anyway. Iden's attention now was only because of Zo. It was definitely not something she was accustomed to, especially when she had a crush on him since she was little.

She opened her mouth but only a squeak came out. Even with Iden dating Zo, old habits die hard. She cleared her throat.

"Well, thank you."

"Shall we go?" Yll asked from where she stood by the door.

"Yes, we shall," Brynd said, grabbing her cloak off the rack.

And off they went to the festival. Ryn really hoped Brynd's friend Tory could provide answers to who might want to damage the Library.

* * *

By the time they left the town gates and entered the edge of the festival grounds, Ryn was sweating under her heavy cloak from walking fast enough to keep up with the boys. She almost regretted wearing it, but knew she would appreciate it later in the day. They toured the grounds together to get a feel for this year's layout. As usual, the food vendors were near the docks where the fish and crab were brought in fresh by boat. This year they had set up a giant barrel with water and crab in it. Using a pole that had a line hanging from it with a bunch of loops at the end, you could try to entice a crab to grab a loop, then pull them out of the water. If you caught a crab, they would cook it for you to eat. Ryn wasn't hungry yet, so she made a mental note to come back and do that later. They searched, but hadn't found Tory's bag booth yet. The goods and wares booths were a maze they could easily get lost in. Probably by design. They would need to keep searching.

The big attraction this year was something called "The Slayer's Staff." It looked like a lighthouse, but around the outside was a huge slide that started at the top, and went all the way down and around the lighthouse to the bottom. The stairs to the top were inside the lighthouse.

"That looks fun," Zo said.

Iden grinned at Zo. "Let's do it."

"Ryn!"

Ryn turned to see her mother rushing to her. "Mama!" Ryn was startled to hear her baby name for her mother come out of her mouth.

She hadn't seen her mother in over a moon. Ever since leaving their cottage and moving to Waatch, Ryn had been on her own. It wasn't until this moment she realized she missed spending her days in their cottage in the woods, reading by the fire with Abby on her lap, and her mother's research spread all over the kitchen table.

Ryette scooped Ryn up into a tight hug, holding her for longer than normal. Long enough for Ryn to feel some of the knots of worry she didn't know she carried in her chest loosen and ease.

When Ryn pulled back, her mother had tears in her eyes.

"It's so good to see you," her mother said.

"You too. Did you find Jett?" Ryn asked. Her brother Jett had been missing since Master Wes had tried to steal Luc's journal and kidnap them.

Ryette glanced back at Lar as he came up behind her mother with Regg at his side.

Her mother snaked her arm around Ryn's waist. "Let's go for a walk, shall we?"

Ryn looked back at her friends as her mother led her away. Yll was already in Regg's arms and she could hear Zo and Iden trying to convince the group to ride the Slayer's Staff with them. She didn't want to miss out on the fun, and her stomach was starting to knot at the thought of what her mother wanted to talk to her about. They walked side by side for a while until they were past the last tents of the festival and alone on the sandy beach.

Unable to stand the tension of what bad news her mother would tell her, she decided to just ask and get it over with.

"So, did you find him?" Ryn asked again.

She didn't like her mother's delay in answering. Ryn loved her brother, even though she feared he had joined with those who wished Ryette harm.

Her mother sighed. Shaking her head, she looked out across the water toward the islands.

"Did you try Viatoro? I'm pretty sure he was headed there to get his magic from them."

"He would need my approval for that," her mother said.

"Can't your mother, err, my grandmother do that?"

Her mother was quiet for a while. Then she said, "I went there. It was tricky to be there and avoid detection, but I have friends. No one's seen Jett. I don't like what that says."

"What does that mean?"

"It means they're hiding him, or worse..."

"What's worse?"

"It's like I told you before. They want my combination of magic. House Viator has been experimenting for I don't really know how long, decades if not longer, to find a way to gain all the magics again. They want to be as Praedo of old, using all the magics for their advantage. House Viator's power has been on the decline for over a century. Having the power to bestow all the magics on one person would allow Viator to dominate the other houses. My great uncle has been the biggest proponent for making Viatoro the center of power. He has this crazy idea the dragon has already returned, and we need to be prepared to fight it. After many years of experimenting, they have hit upon the idea that the combination of travel and spirit is the one that will make it work."

"You said it's why you left your family." Ryn recalled their conversation from before her Debut party. It was the first time she heard about her mother's family, and why she had pretended to be an Ordinary when she was not.

Her mother continued to stare out over the water. "Yes. I had hoped to keep you and your brother out of House politics."

"I don't understand, Mother. Why is this experiment so terrible? Think of it. All the magics united in one person again? All the wonderful things you could do with that!"

"No." Her mother turned quickly to face her, red faced and lips pursed. "It's not wonderful. I've seen those whom they've experimented on. Some of them maimed. Most of them can no longer string a sentence together. They are broken inside and out."

Ryn had a sudden image of the man from the woods. The Schiz guy, tapping his fingers to his head, almost as if he could no longer concentrate on what he was trying to say. He must be one of them, the failed experiments. Ryn thought about telling her mother about him, but something made her hold it back. Perhaps it was Schiz's claim that he knew Ryn's father. She hoped that meant her birth father. Then she realized what her mother was really trying to say.

"You think they've experimented with Jett, and...that's why you can't find him."

Her mother squeezed her eyes shut, and Ryn had to look away. She felt like she'd been punched in the gut. She couldn't breathe. For all their growing up together, she had never felt close to Jett. They had different interests and they had both been kind of caught up in their own worlds, but the thought of him somewhere hurt by the people who should be taking care of him as their heir, was gut wrenching.

Ryn wanted to do something, but didn't know what. She picked up a rock and skipped it out over the water.

"You always did love skipping stones," her mother murmured absently.

Happy voices and screams of delight drifted to them from the festival.

"We should get back," Ryn said, shoes shuffling across the drying sand.

Her mother put out a hand and stopped her.

"There's one more thing. I've returned to help Clayr with this Library pest business. I know you've been involved in helping out. You're a great researcher, but you need to be cautious. There's a lot of powerful people involved in Library politics."

"The tension in the Library is high. Everyone is worried, but I'm certain I can help Clayr."

"That's great sweetheart." Her mother took her shoulders. "But be careful. There's talk of a proposal to move the Library. It's not a rumor. I've seen the new facility on Viatoro. I fear this is another move by my mother to consolidate power in Viator. If they send a delegation to negotiate, steer clear of them. They may try to use you to get to me."

Ryn saw the worry and panic in her mother's eyes, it made the only thing she could say was, "Yes, Mother."

Her mother immediately softened and relaxed. Slipping her arm around Ryn they headed down the beach back to the festival.

Ryn tried to relax as well, but frustration was bubbling inside of her. The Library was so important to her. If she could find a way to help, even in a small way, she would do it.

As the sand ended and the grass began, a colorful, out of the way tent caught Ryn's eye. The sign outside the tent read:

Spirit Magic Readings
Your Future
Your Past
Ancestry Told
Have your spirit read today!

Ryn was startled. "Can Jett..." She remembered her mother had Spirit magic as well, it was hard to get used to "or you, read my ancestry through Spirit magic?"

Her mother frowned as the red, and gold tent panels fluttered in the breeze. "Superstitious nonsense people use to make money. Spirit magic helps you commune with the world around you. It's not a way to read your future, or your past."

But Ryn's eyes stayed on the words 'Ancestry Told' till her mother pulled her away deep into the forest of festival tents.

* * *

On their way back to the Slayer's Staff they ran into Lar, the boys, Yll, and Brynd watching an Ordinary do sleight of hand "magic". He wore a short red and black cape with a tall hat. He took a little girl's hand, told her to watch her hand closely, then shook it up and down three times. He turned her hand over and a robin flew out.

"He has to be using Ancestor magic to do that," Ryn said, skeptical.

"You'd be surprised what you can do without magic," her mother said before she stepped over to join Lar.

Everyone clapped, and the showman bowed with a flourish of his cape. There was something about him, maybe it was the dimple on his cheek when he smiled, or his curly brown hair, but Ryn found herself flushing all over at the sight of him.

Brynd spotted Ryn and came to join her. "Let's check out the vendors."

Ryn reluctantly let herself be pulled away.

They moved to the rows of booths, where local artists and farmers were selling their goods. Everyone drifted off in different directions. Ryn's mother and Lar disappeared, Zo and Iden stopped at a leather shop, and Regg and Yll found someone selling promise necklaces. That left Ryn and Brynd to search out and finally find Tory's bag shop.

On the way to find Tory's tent, Ryn caught a glimpse of the colorful Spirit magic tent again. Ryn pointed it out to Brynd.

"Have you ever had your spirit read by someone like that?" Ryn asked.

"No, but my brother did once."

"Oooo, your incredibly cute brother? The one who sells apples with your mom?"

"No, my older brother. The one who works in the apple orchards with my dad. Anyway, when he was young, before he turned of age, he wanted to do more than work the farm. He went to one of those Spirit tellers and she told him the weirdest stuff. Said he wasn't Ordinary. That he had magic in him, and he should go off into the woods to find his magic."

Ryn's eyes went wide. "What happened?"

"He spent a couple weeks in the woods. Got chased by a boar, a chipmunk stole his food and a bunch of his gear, and he walked into a hornet's nest and got stung multiple times. He came home swelled up red and hungry—with no magic." Brynd giggled.

They stopped at a tent with colorful patchworked bags hanging everywhere. Some had beadwork, or ribbons stitched on them. Others had mis-matched fabrics stitched together in bold patterns. All of them looked fancy enough for a ball, but fun enough for a day out shopping.

"These are great," Brynd said as Tory appeared from behind a group of hanging bags, looking every bit as bright and cheery as the bags did.

"Thank you! Thax has a lot of scraps I can use. How goes the Library investigation?"

"It's going. Did you find out anything from your sources?" Ryn asked, trying not to be distracted by a velvety blue bag that could have come from leftover fabric from her Debut dress.

"Actually..."

Tory was interrupted by the side tent flap fluttering open to admit the magic showman they had been watching earlier. Up close he looked no older than Zo. Ryn felt heat rise to her cheeks to be so close to him.

"Jak!" Tory sounded almost scolding. "Use the proper entrance and save us all from being startled to death, will you?"

"And who do we have here?" The showman held out his hand to Ryn.

She was so taken by him, she froze. The memory of the bird coming out of the girl's hand during the show made Ryn pause. So Jak turned to Brynd, who immediately put out her hand. He took it, bowed to press her hand to his forehead, then he rose, pulling her into a warm hug, as if they had known each other all their lives. Ryn found herself becoming jealous.

"That would be Brynd." Tory said, as Jak released the hug, but slid his hand down to hold hers.

"Delighted, I've heard so much about you from Tory."

"And this is Ryn." Tory gestured toward her.

"Brynd and Ryn. I like it. I could write a poem about them. It would make a great rhyme." The voice came from another young man Ryn hadn't seen enter the tent.

He was bigger and broader than Jak, with wavy brown hair and brown eyes. He wore a fashionably cut coat in a rustic fabric, and a hat with a folded up brim. The grin he gave Ryn was sweet and genuine. She felt herself smile in return.

"And this is Dan." Tory flicked her fingers at Jak's companion.

Dan took Ryn's hand, and with a flourish of his hat, bowed low to her. "A pleasure, my lady." He pressed her hand to his forehead with such a delicate respect Ryn blushed.

"So you boys want to tell us what you've uncovered about the Library?" Tory asked.

Jak, who still hadn't let go of Brynd, eyed the festival goers outside the tent. "Not here. Not now." He turned to Tory. "Weren't you going to have an end of festival bonfire night after next?"

"Yes, who said I was inviting you?" Tory lifted her chin.

"Perfect." Jak let go of Brynd and took her hands. "We'll meet you two nights from now on the beach for Tory's bonfire party."

Then he kissed Brynd's hands, and her fair skin turned bright red.

"Until we meet again, beauty of the Library." Dan gave Ryn another flourished bow, and both boys slipped back out the side flap the way they had come.

Brynd had a hand on her heart, looking like she was trying to catch her breath. "Well, I don't know what to say."

"Say you're coming to the party because Jak already decreed it." Tory laughed.

"Of course!" Brynd smiled.

Chapter Eight

Who would have guessed it was possible for Praedo to transfer his magic to us? If we believed what he said, then he came from the stars to help us fight the dragon. He certainly could do remarkable things, and we came to believe that he was indestructible. We all thought we would die in that final battle, but none of us imagined he would. It was quite the blow and the shock when I held him as he took his last breath.

— Luc's Journals, Volume Six

Zo watched Iden replace his belt with the new one he had just bought from the leather craftsman.

"I really don't think you need a new belt to ride the Slayer's Staff," Zo said.

"I've seen it happen, people lose their pants on those things." Iden adjusted his belt to secure it.

Zo rolled his eyes. "Whatever. Can we go ride the thing now?"

Iden took a deep breath. "I love the smell of new leather."

"I think this is all an excuse to buy a new belt."

Iden's eyes darted back and forth. "Maybe..."

Zo's laugh was drowned out in the giggling of a gaggle of girls Zo recognized from the village. They swooped in to surround Iden.

"Good morning, ladies," Iden said, all smiles, but now that Zo knew him better, he could see how his posture straightened, and his movements tensed.

"But it's lunch time Iden," a girl whose red dress reminded Zo of roses said.

"We haven't seen you in forever, you owe us lunch," a girl in orange like a calendula pouted.

Iden looked at Zo with panic in his eyes. Iden and Zo had been looking forward to this whole day together without work or studies. Zo took in the festival goers around them and saw how many people were actually watching this exchange. He gave Iden an almost imperceptible nod, but with a look in his eyes he hoped would convey how Iden owed him later. Relief came over Iden's face as he turned back to the girls.

"I do, do I? Well lead on then." Rose girl and a girl in forest green both snuggled up under Iden's arms and pulled him away toward the food vendors.

Zo was disappointed at having their plans ruined, but most villagers and Library workers knew Iden, and how the ladies flocked to him. If Iden turned them down to spend the day with Zo it would draw unwanted attention and gossip to them. It stank, but it was better to avoid any suspicion or speculation about their relationship. The Ghost Festival was primarily an Ancestor worship festival. Although there were lots of Ordinaries from Waatch here, the festival grounds felt more like the Library grounds—intolerant to those who didn't worship the Ancestors by dating and marrying in the "proper" way.

As Zo's heart sank watching Iden walk away, out of the corner of his eye he saw someone dressed all in black moving toward him. Zo's eyes shifted and he took in the crisp jacket and pants, the silver rings on every finger, and the jet-black hair framing that flawless face. Before Zo could blink, tall, dark, and handsome stood before him.

"We meet again," he said with a slight bow.

Zo nodded, trying to force away fresh thoughts of that dreaded day not so long ago, and an image of the dead man on the table. He needed to say one thing, and hoped the conversation would die after that. "Thanks for finishing the clinic hours for me the other day, I wasn't in the right headspace to take care of anyone else."

Dark and handsome nodded. "My pleasure. I was happy to help." He put out his hand. "Keir," he said.

"Zo." he took the offered hand, feeling a tingling shock when their hands touched.

"I saw you before at the Healing House. The Headmaster wanted to see you, but you walked out," Keir said.

"I don't have anything to discuss with the Headmaster."

Keir nodded, then turned to take in the giant slide. "Have you gone for a slide yet?"

Zo gazed after Iden, now swallowed up in the growing crowds.

"Not yet."

"Well, let's go then." Keir grinned. He didn't look at all dressed comfortably for sliding down slides, but Zo wasn't going to argue.

At the entrance to the slide, they were given woven sacks to slide on. They climbed the wooden stairs inside the lighthouse structure, waiting in a line that started about halfway up.

Keir stood on the step above Zo, and pulled Zo's collar aside to see his beads. "Hmmmm, I like fiery."

Despite the invasion, and rudeness of the move, Zo flushed at the light brush of his fingers against his collar bone.

Keir let his hand drop. "And healing. You couldn't heal the man in the physician's office. Why not?"

Zo felt his cheeks go hot. "It's personal."

Keir nodded like he understood, like Zo had told him everything.

It was their turn to slide. They put their burlap sacks down. Zo sat on his sack. Keir surprised him by sitting right behind him. His legs on either side of Zo, he pulled him close, hugging him around the middle. Zo's entire backside tingled with a vibration of anticipation. He opened his mouth to— say something? Gasp? He wasn't sure, but the next thing he knew the slide attendant pushed Keir and they were sailing down the slide at top speed. The weight of the two of them combined made them zip down the slide, rising up close to the edge of the curves. Zo found himself screaming and laughing in delight. The slide leveled off at the bottom and roughened till they came to a stop. Zo was buzzing inside, and reluctant to stand up and move away from Keir. His touch sent shivers through Zo's body. Unfortunately, the attendant at the bottom of the slide was quickly hustling them off before the next sliders came down on top of them.

"Let's go again!" Zo said.

"Yes!" Keir grinned, taking Zo's hand and pulling him back to the entrance.

The next time down the slide Zo put Keir in front of him. When they got to the bottom of the slide, Zo's legs were so wobbly, they would hardly support him, but he was grinning from ear to ear as Keir supported him back to the stairs to go again. They rode the slide several more times. Every time Zo was left a little more breathless. On their last run down Zo reached out to steady himself, but the attendant pushed them to go. Zo's fingers slid on a protruding splinter, cutting them. By the time they got to the bottom, Zo's blood was dripping down his hand and arm.

Keir returned their sacks to the entrance and pulled Zo aside to look at the cuts. One of them was fairly deep.

"Heal it," Keir said.

Zo studied the silver ringed fingers that were holding his bleeding hand.

He was almost too embarrassed and ashamed to say it to Keir.

"I can't." He turned his head away, fighting the blush.

"Well, we can fix that," Keir said.

"What?" Zo was confused as Keir dragged him off behind a spice exchange tent into the forest.

"Where are we going?" Zo asked.

"Shhh," Keir said, not stopping till the sound from the festival was silenced a bit by the enclosing forest trees.

Keir stood close to Zo, putting pressure on the bleeding cuts. The light shifted through the trees just right to see Keir's magic beads.

"You have two healing magic beads." Zo frowned. "Your mother and your father are both House Sano?"

That was considered inbreeding, and a perversion.

"Yes." Keir's voice was low and silky. "My parents love power."

So much so they don't care if their son is sterile, Zo thought. Often inbreed kids couldn't have children.

"It allows me to do this." Keir put his hand on Zo's neck. "Follow my lead," he said as Zo felt Keir's mind enter his body.

It was like nothing Zo had experienced before. He had felt his mother's and Regg's mind enter to heal him, but their minds left only the lightest of impressions. Keir's was strong, and powerful. Zo could almost feel Keir grab his inner self and lead him to his injured hand. It was similar to Madame Sano, but much less harsh. There was something exhilarating about the way Keir led him through repairing his hand. When they were done, Keir took him on an explorative romp through the rest of Zo's body, healing sore tired muscles—including the headache that had persisted since he couldn't save the patient in Wilmar's office. Keir explored spots of pain, then slid lower past Zo's abdomen, causing his back to arch with need and want. Keir pulled Zo's mind out of his body. Zo doubled over gasping from the sudden absence of Keir's magic. Before Zo could recover, Keir pulled Zo's mind into his body. They explored all of Keir's hurts, and pleasures. It was Keir's turn to gasp and moan. Zo pressed against Keir, their lips almost touching, but Keir pulled Zo's mind away and showed him a way to heal someone quickly, without them noticing. It was difficult, but with Keir's beacon-like touch, Zo learned it fast. He watched as walls and barriers he didn't know he had placed around his healing magic seemed to evaporate at Keir's touch.

When Keir's mind finally withdrew, Zo was panting and quivering with the sudden withdrawal of their intimacy. Heat rolled off Keir's body, his breath hot on Zo's cheek. A burning desire bubbled up inside Zo. Every bit of him wanted Keir in that moment, but he was frozen in place as if Keir had left a silent command of immobility. Keir stepped back, examining Zo's cuts. The emotional withdrawal, followed by a physical one, left an icy hole of need.

"Good work," he said. "Let's get back before you're missed." Keir said, with a mischievous smile on his face.

He knew very well what he had just done to Zo.

He took Zo by the hand and led him back through the woods to the festival. They had barely passed the spice tent when Zo spotted Ryn searching the crowds. Once she saw him, she ran across the festival grounds toward him, stopping short when she got close enough to see Keir still holding Zo's hand. She frowned, took a deep breath, and looked up into Zo's eyes.

"The lantern lighting is starting, and the parents are looking for you," she said.

"How is it time? It's still early," Zo began, but quickly realized the sun was getting low. Where had the time gone? They must have spent a lot longer healing than he thought.

Keir squeezed Zo's hand, then dropped it. "I must be on my way. It was a pleasure meeting you officially, Zo. I hope you will reconsider that trip to the Headmaster's office."

With that he walked off toward the setting sun. Zo felt his absence like a pull at his gut. He put his hand on Ryn's shoulder as he nearly doubled over with it.

"What's happening?" Ryn asked, slipping her hand onto his back.

"I don't know." Zo's eyes were watering badly, not like an allergy, but like he was crying. "Whatever it is, though, I'm not sure it's a bad thing."

Ryn looked skeptical, but he straightened and allowed her to slip her arm around his waist as they walked to the docks to find their parents, and hopefully Iden.

* * *

At the docks, Iden and his parents were there with Ryette and Lar. Being back in Iden's presence was a relief. Iden had an easy smile on his face, but his blue eyes searched Zo's, knowing something was different. Zo stared back, filling his mind with how they would talk later. Zo and Iden hadn't known each other long enough for Iden's mind magic to read him clearly yet, but Iden was beginning to understand impressions from him. Iden nodded, and Zo relaxed into his comforting presence. It was one of the things Zo loved most about him, that he felt at ease with him.

Keir's intensity had left him breathless, but there was only so long you could be out of breath.

Iden pulled Zo aside on the pretense of watching the first of the lanterns float out onto the waters of the bay, but when they were away from everyone else Iden looked intently into Zo's eyes and said, "Go ahead and play around, but make sure you come back to me."

Zo started at that. He didn't realize he'd been that obvious, but of course Iden could have picked it up through their growing connection. Zo's eyes drifted down to the planking of the dock. He cracked his knuckles on the dock railing, before looking into Iden's eyes and nodding.

Iden led him back to the group and urged everyone to set off for the vendor selling lanterns. On the day of the Ghost festival the Ancestors and their sacrifices were honored. There were vendors from each Ancestral House selling lanterns. Legend had it that if you lit the lantern you could speak to the Ancestor and ask them questions. Once you released the lantern to float upon the water, the Ancestor would answer.

Zo thought it was just superstitious nonsense. He'd never had an Ancestor talk to him via a lantern. Talking to them via his beads, yes, that happened all the time. The lantern was supposed to be a way to communicate in a deeper way with the Ancestor other than by lesson, and for those who had finished their magic studies, it was a way to seek help from their Ancestor.

"Fire or healing?" Iden asked.

Zo opened his mouth to say fire. He had always chosen fire, never wanting anything to do with healing, but today...today his mind felt clear. Like there were paths to new places.

"Healing," he said.

Iden pulled away from him, narrowing his eyes at him like he couldn't quite believe this was the Zo he knew.

Zo chuckled.

Iden, of course, bought a lantern for House Dico. He was always fondest of his Mind magic. He always joked that House Venti was only for blowing hot air.

When they returned, they found Ryn standing alone by the dock, gazing out over the water as the evening sky deepened, and lantern light began to dot the bay. She was hugging herself as if against the cold.

"Something wrong, little sis?" Zo asked.

She gave him a weary half smile.

"When I was young, my dad would always let me help him light his lantern and float it on the water for him. It was his way of including me in the ceremony, even though I don't know my ancestry," she said.

"You can light mine," Iden offered before Zo could. It warmed Zo's heart.

Ryn shook her head. "No, if you believe the tradition, you have to light it yourself to get the answer to your questions. I guess my dad didn't think he needed any answers when he let me do it."

"You could always do Praedo's lantern," Iden suggested. "His is supposed to be for when you don't know who to ask."

"But I thought you had to know your Ancestors to ask Praedo," she said.

"Do you see anyone offering their family trees to the lantern vendors?" Iden said, gesturing to the booths lining the docks.

Ryn opened her mouth, probably to object, but Zo took her by the hand and led her down the docks to the last booth on the end.

"One please," Zo said to the vendor as he handed him coins to pay for it.

The vendor handed Ryn the lantern, and she stood there holding it tight. There were tears in her eyes.

"Don't waste it on a dumb wish," he joked, hoping to make her smile.

She just nodded, letting him pull her back down the docks to where they left Iden.

Ryette and Lar were there now, Ryette holding a lantern from House Pentral.

"I haven't done this since I was a little girl," Ryette said.

Lar shifted his earth magic lantern to lean over and give Ryette a kiss on the cheek. "I'm sorry you were revealed to your family, but it's good to see you embracing your magic."

With that comment, Lar gave Zo a side eye. Little did he know, Zo was opening up to embracing all kinds of things.

As a group they moved to the water's edge. One by one lit their lanterns and set them afloat upon the waters of the bay. Lanterns already dotted the shore floating out into the middle of the bay, shimmering upon the water. Zo lit his lantern with a snap of his fingers. He thought about his healing magic, and the way Keir had made it exhilarating. He had never before felt good about it, but now it called to him. He rested the light wood upon the water and pushed it off.

It's time to heal, Madame Sano's voice came, out loud, not in his head.

Startled, he glanced around, certain everyone around him had heard her voice, but everyone else was absorbed in what they were doing. He considered what Madame Sano would think of Keir, and a shiver ran up his spine.

I will come for another lesson soon, she said. Then her voice was gone.

Somehow Zo wasn't as opposed to spending time learning with her as he used to be.

Zo shook his head to clear it as Lar lit a stick for Ryn so she could light her lantern. She pushed its paper sided glow out into the bay. There was a tear trickling down her cheek. As he watched, she rose to her feet.

"I need to go for a walk," she said.

Zo glanced at Iden, who was deep in thought staring after his lantern as it floated away. He didn't want to leave Iden, but he didn't like the look on Ryn's face.

"I'll go with you," he said.

She frowned at him, but nodded. He liked that even less. He had a bad feeling she was planning something unwise.

She led them back to the festival tents. Most people were out at the bay, just a few people remained to watch over their goods. Ryn strode with determination.

"Where are we going?" Zo asked.

"To get answers," she said.

Zo shrugged, but followed her, cracking his knuckles against his thigh.

At the other side of the festival near the beach, Ryn approached a tent that was a riot of color. Red, orange, and yellow scarves glowed in the torchlight. Sweet-smelling smoke wafted out from the tent, making Zo's stomach twist. Ryn headed right for the tent and reached for the gauzy entrance. Zo grabbed her arm.

"What..." he started, but the glare she gave him made him drop his hand.

He followed her into the tent.

Inside, there was a rug on the ground and pillows piled everywhere. From carved metal balls the sweet smoke drifted and floated, almost with a rhythm to it. No one was inside.

"I think we should go," Zo said.

A voice filled the tent, seeming to come from all directions. "Welcome child, what do you seek?"

Zo opened his mouth to say, "Nothing," but Ryn answered first.

"My Ancestors," she said.

"Come and sit." A woman appeared, from seemingly nowhere, wearing a floating skirt that looked like it was made of scarves, and a jacket with flowers embroidered all over it. "I felt your spirit earlier as you passed by my tent. I've been expecting you."

Ryn and the woman sat on pillows facing each other, both ignoring Zo completely. He felt trapped. He didn't like what was going on, but he couldn't leave Ryn to it, so he sat next to her, wanting to pull her away, but unable to say anything.

"My payment." The woman held out her hand.

Ryn dug in her skirts and came up with a small bag. She took out some coins and dropped them into the woman's waiting hand.

"Wait, just wait." Zo was finally able to say something. "Who are you and what are we paying for?"

The woman's attention finally turned to Zo. The intensity of it made him pull away. Her gaze felt like she was looking through him straight into his soul. As if she could see everything about him, every deed he'd done, all the good and the bad. He shrank before her.

"The girl wants to know her ancestry, and I will tell it to her. I have the power to read spirits."

Zo suddenly realized where they were. He should have realized before. The tent of a Spirit teller. As a kid his parents had always steered him clear of such people. Of course, that didn't stop him. Curious, he had once peeked into a tent similar to this one. When he was caught by the owner, their eyes rolled back while they gasped and shook, and they started calling him a killer. Zo had fled.

"Ryn, we need to go." Zo put a hand on Ryn's shoulder, trying to get her attention.

Madame Maya closed her fingers around the coins. "Too late, the contract has been made. Let's see where you come from, little one," she said, eyes intent on Ryn.

Madame Maya held out her hands and Ryn took them, as if she knew what to do. Ryn's eyes were fixed on Madame Maya. So intent she didn't seem to notice anything around her. Zo's stomach churned, while his chest tightened.

After a long time, Madame Maya squeezed Ryn's hands and stood.

"No. No good. I need more. Wait here." Madame Maya stood and left behind a curtain.

Ryn slumped forward. Zo caught her.

"I think we should leave." Zo tried to pull her to her feet.

Ryn shook her head, pulling out of his grip.

Zo looked back at the entrance, but it no longer seemed clear where the opening was. He was about to scoop up Ryn and make a run for it—he'd make his own opening if he had to, when Madame Maya returned—and Ryn sat up straight.

She placed a milky white ball in front of Ryn. "Gaze inside and tell me what you see."

Ryn stared into the ball, her eyes unblinking. It was creepily unnatural.

"A crystal clear pool with a waterfall," Ryn said.

"No, no, no, look deeper," Madame Maya said.

Ryn squinted. "The waterfall, like silver strands of hair."

"No, that's not it." Madame Maya went back behind the curtain.

Ryn stayed transfixed by the ball, unmoving. Zo was done. Now was his chance. He put one arm under her legs and one tight around her back, but when he tried to lift, she felt like stone. He couldn't budge her at all. He contemplated leaving to get help, but he was terrified of what would happen when he left. Madame Maya returned, and Zo's arms dropped from Ryn of their own accord. He was pushed back onto his cushion. He fought to put his arms out again, but couldn't move.

Madame Maya moved as if he didn't exist.

"Now." She produced a black stone, holding it up for Ryn.

Ryn's eyes immediately shifted to the stone.

"Ryn of the mystery ancestors, come out and show us who you are!" Madame Maya commanded, her arm making a swishing motion in front of Ryn. Then her hand closed around something invisible and pulled with a jerk.

Ryn started convulsing. Zo fought the invisible vise that held him tight. He tried to scream, but nothing came out.

A silvery glow that looked like Ryn and flowed like water exited Ryn and stood before Madame Maya. The rest of Ryn fell backward onto the cushions, pale like the man who'd bled to death. The ghostly Ryn held up her silver water hands and gazed at them in wonder.

"*Nooooo!*" Zo finally broke the restraint holding him to scream.

At that moment Ryette stormed into the tent. Eyes blazing.

"Ryn, I command you to return," Ryette yelled, sweeping her hand from Ryn's ghostly form, back toward her body. Her ghost bent in the middle and flowed backward into Ryn.

Ryette snapped at Zo. "Heal her—now!" Then she turned on Madame Maya. "I told you to stay away from my daughter."

Madame Maya and Ryette raised their arms, to do what, Zo didn't stay to find out. The moment he found himself free to move, he picked up Ryn and ran out the way Ryette had come in. When he was out on the beach he glanced up at the bay, now filled with lantern light.

It's time to heal.

And he went to it.

Chapter Nine

Journal entry ???

I wish I didn't stand out as much as I do. I'm forced to stick to the woods. Most people don't bother me here, but it renders me practically useless to protect her. I saw her yesterday, she was here for the Ghost Festival. I tried to get close, but more than one vendor drove me away. I didn't want to start a scene that would cause the Waatch guard to be called on me. I really need to talk to her. She must not let House Viator take her to his sword. The power is too much, and she is not prepared.

— From the Journals of Schiz

It was dark and still. Ryn had the strong impression of Zo with her, but then he was gone, and it was just darkness.

A lantern shone bright on the dark waters, as it bobbed up and down. Ryn was with the lantern and from it she could see Yll and Regg on the edge of Waatch Bay. They were crouched next to each other with their lanterns lit. Regg closed his eyes, his lips moving with a silent question. Yll set her lantern on the water and gently pushed it away. Regg opened his eyes and sent his lantern after hers. He turned to Yll and wrapped his arms around her, pulling her to him as they watched their lanterns float away. Yll's face was bright in the lantern light as she rested her head on Regg's chest.

Ryn watched her mother release her lantern with tears in her eyes. Lar smoothed her hair back from her face and kissed her cheeks, then her lips. Her mother snuggled into his arms.

As she watched Zo release his lantern with a frown, Ryn realized she was watching the Ghost Festival lantern ceremony, but from the point of view of her lantern. The one she released. Praedo's lantern. She had no idea how she knew this, but she was certain of it. What she saw from the water were scenes she hadn't seen at the time. She had been too intent on her own lantern and question. It seemed silly, but she had asked the lantern, or supposedly Praedo, who she was. As she watched her lantern, a distinct voice had come to her mind:

Look no further than who you already are.

Startled, she had looked around to see if Iden or someone was standing behind her. Nobody was there. Could Praedo have really talked to her?

"What does that mean?" she asked this time. Earlier that evening she was too surprised to ask.

No answer came and the darkness took her again. Something shifted.

She found herself walking along a road with her father. It was early morning, the sun not quite up, but the birds had started to sing in the trees. A mist shrouded the way, making it hard to see ahead. The crunch, crunch, crunch of their feet on the roadway seemed too loud in her ears.

"Where are we going?" Ryn asked.

Her father looked at her, and gave her a sad smile, but didn't say anything.

As it grew lighter, the mist ahead cleared and buildings appeared, lining the road. Though it was that time of the morning when the village should be up and about preparing for the day, nothing stirred. Ryn shivered at the stillness from the homes and businesses they passed. On the right, they passed a strange building made from whole cedar trees layered on top of one another. On the door was the symbol of the sword of Praedo, Dragon Slayer, but above the door was the symbol Ryn had seen around Waatch in places Ordinary mainlanders frequented. It was a tall, leafy tree, much like the one depicted in the history books of the Library. The building had all the trappings of Ancestor worship, but in a way that felt it had supplanted something older.

They continued through the village till they came to the far edge of it. There they found a large building with two stories, the only such building in the village. It was as still as the rest of the village. The only sound was the creaking of a rope swing gently swaying in a light breeze. A short fence surrounded the building, giving it a homey, well-kept look.

Something moved in the forest, and Ryn's father pulled her out of sight behind the tree with the swing. A man emerged from the forest, wearing nothing but a hooded cloak. His feet and legs were dirty, but his face was shrouded in the hood. The man held something wrapped in his arms. He stopped in front of the short gate to the yard, clutching his bundle to him. He stood outside the gate for what seemed a long time before he reached down and unlatched it. His shuffle to the door was like that of a man walking to his doom. Ryn couldn't understand what this place could possibly be that this man would dread it so much.

"What..." Ryn started, but her father shushed her, his eyes intent on the scene unfolding before them.

Ryn watched as the man raised his hand. He held it there hovering next to the door for a long time, then at last, he knocked. The sharp sound in the still morning made Ryn jump.

Nothing happened. The man clutched his bundle then knocked again. At last, someone opened the door. Despite the quiet, Ryn couldn't hear anything they said to each other, *if* they said anything to each other. The man began to tremble as he buried his face in the bundle he carried. She heard him gasp from a sob as he held the bundle out to the person at the door. From the bundle came a tiny cry as the person gently took it from the man. He turned then, wiping his eyes. He seemed to look right at Ryn. His face was angular, but beautiful. The hand wiping his tears shifted his hood enough for Ryn to see his pale hair similar to Brynd's. Then he strode quickly away, pausing only briefly to look at the rising sun, and back at the person, still holding the bundle in the doorway, then he disappeared back into the forest.

Ryn's heart ached. She didn't notice her father had spoken her name till he took her by the shoulders and turned her toward him.

"You must find this place," he said.

Ryn nodded. "Where..." she started to ask, but the creaking of the swing turned into the squeaking of door hinges and the soft whispers of someone close by. Everything was dark again.

"How's she doing?" a voice that sounded a lot like Regg said.

"Still out. The Healers said Zo finished healing her before he brought her here, but they don't understand why she's not awake." That was Yll's voice.

"Give her time. I'm sure she'll rejoin us when she's ready," Regg's voice said.

There was the scraping of a chair being dragged across the floor, stopping near Ryn.

"Did they tell you what happened?" Regg asked.

That was a very good question. Ryn was anxious to hear the answer because she remembered nothing past...what was the last thing she remembered? She remembered water. And a lantern. And a voice...

Look no further than who you already are.

Who had said that? And why?

"I don't know. Mom and Ryette wouldn't say much. Zo said something about Spirit magic, but he was tired and mumbling," Yll's voice.

Ryn felt cold fingers brush her cheek, then what seemed to be a kiss on her head. She fought to open her eyes.

"I came to get you. Something is happening at the Library and your mother has recalled all workers there," Regg said.

"I can't. I promised I would stay with her till she woke up," Yll said.

"Whatever happened, that inquisitor guy is looking for a fish to fry, and the Board of Regents is meeting with your mother," Regg said.

Ryn tried to reach out her hand, but it didn't move. There was silence. Ryn was sure Yll wanted to leave, but she didn't hear footsteps.

Yll let out a little sob. "I made a promise. I can't leave her. I won't betray her again."

"You're not betraying her," Regg said.

"Heal her," Yll said.

"But my brother already did."

"Maybe he missed something."

Regg sighed. "I think the Healers would have caught something like that, but I'll try."

"Just wake her up," Yll said.

Yes, Ryn thought, *wake me up!*

She felt a cold hand go to her neck. She would have flinched away if she could have,

Then she felt a strong sense of Regg, not the girl chasing joke maker, but the Healer. He seemed less confident than he did normally, but his presence flowed through her body, till she felt him whisper in her mind:

I see you Ryn. Come back to us.

Her eyes opened to Regg's face level with hers, and Yll hovering behind him.

"You did it." Yll exclaimed. "You're incredible!"

"I'm not even sure what I did," Regg said.

Ryn pushed herself up. The bed was so incredibly soft and warm her body protested the move.

"I heard you talking," Ryn said, swaying.

"You're awake now, so we'll go and help. You stay here and get better," Yll said.

"No. If there's trouble in the Library, I'm going with you." Ryn put her hand on Regg's shoulder to lever herself up to her feet.

She wobbled, and Regg caught her.

"I don't think that's a good idea," Regg said.

The soft warm bed and blankets called to her, but she steadied herself on the chair. She looked down and found herself wearing a soft, warm shift.

"Help me get dressed," Ryn demanded.

Yll and Regg looked at each other like they didn't know what to do.

Regg shrugged. "I've never had a sister before, but I guess I could learn how to lace up a dress."

"Out!" Yll pointed to the door.

Regg held up his hands, gave them a grin, and slipped out the door.

"Hurry," Ryn said. "Who knows what's going on now, but it sounds bad."

* * *

The Healers weren't happy to let Ryn go, but they had declared her healed by Zo, so they didn't have an excuse to keep her. Ryn, Yll, and Regg pooled together what coins they had and took a carriage to the Library. It was the fastest, and Ryn felt too wobbly to walk that distance. It was a strange sensation. Like her mind and body were not working together. It took a while for her arms and legs to do what her brain told them to. It was frustrating, and caused her to stumble.

When their carriage pulled up in front of the Library back entrance, Ryn spotted Master Nix heading across the drive toward the steps to the back door. Ryn's legs tried to collapse under her when she hopped out of the carriage, but Yll waved down Master Nix.

"What's going on?" Ryn asked when he got close enough.

"Water leak," Master Nix rumbled, his shadow covering Ryn in the cold morning air. She shivered.

"What water? There's no water in the Library," Yll said.

"The heating system," Ryn answered.

Master Nix grunted his confirmation.

"Oh dear." Yll's fingers rubbed her forehead.

Fergus came down the steps from the back door, taking them two at a time. "Master Nix, we need your assistance *now*."

Master Nix hurried up the steps next to Fergus. Yll followed, with Regg supporting Ryn around the waist to keep her from falling on her face.

Inside the Library, Fergus led them to a spot inside the reference section. Norm and Ed were there keeping people back, but Ryn could see the stone floor was cracked and a pool of water had collected around it.

Master Nix knelt beside the pool, running his fingers along the crack.

"How does that even happen?" Yll asked.

Nobody answered.

Ryn pulled on Fergus' arm. "The Board of Regents can't possibly think this is Clayr's fault."

"No, but Clayr just hired a new docent who miss-shelved a bunch of new materials that hadn't been through quarantine. They are definitely blaming Clayr for that." Fergus said, his lips flat and grim.

Ryn felt a sinking feeling in her gut that had nothing to do with how disconnected she felt with herself.

"Those voices," Ryn said.

"What?" Regg asked.

Yll's jaw dropped. "You're right! Those intruders the other night. They said something about water..."

"But nothing happened after we saw them." Ryn gazed down at the water seeping up from the crack in the stone.

"Maybe we scared them off," Yll said.

Master Nix grunted. "I'm heading down below to check the breach. Somebody fetch Zo to come help me," he said as he struggled back to his feet.

"I'll go find him," Regg offered.

"Fine. And grab the first guard or maintenance person you see and have them come clean this water up before the Board shows up. If they get here with the delegation from Viatoro before we get this cleaned up, all our heads will roll, not just those at the top."

Ryn's anxiety rose. "Fergus, where is the Board meeting with Clayr?"

"The Regent's Chamber."

"Can you take us?" Yll asked.

Fergus shook his head. "Nobody's allowed in the Regent's Chamber without a summons."

Ryn felt woozy again. Fergus grabbed her arm when she started to sway.

"I think I need to get you back to your room. Nothing you can do to help now," Fergus said.

Ryn felt an overwhelming nausea but managed to keep from throwing up.

"Alright." She swayed again.

Fergus scooped her up, and she rested her head on his shoulder.

"Maybe you should take me to Zo's room. It's on the first floor," Ryn said.

Fergus nodded. "Good. I can carry you up three flights of stairs, but I'm needed to escort the delegation onto the Library grounds."

Fergus carried her out of the Library, and across the grounds to Zo's dorm room. Zo had graduated from the open dormitory to his own room when he became the head temperature taker for the Library. His room was small, but clean. He didn't have much, mostly clothes, and his blanket and pillow. The quilt on his bed was the same one he had on his bed in his father's cabin in Sooke. She ran her hand over the stitching, wishing she was back in the village playing card games with Zo in the cabin loft.

Yll got a glass of water for Ryn, as Fergus tucked an extra blanket around her.

"You feel better, I need to go. The delegation will be here soon," Fergus said.

"What delegation are you talking about?" Ryn asked.

"House Viator has sent a delegation with the official proposal to move the Library to Viatoro. It's very bad timing. The Board called in Clayr to answer for the new hire who somehow wasn't properly trained and was shelving items without going through quarantine, and now the leak."

With the magical barrier around the Library, new requisitioned items going to quarantine was mostly a tradition, and to give Ryn and Yll's team time to accession them, then shelve them, but with the barrier compromised, quarantine was crucial to make sure other pests weren't introduced into the Library—pests like silverfish, or cockroaches, or book worms.

Ryn shivered under the blankets.

"I'll see you later and let you know how it goes," Fergus said.

"Thanks." Ryn watched him go.

Yll stared at the door as he shut it.

"You should go. Your mother will want you by her side, I'm sure," Ryn said.

"It's not that. I'm really worried about her and what they might do to her. If there's a vote of no confidence against her, where will we go? What will we do? The Library is our whole life," Yll said.

Ryn sank deeper into Zo's pillow. She felt bone wearily tired. "You go. Find out what you can and come back and tell me."

Yll nodded, moving to give Ryn a kiss of the forehead. "Feel better. I'll be back."

Ryn had drifted off to sleep before Yll was out the door.

* * *

Ryn was dreaming again. This time she was high up on the top of the tallest Library spire, but somehow also at the Library door, and by the potted plant at the Library gate. She felt cold, and stiff, and ancient. She watched with three eyes, one from the top spire, one from the door, and one by the gate. Clayr stood with a full Library honor guard, waiting, a breeze blowing her Curator's dress and shawl. Strands of hair slowly escaped her neatly pinned updo. Yll was standing off to the side and behind her mother, but Jeris was at Clayr's side, sending a constant stream of words at her.

"Just because the delegation has arrived days early and interrupted our hearing, doesn't mean it's over," Jeris said.

Clayr only nodded.

Master Ubert strode across the grounds from the Library with Prym in tow, hanging onto her shawl, and clutching her clipboard of papers to keep them from blowing away.

Jeris turned to him. "Master Ubert, what news?" His voice was so silky smooth, Ryn wanted to gag.

Clearly out of breath, Master Ubert collected himself. "There's been a breach in the Library flooring. It's cracked and water from the heating system is seeping out into the reference section."

"What?" Jeris yelled, but just then a clattering of hooves and carriages came down the grand promenade toward the Library gates.

The guards snapped into a salute as the first carriage pulled up to the gate. Fergus stepped forward to open the carriage door, and a man dressed all in black swept down from the carriage, almost as if he was made of smoke.

A man dressed in deep maroon with gold trim followed.

The man in black approached Clayr, took her hand, and bowed to press her hand to his forehead.

Something deep inside the ancient part of…not Ryn, she wasn't ancient, but who she was at the moment, stirred. There was a hot flash of cold anger, and an icy cold dread.

"My name is Zmej. I was charged with bringing this delegation to you. I present to you, the Patriarch in Waiting for House Viator." The man in black stood and opened one arm to bring in the man in maroon. There was something about him that was familiar, even though Ryn had never seen him before. He certainly had the red hair of House Viator.

"Greetings, I am Mik de Viator, I have come as head of this delegation with a petition for the Library Board of Regents."

Ryn, the part of her who wasn't watching the scene unfold, wondered who he was and how he might be related to her mother.

A woman dressed in black stepped forward, handing an old-fashioned type scroll to Clayr.

"We wish to formally declare our intent to move the Library to our newly built facility on Viatoro," Mik said.

A gust of wind shook Ryn, and she drifted back into darkness.

Chapter Ten

Dear Fyri de Sano of the Healing Counsel,
I've heard the most salacious rumor about your son Zo de Ignis...

— Anonymous

Zo stretched, cracked his neck, and stood from Wilmar's worktable. He was still tired from the night before last when he had spent the night healing Ryn. It was the oddest kind of Healing he had ever done, but admittedly he hadn't performed much. Fortunately, this morning had been an uneventful shift, patient-wise, but Wilmar had kept him busy mixing up concoctions for what Zo called "Wilmar's potions wall." They had successfully re-stocked many medicines, and the herbs they had harvested at the end of summer were sufficiently dried to crush despite the cold, damp fall. Zo put his coat on and reached for the door.

"Are you heading over to the Healing House to check on your sister?" Wilmar asked, giving Zo a side eye.

Zo rolled his eyes at Wilmar's not so subtle hint. "Yes, I'm going there, but only to check on Ryn and nothing more."

"Good." Wilmar gave him a huge grin he didn't like at all. Zo knew Wilmar was still hoping Zo would become the first physician with Healing magic.

Zo crossed the street, dodging carriages arriving at the Healing House with healing requests. No one arrived at Wilmar's by carriage. Physicians were for the common people, not Ancestor descendants. Zo turned heads as he snaked between family members waiting to see patients and students chatting, striding down the hallway to Ryn's room. When he found it empty, he went in search of Regg—not that he had a lot of hope in finding him. Regg seemed to spend more time at the Library with Yll than he did studying Healing. The dorm room Regg shared with three other first-year students was empty. He also didn't see Keir anywhere. He wasn't sure how he felt about that. Part of him wished he would bump into him, but another part of him was disquieted by that wish. Since the time he spent with Keir yesterday, Zo couldn't get Keir and the things he'd learned off his mind.

He passed an open door, and heard his name from inside.

"Zo of Fyri, a moment please."

Zo backed up and looked inside the door. It was a large office, with an enormous desk stacked with books and papers and what looked like old scrolls. As Zo's eyes shifted to the man behind the desk, he instantly realized the huge mistake he had made by choosing this hallway.

"Come in, come in!" The Headmaster of the Healing House waved Zo in.

Zo took a deep breath. He was still in the hallway. He could easily ignore the man and walk away, but even though that instinct was strong, he fought against it. Exhaling slowly, he stepped into the office.

"Have a seat." The Headmaster indicated one of the chairs in front of his desk.

Zo sat, cracking his knuckles on his thigh.

The Headmaster's eyes seemed to take Zo's measure, but he remained quiet.

"Was there something you needed?" Zo asked.

The Headmaster stirred out of his thoughts. "Yes, as a matter of fact there is. The Spirit magic Healer was impressed with your healing work on the young Library girl. He says healing a spirit torn from the body is delicate work that usually requires a Healer with Spirit magic."

Zo knew what was coming, but the praise was alluring anyway.

"You have great healing talent. Has no one told you this before?"

"No," Zo said. "I really haven't used my Healing magic much. In fact, I've been avoiding it for years."

The Headmaster frowned deeply, fiddling with a paper on his desk.

"I don't understand your reluctance. Master Don said the healing you performed was near perfect."

"That's kind of him to say, but Madame Sano and I don't really get along," Zo said.

The Headmaster chuckled. "She can be a bit...difficult. I had my own run-ins with her."

Zo's eyes narrowed at that. Madame Sano had always made him feel he was the most difficult student she had ever had. He was actually quite proud of that fact.

The Headmaster waved his hand to dismiss the thought. "Doesn't matter. What matters is that I would like to extend an invitation to study here at the Waatch Healing House. I know you deserve better, as the son of a Healing Council member, and with your talents you should study at the House Sano Healing House, but if you would consider us, we would love to have you."

Yes, I bet you would, Zo thought. The fact that the Headmaster used his mother's name when calling him into his office demonstrated his knowledge of Zo's parentage, but having him mention his mother's position on the Council drove that home. He almost walked out. It smelled of too much drama.

"You already have my brother. Why do you need me?" Zo asked.

"And your brother also has potential, if only he could stop spending so much time with the curator's daughter, but you..."

Zo folded his arms. Silence stretched between them.

"I won't give up my work at the Library, nor will I give up my work with the physician," Zo said at last.

The Headmaster rocked back and forth, as if he was having a debate with himself.

"You won't have to. You can keep both of those apprenticeships and study here."

Zo raised an eyebrow. *Really?* They wanted him that badly. Well, he had one last condition he doubted the Headmaster could accept.

"And you will not tell my mother I am here studying," Zo said.

The Headmaster stood from his desk. He walked to the window behind him and looked out into the gray day. Such a change from the sunny, bright day before.

The Headmaster exhaled. "I will promise not to inform your mother you are here studying with us."

Zo knew that was a huge concession. His mother had offered a large sum of money to the Healing House who could get her wayward son to take Healing lessons. This meant everything. It meant the Healing Master was willing to forgo the possible goodwill of the Healing Council, via Zo's mother, to get Zo to commit to studying with him. Zo almost dared to hope it meant the Headmaster had Zo's interests in mind, and not politics. More likely he was lying and would tell his mother for the money.

The Headmaster came back to his desk and gave Zo a hopeful look.

Last chance to walk out, Zo reminded himself.

He thought about all the times Wilmar had subtly tried to encourage him to study Healing. How good it felt to heal Regg and Ryn. The way Keir had stepped over his barriers and helped him access his magic.

It's time to heal.

"Fine, as long as I can fit it into my schedule, and my other Masters are agreeable, I will take my Healing study here at the Waatch Healing House." Zo almost couldn't believe those words were coming from his mouth.

Nix and Wilmar had been scheming for a while to get him to study his Healing magic, so they wouldn't object.

The Headmaster thrust out his hand. Zo stood and took it.

"Done," the Headmaster said.

Zo wanted to feel bad about this choice, but instead he felt strangely relieved.

* * *

On his way out of the Headmaster's office, Zo's Healing bead began to burn. A healing student was passing by with a tray of food. Zo stopped her.

"Excuse me, I'm going to have a Healing lesson, do you happen to have a quiet room I could use?"

"Sure. Let me set this down and I'll show you." She smiled. Her nose crinkled when she smiled. Zo found himself instantly at ease with her.

He followed her down the hall and into the Healing House mess hall where she deposited her tray then led him down a narrow hallway that led to the back of the Healing House.

"Here you go." Crinkle Nose slid a pocket door open to reveal a meditation room.

"Prefect. Thank you…"

"Ayn," she said.

"Ayn. I'm…"

"Zo of Fyri. I know your brother," she said.

"I'm so sorry, please don't judge me by him." Zo grinned.

Ayn smirked. "I'll try not to. Just close the door when you're done."

"Thanks again."

Zo moved to the middle of the matted floor and sat cross legged to wait. He didn't have to wait long.

"Zo of Ingis, son of Fyri, it's about time!" Madame Sano appeared before him, cross legged and stooped almost in half.

"It's good to see you too, Madame Sano," Zo said, keeping his tone even.

"Don't try to sweet talk me." She shoved a gnarled finger into his chest. "You are far behind on your lessons, and you're only a few moons off from being eighteen and unable to take any more lessons. We have so much to catch up on. It's going to take days. A quarter moon, or a fortnight."

Zo squirmed at that. He had a shift at the Library soon. He didn't have time for an hours long lesson.

"I hear that!" Madame Sano said. "I've got your thoughts." She sighed. "Fine, fine, fine. I'll make it quick if you promise you'll take your lessons every day."

Zo swallowed. He didn't know how he was going to take the Library's temperature, work with Wilmar, take lessons at the Healing House, AND take lessons with Madame Sano every day—plus the mouse thing at the Library. It felt like he was teetering on the edge of having too much, but he absolutely didn't want to give up any of it. He let out a long breath his stress had caused him to hold.

"Fine. I'll meet with you every day from now till my birthday," he conceded.

Madame Sano's wrinkled grin spread across her face and made her eyes twinkle.

"Perfect. Let's get started. This might hurt a bit because you're in a rush."

Her grin took on a bit of a wicked twist, right before she yanked his mind into his body to start his lesson.

After his lesson with Madame Sano, his brain felt like mush from cramming so much information into it. He was on his way to check on Ryn in her dorm room when he crossed paths with Nix who had a gaggle of maintenance workers trailing behind him asking non-stop questions. He looked about to explode, but said nothing. He threw open the door to the Boiler Room as Zo caught up to him.

"What's going on?" Zo asked when they got to Hal's desk.

"Water leak from the heating system into the Library," Hal said.

Zo started. "That's not possible."

Nix gave him a grim look. "I come back from just a few days away and everything is falling apart. I blame you. Come on grunt, let's go find the problem."

Clearly, Nix was trying to get a rise out of Zo. He hadn't called him a grunt in moons.

"I'm not your grunt," Zo snapped back, playfully.

One corner of Nix's mouth twitched up. That was Nix speak for stressed, but amused.

Good, Zo thought, *maybe he won't bite my head off for existing.*

"Grab some lanterns and a ladder so we can go examine the breach," Nix said, striding toward the tunnels.

Zo went to a closet behind Hal's desk to get the requested items, then hurried after Nix. He found him at the junction ordering the water magic workers to cut off the water to the pipes.

"Where is it?" Zo asked.

Nix just waved him on.

Halfway down the north wall tunnel Zo usually traversed when taking the Library's temperature, Nix halted them and pulled out a key. He inserted it into what looked like a solid wall with a small hole in it. He turned the key and the door swung inward.

There's doors in the walls? Zo tried not to look shocked.

Nix led them through a mess of piping and ductwork, then suddenly stopped and reached for one of the lanterns. Zo released it, and saw what Nix had seen before lantern light fell on it—water was dripping from the piping right above them. Nix wasn't satisfied though; he traced where the water was coming from with the light. Eventually he found a spot where the water was coming from the ceiling, but not the piping.

"Pipes are good, but the floor is cracked," Nix said.

Zo swore. "How thick is that floor?"

"At least as thick as your arm is long," Nix said, examining the crack with his own lantern.

Zo swore again. "Earth magic?" He snapped his fingers and tried to ignite them with fire, but nothing happened.

Master Nix set up the ladder to get a closer look.

A shadow moved in the corner of Zo's eye. He shined his lantern in that direction, but nothing stirred.

"More light over here, grunt," Master Nix said from the other side of the piping.

Zo skirted around the ladder to shine his lantern in the spot Nix indicated.

"Not a grunt," Zo said.

Nix harrumphed, then let out a long string of curses under his breath.

Again, something moved, just out of Zo's vision. He set the lantern on some piping, then quietly wove his way to the area where he'd seen the shadow.

The further he got away from the lanterns, the deeper the shadows cast by the pipes. When he was far enough away from the light to have to feel his way around, a chill ran down his spine. The hairs on his arms stood up. Something like a claw hooked itself around Zo's neck.

Zo raised his arms in surrender. "Protector, I'm here to help."

The claw slid away. Zo took a shaky breath. The shadow disappeared, becoming a nebulous darkness. Then it coalesced into a more familiar shape. One with no claws, it appeared to be almost human.

Zo took a tentative step back. He glanced over at Nix, who was still on the ladder muttering to himself. Zo forced himself to lower his hands to try and look calm. He couldn't afford for his own fright to scare away the Protector again.

"What's happening?" Zo asked. "The Library's magic should prevent a mouse from getting in, and Earth magic from being used. Is there something wrong with the Library's magic?"

The shadow moved into a beam of light between two pipes. It shook its head.

"How can magic get past the Library's barrier?"

The Protector held its hand to the light and in its palm, there formed a solid looking stone, then a sword, then a tree branch.

"A rock, a sword, and a branch. I don't understand."

"Hey Zo, can you run back and get me a pry bar from the tool bench?" Master Nix's boomed through the quiet underworld.

The Protector started, head swiveling toward Nix's voice, then it melted into the inky blackness.

Zo sighed. "Thanks Nix," he whispered, then ducked and wove his way back to the light.

He had no idea how a rock, a sword, or a branch could cause the Library's magic to fail, but he was sure Ryn could do some research and figure it out.

Chapter Eleven

Jak,

I hired you a quarter moon ago and I have yet to see the results. You are testing my patience. Get me what I asked for, or you'll forfeit your payment, as well as something you hold dear.

Ryn pulled on an extra pair of socks. It would make her boots tight, but it was better than having her feet get cold. House Viator was a guest of the Library, so Ryn was heading beyond the town walls for the night. She stood too fast and wobbled a bit. She grabbed a chair to cover it. After an afternoon of sleeping she was feeling more together, but if she moved too fast her limbs still took a second to catch up.

"Why a bonfire on the beach in the middle of winter? Isn't it something you do in the summertime?" Ryn asked Brynd.

"Bonfire's too hot in the summer," Brynd said. "And if we find some cute guys, it's cozier."

Ryn rolled her eyes. "I still think I'm going to freeze to death."

Abby sat next to Ryn on her bed with her paws tucked up underneath her in what Ryn called her "nesting pose." Abby's eyes looked at Ryn like she was silly to be going out into the cold. Ryn was inclined to agree.

"You can borrow my heavy wool cloak if you want," Brynd said.

"No, mine'll be fine. Yours would drag on the ground if I wore it. I'm too short for it." Ryn finished lacing up her boots.

Brynd buttoned her cloak. "Let's get going, Tory is expecting us."

"I just hope those Jak and Dan characters have information for us to make going out in the cold worth it."

"Hush now, it'll be fun!" Brynd shooed Ryn out the door.

As they crossed the Library grounds, Ryn kept her eye out for Zo. She hadn't seen him since the Ghost Festival the day before yesterday. She really wanted to thank him for putting her back together. There was no sign of him though, or

Fergus, or even Iden. She was worried about how the repair was going. Clayr had insisted Ryn take the day off. She wasn't sure if it was because Clayr was keeping her away from House Viator, but it was making Ryn anxious to be out of the loop of what was happening in the Library. Brynd had been busy reshelving books all day and got only a glimpse of the delegation. The reference section with the leak was discreetly sealed off.

* * *

Ryn felt a weight lift from her shoulders as they exited the Library grounds, then a bit of a thrill as they hit the nighttime streets of Waatch on their own. It was not something she had done before, especially not alone with Brynd. The town at night had an excitement in the air. It made Ryn feel like she could go anywhere and accomplish anything. Despite the cold, they passed people out walking on the streets. Many of them ducked inside taverns. Ryn and Brynd passed the last eatery and entered the upscale Library manager's neighborhood. Even here, people were out walking, taking the chance to stretch their legs on a clear night. Soon the rainy season would set in, and it would be too wet to be out.

"Do you think we'll ever be managers in the Library?" Brynd asked.

"I suppose. I mean, the longer we work there the more likely we'll move up, right?"

"I don't know. I'm afraid. We're Ordinaries, and if the Board dismisses Madame Curator I doubt whoever takes her place will be friendly to Ordinaries. We might be lucky to keep our jobs."

Ryn hadn't thought about that. Maybe she had, but she was keeping it from her mind. She didn't want to think about it. She didn't want to consider who Jeris would choose to be curator running the Library. They would certainly be of Ancestor descent and probably do what Brynd was suggesting—get rid of all the Ordinaries Clayr had hired to work in the Library. Ancestor descendants had always run the Library before. Clayr was the one who had opened it up to all peoples. As long as a person could pass some basic tests, the Library was open for anyone to work there. The great Ancestral Houses were not pleased. They didn't want Ordinaries seeing their family's dirty secrets. Ryn shivered, but not from the cold. The thought of losing the one thing she was good at, doing research in the Library, was something she didn't want to contemplate. She had lost access to the Library once before, and she couldn't handle losing it again.

Once free of the city gates, the bonfire on the beach was easy to spot. Firelight and music was coming from the section of beach just beyond the docks. Ryn's nose and fingers were cold and the heat of a fire sounded good. The rhythm of the music drew them toward the light.

When they arrived at the fire it was almost too hot to be near. Tory came dancing up to Ryn and Brynd to the beat of some drums, and the rhythm of a flute.

"Glad you could make it!" Tory pointed to some jugs stuck in the sand by the musicians. "Get yourself something to drink. Jak and Dan should be here soon. Jak loves to make an entrance."

Ryn was thirsty from the walk there and the sudden heat of the fire, but instead of moving, she stood gaping at her first beach party. A guy wearing only a vest and short pants was throwing a huge log on the fire. There were people sitting on logs talking and drinking, one girl shrieked with laughter when a guy picked her up and carried her to the bay, splashing in the waves. Other people were dancing in the sand next to the musicians. Ryn felt her cheeks get hot when she spotted a couple sitting in the sand kissing. The whole scene was overwhelming to take in.

Tory returned with wooden mugs. "You haven't gotten a drink yet. Here"—she handed a mug to Brynd—"the night is still young." She winked at Ryn as she gave her a mug. "Just wait."

Ryn sniffed at the liquid in the cup, then took a sip. The liquid burned her tongue. It was nasty, so she just smiled and held it like she would drink more later.

"The party is here!" Jak arrived with the same flourish of his cape he used at the Ghost Festival.

Everybody cheered and raised their cups to him. A girl approached him, pressing a mug into his hand and saying something into his ear. He nodded, moving to where Tory was standing with Ryn and Brynd. Dan trailed behind Jak, also with a mug in hand, his lopsided smile turning into a grin when his eyes met Ryn's

"You remember Ryn and Brynd," Tory said.

"Yes, my beautiful Library workers."

Ryn hoped Jak would reach out his hand to her, so she could redeem herself and take it, but he took Brynd's hand instead and kissed it. Brynd's eyes sparkled in the firelight.

"Jak...Jak...Jak." A small boy with a messenger cap ran up to Jak, and handed him a piece of paper.

Dan watched with interest from behind him.

"Maus!" Jak took the paper then spun the boy around to face the girls. "Maus, I would like you to meet the ladies Brynd and Ryn."

Maus went down on one knee in the sand, took their hands, and pressed them to his forehead. Maus was so tiny, even Ryn had to bend a bit to be low enough for her hand to touch his forehead. This party was much too raucous for a young boy.

"A pleasure," Brynd said.

"Remember these ladies, Maus. It's important," Jak said.

Maus nodded solemnly.

"Now off with you!" Jak, folded the note and put it inside his coat pocket. He must have read it while Ryn was distracted.

"Shall we take a walk and discuss what information I can give you?" Jak asked.

Ryn shivered at the prospect of leaving the heat of the fire, but she nodded.

Dan stepped up to her. "May I?" he asked, offering her his arm.

Ryn took it, and the boys walked them around the fire and off into the darkness of the beach. When they had gone far enough away the sound of the waves lapping on the beach got louder than the voices and laughter coming from the party, Jak led them to a log.

Dan dusted the sand off so Ryn could sit.

"What do you know about what's happening in the Library?" Ryn asked.

"I know you've had a mouse in the house, a water pipe leak, and that poor brand-new docent who's going to suffer the wrath of the Board of Regents for skipping the quarantine of materials," Jak said.

Ryn started, staring at Jak for a long moment. All of those things were Library secrets no one outside the Library should even know about. Some of them were known only to a select few people.

"Oh, don't look so shocked, Waatch's heart beats to the drum of the Library. Nothing that goes on there is truly secret." Jak smiled in the faint light of the bonfire.

Ryn inhaled sharply, then realized her mouth was hanging open.

Brynd recovered her shock first. "Alright, so how is this all happening at once?"

"I asked Dan to look into it."

Dan, who was gazing out over the bay, turned back to them. "House Viator is looking to move the Library to their island."

"We know that. That's still not getting us any closer to knowing how a mouse and Earth magic could get into the Library." Brynd folded her arms.

Dan held up a finger. "Talk on the street is that House Viator has hired someone to sabotage the Library and undermine Clayr's authority."

"But how?" Ryn asked. "I've searched every book I can find about the history of the Library, and there's no mention of how someone could breach the Library's protective magic."

Dan shrugged.

Jak shifted so his eyes flickered in the light of the fire down the beach. "There is a legend. Bedtime stories the people of Waatch tell their children. In those tales, there are objects that can make the Wild magic flee. Have you heard of them?"

Brynd nodded while Ryn shook her head.

"Just bedtime stories meant to give kids nightmares while they sleep," Brynd shivered.

"My mother never told me such tales," Ryn said.

"Proof she's no Ordinary," Jak said.

Ryn glared at him. "How is it you know so much about my family?"

Jak shrugged. "It's healthy for the Ordinaries of Waatch to know everything about the Library and what's going on there. Your little misadventure with Master Wes is no secret."

Ryn shifted on the log.

"Well, if you know so much, it should be easy for you to figure out who is behind the Library sabotage, and how they are getting pests and magic past the protective barrier," Brynd said.

With a flourish Jak knelt in front of Brynd. "We don't have all of the answers yet, but it would be our pleasure to do some more digging." He took her hand and pressed it to his forehead.

Ryn began to shiver as a breeze off the ocean blew past her.

Dan held out his hand to her. "Shall we return to the fire?"

Ryn nodded, letting him pull her to her feet.

Jak and Brynd were already walking back. Jak flashed a coin he pulled out of Brynd's ear. She giggled and let him press it into her hand. They held hands as they walked in the sand.

Ryn stumbled over a hidden piece of driftwood, and Dan caught her by the arm to steady her.

"What's it like, working for the Library?" he asked.

Ryn let him put her hand on his arm as they walked.

"Exciting, fun...stressful right now," she said.

"I've lived my whole life in Waatch and I've never been on the Library grounds."

"How is that possible? Haven't you taken a walk through the gardens?" she asked.

"No, they don't let Ordinary street urchins past the gates. Someday, it would be nice to go there."

Ryn focused on her boots kicking up sand. She hadn't thought about how other Ordinaries might live. Her experience only involved Sooke. The village was inhabited by Ancestor descendants who work in the Library. Ryn, her mother, and Yll were the only Ordinaries—until Yll got one magic, and Ryn found out her mother was the Matriarch in Waiting for House Viator. Villagers had treated Ryn like she was something less, but she had never been denied going places. She had visited the Library grounds with her mother a few times as a child. It made sense now, knowing who her mother really is.

"Well, now you have an excuse to come onto the grounds. I'm sure if you could bring us the information to catch the saboteurs it would be fine," Ryn said, hoping it would cheer him up.

"Ha! The Library guards hate us. We can't set foot on the Library grounds without stirring up trouble."

Ryn pulled him a little closer to her. "We'll figure out something."

Dan's pace slowed, and she glanced up to see him looking down at her like he wanted to say something, but didn't. The firelight from down the beach gave his wavy brown hair a warm glint.

Ryn hated making small talk, but at that moment she wanted to know more about him.

"What's it like growing up Ordinary in Waatch? It was bad in my village. I was teased. They did mean things to me," Ryn said.

"There are lots of Ordinaries in Waatch. The rough part is making a living in Waatch as an Ordinary. The Ancestor descendants can't be bothered to use their magics to help the people around them, and they expect Ordinaries to do all their dirty work, but only the dirty work. Clayr is the first Curator of the Library to allow anyone other than an Ancestor descendant inside." Dan said, his eyes reflecting the bonfire made them glow with passion.

Ryn found herself being taken in by those eyes. They were a rich cedar brown, so open and inviting.

"What do you do?" Ryn asked.

Dan put a hand over the one Ryn was using to hold his arm. "Mostly I am Jak's right-hand man in his um, business dealings."

"You look very young to be a businessman," Ryn said.

"Jak and Tory and I have fended for ourselves for a long time. You learn some things along the way. If we didn't pick up the business, we wouldn't have survived."

They came to a support pillar for the docks and Dan stopped and leaned against it. He took her hands in his. In the shadow of the docks she could just make out his face, but somehow there was still a light in his eyes. They were earnest when they looked into hers.

"Do you really think we can figure out what's going on in the Library?" she asked.

He smiled. "If there's anyone in Waatch who can find a criminal mastermind it's Jak."

"What about you?"

Dan shrugged. "I suppose I have my uses."

She stared up into his face as he stared down into hers. She began to tremble. She had never kissed anyone before, and she wasn't certain she knew this boy well enough to be kissing him. At the same time she wasn't sure she wanted to push him away either. She reached around him and drew him into a hug instead. He was warm, and despite being large, his muscles were firm. She pressed her ear against his chest and listened to his heart beat fast.

He kissed the top of her head and she shivered.

"Let's go get warm by the fire." He took her hand, pulling her back to the party.

When they got back to the bonfire Ryn was surprised to find most everyone at the party had paired off and were in various stages of kissing and making out. Most shocking was Brynd sitting on a log with Jak, arms tight around each other while their mouths were locked together. Ryn's eyes quickly darted away, her face going hot again. It felt far too intimate a moment to be displayed around so many people. Dan led her around the fire to where they had left their drinks. Ryn mumbled an apology when she accidentally kicked two guys making out in the sand. She had to do a double take to make sure it wasn't Zo.

Dan settled her on a log with her back to the woods, and set off to fill his cup. She watched Brynd and Jak together. He had his fingers twined in hair and there was a flash of tongue. They never seemed to need to come up for air. She looked away into the fire. She knew she had blown it and lost her chance.

Her gaze drifted to the two young women next to Jak and Brynd making out. It seemed everyone was happy tonight.

Something crashed through the forest behind them. Ryn leapt up, spinning toward the trees, and backed right into Dan. He slipped an arm around her.

"You're trembling," he said.

"Something's out there."

"Of course something's out there, it's the forest. Animals live there," Dan said.

She sat back down, but glanced over her shoulder.

"Don't worry," Dan said as he poured juice into the cups. "There's enough steel here to take care of racoon. What has you so jumpy?"

"I don't know."

He handed her a cup.

She took a sip and spit it back out when the burning hit her tongue. She had forgotten it wasn't just juice.

The fire was warm and bright. The front of her felt wonderful, but her back was cold. She shivered. Dan moved closer and slipped an arm around her so he was between her back and the cold forest. She tensed at first, but eventually nestled into his warmth. They sat quiet for a long time. A log on the fire crackled and popped. Ryn stared into the fire. She preferred that to watching Jak and Brynd make out. It looked like her and Dan were the only ones there who weren't kissing.

Dan stood and stretched. "Time to take you home."

He walked over and kicked Jak's foot. The two of them raised their faces to him like they were in a fog, as if they had been sleeping. Their lips were red and swollen in the firelight.

"Time to go," Dan said.

"The night is still young," Jak said with a sneer on his lips and steel in his voice.

"Not for Library workers," Dan said.

It was a subtle reference to the curfew for Library workers. So far Ryn and Brynd hadn't been out late enough to break it. They passed Tory on their way out, but Dan said it wasn't wise to interrupt her with her man to take their leave of the party, so they kept going. Jak and Brynd walked with their arms around each other's waists—Jak stopping every once in a while to steal a kiss until Dan and Ryn prodded them forward. Dan just held Ryn's hand. Not too tightly, just firm and sweet. Eventually he took to swinging her arm playfully, like they were small children. Then he tried to duck under her arm and turn around as if they were dancing. He didn't make it, of course, he was so much taller than her and her arms were so much shorter. He fell on his rump, giggling. Ryn had to laugh too.

On the walk home it was Dan's turn to pepper Ryn with questions about growing up in the village. He reverently nodded when she told him she was adopted.

"Jak was too. My father adopted him after his mother died."

Ryn was curious what age Jak had been, but didn't ask. "So he's your brother?"

"Yep. It's legal and everything," he grinned.

Ryn hadn't realized it could be illegal.

"This is as far as we can go," Dan said. "Can't risk being seen by the guards."

Ryn looked around and realized they were a block from the Library. She hadn't noticed they'd walked that far.

"You're serious about the Library grounds thing, aren't you?"

Jak groaned and pulled Brynd with him to lean against an ink shop. He kissed her then buried his face in her neck. "I don't want you to go." he mumbled against her skin. She put her arms around his neck.

"I don't want to go," Brynd said.

Jak took Brynd's hand. "We're just going to go for a walk. I'll have her home soon."

Ryn gave Brynd a glare, worried about her walking the streets late at night with this practical stranger.

"I'll be fine," Brynd whispered in her ear then disappeared around a corner, arm and arm with Jak.

Dan took Ryn's hand and bowed to her, before kissing it. "I shall endeavor to find a clue for your mystery so I can see you again."

"Looking forward to it," Ryn said.

It was late at night. The grounds were only a block away, but she looked down the street nervously.

"Do not fear. You will be safe on the streets."

Ryn gave him a puzzled look, but nodded and hurried across the street and down a bit to the Library gates.

Jak and Dan were certainly unlike anyone else she had met. She had grown up surrounded by boys whose only interest were girls who did magic. Now here were these two guys who knew she was Ordinary, but didn't care. That was enormously appealing. There was also a bit of mystery surrounding them. She wasn't sure if she liked that or not. Dan wasn't as cute as Jak, but he was sweet and respectful, and he seemed to really like Ryn. No one else had wanted Ryn as anything but friend before. She couldn't stop smiling, and her feet were almost dancing along the cobblestones.

She passed Bart and Norm standing guard, their quiet nods of acknowledgement put her instantly at ease. Home and bed were just a garden away.

As she passed the Boiler Room, she saw a familiar figure moving much slower than normal.

"Wait up!" Ryn ran to catch up to Zo.

He turned and Ryn stopped in her tracks.

"What happened?"

His shrug was so slow it made her feel tired. "Leak is almost fixed. Nix made me leave to get some rest."

"I met with some people tonight who think it's sabotage," Ryn said.

"Funny you should say that." Zo paused as three Library workers walked by. "As much as walking up all those stairs to your room sounds horrible, let's talk there."

Zo was wobbly on his feet, so Ryn slipped her arm around his waist. Not that it would do much good if he fell, as he'd probably take them both down with him, but the support seemed to steady him.

Inside her dorm room, Ryn lit a fire in their small fireplace and put a kettle on. Once they were huddled around mugs of chamomile tea, and Ryn began to feel her toes again, she prodded him to explain.

He frowned. "I saw the Protector again. At the site of the crack in the flooring. I asked if there was something wrong with the Library's magic and it shook its head no."

Ryn nodded. "That seems to be the consensus."

"I asked how the Library's protective magic could be penetrated, and in its shadow hand appeared a rock, a sword, and a branch. Do you know what that could mean?"

Ryn thought back to all the books she'd been reading about the Library lately. "Nothing comes to mind, but I wasn't looking for references to those things. Maybe a second look at my sources would help, but I did hear something tonight about Waatch legends of objects that make magic flee."

Zo cracked his neck, and stretched out his feet, leaning back into the chair. He yawned.

"Who was it that told you these things?" he asked.

"These boys we met. I don't know if you remember that girl with Brynd on the street the other day. Her name is Tory, she introduced us. They seem to know a lot about what goes on in Waatch and the Library. They even knew who my mother was."

Zo sat up. "You shouldn't tell Library secrets to strangers."

"I didn't. They knew everything without me saying a word. I have no idea how."

"Sounds creepy," Zo's voice got a little sharp.

Ryn shifted in her seat. "They seem nice enough. The one who walked me home told the funniest stories. Reminded me of your stories."

Zo rubbed his eye and yawned again. "I need to meet these guys."

Ryn nodded. "We'll see."

"Not 'we'll see.' Next time you go to meet them, I'm coming." Zo finished his mug of chamomile. "Now I'm dead on my feet, I'd better go back to my room."

He stood, wobbling a bit.

"Why don't you sleep on my bed till Brynd gets home? I've got some reading to do anyway. I still have that guidebook on Waatch that Master Wes gave me. I want to see if there are any of these legends Jak and Dan mentioned in them."

Zo raised an eyebrow. "Jak and Dan huh?"

Ryn blushed.

He sat on her bed, pulling his boots off.

Ryn cleared her throat. "Hey, I wanted to say thanks for healing me after what the Spirit magic lady did to me. I know how using your healing is problematic for you."

His gaze held her eyes. "You're welcome, and you should have never trusted that Spirit teller. The way she used it was dangerous. We could have lost you." His voice was strong, with an angry edge to it.

Ryn bowed her head and nodded. He was right, but at the time she couldn't resist the temptation of finding answers about who she was and where she came from.

He continued. "Fortunately, I met someone who taught me about Healing magic right before the Spirit lady. Something I've never felt before. Healing you came easy. And now...Well, when I went to check on you at the Healing House, I ran into the Headmaster."

Zo yawned so long Ryn asked, "And?"

"I agreed to study Healing magic."

"Wait...what?" Ryn couldn't believe what she was hearing. "How?"

Zo flashed his toothiest grin. "Bed sounds great. Wake me when it's time to go home."

With that, he laid his head on her pillow and was fast asleep in minutes. Ryn sighed, shaking her head. Only because he looked so tired, did Ryn resist poking him back awake and demanding the story.

Chapter Twelve

Jayn de Viator, Matriarch of House Viator,

I agree with all your arguments about the Library. The building is old and run down. I blame its decline on the current Ordinary leadership. The facility you have built is the most modern and beautiful building on all the islands. I feel it is time for changes to be made, and if the current leadership doesn't agree, then we will need to look into eliminating it. You have my support, and I will do whatever it takes to make this move happen.

Jeris de Veni, Library Board of Regents

Zo took a deep breath before he attacked the steps to the Waatch Healing House. Different thoughts and emotions battled within him. The first to rise up was an old familiar fear he realized he always covered with anger. The fear that he would never be a good enough Healer. His mother desperately wanted a strong heir to her Healing magic. Tradition taught that for his mother's inheritance he would have to be a girl, but many people thought that was just superstition. His mother must have thought that too, because she placed a huge amount of expectation on her oldest born son. She wanted him on the Board of Healers alongside her, increasing her family's power in House Sano. As he climbed the steps to the Healing House, Zo realized that pressure had been too much for him. It made him hate his magic. Now, as he raised his head to gaze on the morning sun shining on the carved front door of the Healing House, he realized fear was being replaced by something new—anticipation. Wilmar had done his job well. Ever since Zo met him, he'd been advocating Zo pursue Healing—and he was right. Zo dared to let his chest swell with a sense of hope and pride in his new adventure. He was going to study Healing magic, and he was going to do it on his terms and in his way. This was a worthy power to pursue.

Once Zo entered the Healing House, he began looking for Regg. He was supposed to meet him in the foyer, but as usual these days, Regg was missing. Zo figured it couldn't be too hard to find the right classroom, so he began walking the halls peeking his head into rooms to find his class. He stopped when he caught a glimpse of a black suit coat with silver embroidery. Keir's silver ringed fingers were pulling a book off a shelf, but he seemed to sense Zo's presence and turned.

Keir smirked. "It's good to see you here where you belong."

Zo stepped into the room. It was the Healing House's library. The walls were lined with shelves filled with books. A table was pulled up next to the window and the morning sunshine slanted onto what looked like someone's research in progress.

"I suppose I have you to thank for it. Because of you I was able to heal my sister, and the magic is coming much easier," Zo said as Keir took his book to the table with the rest of the research.

Keir set the book down and leaned against the table. "I'm glad I could help. I'd be happy to assist you with your studies." He waved at the books on the table. "I do have brains as well as talent."

Zo found himself next to Keir without remembering crossing the room, as if he was pulled there.

"I'd be happy to give you private lessons." Keir's voice was low. His finger traced Zo's collar to the spot right below Zo's Ancestor beads.

Zo shuddered thinking about what Iden had said about messing around. Zo didn't want to mess around. Iden had Zo's heart, but the thought of Keir's touch pulled at Zo's abdomen in ways that made his breathing shallow.

To distract himself, Zo read the titles of the books on the table.

Dueling Magics: How to Protect Yourself with Your Magic

Magic and Its Improper Uses

Zo frowned, holding up the last book. *"Killing with Magic?"*

Keir shrugged. "It's a research project."

"Sure," Zo said, returning the book. "Do you happen to know where the Healing the Mind class is at?"

"Zo," Regg's voice came from the doorway. "Sorry I'm late. There were so many people on the streets this morning. You'd think with it being winter people would stay inside more."

"It's a sunny morning. People like to soak up the sun when they can, and you live here in the Healing House. If you didn't go to the Library to have breakfast with Yll, you wouldn't have this problem." Zo shivered as he left Keir and joined Regg at the door.

He bid Keir goodbye and tried to shake off the need Keir generated inside him.

"How is this Mind Healing class anyway?" Zo asked Regg.

"Master Don is as boring as a decrepit Ancestor. I have to fight to stay awake."

"Great," Zo said.

"Hey Regg." The cute sandy-blond haired girl with the crinkle nose was standing outside the door to a room.

"Hey Ayn, this is my brother Zo. He's new. Ayn's House Dico and she's wanting to go into Mind Healing. She's really good at it."

Zo nodded. "We met the other day. That sounds like a complex form of Healing. You must be loads smarter than Regg here."

Ayn laughed. "I wish I could duplicate his subtlety. He's a master."

Zo eyed his brother. "That's true."

Regg blushed with a shrug as they entered the classroom.

* * *

Later that day, Zo sat in the middle of a pile of fabric he had spent the evening tearing into strips to make bandages. Now he was neatly rolling them up and storing them in a basket. Wilmar said it was his fault for using so many on the stabbing victim, but there hadn't been *that* much blood. While he worked, Wilmar was treating Nix for a shoulder burn he'd sustained from stumbling while carrying out the broken pipe from the Library heating system. Zo was listening to Wilmar and Nix bicker about whether Nix's job was too dangerous for him.

"That Boiler Room is seriously too hot, you're going to die from heatstroke one of these days," Wilmar scolded as he applied some of the salve he had used on Zo's burns in the past.

Nix waved his free hand. "I'm used to it. Young Zo here though—he's the one you should worry about."

"And I do—I worry about both of you."

Wilmar must have applied the medicine to a particularly tender area, because Nix winced.

Nix's gaze shifted to Zo. He frowned.

"He does look worn through, now he's taken on the Healing apprenticeship. I must admit I expected him to drop one of *us* if he signed on with the Healing House," Nix said.

"Oh, and you were expecting that to be me?" Wilmar countered. "The boy has a shot at being the only Healer who is also a physician. The potential for such a combination has no limits."

Nix glared at Wilmar. "And he signed an unbreakable contract with the Library. He can't practice Healing from jail."

"A contract you could deem fulfilled and let him out of..." Wilmar started.

"Whoa, whoa, whoa," Zo interrupted. "Keeping all three is my choice, and I'm handling it just fine by the way, so you two can just go back to fussing over each other."

Nix and Wilmar both stared at him for a long moment. He could tell they both wanted to object, but for once Nix took a lesson from Wilmar's book and said nothing.

Zo cleared his throat, then cracked his neck. Wilmar shifted his attention back to Nix's shoulder.

"You need to survive long enough to retire, you know," Wilmar said quietly.

Zo wasn't sure if he was talking to him or Nix.

When the silence that followed got awkward, Zo decided to change the conversation.

"Do we really need this many bandages? This looks like we're preparing for a battle or something."

"You can't be too prepared." Wilmar put the lid on the jar of the burn cream.

"Nothing good is coming, that's for sure," Nix added.

"How does someone get through the Library's barrier, and security anyway?" Zo asked.

"Not easily," Wilmar said.

"There are legends, but nothing I've paid much attention to over the years. The Library certainly has not." Nix winced as he shifted to put his shirt back on.

"Do not put your shirt on," Wilmar said.

Nix smirked. "Not in front of the child."

Wilmar rolled his eyes at the ceiling. "Not that, the fabric will stick to the burn."

"Given that it's freezing cold and rainy outside, I guess I'll have to spend the night." Nix's face was serious, but there was a twinkle in his eye.

Wilmar sniffed. "Yes, I suppose you do need extra attention tonight."

Zo felt his cheeks go hot.

"You're embarrassing the young one." Nix stood and moved closer to Wilmar.

"I think he can handle it."

Zo put all his focus on the bandage he was rolling, certain those two were going to make things even more awkward, but a knock at the exam room door stopped everything.

Wilmar opened it. "How can I help you?"

He shifted to reveal Keir standing at the door.

"I came to see if Zo was here, and if I could borrow him for a Healing call." Keir's eyes found Zo at the worktable.

Zo could tell Wilmar was torn. He absolutely wanted Zo to be studying Healing, but he also jealously guarded his apprentice time with Zo.

Keir's gaze shifted to Wilmar. "I promise to return him."

"All right, fine. Just be back all the earlier to finish those bandages," Wilmar grumbled.

Zo slid down from his stool, cracking his back. His bottom was numb from sitting for so long.

Nix's fingers brushed Zo's arm as he passed, stopping him. "If you need us for anything, send us a message."

Zo nodded, pulled on his coat and cloak, and stepped out into the night with Keir.

"Where are we going?" Zo asked.

"Upper west side," Keir said, climbing into a Healing House carriage.

Zo had only just started practicing his Healing. He didn't feel prepared to make a house call yet, and he certainly didn't feel prepared to go to any influential Ancestor family on the west side of town. But Keir beckoned to him.

"Where's the Healing Master? Shouldn't we have one with us? I wasn't aware students could go on calls by themselves," Zo said, joining him.

Keir didn't acknowledge Zo. He banged on the ceiling and the coach lurched forward.

Neither of them spoke, but the energy between them crackled. Zo wished he hadn't sat next to Keir. The memory of Keir's Healing touch stirred inside him. Zo almost got up and switched to the other bench when Keir took Zo's hand. Zo suppressed a shiver. He looked over at Keir, who gave him a weak smile.

"I'm so glad you agreed to join us at the Healing House. I wish you would do it full time. You will wear yourself ragged doing all of them."

"You sound like those two I just left. I'm fine. I would be sharper if I wasn't up all night repairing damage to the Library."

Keir withdrew his hand, much to Zo's relief. "Nasty business that is. There's definitely something bad brewing between the Houses. We need to be prepared."

"Prepared for what?'" Zo's suspicion level rose.

"To defend those we love," Keir said.

"Again—from what? The Ancestral Houses haven't been at war in many years."

"You never know."

His eyes searched for Keir's two Healing beads in the dim light of the carriage.

Zo lifted his fingers filled with flames. "I have fire to defend myself. How will you defend yourself with only Healing?"

Keir's eyes went in the direction of the driver, and even though it would be hard to hear anything, he said, "Later."

* * *

When they reached the house, they were greeted by a servant in distress. Apparently, the youngest child of the Ancestor family had fallen down the stairs and had not woken up. The servant led them to a large bedroom on the second floor, up the grand staircase. The layout of the house reminded Zo of his mother's estate, but smaller. The young boy was pale and unconscious on the bed.

"If this is a brain injury, shouldn't a Mind Healer be on this call?" Zo asked.

Keir turned his palms up. "They sent us. I think we're up to it."

Zo didn't feel so confident. Keir directed the family to put chairs on each side of the bed.

"You take that side," he told Zo. "Put your hand on the right side of the neck and I'll take the left. Don't worry, we'll do this together."

Zo felt awkward with an audience. The mother and father, and what looked like the child's three older siblings, were all in the room, along with a few servants. Zo shrank under their watchful gaze, but Keir seemed to preen at the attention.

"Now, with me," Keir said.

Taking Zo's hand, they both dived into the child.

There were some minor injuries, bruises and such, but he must have hit his head hard, because there was bleeding in his brain. Zo shrank back. He had never dealt with something so complicated, but Keir took his mental hand, and together, as before, they began to work. It was exhilarating and exhausting as Keir had a real power in his healing. Somehow, in some way Zo couldn't detect, Keir also used the healing connection to soothe Zo, to play with certain spots inside that caused tingling aches to flood through his body. Zo thought it would be distracting, but he was more alive and focused than ever before.

The Healing seemed to take forever, and yet no time at all. When they were finished it was late, but not as late as it felt like.

To the family's delight, the little boy woke—and asked for some cake. Zo and Keir were celebrated all the way out the door, taking their fee along with loads of sweets, and invitations to return for dinner sometime.

"Is it always like that?" Zo asked, handing a teacake to Keir who produced a linen bag to fill.

"Most of the time," Keir said.

"If I was tired before, I'm dead now. Drop me at the Library dorms, will you?"

Keir nodded to the home next to the one they just left. "One more stop."

Zo groaned.

As they mounted the steps to the home, Keir handed Zo the bag of treats and opened the door.

"Do you know these people?" Zo asked.

Keir flashed him a smile warmed by the glow from the front windows. "They're my parents."

Before Zo could back out, he was ushered into the front room where Keir's parents were entertaining guests, one of which was Iden.

Iden flashed Zo a surprised grin. "And where have you two been so late this evening?"

Zo covered a yawn. "Healing call."

The two people in chairs next to Iden were his parents. Zo had met them a few times.

"Mom, Dad, I'd like to introduce you to the newest student at the Waatch Healing House, Zo of Ingis," Keir said, standing behind his parents with his hands on their shoulders.

Keir's mother almost choked on her tea. "Not Fyri's son?"

Zo tried to wave Keir to stop, but it did no good.

"Of course!" Keir said.

"Interesting. She's been looking for you." Keir's dad sipped his tea.

Zo frowned. "And it's going to stay that way."

"Of course, of course." Keir's mom waved at Iden and his parents. "And this is..."

"I know them, thanks," Zo said, moving across the room to stand by Iden.

Keir's mom gave Iden and Zo a look Zo didn't know how to interpret.

"He's not your usual plaything that you bring home. Your tastes have much improved," she said, looking Zo up and down appraisingly.

Zo shifted uncomfortably, while Iden's mom looked scandalized.

"Anyway, where were we?" Keir's dad started.

"We were discussing House Viator's attempt to move the Library to their island," Keir's mom said.

"I don't know of any Ancestral House that will stand up to House Viator to prevent them from taking the Library," Iden's dad said.

"There's always House Pentral." Keir's dad sipped at his tea again.

Iden's mom laughed. "The animosity may have increased after those two Houses mixed their bloodlines, but Pentral has been shying away from an all-out fight. There's something very wrong there. You'd think Spirit magic would give them the passion their Ancestors had. I wouldn't count on them standing up to Jayn, she's just too powerful a Matriarch."

Iden's dad shrugged. "I know House Dico's certainly not going to do it. We can't read everybody's mind, nor can we change it."

"Neither will House Sano," Keir's dad said. "The Healing Council will not allow hostilities."

"So there's no hope?" Iden asked. "We just let Viator take the Library?"

Flames curled around Zo's fingers. "There's a whole army of Library workers they will have to get through first."

"Easy now, young Zo," Keir's dad said. "Let's not count Clayr out yet. She's tough, and smart. I'm sure she's got a trick or two up her sleeve."

The adults droned on about which Houses could align with each other for protection and defense. Zo caught himself nodding off. He was afraid he would pass out on the floor. There was potential important information in their conversation, but he was so exhausted he couldn't focus.

"Keir dear," Keir's mother said. "Why don't you take these young men home?"

Keir bent to kiss his mother on the cheek. "Yes, Mother."

"Don't have too much fun on the way home," Keir's mother gave them a sly smile around her teacup.

Iden's mother's cheeks turned red. Iden had told Zo how his parents had rushed him into betrothing Prym at Iden's grandparents' urging, as well as a rather forceful Jeris. They had been relieved when Prym's scandalous behavior with Master Wes had given them a clean out of that marriage contract. They had accepted Zo as a close friend of Iden's, but didn't seem willing yet to acknowledge their relationship. They also didn't seem wholly opposed to it either. Time would tell how that would go, but Iden's mom clearly wasn't ready to be as forward about it as Keir's mother.

Zo's yawns were huge and loud as they said their goodbyes to the parents, and piled into the Healing House carriage.

Iden sat next to Zo and held his hand. Zo was too tired to care and it felt good. Keir said nothing.

When they pulled to a stop in front of the Library dorms, Iden opened the door.

"Zo, may I speak to you in private?" Keir asked.

Iden squeezed Zo's knee and let go. "I'll see you in the morning for breakfast." Iden had the same look in his eye that he had on the docks at the Ghost Festival.

Zo nodded, really wanting a meaningful goodnight, but he let Iden go, closing the carriage door behind him.

"Hurry, before I fall asleep on you," Zo said while yawning.

"Sure, sure. I just want to ask, since you've mentioned it in the past—have you ever thought about how Healing magic might be used for defense?" Keir asked.

"How could a magic meant to help people heal be used in battle?"

Keir shrugged. "I have some ideas." He handed Zo a small, black notebook. "Read this, and next time we see each other tell me what you think."

Zo could barely see the book through his tired, watery eyes. "Sure, I'm off to bed."

As Zo moved to climb out of the carriage, Keir put an ice-cold hand on Zo's arm. Zo shook all over from the impression Keir left, inside and out.

"Please seriously consider what the book has to say. I think it might be the answer to everything the parents were discussing tonight," Keir said.

Zo nodded.

"And don't let anyone else see what's in that book. It could be dangerous."

Zo thought that statement should disturb him more than it did, but at the moment all his brain could do was calculate how much sleep he would get before his morning Library shift if he got in bed in the next few minutes.

Chapter Thirteen

If we could just get those lazy-assed Ancestor descendants to use their magic, we might be able to harness all that power. Who in their right mind decided we shouldn't use our magic, but should save it? For what? Is our magic diminishing with use? If they don't want to use their magic as a profession, at least they should use their magics for a good cause, and I say saving the Library from House Viator is a good cause! You have my vote against this move. I won't allow this travesty to play out.

Jordan de Mare, Library Board of Regents

"I think Zo must have misunderstood the Protector. I can't find a single thing about stones or branches," Ryn said.

"Don't forget the sword!" Yll turned the page of the book she was thumbing through.

"It's ridiculous. We've been through half the books in the Library by now." Ryn slumped down in her chair.

Yll chuckled. "Not true—I'd say a third."

"There's nothing here." Ryn gestured to the pile of books on their desks. "Let's go back to the reference section and try again."

Yll stretched as she stood. "I don't think it will get any better, but I'm up for stretching my legs."

Ryn gathered the books they had been searching and put them on the return cart. A docent would reshelve them for them. It was kind of funny that Ryn and Yll's job was shelving new books, but they didn't have to shelve existing books.

By some unspoken agreement they took the long way around to the Reference section, stopping by the foyer to soak up sunlight, then making a stop in the objects room. They had searched it three times already. Although there was a sword there, it was a replica of Praedo's sword, and there were no stones, or branches. Ryn always marveled at the centuries-old reproduction. It had a presence to it. Despite that, she dismissed the idea that it could be the culprit damaging the Library's magic. It had been a part of the Library's collections for longer than anyone could remember and had never affected the Library before.

On their loop back around, Ryn's feet took her as they always did, down the hallway to the carved door with no handle. Somehow her feet seemed to have a mind of their own, or maybe it was just the way she seemed to be drawn here when she was in this part of the Library. Yll must have known where she was headed, because she followed. Ryn swore every time she passed it the door looked different, but that wasn't possible. What was behind it? And why was she always drawn to it? Something there made her feel she belonged. If only she could find a way inside. Maybe it held answers.

Today though, there were voices coming from the hallway. Ryn put out her arm to stop Yll. Ryn cautiously peeked around the corner. Master Ubert and Prym were standing in front of the door, halfway down.

"Where's the keyhole?" Master Ubert said, leaning into the carvings. "Do you have a key?"

"I don't know, I've never seen one," came Prym's voice.

"Well, there should be a key and you should have it. Useless. There shouldn't be any locked doors, I am an Inquisitor, all Library materials should be open to me," Master Ubert said.

"Stupid door has always been locked. I don't understand how anyone could use the materials inside if the door is never open," came Prym's voice again.

"This is an outrage. I must see the curator at once to open this room for me." Master Ubert's voice was full of indignation.

"I couldn't agree more, I'll take you right to her office."

Ryn watched them retreat down the hall, grateful they hadn't noticed her and Yll standing at the opposite end.

"Well, I certainly hope they don't let those two in," Yll said.

"Agreed." Ryn ran her fingers down the wall till they got to the door.

Today it appeared as a paneled door, but she thought for sure she had seen carvings on it in the past.

"Come on, it's getting late and I have a date tonight. Let's get the reference section search over with," Yll said, suddenly sounding too loud in Ryn's ears.

Ryn shook her head to clear it. "Right."

Brynd and her had a date that night as well, but Ryn wasn't quite ready to tell Yll about Jak and Dan. They felt like a secret she didn't want to share yet, especially not after Zo's reaction to them. Best to leave it to Zo being the only one who knew about Jak and Dan for now.

In the reference section Ryn wandered away from the Library history references and started searching for books about trees and fruit. She found a few that sounded promising.

"*Planting Seeds in the Library*- do you think it will tell us why a branch could counter the Library's magic?" Yll asked, looking over Ryn's shoulder.

"I'm not sure, but I have a hunch." Ryn copied down the directions for the four books she deemed promising and they set off on their search.

The first book on her list took them to the first-floor botany section of the Library, but instead of finding the *Planting Seeds* book, there was a wooden placeholder stuck between the books. Written on the stick were the words: "If found, send to Dayna in serials."

"Who's Dayna?" Ryn asked.

Yll shrugged.

They set off to find the other three books. All of them had the same wooden placeholders with the same message on them.

"This is so weird, what is going on?" Ryn asked.

"Let's ask."

They asked Brynd, then a couple docents, and a researcher, but no one knew who Dayna was.

"Great, another dead end." Ryn slumped against the wall.

"Let's ask Mom," Yll suggested.

"She's busy, and stressed."

"But if we find something useful, that could be a help, it would take away some stress." Yll's eyes were bright with desperation.

"Alright."

Norm was standing guard at Clayr's office door, and told them Clayr was in a meeting.

"Will you let Mom know I'm here waiting at least?" Yll asked.

After a long moment he slipped in the door, not letting them get a look at what was happening inside. Ryn paced in front of the door till it opened and he admitted them.

The sight that greeted them took Ryn aback. Clayr's desk was piled with books. She sat at her desk pouring over them while Ryn's mother sat on the other side doing the same. Ryn almost giggled, it looked so much like when Ryn and Yll did research together.

Lar was standing at the window looking out at the rain-soaked drive. He seemed lost in thought.

Clayr looked up from what she was reading, rubbing her eyes. "What's the problem, girls?"

"Everything." Yll rounded the desk to put her arm across Clayr's shoulders and give her a hug.

Ryn joined Lar at the window. He stirred and gave her a slight smile in greeting.

"Where's House Viator?" she asked. The carriages that had carried the Viator delegation were gone from the carriage house.

Ryn turned to see her mother and Clayr exchange a look.

"They're in Sooke at the moment, visiting various Regents," Clayr said.

That would explain why Ryn's mother was in Clayr's office and not hiding out at home in Sooke.

"What is it you need?" Clayr asked. "We're somewhat rushed to find what we're looking for after the interruption by Ubert."

"You didn't give him the key, did you?" Yll asked.

Clary startled. "How did you...Nevermind, no, there is no key to that room."

"We were looking for some books and instead of the books we found placeholders that said they were lost and to send them to Dayna if they were found. No one we asked knew a Dayna. Is there a Dayna working in the Library?" Ryn asked.

Clayr and Ryn's mother exchanged a look Ryn couldn't read, but Clayr just chuckled.

"Not that I've heard of. Must be old. What were you looking for?"

It was Ryn and Yll's turn to exchange looks. "We're trying to figure out what the Protector meant by the stone, the branch, and the sword. I had this thought to look for trees."

Clayr gestured to the books on her desk. "Welcome to the party."

"Have you found anything?" Ryn asked.

"Not when we keep getting interrupted," Ryn's mother said.

"I had to stuff Ryette and Lar in the closet when Ubert showed up earlier," Clayr said.

"We've found references to the fact that there was once a tree here on the Library grounds. Do you know what happened to it?" Yll asked.

Ryette pushed a book across the desk to Ryn. "There are many sources that talk about the tree, but they skip over the construction of the Library, and go straight to filling the Library with books."

Ryn gazed at the pages. It was a picture of the tree similar to the ones she'd found in other books, only more stylized.

"I thought for sure I'd seen plans for the construction of the Library somewhere, but I haven't been able to locate them. Maybe I just dreamed it," Clayr said.

"Do you think the 'branch' mentioned by the Protector could come from this tree?" Ryn asked, running her hands over the picture in the book.

"I don't see how. That was a couple thousand years ago," Ryette said.

"Stranger things have happened." Clayr leaned back in her chair.

Ryette scoffed.

"There is an Ordinary bedtime story told to children in Waatch that says the tree wasn't cut down, that it lives inside the Library," Clayr said.

"That's preposterous," Lar piped up from his place at the window. "Have you seen any signs of a tree growing inside the Library? Where's the roots? Wouldn't it by now be growing into the Library? Or taller than it?"

Clayr lifted her hands. "I'm just telling you what is said."

A thought that had been niggling the back of Ryn's mind suddenly came out fully formed. "I know I messed up a few moons back, but do you think I could get access to Luc's journals?"

Ryn put a hand to her mouth, hardly believing those words had popped out of her.

Clayr and Ryn's mother both frowned. Lar turned from the window.

"Sorry, I don't know what I was thinking," Ryn rushed to add.

Lar stepped over to the desk. "I think this might be the answer we have been looking for."

Clayr's face turned thoughtful.

Ryn raised an eyebrow at her mother.

"We have been thinking of accessing those materials, since they predate the Library and may hold some clues, but with Ubert watching every move we make it's been impossible to retrieve them," Ryn's mother confessed. "We wish to keep the knowledge of where they are stored secret."

"But if we had *you* access it..." Clayr drummed her fingers on the desk.

"Ubert hasn't paid any attention to the girls, despite the research they've been doing after hours." Lar said.

Ryn shot her gaze at him. How did he know what they'd been doing?

"Alright, I'll give you access, but not tonight. Come in early tomorrow and I'll give you the key," Clayr said.

Ryn felt a thrill run through her. Maybe they were finally going to get somewhere.

* * *

The boys were both dressed well in the latest fashion, but not as flashy, wearing capes instead of cloaks despite the chill. Winter solstice was rapidly approaching, and it was dark even though it was only early evening. Dan offered Ryn his arm. Somehow Jak and Dan made her feel safe even though she was pretty sure they didn't have any magic.

Jak took the lead with his arm tight around Brynd's waist.

"Where are we going?" Brynd asked.

"You'll see," Dan answered.

Their walk took them from the respectable part of town into the shadier parts. Brynd was pressed close to Jak and they were having a quiet conversation. Despite the area of town they were in, both Jak and Dan were perfectly at ease. After passing a particularly dark alley, Ryn pressed closer to Dan. He shifted his arm to her shoulder and pulled her closer, but stayed relaxed. Dan started throwing jokes, and Jak responded with insults and a rude gesture.

When they came to a building that loomed over them almost as much as the Library did, the boys led them through a series of stairs, hallways, and rooms till Ryn was completely turned around and lost. They eventually came to a door at the end of a long hall. Maus sat looking very serious behind a desk that dwarfed him. A man sat on the desk suppressing a smile. He stood.

"It's good to see you, boss," the man said.

Jak clapped him on the shoulder. "It's good to have you back."

The man opened the door for them and they entered what could only be described as an unusual office. There was another enormous desk, this one elaborately carved, in the middle of the room. It was polished to a shine, but piled with all sorts of odds and ends and unusual objects. The chair was more elaborate than anything Ryn had seen, and that included chairs in the Jeris' house. It had the appearance of belonging to some high-powered Ancestor.

"Welcome to The Office," Jak said.

He sank down into the chair with a sigh and pulled Brynd onto his lap. She put her arms around his neck and he pulled her closer to him and into a long, drawn out kiss.

Ryn noticed another doorway off to the side of the office.

"Is this where you live?" Ryn asked, peeking into the room.

It was a simple room with two beds and a dresser. It was quite the contrast to the ostentatiousness of the office desk and chair.

"Yes," Dan said, as he lit a lantern on the dresser.

Ryn's eyes were immediately drawn to a portrait hung over it. It was of an older man who bore resemblance to Dan with greying hair, and wrinkles that spoke of laugh lines as much as sorrow and pain. His right eyebrow had a jagged scar through it. The man had one arm around each of the two boys who were unmistakably a much younger Jak and Dan. The young Jak was scrawny and thin, shorter than Dan. Dan was thick and robust looking, and had a healthy wave to his thick brown hair and a warm smile. Both boys grinned in happiness while the man's clear pride in the boys beamed out of his eyes and off the canvas. The picture gave Ryn the feeling of home, of peace, and the love of a father filled with pleasure in his children. Ryn got tears in her eyes and turned away.

"How was the Library today?" Dan asked.

Ryn sighed. "Less than fruitful. Our research isn't turning up much, and that inspector..."

"Master Ubert," Jak said, pulling away from a kiss to say it, proving he'd been listening.

"That's the one. He tried to get into this strange door in the Library. It seems to have no way inside, but it's clearly a door," Ryn said.

Jak's gaze shifted to Dan's. Some unspoken something passed between them.

"You don't say," Jak said.

"What about you? What have you found out?" Brynd asked, running her finger down Jak's jawline.

"We think we may be on to something. That's why we invited you out tonight," Dan said.

"There's someone in our..." Jak paused. "Business that has information for us."

Ryn's stomach grumbled. "Great! Let's go, I'm hungry."

"Not quite yet. The place doesn't open till later. That's why we came here first." Jak said.

"Actually," Dan said, looking Ryn and Brynd over. "We probably need to get you something a little fancier to wear."

Ryn looked down at her old blue dress. It was nice enough.

"Fancier than this?" Ryn waved her hand down her front.

Jak and Dan exchanged another look.

"Yes." Dan said, his cheeks blushing.

"Alright. How do we do that?" Brynd asked.

"Thax," Dan said.

"Thax," Jak grinned from ear to ear.

"After you." Jak bowed with a flourish.

"I don't know about this, Brynd. I can't afford to pay for it," Ryn whispered as they followed Jak and Dan out of The Office.

The man outside the door raised an eyebrow. Maus had his feet up on the desk, but jumped up at the sight of Jak.

"Maus—run tell Tyndyl the Barons are coming and need to speak with Master Cobb, and I don't care if he's in the middle of something—this is urgent."

Maus was already halfway down the hallway as he called over his shoulder, "Yes boss!"

"Shall we take the scenic route, or the less scenic route?" Jak asked.

Dan looked down at Ryn and frowned in concern. "Less scenic seems wisest."

Jak nodded and it soon became clear that he wasn't talking about a less scenic route through the building, because the succession of rooms and stairs was no less complicated on their way out. Ryn was almost convinced even Jak and Dan didn't really know where they were going and were just guessing. Except they did it with confidence... with a lot of confidence.

They left the building, the boys leading them down several streets.

"Maybe we can just borrow some dresses." Brynd finally whispered back.

Ryn still felt skeptical. It had rained all day and the cobblestones were still wet. Ryn couldn't imagine anyone letting her borrow a brand-new dress where the bottom would most likely get wet and dirty.

Soon Ryn recognized the street they were on as being one that was close to the Library. Jak stopped in front of a shop door. There was no sign over it, but there were dresses and suits on display in the window. Dan pounded on the door.

"Open up, Thax!" Jak yelled. "I have a fashion emergency!"

Ryn giggled, but she saw the curious neighbors move away from their windows. She imagined them rolling their eyes.

Dan pounded the door a few more times before Tory opened the door.

"For the love of the Ancestors, Jak, we're closed." She tried to shut the door on him.

"We need some dresses for Tyndyl's place," Jak said.

Tory glanced back into the darkened shop. "Fine. Come in." She waved them in. "Thax! Customers."

Tory lit some lanterns, and Ryn's eyes were dazzled by the different dresses on display around the shop. No one appeared.

"Thax!" Tory shouted.

She waved for them to follow her. Toward the back in a corner stood a man draping and pinning fabric to a dress from. He was muttering to himself.

"Thax!" Tory shouted again as loud as she had from the front of the store.

The man jumped, stabbing himself with a pin.

"Ow! Tory, do you need to shout?"

"Apparently, because you ignore me otherwise. Jak and Dan, and some new friends are here."

Thax turned to them, his eyes unfocused at first as if he was thinking of something else. Then his gaze became intense, like he could see right through Ryn's soul.

"And who do we have here?" Thax asked.

Tory gestured to Brynd. "This is my apple-farmer friend turned Library worker."

Thax bowed to Brynd, then took her hand. "So charming."

"And this is..."

"The Matriarch of Viator's granddaughter," Dan said, folding his arms.

Thax bowed, took Ryn's hand, and pressed her hand to his forehead.

"An honor," Thax said.

Ryn shifted uncomfortably. "But I'm not really, I'm adopted."

Thax lifted his eyes to her. "Adoption makes you every bit a part of that family, as if you were born into it."

"Except for the having magic part," Ryn said.

Thax waved away her comment like magic meant nothing. "Now, what can I get for you?"

"We're having dinner at Tyndyl's tonight, and we require appropriate attire," Jak said.

Thax gave Ryn one more look that seemed to see all of her, even her broken parts, then he turned. "I have just the dresses." He winked.

* * *

Tory brought a confusing array of bits and pieces she helped Ryn put on. When she finally emerged from the dressing room, someone gasped.

Ryn looked up from the shimmering blue skirt her fingers were smoothing, to find Jak and Dan changed and waiting for them. The boys were dressed in the latest fashion, trousers in dark fall browns with waistcoats and coattails embroidered with intertwining fall flowers and leaves. Dan's mouth was slightly open, and his eyes fixed on Ryn. She felt herself blush.

Jak had Brynd in his arms, kissing her nose, her cheek, her lips.

"You're going to wrinkle her dress!" Tory scolded, pulling Brynd away from Jak.

Thax was standing by the counter, nodding his approval. "You all look fabulous. I'll have to design something just for you." He tapped his finger to his lips, then narrowed his eyes. "Yes, I think something for the Winter Solstice Ball."

"I don't think I'm going to the Ball." Ryn had never been before, but she realized she was old enough to go now.

Ryn looked down at herself. The dress seemed perfect to her, the color of the clear blue sky fading into night at the hem, plus a shapely waist and long sleeves. The only drawback was the sweetheart neckline. Everyone could see she didn't have any magic. She hadn't worn her carved bead necklace since she had pretended they were real to gain access to Master Wes' class. It was a childish thing she left behind, so now her neckline was noticeably bare. Certainly a collar that hid her Ordinariness would make it better. Then she noticed she wasn't tripping over the hem.

"How is it this dress is the right length for me? Dresses always have to be shortened for me."

Thax took her hands. "Don't you worry about that, just go and have a good time."

He kissed her on the cheek, then spun her around and gave her hand to Dan.

"Thank you Thax," Jak said.

Thax gave him a sly smile. "For you, anytime. It's time for you to come in and let me spruce up your wardrobe."

"Maybe next moon." Jak held his arm out for Brynd to take it.

"But the midwinter ball is coming." Thax narrowed his eyes at Jak. "I have all kinds of ideas for you."

"I appreciate your dedication to your craft Thax," Jak said as he led them all out of the shop and onto the street.

"Have a good time!" Tory called to them as Dan closed the door.

"Oh boy, narrow escape," Jak said.

"It's a good thing he didn't have his measuring tape on him for sure, he would have measured you for the hundredth time," Dan laughed.

"Wait." Brynd stopped. "Don't we need to pay for the dresses?"

Jak leaned in close, kissing Brynd's head. "Don't worry about it."

To Ryn's surprise, outside the shop a carriage stood waiting. Jak and Dan helped the girls in, their skirts almost too voluminous for the coach. For once she felt pretty and wanted. No one in the village had ever paid her this much attention.

The voyage through Waatch was short, and all too soon the coach stopped at a nondescript door on a random street.

"We're here," Jak said as he opened the carriage door.

Ryn looked up and down the street, but couldn't find a restaurant anywhere.

"Where? I don't see anything but an abandoned building," Brynd said.

Jak jumped down from the carriage and held his hand up for Brynd to take. "Do you trust me?"

"Yes," Brynd said as she took his hand and let him help her out of the carriage.

Dan helped Ryn out, then they stood in front of the plain door.

Ryn glanced around nervously. "Now what?"

Jak grinned, then gave a pattern of knocks on the door Ryn knew she could never duplicate. A man dressed all in black opened the door.

"Password," the man said.

"Four dragonflies at night," Jak answered.

"Enter," the man stepped out of the way.

Jak and Dan led the girls into a dark room. Once inside, the doorman shut the door. It was pitch black. Ryn gripped

Dan's hand and he pulled her closer to him. A door, opposite the one they came in, opened and music floated in.

When they passed through the portal Ryn couldn't believe her eyes. There were three tiered floors of tables, layered with fabric and flowers. Diners talked, and ate, plates clinked, while music floated above it all.

"It's a private dining club," Jak said.

"Very private," Dan added.

A woman in a formal black gown approached them. frowning. "I haven't seen you in a while, Jak."

Jak smiled. "Candy! Been busy. How are you doing?"

"Nothing stops you if you want something." Candy glared at him. "Tyndyl has your usual table waiting. Follow." Her eyes never shifted from Jak's as she spoke.

Ryn's attention drifted to all the women in their formal gowns, and the men in waistcoats and jackets, all embroidered elaborately. Most everyone here had open collars and necklines that proudly displayed their beadscars. This place, like her village, was filled with magic. Maybe she should have put on the beads her brother had carved for her so she wouldn't feel so exposed by her open neckline.

Dan leaned over and whispered in her ear, "Don't worry, power lies in more than magic."

Ryn took her hand from her collarbone, trying to hide her discomfort.

"Jak!" A barmaid called from behind the bar. "You still owe me."

Jak launched a small pouch at her in an underhanded toss so quick Ryn had no idea where he had gotten the pouch from. Then she remembered how good he was at sleight of hand. At the end of the bar a serving girl stood with a tray of drinks in her hands. Jak wrapped an arm around her waist, and she spoke into his ear. Candy frowned at Jak.

Candy turned and led them down a short hallway. She waved them in, but before Jak could enter, she slammed her hand into the doorway, barring his entrance.

Jak smiled. "Send for Maus, will you please?" he asked her.

"You best be coming to see me soon, or I'll gut you," she snarled.

Jak smiled. "I love you too, Candy."

She removed her arm and backed away.

Dan chuckled. "I told you that one was a mistake."

"Yeah, yeah, yeah." Jak waved his hand.

"Hmmmm...Now where did we last leave off?" Jak said. "Oh yes..." He bent to kiss Brynd.

Brynd put her hand on his lips. "Candy?"

"Long story. Nothing to worry about," Jak said, pulling out a chair for her.

The cut crystal goblets sparkled in the candlelight as Dan held out the cushioned chair for Ryn to sit. Ryn was completely dazzled.

"Jak!" Maus came bounding up to the table in a manner most inappropriate for the setting, but no one even turned their head.

Jak let the boy embrace him. "Did you run that errand I asked you?"

Maus nodded his head and handed Jak a note.

Jak opened and read it.

"Excellent, our informant will meet us here soon." Jak folded the paper and tucked it into his jacket pocket.

"Informant? The businessperson you were talking about earlier?" Ryn asked.

Dan nodded, taking a sip of water from his glass.

"You look hungry. Maus, run off to the kitchen and tell Sal to get you something to eat." Jak patted Maus' shoulder, who then nodded and disappeared around the curtains.

"Is that your little brother?" Brynd asked.

Dan shook his head. "Not by blood, but in a way."

The server brought them plates with a soft cheese, winter greens, and pine nuts, topped with some kind of glaze. Ryn nervously picked up the outside fork. She hadn't had much occasion to eat at fancy places, but her mother made sure she taught her how to properly eat at a table. Ryn hadn't understood it before, but now she did, knowing that her grandmother was the Matriarch of House Viator.

"So, what's it like being adopted?" Jak asked.

Ryn choked on her salad and started coughing. Dan patted her on the back.

Ryn looked at Dan, confused. Hadn't he told her the other night on the beach that Dan's father had adopted Jak? She had no idea what kind of answer Jak was after.

"Great, wonderful, difficult?" Ryn said.

"Humor me." Jak gave her that focused gaze of his.

Ryn got quiet and the sound of the other diners got louder. "I don't know. I mean, I love my family and wouldn't trade them for anything, but I still have this feeling inside like I don't fit in. Like no matter how much they love me, I still feel adrift, like I can't quite claim them as mine. It's weird, I know." Ryn shrugged.

Jak nodded. "As much as Dan is my brother, and his father has been everything I could ask for, I haven't felt whole since my mother passed."

"Do you know your birth father?" Ryn asked.

Jak shifted.

The server entered, clearing away the plates. Jak whispered something to her and she nodded. Another server entered with plates of broiled sea bass, with juniper berries on top.

Ryn took the hint that Jak didn't want to discuss it. "You mentioned before that there were stories about objects that could disrupt magic. Any idea about what those might be?"

Dan picked up his fork and knife and delicately balanced the fish on the backside of his fork. "Some stories say any object that is derived or adjacent to the Wild magic could enhance or negate magic. Depends upon the type of magic."

"They also say it could be anything from lake water to a burning ember. Who knows, myths and legends can get fancifully embellished by the teller of the tale." Jak wiped some butter from his chin.

Maus came scurrying around the curtains like the creature he was named for. Jak bent to him as Maus whispered into his ear.

"Seems our informant has arrived." Jak waved a server over. "Can I get another chair please? Maus, will you escort the gentleman here?"

Maus ran off, and the server put a chair at the corner of the table between Jak and Dan.

Jak and Dan held each other's gaze. Dan nodded slowly. Ryn shifted in her seat.

A man who was not dressed for the private dining club came into view trailing Maus. His brown wool coat was undone, and his hair was disheveled. His right hand was inside his coat, like he was holding something.

Maus moved around Jak's chair and came to stand to the side and behind him like he was three feet taller and protecting Jak.

"Cobb, it's good to see you. Have a seat." Jak gestured to the chair.

Cobb nodded, but winced as he sat, slightly hunched over.

"What do you have for us?" Dan asked.

The man shifted slightly to look at Dan. His face was pale in the candlelight, and the way he held his jaw, Ryn was certain he was about to throw up. Ryn scooted her chair back from the table.

Cobb focused on Jak. "I'm sorry boss...I tried... Evclesco...kill the roots." He pulled a bloody hand out of his coat.

Ryn and Brynd gasped.

He plunked a rock down on the table in front of Jak, then collapsed.

Chapter Fourteen

Madame Curator Clayr,
Yes, I know Jak and Dan. They are well known in certain circles in Waatch. I, being a physician, get to know all the non-Ancestral circles. Even though those boys are young, around the age of eighteen, they hold a great deal of power and control with the common folk. I believe many of their business dealings are not exactly legal, but I'm not one to point fingers at those kinds of activities. I've seen them do some kindhearted things, but I don't think I would advise you to lift the Library ban against them. I don't completely trust those two.

Your humble servant, Wilmar

Zo sat at Wilmar's workbench crushing dried leaves that gave off the scent of grass in the summertime. Wilmar insisted they be crushed into a fine powder. It was a long, tedious task, so one hand held Keir's book, while the other pounded the herbs with the stone pestle. The book had notes and copied quotations from different sources. It began with a discussion of how to use Healing Magic, and how it controlled the different systems of the body. It was mostly a discussion about restoring the proper blood flow when there was a blockage, or when the heart wasn't pumping to all the extremities. It was interesting, but nothing groundbreaking. He turned the page and everything stopped.

The Forbidden Art of Using Healing Magic to Kill.

Zo stopped. He had to read it again to even believe what was written on the page.
The first sentence began:

The big secret no one is willing to discuss is the reverse of Healing magic. The few people who have written about it or talked about it in the past were brought before the Healing Council and never seen again, but there are a few sources still out there. The applications of this art could be applied to euthanasia of patients, as well as how it could revolutionize combat...

Zo felt bile burn the back of his throat. He snapped the book closed just as Wilmar came into the workroom to check on why the herb pounding had stopped. He eyed Zo and his face grew concerned.

"What's wrong?" Wilmar asked.

The door to the exam room burst open and two young men came in carrying a man covered in blood.

"On the table," Wilmar directed them.

They were dressed in formal attire, but the curly haired cute one was covered in more blood than his burly companion. Zo's next shock was to see Ryn and Brynd walk in behind the two men. He forced himself to set aside his questions for Ryn and focus on the patient.

Wilmar's hands were already pulling aside layers of clothes and checking for a pulse.

"This man is dead," Wilmar declared.

"Yes," Curly Cutie agreed.

"Why did you bring him here, Jak? Don't you have people who handle these kinds of messes?" Wilmar waved at the body.

Zo examined the curly one named Jak more closely. He did not like what he was hearing.

"I do, but I need you to confirm cause of death for me. This man claimed he knew who was sabotaging the Library, but he died before he could tell us," Jak said.

Zo's eyes found Ryn. She shrank back into the wall at his gaze. Oh, he definitely was going to have words with her.

"Zo, take a look at this." Wilmar had the man's clothes open to expose his chest.

The stab wound was in the exact same place, the same size with the four-point star, and the same entry point as the man Zo had lost. Wilmar held his gaze in a way that told Zo he was thinking the same thing.

"We have seen a wound similar to this recently. Cut his clothes off. I want to see if there's any other wounds on him," Wilmar said.

Ryn moved to the patient's bench and sat. She was looking green.

Zo took the scissors from the drawer and started cutting at the jacket sleeves. The coat was thick wool, but Wilmar's scissors were sharp enough to cut through several layers of fabric. The jacket shouldn't have been a problem, but something was preventing the scissors from cutting. Zo stopped, pulling down the cuff on the sleeve. A small metal tag fell out onto the floor.

"What's that?" Wimar asked.

Zo picked it up. One side was smooth and shiny, like it had been rubbed often. The other had an engraving on it.

"*Kill the roots*," Zo read.

Ryn gasped, her hands going to her mouth.

"He said the same thing right before died," Jak said.

Burly guy crossed his arms, shifting his weight from one foot to another.

"What does it mean?" Zo asked. "The last guy we found killed this way said the same words."

"As well as the two mysterious men we overheard in the Library," Ryn said.

"Can I see that?" Jak asked.

Zo handed him the piece of metal.

Jak held it up to the lantern overhanging Wilmar's worktable, then turned it over in his fingers several times.

"It looks as though there used to be something on the back," Jak said.

"Let me see." Ryn came forward, and Jak handed her the metal. "Maybe. It's very faint though. What would erase an engraving on metal? Don't people write on metal so it won't fade?"

"If it's shallow enough it could disappear from constant rubbing," Burly guy said.

Jak pocketed the piece of metal.

"Zo, take a look at this," Wilmar said, pointing to the man's collarbone.

Zo shifted to get a better look. Wilmar was pointing at the man's bead scars.

"Earth and Water? Are those the symbols I'm seeing?" Zo asked.

Jak nodded. "Yes, those are Cobb's magics."

"So, let me get this straight." Ryn was fanning herself, sweating, and looking even more green. Zo used his foot to slide a bucket closer to her. "We have two dead men, both with the same wounds which caused their deaths, and both of them saying 'Kill the roots' before they died, and one of them has a piece of metal on them with the same words, plus he has the magics needed to damage the flooring and heating system in the Library?"

Zo remembered something Iden had pointed out. "We also found mouse droppings on the first guy. I dismissed it at the time, because it was too coincidental and lots of people who've lived on the streets come in with things like that on them, but now I'm not so sure."

Ryn's eyes got wide. "Dan, can I have that stone the guy dropped on the table?"

The Burly one, Dan, looked at Jak whose lips were flatlined, but he nodded. Dan took a rock from his pocket and handed it to Ryn.

"Do you mind if I keep this?" she asked them.

Dan held Jak's gaze for a long moment. Jak shifted from one foot to another.

"Sure," Jak finally said, rubbing the back of his neck. "We need to go and get the girls home. How long do you think your exam will take?"

Wilmar rolled his eyes. "You're going to wake me in the middle of the night to collect this body, aren't you?"

Jak shrugged with a slow grin.

Wilmar sighed. "Fine, fine. You can come after midnight, I should be done by then."

"Excellent, and now—" Jak turned to the girls, but Zo had moved between them and the door.

Ryn cleared her throat. "Zo, these are the two I told you about. Jak, Dan, this is my brother Zo."

Jak seemed a bit startled, but stuck out his hand in greeting.

Zo stood immovable with his arms crossed. His eyes narrowed at Ryn. "I thought we agreed you would have me there the next time you saw these two."

"You agreed," Ryn frowned at him.

"It's a pleasure to meet you, now if you'll excuse us." Jak took Brynd's hand and tried to move around Zo.

"I'll take the girls home," Zo said.

Wilmar eyed him but said nothing. Zo knew Wilmar needed help with the exam, but he wasn't going to let these two take Ryn and Brynd anywhere else tonight. The fact that they showed up with a dead body from what looked like a date did not sit well with him. He felt a flood of brotherly protectiveness.

Jak locked eyes with Dan for a moment, then shifted his gaze between Ryn and Brynd. His lips shifted to a smirk, and he let go of Brynd. "If you insist, but you should know there's someone out there killing people for information on the Library, and Dan and I are handy in a fight."

"I'll handle it."

Jak backed off, giving Brynd a kiss that made Zo miss Iden. The two stalked past Zo, who was grateful that Dan had only pressed Ryn's hand to his forehead. Then they were gone.

"Stone?" Zo turned to Ryn.

Ryn held up a black pockmarked rock between two fingers. "Yes, I might be wrong, but I have a weird feeling this is *the rock*. It only makes sense." She pointed at the body on the table. "If he has the right magic..."

Brynd moved in closer to look at the stone. "And legend says there's objects that can negate magic..."

"Then this is our saboteur." Ryn fanned herself as she moved to examine the face of the body on the table.

"Can't be, he's dead. Apparently, so is the guy who deposited the mouse in the Library," Brynd said.

"Can I see?" Zo asked, indicating the stone. Ryn held it up between her fingers and he examined it more closely. It was hard to tell from an image the Protector created from smoke, but he was inclined to agree with Ryn's pronouncement.

"Hmmm. Would it be alright if I took it to run an experiment?" Zo asked.

Ryn turned it over in her fingers. "Yes, but if it turns out to be what we're looking for we need to give it to Clayr."

"Will do," Zo said.

Ryn released the stone into Zo's waiting palm.

* * *

Zo rolled the rock around in his pocket, as they left Wilmar's. It could have been his imagination, but something about the rock felt different.

He looked over his shoulder in the direction Jak and Dan had gone. "I don't know Ryn, those two guys feel like trouble."

"And creepy Healer guy is better?" She shot back.

He had to admit she had a point. After reading Keir's book, Zo was starting to have a lot of doubts about Keir, no matter how he made Zo feel inside.

"Keir has nothing to do with the boys you're hanging out with. There's already enough going on with the Library stuff, and you don't need to add dangerous dates on top of that."

"They're not dangerous," Ryn protested.

Zo glared at her.

"I mean, they seem to be extremely well connected and in charge of a lot of things for a couple of guys who are only a year or so older than me, but they come from Waatch. I'm sure growing up here is different," Ryn said, her jawline set like she when she was determined to do something.

"I feel safe with Jak," Brynd piped up.

Zo sighed. Despite the conversation, he was on high alert as they took the main street running from the Wilmar's toward the Library. His gaze attempted to penetrate every darkened alley and cross street.

"You didn't have to send them home. You could have let them come with us," Ryn said.

Bryn tilted her head backward. "I think they are following us."

Zo looked behind him to see two tall figures and a child walking far enough behind them he couldn't make out any faces.

"Great," he said, picking up the pace.

Ryn grunted, but didn't complain even though she was breathing hard from keeping up with him after a couple blocks.

"We're almost to the Library, and whoever they are, they won't dare follow us there," Ryn said.

When they were only a couple blocks from the Library, the light from a shop window revealed Iden walking toward them. Zo breathed a sigh of relief.

"Hey, where are you headed?" Zo asked.

Iden looked up, startled. "To find you." He smiled.

Zo's heart warmed. "Let's head home."

Iden put his arm around Zo's waist and pulled him close. But when the lamplight from the Library grounds hit them, Iden's hand slid away. Zo found himself wishing it hadn't. He really needed Iden tonight.

They escorted the girls all the way to their dorm room. When Ryn gave him a hug, she was trembling. Zo couldn't tell if it was from the cold, or what she had seen that night. He rubbed her back with his hand and vowed to keep a closer eye on her.

"We'll figure it out. I promise we'll figure it out," he said.

Ryn nodded into his chest then pulled away from him. She said good night and disappeared into her room. Zo pressed a hand to her door. At least she was safe here.

"You look tired. Let's get some sleep," Iden said.

Zo turned to him. "No. Come help me with a little experiment," he said, holding up the rock.

* * *

The night shift in the Boiler Room was hot and noisy as ever, but the tunnel to the underbelly of the Library was cool and quiet.

"Something's bothering you," Iden said, slipping his arm around Zo's shoulders.

Zo glanced behind him, but they were alone in the tunnel.

"It's been an unsettling night," Zo said.

"Tell me."

"Beyond my sister and Brynd dating two guys that seem pretty shady, and the body they brought to Wilmar's…"

"A what? Body?"

"Yes, same wounds as the guy I lost that day." Zo's voice hitched. He couldn't say more. That day still shadowed him.

"Interesting, go on."

"I've had someone give me something rather disturbing."

Iden said nothing, but walked quietly beside Zo waiting for him to elaborate.

It felt very strange to say it out loud, especially in the quiet lull in the conversation Iden had created. Zo took a deep breath.

"Someone gave me a book. It talks about something I've never heard spoken of before."

Iden squeezed Zo's shoulder in support and encouragement.

Even though he didn't intend it that way, his voice came out as a whisper. "It talks about using Healing magic to kill."

Iden almost stumbled over his feet. "What?"

"I suppose it makes a lot of sense, if you have access to heal an organ you have access to stop it as well," Zo said.

"That Keir guy gave you this information, didn't he?"

Zo nodded, fiddling with the handle of the lantern he carried.

Iden took a deep breath.

Oh no, here it comes, Zo thought.

"I'm not one to tell a person who they should and shouldn't associate themselves with, but after meeting with Keir's parents the other night, and now this, I'm not sure he's somebody you want to be spending time with."

Zo frowned. "I just said the same thing to Ryn about the guy she's dating."

Iden chuckled. "It's very good advice. You tend to know what's right."

Zo sighed. Iden was right. There was something creepy about Keir and his behavior, but there was also something exciting about him. The boys Ryn and Brynd were with must have a similar appeal to them. Still, Zo felt he was better at controlling situations than Ryn. She was too much of a people pleaser. Without magic, Ryn was vulnerable to the dangers those two boys put her in. He winced inwardly at how angry she would be at him thinking that way.

They came out of the tunnels and into the exchange. There was a full crew of water magic workers directing the water through the newly repaired pipes to heat the Library on a cold autumn night. It was late in the season, and the winter solstice was upon them. Soon winter cold would have its grip on the Library and everyone.

Zo pulled the stone out of his pocket and held it up for Iden to see.

"Now, let's see if this is what Ryn thinks it is." Zo stepped across the barrier threshold that put him squarely into the Library's protective magic.

He looked back at the workers and drew Iden further down the tunnel under the Library.

"What exactly is that rock supposed to do?" Iden asked.

Zo looked back down the way they came and judged they were probably far enough not to be seen.

"If I'm right, this rock is how the saboteurs of the Library have been introducing pests, and damaging the heating system in the Library."

Iden shifted his stance in a way that said he didn't quite believe Zo, but he didn't quite disbelieve him either.

"Here goes."

Zo handed Iden the lantern he was carrying, held up the rock between two fingers, then snapped the fingers of his other hand right next to the rock.

Flames leapt into Zo fingers.

Iden jumped back.

"Great Ancestors!" Iden exclaimed.

He reached out and delicately took the stone from Zo's fingers, examining it.

"Walk that way," Zo said, gestured with his chin down the tunnel.

Iden held up the stone and began walking backward down the tunnel. Zo worried he might back into a hot pipe, but he said nothing. Once Iden was about a horse length away from Zo the flames went out, and Zo felt his hair stand up, and his magic became muffled.

Iden gasped.

"I think we found it," Zo said.

Iden twisted his hand and sent a burst of wind down the tunnel toward Zo. His mouth dropped open. He examined the rock closer, then tossed the rock back to Zo.

Zo snatched it out of the air and flames leapt back to his fingers.

"Now to find the branch and the sword."

Chapter Fifteen

Clayr,

Enclosed is a list of delegates whom we are taking to Viatoro to inspect the new facility. I think you will see that it is a fair split between those who are in favor of the move and those who have some objections. This list has been voted on and approved by the Board. Make sure all of these delegates are ready to sail with the tide tomorrow morning.

Jeris de Venti, Library Board of Regents

The cave Ryn stood in didn't smell damp or musty like she thought it should, despite the rain falling outside the cave door. It smelled dry, clean, and warm. Ryn's dad sat at a desk pouring over a stack of books. Ryn shifted. The sound of her feet scraping on the rock floor caused her dad to look up from his work. Shock passed over his face.

"Ryn, you're here. How are you here?" His brow furrowed as he ran his thumb across his eyebrows.

Ryn took in the walls of the cave, which sparkled a bit in the lamplight. "I don't know."

Her father didn't get up, didn't approach her. He stayed rooted in his seat like he was at a complete loss as to what to do.

"What is this place?" she asked.

Her father's gaze took in the cave. "The alleged place where Luc left his cask of leftover beads. The ones that give all of Praedo's power."

"Really? Where?"

Her father turned back to the book on his desk. "I'm still looking."

Ryn stepped up next to her father and read:

The years have now passed, and in solitude,
I've sought my shelter, far from human crowds,
Among the high mountains and under the clouds,
Within the green woods Praedo once renewed.

She looked around the cave again. This was really the place?

"May I?"

Her father gestured for her to take the book.

And now, I've grown old, in a cavern I stay,
And search with my lyre for perfect refrain,
Till under the echoes of earth's arcane,
A deep song of bones calls my heart to play.

I carry the tale of Praedo with me,
His magic, his legacy, close to my breast,
His spirit I've guarded, his memory blessed,
And now I release it with this, my song, free.

"This is what it's all about isn't it? Praedo's power. This is why the Library is in danger," she said.

"Perhaps. There are many factions who would like to get their hands on those beads first. Having control over the Library and its resources could lead them here. The Library is where I found the clues to this place."

"But you've been here for years and haven't found them," Ryn pointed out.

The wooden chair her father sat in creaked as he shifted in it. "It took me a long time to find the cave. Now I'm in a race against time to find the beads before someone else discovers the cave."

"And the orphanage book? Why is that so important?" Ryn asked.

Her father stood and paced. "I think it's connected somehow. Your parents..."

* * *

Bang!

The window over her bed flew open, dumping cold air and rain on Ryn's head.

"What the..." Ryn's sleep filled eyes squinted to see a face staring down at her from her window.

She hurtled out of bed, gasping as she scrambled out of the way, heart pounding. She should scream, do something to bring people running, but her breath was gone.

"Jak!" Brynd called from her bed.

Ryn shook her head and looked again. It was Jak outside her window. *On Library grounds.*

"How?" Ryn rushed over as Jak climbed through to reveal Dan right behind him. It was still before sun up, but light enough to see the guys had climbed the tree that grew outside their window, the trunk of which grew close to the Library grounds wall. At some point the branch had been cut to prevent it from growing into the window, but it had continued to thicken over time. Apparently, it was sturdy enough for two grown teenagers to climb.

"What are you doing here?" Brynd asked as she closed Ryn's window behind them.

Dan looked into Ryn's eyes. She flushed at how sweet and earnest his gaze was. "We found a clue, and thought we should bring it to you."

"And risk getting caught on Library grounds?" Brynd folded her arms.

"It seemed important." Jak put his arm around Brynd and kissed her head. She relented and tilted her face up so he could kiss her proper.

"So what's this news?" Ryn asked as she put kindling on the embers of their fire to warm up the room.

Dan hung his wet cloak on the coat rack. "We were able to find a jeweler who could make out the etching on the metal tag."

Brynd took Jak's cloak from him and hung it next to the others. "Aaand?"

"It's a wolf's head." Jak caught Brynd's hand and pulled her close to him.

Ryn put a kettle over the fire then joined Dan at the table. "So an engraved piece of metal that says *Kill the Roots* on one side and has a picture of a mythical creature on the other. What does it mean?"

Dan put his hand on the table, like he wanted to take Ryn's hand, but didn't. "The wolf's head is the symbol of an underground organization. Goes by the name of Evalesco."

"To become strong—to dominate," Ryn translated from the language of the Ancestors.

"That's one way to translate it," Dan said.

"Very secret, very deadly," Jak said.

"Yeah—two people are dead. Didn't that man Cobb mention Evalesco?" Ryn said.

Dan nodded. "He did. Everyone in Waatch avoids dealing with them," Dan said.

"Clearly not everyone," Brynd said.

"So—highly secret organization is giving out metal pieces that say, *Kill the Roots*, but to what end?" Ryn asked.

"We are not sure. This is where we need your help." Jak looked straight into Brynd's eyes.

"Anything," she said.

Jak nodded. "We need access to the Library to find out what *Kill the Roots* means."

"That would be impossible, even if you weren't forbidden on Library grounds. Only workers, researchers, or students are allowed into the Library," Brynd said.

"We heard you found a way." Jak shifted to stare Ryn in the eyes.

"And how is that?" Ryn demanded.

"Look, Library workers talk. Talk is overheard, in taverns, in ink shops—I have ears everywhere."

She inhaled sharply and choked. The kettle started to whistle. Brynd moved to take it off the fire and grab some mugs.

"The only way I know of would require the cooperation of my brother, and you didn't exactly make the best first impression," Ryn said.

Dan looked thoughtful accepting a mug of chamomile tea from Brynd.

Jak joined them at the table. "Then we'll just have to make a better impression."

"Tell us what sources you're thinking of, and Brynd and I will look it up for you," Ryn said.

Jak took a sip and shook his head. "It's not that simple, there are hidden codes only..."

There was a knock on the door.

The boys stared at each other for a second then quickly scrambled under the beds.

Brynd made sure the blankets hung over the sides to cover them, then opened the door.

Fergus stood there in the rain.

"May I come in?" he asked.

Ryn joined Brynd at the door, but she knew she wasn't tall enough to block Fergus' sight.

"We aren't dressed yet. Can we help you with something?" Ryn asked.

Fergus' eyes glanced at the damp cloaks on the rack then fixed on the table, but only for a moment. The look on Fergus' face told Ryn he'd counted mugs. His eyes lingered on Ryn for a moment. The hurt look in his eyes that ended in a frown made Ryn's stomach drop. She didn't want to hurt Fergus again.

"Madame Curator wants to see you immediately. There is a meeting with the delegation from Viatoro and she wants you there," he said.

"Me? Why me?" Ryn asked.

Fergus gave a slight shrug. "She didn't say. I'll wait out here in the rain while you get dressed."

Ryn fought hard not to look back to the guys. "Give me a few, and I'll get ready."

Fergus stepped back and Brynd shut the door.

"What do we do?" Ryn whispered.

"Get dressed. Madame Curator has summoned you!" Brynd's harsh whisper came back.

Ryn glanced at the beds where they were still hiding.

"I'll take care of it," Brynd whispered in her ear.

Ryn nodded, and ran to her cabinet to pull out her best researcher dress.

When she was dressed and pulling on her boots Dan emerged from under the bed.

"I'll wait here for you," he whispered.

Ryn shook her head. "I'm pretty sure Fergus suspects something. You should go."

"Alright." He pulled her into an embrace and kissed the top of her head. "Send word with Maus when you're done, and I'll come. We have more to talk about."

"How do I find Maus?"

"Maus will find you."

Ryn stiffened, but then relented and melted into his arms. "I will."

Dan slid back under the bed and Ryn counted to ten before opening the door and stepping up to the waiting Fergus.

Fergus eyed the inside of the room before Brynd closed the door.

Ryn took his arm, and he relaxed a little.

"You know you can talk to me, right? I've kept many of your secrets."

Ryn nodded as they descended the stairs. "Sometimes we hold things to protect those we care about."

Fergus' exhale sounded exasperated. "Just don't be upset when the same thing happens in reverse."

He stopped at the bottom of the stairs and looked into her eyes. "I'm your friend, Ryn, I'm here for you. For whatever you need."

Ryn hugged his arm. "That means the world to me."

"*Girls.*" Fergus shook his head.

Ryn let Fergus escort her across the Library grounds. She wished she could tell Fergus what was on her mind, but she didn't want to get Jak and Dan into trouble. She was certain

Fergus would have no choice but to do something about them. She wasn't completely sure about Jak and Dan yet, but she didn't think they were bad, or deserved the Library guard to be brought down on them.

With all of that on her mind, she still enjoyed the quiet moment walking in the rain next to Fergus. He made her feel safe and at peace, even in the face of what was probably trouble. Her mind drifted back to the dream Jak had interrupted. Something was very odd about her dreams. Her dreams used to be the normal kind of weird things shifting from one scene to another. Sometimes when someone had bullied her she dreamed about being chased. Lately though, her dreams had a reality to them. Like she had been in the cave with her father. Like she had been on the road with her father. Like she was the Library when the delegation arrived.

"Ryn!"

She heard her name called, but the voice was unfamiliar. She scanned the area for who had called her name. Then she saw him, hurrying down the path past the winter stumps of the rose bushes.

"Ryn! Wait up," he called again. It was the man she saw in her dream. The one with the red hair that looked so familiar.

"Can I help you?" Ryn asked when the man caught up to them.

Breathing hard and out of breath the man put out his hand. "Mik de Viator, younger brother to Ryette de Viator. I'm your uncle." Mik grinned.

Her uncle? Her mother had a brother? No wonder he seemed familiar.

Ryn tentatively took his hand. "Well, you already know my name so, nice to meet you."

"I've been trying the entire time we've been here to meet you. It seems you are a busy girl and hard to catch," Mik said.

"I have been a bit busy," Ryn said, plus she had been avoiding the delegation precisely because she was hoping to avoid meeting anyone from House Viator. Her mother didn't trust them, and after Master Wes from Viator tried to kidnap her, she didn't trust them either.

"Well, it seems we have some time now," Mik grinned as he let go of her hand.

Fergus shifted uneasily.

"Actually, I'm on my way to meet with Madame Curator," Ryn said.

"That's perfect, because I am as well. Can we walk together? I would very much like the opportunity to get to know my niece." Uncle Mik held out his arm for Ryn to take.

She slipped her hand back onto Fergus' arm, and they continued on their way.

Uncle Mik's brow furrowed. "I take it your mother hasn't mentioned me."

"No, she hasn't, but I recall now finding your name in a book on House Viator. I wasn't sure if it was true," Ryn admitted.

Uncle Mik sighed. "I'm sorry Ryette has such a strained relationship with the family. We really do wish that was not the case."

I bet you do, Ryn thought.

"Your grandmother and I, well all of House Viator, would like to get to know you. All we know is that Ryette is your mother and that you're a researcher in the Library."

"Assistant researcher," Ryn corrected.

Uncle Mik shrugged. "The fact that you went from being a student to a research position is quite remarkable. Your grandmother is quite proud. She would like to meet you. This is a formal invitation to spend some time on Viatoro in your Ancestral House."

Fergus' hand covered Ryn's on his arm and squeezed. He must have felt her hand start to tremble. Viator wanted her to come to their island. They already had Jett there, she was sure of it. Something must be wrong, because now they wanted Ryn. They must think she was Ryette's biological daughter.

Ryn tried to speak, but it came out a squeak. She cleared her throat. "That sounds lovely, but I am heavily involved with my duties here at the Library. I hardly get even one day off per quarter moon."

"I think we can arrange something." Uncle Mik winked at her.

Ryn squeezed Fergus' arm tighter. He pulled her in closer, his free hand resting on the hilt of his side sword.

At Clayr's office door Fergus put out his hand to stop Uncle Mik.

"You need to wait out here. Madame Curator needs to speak to Ryn alone," Fergus said.

Uncle Mik nodded, then sat in one of the chairs outside Clayr's office.

Fergus slipped his arm around her waist and gave her a side hug.

"Good luck," he said, then opened the office door for her.

"Thanks. Thanks for understanding," she said.

"I wouldn't go that far." He grinned, and she walked past him into the office...

...and immediately wanted to walk right back out.

"No," her mother was saying. "This is a terrible idea. I won't allow it. Do you know what they'll do?"

Clayr looked up from her desk. "Ryn, come in and have a seat."

Ryn watched Lar close a book and return it to the shelf behind Clayr's desk. He came to stand close to Ryn's mother, putting a reassuring hand around her shoulder. Ryn's stomach twisted.

"What's going on?" she asked.

Clayr looked at Ryn's mother for a heartbeat, then turned to Ryn. "The Board of Regents has decreed that the Library is to send a delegation to Viatoro to inspect this new facility they have built to replace the Library. The Board has chosen the delegates, and you are one of them."

Ryn's jaw dropped.

"No," her mother said again. "This is my mother's ploy to get Ryn there. Now that she knows about Ryn, she wants her on her side. She'll never believe Ryn's adopted. I'm certain she already has Jett, I'm not letting her have Ryn as well."

Clayr's chair creaked as she leaned back in it. "Unfortunately, Ryn works for the Library, and is therefore subject to whatever the Board decides for her. I cannot overrule the Board. I can make suggestions, but whatever they decide goes."

Ryn's mother turned on her best friend. "So make the suggestion, and make it firm. Ryn is not to go to Viatoro. She is not safe around my family."

"Come now sister, I am hurt."

Ryn jumped at the deep voice behind her. She turned to find the man dressed all in black she dreamed of speaking for the delegation when they first arrived. He was accompanied by Uncle Mik, whose sparkling green eyes danced with mischief at his words. They were followed by Jeris, and Master Ubert the Inspector.

"Excuse me, I didn't hear a knock," Clayr's tone was sharp.

"Since when does a Regent need to knock?" Jeris folded his arms, feet planted in the middle of the office next to the Inspector.

The door opened again to admit Prym with a notebook and a pencil ready to write down every word said. She shot Ryn a wicked smile.

Ryn turned back to her mother, who was pale as a bed sheet.

"It's good to see you sister, the family misses you. Mother is anxious to be in touch," Ryn's uncle said.

Her mother's face was devoid of emotion. "I bet she is."

"Come home. All will be resolved." Her uncle placed his hand on the back of Ryn's chair. Her mother stepped forward, but Lar held her back.

"And who are these people?" Ubert asked, waving his hand at Ryn's mother and Lar. "I haven't seen them on the list of workers."

"Independent private document handlers. They collect documents for the Library," Clayr answered.

Prym started scribbling notes in her notebook.

"I see," Ubert said, but he didn't look convinced. "I have come to protest a delegation of Library managers leaving before I have completed my investigation. A potential guilty party could escape on this expedition. I recommend you wait until my findings are complete."

Clayr turned to Jeris. "I have no objection to that," she said.

"Unfortunately, the trip cannot wait. The sooner we can hear the findings from the delegation about the proposed move, the better. It is a huge undertaking to move the Library, and if the Library is deemed unsafe we need to be in a position to move the materials quickly," Jeris said.

Master Ubert threw his hands up. "I don't know why you hired me if you aren't going to listen to my recommendations."

Jeris turned to him. "Don't worry, we are prepared to listen to all of your suggestions."

"Fine. Go, but if our culprit slips away because of this trip, you will not be hanging it on my head." Master Ubert turned to Prym. "Make sure you write that down word for word."

Prym nodded, scribbling.

"We'll see you on the boat tomorrow then," Jeris said to Clayr.

Ryn's uncle patted her shoulder. "I can't wait."

The intruders left them in Clayr's office. The man in black lingered.

"Is there something I can do for you, Zmej?" Clayr asked.

Ryn choked. That was the name she had heard, she remembered now.

"Nothing Madame Curator, just a word of promise that my security team will guarantee the safety of the delegation, if that is a concern," Zmej said.

"That will be all," Clayr said.

Zmej turned and walked out of the office.

Ryn's mother took a deep breath. "I vowed never to set foot on that island again," she said, walking over to wrap her arms around Ryn.

"You don't have to. We will be perfectly safe. They can't move against us as members of the delegation," Clayr said.

"I'll go with her," Lar said.

Ryn's mother nodded.

Clayr opened her mouth to object.

"Not as part of the delegation," Lar added.

"But aren't we supposed to be researching Luc's journals to find clues about the ancient tree and the Library's magic?" Ryn asked.

"It'll have to wait till we return," Clayr said.

There was a knock at the door, and it opened to admit Zo. He strode into the office and right up to Clayr's desk.

"I found the culprit."

He put the black rock Jak had found the night before on the desk. Then he snapped his fingers and flames leapt into them.

Gasping, Clayr jumped back.

"This is how they've been sabotaging the Library."

Chapter Sixteen

Holly de Venti, Master of Library Legal Collections
My dear, it was so good of you and your husband to visit. I think we should do it again soon. I've heard rumor there's been developments in the status of the investigation at the Library that could help sway the opinions of various Houses. You should bring any news that you have. Also, we should discuss our sons. I've heard that Iden is single since his engagement to Prym de Vivus was broken. I know you follow a more traditional Ancestral path, being from House Venti, but I think our sons would make a good couple. We'll discuss it over tea!

Myrta de Sano, House Sano Healing Counsel

Lar grabbed Zo's forearm.

"What in the name of the Ancestors are you doing—put it out!"

Zo shook his hand to extinguish the flames.

Clayr leaned forward, slowly extending her hand to pick up the stone, as if it would burn her.

"How is this possible?" she asked.

"Remember I told you about what the Protector showed me—a rock, a branch, and a sword. I believe this is the rock," Zo said.

Ryn joined Clayr next to her desk. "It is...I can't believe it."

Clayr held the rock up.

"Where did you find it?" Ryette asked.

Zo glared at Ryn, who shrunk down a bit.

"Ryn?" He deferred to her, hoping to get some answers about what went on the night before with Jak and Dan.

"Uhhhhh," she started.

"I've seen a picture of this in Luc's journals, I'm sure of it." Ryette took the rock from Clayr's hand.

Zo narrowed his eyes at Ryn, who blushed, but shook her head slightly, her eyes pleading.

Zo sighed. "We took it off a man who was brought to Wilmar's with a knife wound. The man was, unfortunately, beyond our help."

Ryn looked relieved. He hoped she appreciated him covering for her, and that it wouldn't end up coming back to bite them both. If something happened to her because of it, he would never forgive himself.

Lar took the stone from Ryette, his fingers running over the pock marked surface the way he did when he used his earth magic to track something.

"This stone is full of...something. It feels like magic, but not one I've ever encountered," Lar said.

"So, a rock with the power to negate the Library's magical barrier is found on a dead man," Clayr said.

"Along with a silver tag that had the picture of a wolf's head on one side, and the phrase *Kill the Roots* on the other," Ryn added.

Zo gaped at her, wondering how she knew there was a picture of a wolf on the side that had been erased.

Ryette sank into one of the chairs next to Zo. "Evalesco."

"How do you know this?" Lar asked Ryn.

"I was at Wilmar's with Zo," Ryn said.

It was Lar's turn to stare her down. She gave him a slight shrug.

Zo couldn't take it anymore, and opened his mouth to spill what he knew about Ryn. Maybe Ryette could talk some sense into Ryn about her new 'friends.' Before he started Lar cut him off.

"This is bad. If Evalesco is behind the plot against the Library, everyone here is in danger," Lar said.

Ryette reached out and took Ryn's hand.

Lar and Ryette exchanged a look. "This expedition needs to be canceled. Master Ubert is right about one thing, the saboteur could be with the delegation, and if Evalesco is running around Waatch...I can't protect you if I go with Ryn," he said, staring into Ryette's eyes.

"Unfortunately, it's too late," Clayr said.

"And I can take care of myself," Ryette added.

"Against Evalesco?" Lar asked.

Ryette shifted in her seat, but sat up taller. "Yes."

"Who is in the delegation going to Waatch?" Ryn asked.

"Couple of Regents, and the Head of Collections, as well as the Head Researcher," Clayr said.

"Regent Jeris?" Ryn asked.

Clayr nodded.

"He's definitely top of my list of who could be behind this. He's so anxious to move the Library," Ryn said.

"That's an accusation I would keep to myself if you want to keep your job." Clayr gave Ryn a stern look.

"Or Prym," Ryn added.

"Prym is a child," Lar said.

"I would say my mother, Jayn, is most suspect. All the more reason for you not to go," Ryette added.

"Personally, that inspector guy gives me the creeps," Zo said.

"And with Clayr away, the Library will be unprotected," Lar said.

Clayr sat down at her desk, placing the rock upon it. "I disagree with all of these. There's no way a Regent who is sworn to protect the Library would try to destroy it, nor would his family. Master Ubert is an outside party with supposedly no interests in the Library, even if his behavior appears biased. It's possible the Matriarch of Viator would have motivations to make me, and the Library look incompetent to support her arguments to move the Library, but I don't see your mother being involved with Evalesco, no matter how desperate she is."

"Maybe at one point in my life I would agree with you, but I'm not so sure now. Her desperation seems to have grown," Ryette said.

Zo watched all their eyes shift to the rock on Clayr's desk.

Clayr placed her hand over the rock, sat for a moment, then closed her fist around it and handed it to Ryette.

"Take the girls. With the rock you can Travel into the rare books vault. You've seen inside, you can magic yourself into it. Ryn's the only one besides me who has opened the box that contains the journals. If you've seen the picture in Luc's journals, it's possible there's more information there. Find what information you can. Take Yll and let her use the stone. She'll know what to do."

Zo's gaze shifted from the rock to Ryette's face, her mouth forming a large oval shape.

Her hand closed around the rock. "I hope this works. I'd hate to Travel magic us into a wall. So strange to think of doing magic in the Library."

"Hurry, there's not much time," Clayr said.

Ryette nodded and stood.

Ryn started to follow her, then changed directions and wrapped her arms around Zo.

Conflicting emotions wrestled for control of him. He desperately wanted to take her away someplace safe, but knew that was impossible. He squeezed her back, hoping she would catch all his feelings.

"Be safe. I'm going to miss you," she said into his chest.

"You too. I'll keep you updated on what's happening."

She let go, nodding and wiping a tear from her eye, then she followed Ryette out of the office. Zo's shoulders tightened at the prospect of her going with the delegation. He cracked his knuckles on Clayr's desk. He was tempted to argue Clayr into making Ryn stay one more time, but his father grabbed his shoulder.

"I'll take care of her. You watch over Ryette."

Zo nodded slowly.

Clayr stood. "Everything will be fine. I fear time and distance has caused Ryette to vilify Jayn a bit too much. It's going to be a perfectly civilized discussion."

"About moving the center of power to an island controlled by one Ancestral House," Lar countered.

This wasn't helping. "Right, I have a shift at the Healing House, I gotta go."

Zo left the office to find Fergus waiting for him outside. *Great.*

In a hushed voice, Fergus started in while they walked through the aisles of books on their way to the back door.

"I think Ryn's into something shady. I don't know what, but I'm concerned," Fergus said in a harsh whisper.

"I agree," Zo said.

"What can we do?"

Zo released a long, exasperated breath. "Unfortunately, her contacts are producing information that we need, so not much at the moment. Good news is she's going with the Library delegation to Viatoro so that element won't be an issue for a while."

"She's what?"

"They didn't tell you?" Zo glanced at Fergus.

"No. Well, yes, I knew about the delegation, but not everyone who's going. Even though we are in the curator's confidence, it still feels like guards don't get to know what's happening until it explodes in everyone's face."

"That's unfortunate."

"Tell me about it."

Zo stopped at the back door. "Look, my dad's going with her to watch over her. What we need to focus on is what the saboteurs might get up to with Clayr gone. Keep your eyes and ears open. I have a feeling we're going to be in for a fight."

Fergus straightened. "Right. Let me know if you find anything."

"Will do."

And with that Zo was out the door and down the steps, hurrying across the Library grounds toward the gates. He was running late to the Healing House for his lessons. Part of him wanted to slow down and not care, but the part of him that hated to be late anywhere was in control.

As he strode through the streets of Waatch, his mind desperately tried to make logical sense of all they had discovered. If he could just figure out who was behind this mess, everyone would be safe. Unfortunately, his mind jumped from one line of thinking to another, too quickly for him to sort it out. He was almost at Wilmar's door when he realized he was supposed to be going to the Healing House.

He changed course and crossed the street, taking the steps two at a time.

Keir, who was sitting in the foyer lounge, jumped up to intercept Zo as soon as he walked in the door.

"Where have you been? Did you read the materials I gave you?" Keir asked.

Zo glared at him. "I have concerns."

"Let's talk about them."

Zo moved to go around Keir. "Not right now, I'm late."

"Tonight then? Can we have dinner?"

Keir's fingers brushed Zo's hand sending shivers up his spine.

"I don't have much time between here and my shift with Wilmar."

"I'll get a basket of food and we can eat in Wilmar's garden."

"Sure."

Keir finally stepped out of the way, and Ayn, the Mind Healing student, took Keir's place in front of Zo.

He was losing his patience. "What? I'm late."

"Headmaster wants to see you in his office. Now." The look on her face was one of concern.

Zo's heart rate jumped up. Had he done something wrong? Of course he'd done things wrong, but had he gotten caught?

Zo swore under his breath and let Ayn lead him to the Headmaster's office.

Ayn put her hand on Zo's arm. Surprised, he looked down at her.

"I'm really sorry," she said, then hurried off.

Now his gut was twisting.

Zo knocked.

"Come," the Headmaster's voice said.

Zo opened the door. There was a woman seated across the desk from the Headmaster. She stood and turned to him.

Zo's jaw dropped.

It was his mother.

A very long string of curse words flooded Zo's mind. He was afraid some of them had slipped out of his mouth as well.

His mother spread her arms like he was five years old and would run into them.

"My darling, it's so good to see you."

He turned to the Headmaster and glared at him, hoping he would feel his anger like daggers piercing through him.

The Headmaster held up his hands. "This wasn't me. I promise I kept our bargain."

Zo spun on his heel and headed for the door, only to pull it open and find a big, muscly guy wearing a House Sano guard uniform blocking the door. Zo turned to his mother, hand still on the door latch. His heart pounded.

"Please son, we need to talk," she said, gesturing for him to take the chair next to her.

Zo flung the door shut and plopped himself into the chair, arms folded to keep them from shaking.

"When I heard you were finally studying Healing, I was so excited, I came at once," his mother said.

"Yes, I bet you did." Zo was still glaring at the Headmaster.

"I want you to come home. This school is inadequate, the Healing House on Sano is where you were always meant to study," she said, apparently oblivious to the fact that the Waatch Headmaster sat right there.

"No. I'm not going," he said, his chest tightened.

"I assure you I can get you out of all your present obligations if that's what you're worried about."

There she was. Flaunting her power as a Healing Council member. He hated that more than anything.

"So you can make me into whatever creature it is you want me to be? Isn't that what you were attempting to do when you tried to take my fire bead?"

At that comment, the Headmaster choked. He of all people, running a Healing House, dealing with Mind Healing, would understand the ramifications of what happened when a child was stripped of their magic. Zo only heard rumors, but it was likely the Headmaster had seen the results.

His mother bowed her head and her voice got quiet. "That's not fair. It was a brief moment of weakness, and I've apologized profusely for it."

"Not to me," Zo stood.

The office went still and quiet enough Zo could hear the rain outside the window.

"Can we at least have dinner and talk?" There were tears in his mother's eyes.

It made him want to put his fist through a wall.

"I have plans."

"Breakfast then?"

"I don't eat breakfast."

"Lunch at The Dining Room?"

Zo wanted to scream.

"Please?"

"Fine." And with that he turned, yanked the door open, and pushed past the wall of muscle standing in his way.

Normally he would have taken a moment to appreciate that muscle wall, but he wasn't in the mood.

Chapter Seventeen

Ryn led her mother to her desk, feeling quite proud that the stack of research on it rivaled her mother's desk at home. The fact that Ryn had a desk in the Library, that she was an official worker, and an assistant researcher made her giddy to show her mother where she worked. Yll was at her desk, buried beneath a stack of books to be indexed and shelved, but with her nose in yet another Library history book.

Ryn cleared her throat. Yll did a double take to see Ryette standing there.

"What's going on?" Yll asked.

"Your mother has a special assignment for us. She told us to bring you along and that you would know what to do," Ryn's mother said.

Yll looked down at her research and frowned, but stood up and nodded.

Ryn's mother led them to the entrance to the hidden staircase Ryn had used to get Luc's journal the first time. It led to the restricted section. Ryn shook her head in confusion.

"Didn't Clayr say something about a rare books vault?" she asked.

Her mother nodded. "This is hopefully the closest out of the way place to do what we need to do." She held up the stone.

"What is that?" Yll asked.

Ryn's mother tipped the *Sneaky, Clever Dragons* book and let the bookcase swing inward. The three of them ducked inside.

Once the bookcase door had been secured Ryn explained, "Zo has confirmed this rock is *the* rock the Protector was talking about and it allows magic in the Library."

Yll's gaze shifted back and forth between them. "Wait, what?"

"Just hold on," Ryn's mother said, wrapping her arms around the two of them.

Wind that shouldn't belong in the Library swirled at their feet, growing until it was spinning all around them. Traveling with her mother was much smoother than with anyone else.

There wasn't any dust, but Ryn buried her face in her mother's shoulder anyway. When the swirling stopped, they were in a dimly lit room. There was only one lantern and it was trimmed low. Her mother used the lantern to light another hanging on the wall. A large, sculpted urn on the table made it distinctive to any other section of the Library. No wonder her mother could remember it.

"Good, lantern's still hot. That means the guards recently made their rounds. We have a little bit before they return," Ryn's mother said.

Yll stood wide eyed. Her hair was disheveled from the Traveling, and her jaw hung slightly open.

Ryn snapped her fingers in front of her face.

Yll shook herself. "I can't believe we just Traveled inside the Library."

"I'm just happy it worked, and we are here and not inside the stone walls," Ryn's mother said.

Yll shook her head. "That could have happened? Why did no one tell me that could have happened?"

"Come on." Ryn grabbed her hand and dragged her down the aisle after her mother.

They passed rows upon rows of little locked doors. Her mother turned down this aisle, then turned down that aisle. In the darkness Ryn got all turned around. Every row of little doors looked the same as the last, but her mother's stride didn't hesitate in the slightest. Ryn clung to Yll's hand. The darkness and the shadows they cast in the lantern light gave an eerie feel to the place. Somehow in the dead quiet Ryn could swear she was hearing whispers.

She was watching the little doors as they passed them, trying to pinpoint where the sound was coming from when she almost bumped into her mother, who had stopped abruptly.

Her mother stood in front of a row of little doors. She pointed to one of the larger of the doors. It was fifth up from the bottom, but higher than Ryette's head.

Her mother stared at the door. She grabbed Ryn's hand and squeezed it.

"Let us hope the answers we need are in there so we can catch the criminals, and you won't need to go to Viatoro," she said.

Ryn's brow furrowed as her and Yll exchanged a look. Ryn highly doubted Luc's journals would tell them who was sabotaging the Library.

"What's so awful about Viatoro?" Yll asked.

Ryn's mother turned and gave her an appraising look. After a moment she sighed. "I told you my mother's marriage and mine were arranged, right?"

Ryn nodded.

"It wasn't just to join two powerful houses that historically didn't get along. My grandparents had found some source, or maybe just believed in some tall tale about someone using their magics to add an additional magic to their abilities."

Yll gave her a raised eyebrow.

"I know, it seems preposterous, but House Viator had been the center in the Ancestor world for travel, courier, and delivery service. The new movement against using magic for mundane tasks lost big clients as well as making it harder to recruit new Travelers. My grandparents had been studying the Origin and Praedo. After reading the tales of the magic Praedo performed they became dissatisfied with only two magics. They felt the way of reviving House Viator's dominance, and to boost magic use, was to control all the magics-and be the ones to distribute them. They set about experimenting with different magic combinations and mythical tales of how to add more. All of these attempts failed."

"Then why...?"

Her mother held up her hand to forestall questions. "Their latest and greatest idea was to use Travel magic and Spirit magic to somehow imprint magic onto the spirit. Problem was the rift between House Viator and House Pentral meant there was no one who actually had those two magics."

"So they arranged a marriage," Yll said.

Ryette nodded. "Two actually, my mother's and mine. I was less than cooperative, but they managed to manipulate me into having a child with those two magics. I wasn't willing to try it, nor am I willing to let my child attempt it."

Her mother's eyes became unfocused as she stared off into the darkness. "Though I fear they have already gotten Jett to attempt it." She wrapped her arms around herself and shuddered.

Ryn knew this was her mother's fear. She reached out a place her hand on her mother's shoulder.

"My worry is that they'll take you—thinking you're my birth daughter—and attempt to try it with you. There is rumor that the experiment involves touching Praedo's sword embedded in the ground at the Origin. Given what has happened to those who have magic, I fear what would happen to an Ordinary who touched the sword."

Her mother shook herself. "But we're going to find the answer so that doesn't happen."

She pulled a key from her pocket and fit it into the lock on the door she had pointed to earlier. Inside was the same box Ryn had seen before, which held Luc's journals. Her mother pulled it out of its vault and sat it on the floor.

"Now it's your turn." She looked Ryn in the eyes.

Ryn swallowed, wiping her sweaty hands on the sides of her skirt. The last time she did this was quite a shock. She rubbed her palm where there was still a small scar. This time she was prepared for it, but nervous it wouldn't work for her again.

She pressed her palm to the top of the box. Immediately something stabbed her palm. Blood flowed through the channels of the carving of Praedo's sword. She pulled her hand away and the sword glowed. The box popped open. She was surprised to find not one book, but several inside. None of them was the one that had called to her and made her take it away.

Ryn gave her mother a quizzical look.

"Oh, don't worry, that journal is locked up tighter now," her mother said.

Ryn pulled a handkerchief from her pocket and bound her hand before reaching in to remove a journal, the leather binding hard and smooth. Her mother placed her hand over Ryn's.

"Aren't we taking these so we can study them?" Ryn asked.

Her mother shook her head and looked to Yll.

A deep growling came from Yll's throat. "Mother told me she wouldn't tell anyone."

Ryette took the journal from Ryn's hand. "She hasn't. She just told me that you would know what to do."

Yll nodded. "I guess I need that rock."

Ryn's mother pulled it from her pocket, and placed it in Yll's hand.

Immediately Yll began to shift, her body shrinking, her face elongating, and feathers growing to cover her body. Instead of the robin red breast Yll usually preferred, she became the eagle Ryn had only seen her become once—on the steps of the Library when she attempted to stop Thalya from stabbing Regg.

In one talon she held the rock, with the other she held the book open. With her beak she began flipping through the pages of the journal, her eagle eyes intent on each page.

"What's she doing?" Ryn asked.

Her mother stood slack jawed. "In rare cases those shape shifters who shift into birds develop an incredible memory. Yll must be memorizing each page, and quickly!"

Yll's bird head gave them an affirmative nod.

Ryn didn't know how to whistle, but she wished she could to show how impressed she was.

Yll squawked, and Ryn's mother took the first journal, and opened a new one for her. She was going through the books incredibly fast, but Ryn was aware of how much time had passed since they entered the vault. She noticed her mother watching down the aisles, probably thinking the same thing.

"We have permission from the curator to be here, so we can't actually get in trouble, right?" Ryn asked.

Her mother stared over Ryn's head and out into the darkness. "The rare book vaults are not the sole responsibility of the curator. She is more of the arranged caretaker. The Library Board is the one to grant permission to visit the vaults."

"Then how is it she can send you here, and that you have a key?"

Her mother shifted. "There are things in the rare book vaults even the Board doesn't know about."

That didn't really explain anything.

"Don't worry, we took the only lantern," her mother said.

Great, so some Library guard could be out there roaming around in the dark and we wouldn't know it. Ryn focused her ears, straining to hear footsteps.

Yll nipped at Ryette's hand and she pulled out another book.

"Hurry," her mother whispered.

Yll nodded again.

Straining to hear something definitely made Ryn hear things.

"What was that?" Ryn said.

Her mother shook her head. "I didn't hear anything."

"I'm going to go check."

Her mother pursed her lips and shook her head, but Ryn stood and crept quietly down the aisle.

"Don't go far. You'll get lost in here. It's designed that way," her mother's voice was anxious.

Ryn was about halfway down the aisle when she stopped. A cold gentle waft of air brushed her cheek, almost like a touch or a caress. She searched for where the air had come from, but all she could see was vague outlines of little vault doors barely illuminated by the lantern her mother still had.

A little further down the aisle she thought she saw something. The shape of it reminded her of the Protector of the Library. Tentatively she crept forward, trying not to make any sudden moves that would disturb the Protector. When she got closer, she couldn't exactly see it, so much as feel it. The Protector began waving at her wildly. In its hand appeared a rock, the bump in the middle, and pockmarks matching the one presently in Yll's taloned claw. The Protector waved its hand making it disappear, and making a motion as if to throw it away.

"What's wrong?" Ryn asked.

The Protector repeated the sequence, starting with the rock in its hand and then making a motion as if to throw it away.

"We need to..."

The Protector repeated the motion again.

"...get rid of the rock?"

The Protector rolled its hand, like it wanted her to say more.

"Take it out of the Library?"

The Protector nodded.

"The rock is hurting the Library?"

More.

"Damaging the protective magic?"

The Protector's nodding became vigorous.

"Alright, sure. We'll make sure we take it with us."

The Protector looked relieved.

Footsteps sounded somewhere behind the Protector. It turned, then disappeared.

Ryn ran back to her mother and Yll.

"Someone's coming!"

"We're done," her mother said, closing the box.

Ryn placed her hand on top, the fiery glow traced the carved tree, and the box clicked closed, and locked. Her mother returned the box to its vault and locked the door.

"Let's go," she said, just as Yll finished returning to a human form.

Her mother extinguished the lamp, wrapped them in her arms, and the spinning air twirled round them till the vault disappeared.

* * *

When their feet hit the curator's office floor, Clayr came out of her seat waving for a startled—looking guard to leave.

"What are you doing?" she hissed at them.

"We were in a hurry, and I needed someplace I could visualize easily."

"Now I'm going to have to explain this to Errol."

"He keeps your secrets."

"He does, but if they take my position away from me, he will be obligated to answer whatever questions are asked of him." Clayr sat herself behind her desk. "Did you get the information?"

Ryn's mother nodded. "She has it. All we need to do is help her sort through what she is relevant, and we can solve this mystery."

Clayr shook her head. "There's no time right now. We sail tomorrow morning with the tide. We'll have to work on it during our trip. Yes, that means you're going with us, Yll."

Yll said a quiet, "*Yes.*"

"But I'm certain the answer is in Luc's journals. We know already that someone used the rock to negate the Library's magic. The only answer we need to find is if there is, indeed, a tree growing inside the Library, and who would know about it. With that knowledge we should be able to unmask who is sabotaging the Library. I'm pretty sure it's all connected to House Viator's wanting to move it, and then you don't have to go."

"It's not that simple. Even if it is Viator behind this, we'll still need to go. The stone, please." Clayr held out her hand.

Ryn's mother reluctantly handed it over.

"Wait!" Ryn said. "While we were in the vaults I saw the Protector. He said we needed to take the stone out of the Library. It's damaging the protective magic." She reached her hand out to cover Clayr's with the stone.

Clayr's wide eyes met Ryn's.

"Take it." She gave it back to Ryn's mother. "You know where to hide it."

Her mother nodded.

Clayr held Ryette's gaze for a heartbeat longer. Long time familiarity as friends passed information in that one look, then Clayr turned on the girls.

"Off with you two! You need to pack. Time is wasting!"

Ryn nodded, and she and Yll headed for the door. Once outside, Ryn turned toward the way to the back door, but Yll grabbed her arm.

"The orphanage book, this is your chance to get that book binder on Viatoro to look at it," she said.

Ryn's eyes went wide. She couldn't believe she had almost forgotten.

"Yes!"

They raced off to Ryn's desk to retrieve the one book that had permission to leave the Library.

* * *

After they left the Library and Ryn had packed all her things, it was still early, so Ryn left her room hoping she could find Zo. She really wanted to talk to him about what she'd seen the Protector do in the vaults. She inquired at the door to the Boiler Room, and Norm told her he hadn't returned yet from the Healing House. Ryn nodded, disappointed. She had said goodbye to him in Clayr's office, in case she didn't see him before she left, but she was really hoping that wouldn't be the case. Walking the garden path toward the Mess Hall, she ran into Brynd.

"Dan sent Maus looking for you."

"Oh! So much happened I completely forgot. Where is he?" Ryn asked.

"Maus said you could find him across the street in the pen and ink shop."

"Thanks! I'll see you later."

"Better, I want to hear what happened this morning!"

Ryn made her way to the west gate of the Library. That gate was closest to all the shops and eateries.

Ryn crossed the street and found the pen shop a few doors down. Close enough for Library workers and researchers to run to if they ran out of ink, or had broken a nib.

She opened the door to find Dan bent over a table, examining a pen. He looked up and smiled at her, waving her over.

"Have you ever seen something so beautiful?" he said.

Ryn looked at the blue lacquered shine and golden nib.

"It's lovely," she said.

Dan chuckled. "I was talking about you."

"Oh!" Ryn looked up at him and blushed.

Dan waved to get attention. "Can you get this one wrapped up for me?"

The penmaker bobbed his head a bit in a small bow to Dan. "Of course."

He took the pen and went into the back.

"So what was the meeting with the Curator all about?"

"The Board of Regents are sending a Library delegation to Viatoro to be dazzled into moving the Library to this new facility they built."

"Ha! I wonder who they suckered into going on that trip."

"Me. I've been chosen to go, though I'm sure my grandmother, who really wants to meet me, had a hand in that choice."

Dan's eyes bugged out, and he choked. "You can't go. That whole scene is going to be a den of snakes."

"My mother said something similar. She doesn't want me to go, but Clayr has no choice but to bring me. I work for the Library, and the Board has assigned me to go."

The shopkeeper returned from the back with a black box wrapped in a gold ribbon. He handed it to Dan, who turned and presented it to Ryn.

"A shiny new pen for a beautiful lady. Take it with you and write me letters with it." He grinned.

Ryn was taken aback. Her mother had pens, but none this nice.

"That's an awfully expensive gift for someone you just barely met," she said.

"Maybe, but I really do want you to write me while you're gone. Please?"

Ryn lifted the box from his hands. It was heavier than she expected.

She nodded, but she had no idea what this trip would be like, nor was she sure she would have time. It was going to be the furthest she'd ever traveled from home, and she hadn't even pondered what that would be like.

"Thank you," she said, holding the box close.

It all felt awkward. She'd never had a gift from anyone outside her family besides Yll.

"Let's go for a walk," Dan said.

Ryn thanked the shopkeeper, then let Dan hold the door open for her. They strolled the street for a while in an awkward kind of silence. Ryn realized the Library was across the street, and that Dan had a wary eye on the Library walls. She took his arm and changed course, dragging him down a narrow alley between shops.

The alley itself was lined with cute shop windows filled with goods that would appeal to those who did research for a living. Book shops, candle shops, paper shops—a shop that specialized in fancy bookmarks. They came across a tea shop, and Ryn immediately lifted the latch and went inside. The smells of dried mint, lavender, chamomile, and roses all mixed together washing over the senses, relaxing her. This was home and peace.

Dan chuckled. "You're a tea girl, huh."

Ryn nodded as she opened a test jar and inhaled. This one was made of dried berries, and maybe some ginger? The combination was intriguing.

Dan picked up a jar that looked more medicinal than for pleasure drinking. His nose wrinkled.

Ryn put a jar that smelled of apples and spices under his nose.

"I like it!" He grinned. "Makes me think of the Winter Solstice feast."

Ryn nodded, put the jar to her nose, and inhaled deep. In her mind she could see her parents by the fire. The smell of her mother's apple tart baking in the oven. She and Jett playing a pebbled stone game.

Ryn asked for a small pouch's worth of the tea from the teamaker, who scooped some into a small bag and handed it to her. Ryn fished around in her pocket for her coins.

"I got that," Dan said, handing the woman a coin.

Ryn thought to protest, but decided against it. In her experience it was embarrassing for the person offering to pay if she objected. She and the teamaker happily exchanged ideas about the best ingredients for tea, and then Dan was pulling her away, back out into the alley.

"Are you hungry?" he asked.

Her stomach growled.

Dan chuckled. "I guess that's a yes."

He took her into a bakery, and they discovered they both enjoyed sliced chicken, bacon, and cheese, so Dan got one large sandwich and they split it. Their conversation turned to all their likes and dislikes. They had many things in common. After lunch, they came out of the alley onto a street that was one ring circle out from the Library. They walked it, Ryn on his arm. Dan walked tall and straight, occasionally bending to hear Ryn better.

"What made you want to work in the Library?" he asked.

"Hmmm—I love books, I love the hunt for a particularly difficult book or document."

"Books are nice," he agreed.

He didn't ask any more questions, but she could tell he wanted to know more.

She thought about what she really wanted to share with him. She really didn't know him at all, and Jak seemed to know more about her than she did, so what did he really want to know?

She shrugged. "I guess the biggest reason is because I'm hoping I'll find evidence of my birth family. I want to know who I am. I want to know if I have magic before I'm too old to inherit it."

"You don't need magic. I don't have any. I'm still wonderful, and so are you." He grinned at her.

"I suppose."

They crossed the street. Into the north neighborhood. Tall bushes grew in front of the wall around a brick house. Dan pulled her behind the bushes.

Ryn looked up at him in surprise. Dan took advantage of her slightly slack jaw and leaned down to kiss her. His lips and mouth warm against her slightly cold lips and chin. It was a weird sensation. He tasted of...something, she couldn't quite place. His nose blew air into hers. She was having a hard time breathing. He took his tongue and licked her lips, running it along her teeth, like he was looking for something. She realized he wanted her to open her mouth, like she'd seen Jak and Brynd do. Tentatively she parted her teeth. His tongue darted in and slid along her tongue. His breath was blowing out harder into her nose. She pulled away gasping for breath.

He didn't say anything but pulled her in and held her close.

"I don't want you to go," he moaned.

"It won't be for long," she patted him on the back.

"I should go with you."

"I'll be fine." She wasn't sure she would be, but she was annoyed at everyone's overprotectiveness. "Besides, you need to take advantage of the leadership of the Library being gone so you can do your research."

He pressed his cheek to the top of her head. "I know."

Ryn let go of him. She hadn't enjoyed that kiss at all. Maybe it was just because it was her first time that it felt so awkward. Maybe she needed to give it another try. She reached her hand out, running it along his chest. Then she tilted her head up, looking into his warm brown eyes. He took her back into his arms and kissed her again.

Chapter Eighteen

After the horrible encounter with his mother, Zo decided he'd had enough of the Healing House for the day and left without doing the lesson he was supposed to take. He was already finished with his shift at the Library, so he crossed the street to Wilmar's and entered the work room letting the bells at the top of the door announce his presence. Wilmar came shuffling in from the garden, wet with his nose all red. He must have been out there for a while.

"Young Zo, what are you doing here? I thought you were at the Healing House today."

Zo fought to get his emotions under control. "I decided to skip it."

He took down an apron from a hook and cut down a bundle of herbs hanging from the ceiling.

"It must have been particularly bad if you're willing to grind milkweed. Better put on some gloves." Wilmar eyed Zo with that furrowed brow that told Zo he was worried about him.

Zo set the bundle on the table, inwardly cringing he hadn't noticed what herb he had cut down. He washed his hands in the basin, hoping the short exposure he had wouldn't affect him. Once his hands were dry, he dug around in the drawer to find a pair of gloves that fit him. Wilmar's fingers were shorter and stubbier than Zo's.

Wilmar worked at patting dry and bundling the herbs he had brought in from the garden. Once Zo was seated at the table, and attacking the milkweed with his pestle, Wilmar attempted conversation.

"You want to talk about it?" he asked.

Zo, as always happened when he worked with a highly toxic herb and couldn't touch his face, had to keep his fingers from rubbing his suddenly itchy nose and eyes.

"Something happen with the Healers?" Wilmar tried again.

"Someone told my mother I'm studying Healing, and now she's here."

Wilmar pulled a length of twine from the spool, then cut it.

"What is it you fear?" he asked.

Zo's hand moved to the beads around his neck, stopping when he realized what was on his gloved hands. "Nothing."

Wilmar raised an eyebrow at him.

They both worked in silence for a while. Wilmar shook the bundle he was working on one more time, then began hanging it from the rafters.

The silence grated on Zo's nerves. He glared at Wilmar.

"When I was ten, she tried to take my fire bead from me."

Wilmar, who was as Ordinary as anyone could get, gasped.

"That's abuse," he said.

Zo nodded and resumed his attack on the herbs. "I haven't really seen her since."

"And now she's here."

"And now she's here, come to ruin my life," Zo said.

Wilmar didn't respond to that. It was one of the things Zo loved about him, his ability to know when to push, and when to let things go.

The bells rang to announce a patient. Zo took that as an excuse to clean up the milkweed and be done with it. It was a relief when the powder was safely in a jar and everything had been cleaned up.

The patient had a severe headache that had lasted several days. Zo mixed up the appropriate powders while Wilmar watched. Once the patient was on their way, another came. This became a steady stream until the windows began to darken. Zo was lighting the lanterns after the last patient left, while Wilmar was cleaning up bloody bandages, when the doorbells chimed.

Zo looked up to find the huge bulk of Nix standing in the doorway grinning.

Wilmar let out a squeak, running over to pull Nix into a tight hug. The door shut and Nix shifted Wilmar to the side to reveal Iden standing there with a huge basket on his arm.

"Where's my squeaky hug?" Iden demanded, throwing his arms wide.

Zo grinned. In two steps he was across the floor, grabbing Iden behind his neck, and went in for a full-on kiss.

"Now look what you've done to the children," Nix said.

Wilmar wasn't even watching. He was still clinging to Nix, his head on his shoulder, with a contented grin on his face.

Zo reached behind Iden, turned around the closed sign, and pulled the blinds shut.

"We brought you two dinner." Iden held up the basket.

"How did you know I was here?" Zo asked.

"A little birdy told us," Iden said.

Nix grunted. "Your mother has House Sano guards scouring the Library grounds in search of you."

Zo groaned.

"She told me we would have lunch tomorrow," he said.

"Apparently she can't wait," Iden said.

Wilmar took the basket of food from Iden.

There was a knock at the door. Zo opened it to Keir standing there in his usual formal black coat, accented by all his silver rings. Zo's pulse jumped up.

Keir glanced past Zo's shoulder to where Nix and Iden were standing. "I'm here, as planned." He held up his basket of food.

Zo groaned inwardly. He had completely forgotten Keir was going to bring him dinner.

"I'm sorry Keir, but Nix just brought us dinner. Some other time?" Zo hoped Keir would agree and not make it anymore awkward than it already was.

Keir's face darkened into a frown. His eyes dropping to the basket he carried. Then he looked up with a smile. "Sure, but you must promise to join me. Some friends and I are getting together soon."

Zo resisted the urge to glance over his shoulder at Iden, but he could hear his voice: *Play around, but make sure you choose me.*

"Sure. Next time," Zo said.

Keir straightened his stance, then nodded and drifted back into the night.

Zo slowly closed the door, his pulse still racing. He was embarrassed Iden knew he'd told Keir he'd have dinner with him. He'd have to explain to Iden later that it was just to get Keir to move out of his way this morning. Compared to Iden, Keir seemed like an immature guilty pleasure. Tonight Zo needed Iden, not edgy, dark, and mysterious.

Zo turned and followed Wilmar through the curtain that separated his workspace from his living space. Zo had never eaten in Wilmar's living space before. There was a small table there with four chairs, as if Wilmar hoped for guests. He set the basket on the table, and went to his cupboard for dishes.

"Are sure you don't want to go with dark and mysterious?" Iden said, opening the basket and extracting fried fish, and a really yummy potato dish Iden's mom made, along with some winter kale with pine nuts, something Zo had seen Nix eating before.

Once everyone was seated Nix said, "We should give thanks to the Ancestors?"

Zo rolled his eyes.

"For what?" Wilmar asked.

"For bringing me to Waatch so that I could find you." Nix took Wilmar's hand and kissed his knuckles.

Wilmar blushed.

Iden shook his head. "Cheesy, but I love it."

They passed around the plates of food and listened to Nix tell Boiler Room horror stories, while Wilmar told physician horror stories. Iden and Zo were in stitches holding their sides because they hurt from laughing. Zo was sure those events weren't funny at the time, but the way they both spun their tales now was hilarious. It felt good. The tension left Zo's body and a deep sense of contentment washed over him.

"Tell me how you two met," Zo said.

Nix's eyes were on Wilmar, who fidgeted with his napkin. "It was a fine night under the harvest moon..."

Wilmar blushed. "Don't be dramatic, it was wet and muddy."

Nix growled, "Let me tell the story..."

Pounding sounded on the front door, with a faint yell of help.

Wilmar and Zo jumped up. Wilmar made it to the door first. A woman clutching her stomach fell through the door.

She managed one more weak "help" then she passed out in Wilmar's arms.

"Clear the exam table," Wilmar said.

Zo and Iden scrambled to remove bottles and towels that had been left out. Nix scooped the woman up from Wilmar's arms and gently placed her on the exam table.

"Let's see what we've got," Wilmar said, as Zo handed him a pair of scissors to cut away the clothing soaked in blood.

Zo hissed through his teeth when he recognized the wound. "Another one? What is with these people?"

Nix frowned. "Have you informed the city guard about this?"

Wilmar shook his head. "The first one could easily have been a random stabbing. The second—I promised Jak not to say anything."

"I think it's time," Nix said.

Wilmar nodded. "I'm planning to save this one. Let's get to work."

* * *

The four of them worked through the night. There were a few moments Zo thought for sure they were going to lose her, but they managed to repair the damage, and get her all stitched up. While Wilmar was stitching, Zo used a small amount of his Healing to help out. For the first time ever, a small sigh of relief bubbled up inside at the use of his Healing. He knew the Healing House would drive Wilmar out of Waatch if they found Healing magic being done in the physician's office for free, so Zo was very subtle about it. He didn't heal her completely, but he did bring her back from the brink.

In the wee hours of the morning, with the patient bundled up and resting, Zo and Iden collapsed onto the patient bed Zo had slept in when healing from his shoulder injury a few moons back.

"You're going to turn me into a healer," Iden murmured as he pulled Zo close to him so they both fit on the bed.

Tired, exhausted, and emotional from the day, Zo snuggled up against Iden's warmth and began to drift off, but not before he smiled at how good healing and Iden felt.

* * *

As sun beams slanted through the crack in the curtains, the woman on the table began moaning. Zo reluctantly lifted Iden's arm and slipped out of bed. The woman squirmed as if in pain.

"Wilmar," Zo called.

The woman's eyes opened and she grabbed Zo's shirt. "They're going. They're going to the Island." Her voice was raspy and in need of water.

"Shhhhh," Zo tried to quiet her while extracting her hand to pour her some water.

She grabbed his arm. "They're in danger. The Library delegation. More death."

"Who are you?" Zo asked.

"Work...for the Library..." she gasped.

"Who did this to you?"

She shook her head. "Dark...black...like a researcher..."

Her gasping became shaking.

Wilmar entered, and with his usual soothing manner managed to calm her. Zo mixed some powders into her drink and held her up so she could swallow. After a few minutes her breathing smoothed out into the soft rhythm of sleep.

"Did you hear what she said?" Zo asked.

Wilmar and Nix were exchanging looks Zo guessed only the two of them could interpret.

Iden stirred and sat up. "What's going on?"

"I have to go. I need to warn them. Someone in black. That could be a few people. I have to pull my sister off that ship!"

Zo took his jacket from the coat rack. Pulling it on, he opened the door—to see a couple House Sano Guards standing watch on the porch of the Healing House. Zo quickly shut the door.

"Can't go that way," he said.

Wilmar lifted the curtain to look out. He frowned.

"Out the back. Use the garden gate into the neighbor's. You can slip out through their garden," Wilmar said, pointing to the back door.

Zo nodded. Iden slipped on his coat and followed Zo into the garden. They passed through the gate and into the neighbor's yard, then hopped their fence onto the street. Zo broke into a run. He didn't know exactly when the ship was sailing, but he had to make it there before Ryn got on the boat.

"When does the tide shift?" Zo asked Iden.

"Do I look like I know the tide schedule?"

Zo kept his eyes out for a carriage to hire, but this time of the morning they were all carrying Library researchers and managers to the Library. Zo pushed harder, ignoring the stitch beginning in his side. They were about to skirt the Library grounds on their way to the North gate of Waatch, when two guards in House Sano colors turned the corner. Iden pulled Zo back and they sped down a side street. They were almost to the next cross street when House Sano guards appeared at the end of the street. Zo spun around to find more guards behind them.

Zo snapped his fingers and flames leapt into his hand. One of the guards lifted his hands and a rush of wind assailed them, fanning Zo's flames so they threatened to catch Iden on fire. Zo extinguished his hands.

"Zo, look out," Iden yelled as he lifted his hands to blow his own magic wind down the other direction.

It was too late, the guards from behind rushed them, and pinned Iden and Zo against the wall of a building. They yanked Zo's hands behind his back and tied them.

"You can tell my mother this isn't helping my opinion of her," Zo said with the side of his face smashed against the wall.

"Orders are orders. She didn't say how to bring you, just to bring you. If you hadn't tried to fight, we wouldn't have to be rough," the guard said in Zo's ear.

"Bring them," another guard said.

They pulled him away from the wall and to Zo's distress he found they had treated Iden the same. Zo had hoped they would let Iden go so he could warn Ryn.

"We have important information for Madame Curator," Zo said.

The guard holding him shrugged. "Not our problem."

"Hey, I'm not even House Sano," Iden protested, struggling against his bonds.

"We were told to bring the son of Fyri and anyone with him to Madame Councilor. Let's go."

Kicking and protesting all the way, Zo and Iden were bundled into a wagon. Zo's heart burned with anger and panic for Ryn. He'd told his mother he'd meet her for lunch. If anything happened to Ryn, he was going to burn the Healing House to the ground for this.

Chapter Nineteen

Fyri,

What in the name of the Ancestors are you doing seeing Zo in Waatch? Are you forgetting the Waatch court documents I have which state that you are not to see him without my presence? I am not presently in town, therefore you need to stay away from our son. Do you hear me? He's not yet eighteen. When he turns eighteen, he can choose to see you if he wants, but until then, stay away!

Lar

The morning was chill and damp from the rain overnight, but the sun was rising, shining in that sliver of clarity between the mountains and a layer of clouds. Ryn shivered beneath her heavy cloak. It wasn't just the cold, but nerves. She'd never been on a ship before. Her dad had taken her out in small row boats to fish, but the ship tied to the dock was massive compared to what she'd been on before. There was furious activity on the docks; people loading crates and trunks, men shouting. There was a constant stream of people back and forth in front of Ryn. She felt small and in the way. She inhaled deeply the smell of the ocean, with the undertone of cedar trees from the forest nearby. It was a smell she loved and never wished to be parted from. A gull flew by, yelling at her for something to eat. She closed her eyes and tried to imagine making this kind of trip in calmer times, with less at stake.

"Mother and Lar still aren't here," Yll said, interrupting Ryn's thoughts.

Ryn's anxiety spiked. "We need to get on the boat soon, but we can't go without them."

Her eye was caught on someone running down the docks toward them, but it wasn't someone Ryn expected to see.

"Ryn!" Tory waved at them. She was carrying a large, flat box.

"Tory, what are you doing here?" Ryn asked.

Tory slid to a halt in front of them, slipping on the wet dock. She caught herself, scrambling to keep from dropping the box while she cursed Thax for his last-minute errand.

"I'm so glad I caught you before you left," Tory said, presenting Ryn with the box.

"Thax sent this to you with his compliments."

Ryn's eyes got wide.

"Oh, don't be so shocked. There will likely be a formal dinner and Thax is sure you don't have something appropriate to wear." Tory emphasized the last with a roll of her eyes.

Ryn lifted the lid and peeked inside the box. Inside was a deep maroon dress with gold embroidery stitching. It was House Viator's color. Tears pricked Ryn's eyes. She took a deep breath to keep from crying. A dress for her to wear in House Viator in their colors, which declared her to belong to that house.

"I don't know what to say," her voice trembled. She wasn't sure she fit in with House Viator, but somehow seeing that dress eased a knot in her chest. At least she would blend in, and maybe, just maybe, she wouldn't feel like such an outsider.

Tory put an arm around her shoulders.

"Tell Thax thank you."

Tory pulled away, giving Ryn a sly grin, and a twinkle in her eye. "Thax always has multiple things up his sleeve. There's a catch. The dress is not hemmed, you'll need to take it to the tailor there on Viatoro."

Ryn wasn't sure what that meant, but she was still grateful. She nodded, then reached out and gave Tory a hug, fighting to hold back the tears that were threatening to spill out.

"I'll see you when you get back," Tory said.

"Keep the boys out of trouble for me, will you?" Ryn asked.

"Oh honey, nobody's able to do that!" Tory laughed, then bid them farewell as she sauntered back down the docks, catching the attention of every young man she passed.

Regg passed Tory without even a glance at her, coming straight up to Yll with a pack slung over his shoulder.

Yll threw her arms around him. "What are you doing here? I thought we said goodbye last night."

Regg grinned. "Dad got leave from the Healing House for me to go with you. He seems to feel he needs me to help out."

"Why not Zo?" Ryn asked. She would really feel much better if Zo was with her.

Regg pressed his hand to his chest. "I'm hurt you think my brother is better than me," he said.

Ryn stammered, "No, no, not what I meant. Of course it'll be great to have you along, and of course Zo can't get out of his Library duties."

It had been a dumb thing to say. Hopefully Regg would forgive her.

His focus seemed to be all on Yll at the moment as he pulled her into a tight hug and kissed the top of her head.

"I'm so glad I'm coming on this trip. I was so worried about what trouble you two might get into without me. Where's the fun in that?" he said.

His tone was light, but the look on his face was relief, with maybe tension, as his eyes followed one of the Regents walking past on the way to the ship.

One of the dock hands approached Ryn and Yll.

"We're almost ready to go. We need to load your trunks," he said.

Ryn and Yll glanced at each other, then down the docks, but to Ryn's relief she spotted a large group headed their way. Clayr and Lar were among them.

"Yes, please, and can you take this as well?" Ryn offered him the box with the dress.

"Sure." He took the dress box and her trunk and headed for the ship.

Included in the group of people surrounding Clayr was Regent Jeris, the Collections Manager...and Prym, notebook still in hand.

"How is she going?" Ryn asked. "I thought she was supposed to be writing the inspector's report."

As if Prym heard them, she walked straight up to them and said, "The Inspector sent me to keep an eye on you all and report back any suspicious activity."

With a sniff and a tilt of her nose upward, she continued down the dock trailing in the wake of her father.

"Oh boy," Yll said.

"You've got that right," Regg agreed.

"This trip is going to be like walking through a maze of traps," Ryn said.

Clayr put her arm around Yll and guided her toward the ship.

"Let's just get it over with," was all she said.

* * *

Halfway to the ship, with a puff of air Uncle Mik appeared at Ryn's side. She jumped back and let out a squeak. It was too close of a Travel magic landing for her.

"Oh sorry!" Uncle Mik reached out a hand to steady her. "Didn't mean to come in so close."

"That's alright." Ryn was attempting to calm her racing heart, and act natural, like this sort of thing happened to her all the time, when it didn't.

"I don't know why Madame Curator is insisting on this antiquated form of transportation for the Library Delegation, when we have plenty of Travlers from Viatoro who can take you all there, quickly and safely." Uncle Mik fluttered his hand toward the boat.

Ryn took in the huge craft. It didn't look antiquated at all. In fact it looked quite sturdy and majestic. Uncle Mik did have a point—Travel magic would be faster, but Ryn wasn't sure she trusted some stranger from Viatoro to Travel her to the island. She had trusted that Thalya girl Jett had been dating, and it had almost got her kidnapped.

Ryn forced a smile. "I'm sure she has her reasons."

"Annoying, but it does give us an opportunity to get to know each other." Uncle Mik flashed a huge smile. "Not much to do on a boat for a few days but chat."

Ryn swallowed hard. *Oh boy.*

"That sounds wonderful," she managed to say, but her stomach fluttered in nervousness. She was certain the Patriarch in Waiting was not going to find her, or her story, entertaining at all.

* * *

The salt sea spray and crisp breeze at the bow of the ship was cold, but invigorating. Ryn never felt so alive as the ship cut its way through the water. Wind in her hair at the front of the ship felt like she was flying. A thought floated through her mind that she should ask Yll what flying is like. She was only slightly queasy. They had warned her she could be sick, but the fresh air helped. Her nose and cheeks were numb from cold, but she was reluctant to move to someplace warmer.

"It's so beautiful, even in winter," Yll's voice came from beside her.

Ryn startled, turning a half smile to her.

"That's right, you took a boat out to Saarimuto last summer."

Yll nodded, eyes fixed on the waterline horizon.

"The islands are so beautiful," Yll said.

"I wouldn't know." Ryn didn't even try to keep the bitterness from her voice.

Yll picked up on it. "I'm sorry, Ryn. I remember when we were small and we'd pretend your log fort was a ship and we'd sail to the islands to get our magics."

Ryn felt a little guilty for taking out her frustrations on Yll. Ryn had embraced the fact that her talents were in the Library and in research, but she still hadn't found the origins of the orphanage record. She had to find the orphanage where her father adopted her. She was certain they would have information about her birth parents. There was still a remote chance she had some magical heritage, though time for finding it was slipping away from her quickly. While she'd been embroiled in this whole Library mess, she was neglecting her own search, and possibly her only chance at finding and learning a magic.

She thought about the orphanage book tucked safely into her trunk. If the book binder in Waatch was correct, the answer to the mystery of the origins of her orphanage book may be on Viatoro-along with so many other mysteries swirling around her.

Ryn looked up and down the side of the boat, but no one was near to them.

"Have you started writing Luc's journals yet?" Ryn asked in a hushed tone.

Yll pursed her lips as a sailor passed them. Once he moved away she bent closer to Ryn.

"No. Mother thinks I should wait till we get back from Viatoro. She's afraid someone will see it, and possibly steal it."

Ryn nodded. "It's too bad. This would be the perfect time for us to puzzle out if there's any useful information in those journals."

"Hmmm. Usually, I don't really remember it until I write it down, but I'll try to see if I can remember any of it in my head. Maybe I can find something useful."

"Perfect."

Ryn spied Uncle Mik moving toward her. She waved at Yll to cut the conversation.

"Hello ladies." Uncle Mik offered his arm to Ryn. "Shall we promenade around the deck?"

Ryn raised an eyebrow at him.

Uncle Mik laughed. "A fancy term for taking a stroll."

"Oh, sure." Ryn took his arm.

"If you'll excuse us," Uncle Mik said to Yll.

"Sure." She turned back to watching the ship cut through the ocean waves.

Ryn's hands were cold and her hand in the elbow crease of Uncle Mik's wool jacket was warm.

"So tell me about yourself. How old are you? When's your birthday? Where did you grow up? Do you have any other siblings? What did you like most growing up? What's your heart's desire?"

"Uhhh," Ryn started. That was an awfully long list that made her head spin.

Uncle Mik chuckled. "Just tell me what you can."

Ryn hesitated. What could she really share with him? She supposed House Viator already knew where the cabin was in Sooke, but did she want to share her heart's desire with a stranger?

"If it helps, I'll tell you about myself. It'll be an exchange."

"Sure. Ummm—I just turned sixteen. My birthday is at the end of the Ghost Moon. I grew up in the village of Sooke, not too far from Waatch. Mostly members of the Board of Regents live there, and Madame Curator."

"We visited there. Lovely place. Has a great view of the Dragon Mountain."

Uncle Mik stopped them as a sailor passed in front of them to climb into the rigging.

Uncle Mik pointed to his chest. "I am two years younger than your mother. The baby of the family." He chuckled again. "I have lived on Viatoro my whole life, but have had the opportunity to travel about. I've been to every island and several places on the Mainland. We do live in a wondrous part of the world."

Uncle Mik moved them forward. "What else?"

Ryn had to think back to what else Uncle Mik had asked. She wasn't sure what Uncle Mik was fishing for with the "siblings" question, and she knew it would be hard to explain Zo and Regg, so she skipped that question. "When I was young, I liked to skip stones across the river and play in my log fort." To be honest, she still enjoyed those things. She hadn't seen her log fort in a while. She needed to spend some time at home soon.

"As a boy I too enjoyed skipping stones across Viator Bay. Your mother and I would also play hide and seek—which becomes interesting when you add travel magic to the game. Your mother was particularly good at hiding." Uncle Mik's laugh sounded bitter.

Ryn hadn't thought about that before. Did kids with magic play with it? That must be a great way to practice.

Uncle Mik nudged her shoulder. "Heart's desire?"

Ryn flushed. How did she tell someone who probably thought she was a secret descendant of House Viator, that she'd dreamed her whole life of having magic. She knew he was going to use it to entice her to Viator's side of things. She settled on something a bit more generic:

"To fit in. Wherever I go, I don't seem to fit in." To Ryn's dismay her voice cracked on that.

Uncle Mik bit his lip, like he was keeping himself from saying the exact things Ryn had been thinking he would say.

Uncle Mik stopped, and turned to face her. "Ryn, I promise you will fit in House Viator. You are our family. We are so happy to have you."

Ryn looked up into his green eyes. They sparkled with happiness. She discovered, unexpectedly, that she wanted to be a part of House Viator. Her eyes filled with tears.

"Thank you," she managed to say.

Uncle Mik enfolded her in a tight hug.

* * *

That night was a formal dinner with the captain. The table was small for the number of people dining at it, so they were squished in together. Fortunately, Ryn was squeezed in next to Yll. Unfortunately, she was also pressed up against Prym. She hadn't really seen much of her since the incident with Master Wes. They had managed to avoid each other in the Library. The only times she'd seen her lately was in the company of Master Ubert. As if growing up being bullied by Prym wasn't enough, the whole debacle of Prym sabotaging Ryn's chances at getting a Library job through Master Wes just made matters worse. At the time Ryn had almost started to have sympathy for Prym with the way Jeris treated her, but stealing all of Ryn's hard work and claiming it as her own had been too much for Ryn. She didn't know what Jeris' game was with making Prym Master Ubert's scribe, but she was pretty sure there was some sort of ambition for power behind it.

Ryn nervously fingered the lip around the table, which stopped dishes from sliding off.

The captain stood and raised his glass to his guests. "Welcome aboard the *Wolf's Bane*. She's a fine ship constructed in the year..."

The captain went on to give a long history of the ship and the battle of Sand Point in which the ship sailed under House Viator's flag. Ryn was only partially listening, because her mind had caught on how the ship was named for a mythical land creature—the wolf, and now the symbol of the wolf seemed to be a clue to who was behind the sabotage of the Library. Her eyes narrowed at the captain. Could he have something to do with what was happening? The captain had a wide, open face, and a friendly smile. Perhaps not, but the idea put her on edge. Wolves seemed to be surrounding her. She had heard campfire stories told to scare children while out in the woods late at night, but everyone knew wolves didn't exist. Maybe it was common to name ships after children's tales? Ryn had no idea. She hoped it was just a coincidence.

The captain finished his history with a tale of how the ship had narrowly escaped raiders who had tried to take the ship and its cargo. The tale should have captured Ryn's attention, but instead she was focused on how the bowls and cups were heavily weighted at the bottom. She stifled a yawn. It had been an early morning and a long day.

"A moment of silence to give thanks," the captain said, then bowed his head.

Ryn scanned the table, watching heads bow. Some lips moved, but others did not.

"I don't understand," she whispered to Yll.

Yll leaned closer to her. "Sailors don't worship the Ancestors, even if they are of Ancestor descent."

"Why not?" Ryn asked, but she had drew several warning looks from around the table so she dropped it.

The captain engaged Clayr in a discussion about moving the Library and its contents, and about what the logistics that would involve.

Clayr reached for her glass. "Captain, wouldn't you agree that shipping the Library's contents across the water to Viatoro is dangerous? How much of the Library's content would you expect to lose in such an endeavor?"

The captain sat back. "I mean, I suppose it would depend upon the time of year. The summer time would be the least likely to have storms, but unless I had use of some help from House Venti and Air magic the shipments might be slow at that time or year. Of course, any other time of year would run the risk of storms. There's always a possibility of losing a ship to a storm, though that hasn't happened in a while. Most ships these days are built sturdy like the *Wolf's Bane*."

Ryn perked up. "What about raiders? You just told a story about raiders and fighting them off. Would the Library's contents be in danger from being stolen by such people?"

The side table conversations got quiet.

The captain shifted.

Jeris came partway out of his seat. "No one would dare challenge the Library in that way."

Clayr's eyes narrowed at Jeris and Mik. "You don't think any of the other Ancestral Houses might be interested in possessing the Library's contents? Even if it was just one shipment, imagine the disruption if I have to go to Ingisapan to research property records because the records were taken to that island."

"I doubt the firestarters would steal Library records," Jeris sputtered.

The point was taken though. Ryn stared down the table where Clayr sat at one end. Ryn was sure she understood why Clayr had insisted the delegation come via boat—so they could see firsthand the dangers of shipping the Library across the water.

"What about shipping the Library via Travel magic?" Prym piped up. "Isn't House Viator renowned for their Travel shipments?" She stared at Uncle Mik.

Uncle Mik's lip twitched up in a partial smile over his clasped hands. "It's complicated."

The table got very quiet. All that could be heard was the occasional creak of wood.

"This has been a lovely meal, but we've had a long day, the girls look like they're about to drop." Clayr glared at them to back her up. Ryn and Yll obediently yawned. "We should like to retire. When do you think we will make landfall on Viatoro?"

The Captain appeared disappointed. "Of course. We should arrive day after tomorrow."

He stood, and all the rest of the company stood with him. Ryn was relieved as they made their way out of the cabin. As they shuffled off to their various sleeping arrangements, the girls headed for the one cabin which had been given to the women of the delegation.

Regg and Lar were waiting outside the captain's cabin for them. Regg put his arm around Yll.

Uncle Mik pulled Jeris aside, whispering something to him. Jeris and he walked off across the deck of the ship.

Lar watched them go, then herded the girls and Regg toward their cabins.

Ryn lay next to Yll in the too-small bed, with an even larger lip to hold them in than the table. She tried to ignore the rocking of the ship and imagine it as some large swing. It didn't really help, but sleep eventually came. She dreamt of ships full of books sinking into the sea. When she woke in sweat, she hoped it was just a regular dream, and not one of the seemingly real dreams she'd been having.

Chapter Twenty

Holly,

My dear, we are living in Waatch. Nobody's going to Exile. And please don't lie to me. I know you're aware Iden is dating Fyri's son. I thought we could be frank about it since you seem to be embracing the idea. My son has far greater potential than Fyri's boy, trying to deny his Healing magic. He's a disgrace to House Sano, but Keir-Keir had more Healing power in his baby toe than everyone on the Healing Council. You should still consider my offer.

Myrta de Sano of the Healing Council

To Zo's surprise when the wagon door opened, they weren't in front of the Healing House, but the Dining Room. The restaurant where Zo had promised to meet his mother.

"What the..."

Iden grinned. "Your mother has style, I'll give her that."

Squinting as the clouds parted for a ray of sunshine, Zo tripped and would have landed on his face if the House Sano guard hadn't had such a tight grip on his arm. Zo bit his tongue on the suggestive comment that came to his mind, then immediately wondered why he still cared.

The guards dragged Zo and Iden up the grand entrance stairs to the front doors. The Dining Room Host looked startled at the sight of them, but must have known they were coming, because he just nodded, then led them into the restaurant like they were normal diners. He didn't seem concerned about discretion, because he took them winding in between tables of diners. Fortunately for the potential embarrassment of it all, it was late for breakfast and the place wasn't packed.

At the back of the Dining Room, the Host stopped at Fyri's table. She was gently tapping with her spoon on a soft boiled egg held on a filigree silver egg pedestal. The House Sano guards pulled out the chairs opposite her and shoved Zo and Iden into them, then stepped back a pace.

Zo's mother looked up as if she was surprised to find them there.

"Oh Zo, there you are! I was worried sick about you. Imagine my horror when I found out the nasty rumors of Library troubles were true, and that you have been involved. I couldn't wait one hour more, I needed to see you and make sure you're alright. It was so wonderful of my guards to find you and bring you." At that Zo's mother put down her spoon, spreading her arms as if to embrace Zo from across the table.

"And who is this?" She asked with a flick of her spoon toward Iden.

Zo opened his mouth. He so much wanted to spit out that Iden was his boyfriend right in her face, but the words wouldn't come out. That barrier of protection wouldn't lower itself. Even with Iden's eyes twinkling at him, daring him to throw it out into the world, Zo couldn't do it. Although living in Waatch was making him more comfortable with his relationship, he knew the fact that his mother represented the leadership council of House Sano made his stomach twist. He really wasn't sure how much power his mother had to ruin his life.

"My...friend." Zo felt instant shame he couldn't say it out loud.

"Does your friend have a name?" His mother moved onto a plate of cured meats and cheeses.

"Iden de Dico. I'd offer you my hand, but I'm kind of tied up." Iden showed his tied hands as best he could from behind his back.

"Untie us, mother," Zo demanded.

Fyri gave him a grim half smile. "I just need to make sure you're safe."

Zo glanced around at some of the other diners who were covertly watching the scene while they ate.

"At least let Iden go. He's not a part of this." Zo let loose a growl in his voice.

Iden shot Zo a hurt look. Clearly he wanted to be a part of it, but Zo wanted him safe and away from Fyri.

"Very well." She flicked her fingers. The guard behind Iden stepped forward with a long knife and cut the cords binding Iden's hands.

Iden rubbed his wrists, but didn't leave the table.

Zo's mother set down her knife and fork and a waiter took away her plate. She folded her hands in front of her and fixed Zo with her penetrating stare. The one he remembered so well from his childhood. The one that said she'd thought long and hard, and had come up with the best punishment for his misbehavior.

"Zo darling, I have much regret about the past. Your father overreacted to a small moment, but I am thrilled that you have finally changed your mind about your Healing. It does my heart proud to hear from the Headmaster that you are his top student."

Really? Zo hadn't heard that from anyone. He was pretty sure the Headmaster hadn't seen Zo. Mostly because Zo hardly had a chance to study anything yet.

"Top student in Waatch is quaint, but you are almost eighteen, and ready to finish your lessons. You need to be studying at the Healing House on Sano."

"We've already discussed this mother. The answer is no."

"It's not open for debate. I am your mother, and I have indulged your father for far too long. Look at you in such a state; you barely know how to Heal and are almost aged out of your lessons. It's a travesty. I am invoking my parental rights. According to the law you must obey me until you are eighteen."

Zo's jaw dropped. That can't possibly be true. He'd never heard that before.

Elbows on the table, Iden's eyes narrowed at Fyri. "That's quite an antiquated Ancestor law to evoke here in Waatch."

Fyri shrugged. "I already have research lawyers in the Hall of Regents drawing up the paperwork. I'm also in the process of getting your contract with the Library struck down given your father arranged it and you made it without my consent."

"What?" Zo started to rise out of his seat, but the guard behind him shoved him back down.

Fyri's eyes went distant, and a slow smile crept across her face. "I can't wait to get you home. It's been so long since I've heard the pattering of feet on the stairs. That burn spot is still on the wall, by the way."

Her eyes snapped back from whatever fantastical place her mind had gone. "I've entered into contract negotiations with a fine family. You are to be betrothed to the loveliest girl from House Illusio as soon as we get home."

Zo stood so fast his chair toppled behind him.

"No," he said in a voice so low and deadly, he scared himself.

For the first time Fyri looked shocked.

"Believe me, she's the loveliest of creatures, and from a fine family. Exactly what you need to advance in power in House Sano."

"*No.*"

And with that he straightened his back as best he could with his hands tied behind them, turned, kicked his chair into the guard standing behind him, and strode for the exit. Iden joined him, helping push past the guards. Zo's face dared them to stop him.

This time, they backed down.

"You can't deny me. I'm your mother and I own you till you're eighteen."

Zo did his best to make a rude gesture with his tied hands, but feared it lost its impact.

"You go and settle all your affairs. We leave in two days," Zo's mother called after them.

Iden grabbed a steak knife off a table and cut the cords binding Zo's wrists.

Zo turned to face Fyri. "Goodbye, Mother."

"I will have your custody paperwork tonight. You will be on that boat!" His mother screamed.

Zo and Iden hit the front doors, and were gone.

* * *

Zo's feet took him out of Waatch toward the docks. He knew he was too late, but his feet still took him there. Iden walked beside him in silence. It wasn't till they were on the beach staring at an empty dock that Zo let loose. He screamed, then started throwing rocks, sticks, branches, anything not buried in the sand. Iden stood quietly by, arms folded, looking thoughtful.

After chucking a particularly heavy branch into the water, Zo examined his now cut and bleeding palm. Iden finally stepped forward and grabbed his hand. He wrapped it in a handkerchief he pulled from his pocket and squeezed it tight.

"How can she think she could do this to me? She can't do this to me, she has no right or power over me, I am of age already and living on my own. You would think that seven years would have changed things, but nothing has changed. She's still conniving and controlling. You see? Do you see why I didn't want to be a Healer? It's all she cares about. She's obsessed with me being on the Council of Healers with her. Healing isn't even my patriarchal magic. I won't pass it on to any offspring. Her behavior is ridiculous. Someone's got to see that she's unhinged. How can she even think about enacting some law no one even uses anymore?"

Iden continued to squeeze Zo's hand, like he was pinning him to the spot right there in front of him.

"My mother has some experience with Ancestor law. We can see what she can do," Iden said in a low voice.

"Betrothed? Betrothed? How can she even think of such a thing, she doesn't even know me."

Iden chuckled. "I've been there."

Zo remembered Iden was briefly betrothed to Prym this last summer.

"You got out of it. How do I get out of it?"

Iden smiled. "Tell her the truth. At this point you're not afraid of her rejection."

"No, I'm afraid of what she'll do with the information."

As he stood on the beach with Iden still holding his hand, a memory flooded his mind. A moment he hadn't thought of in a while. Maybe he'd buried it. He was a young student in the halls of House Sano. Two older boys had been caught kissing in a closet. House Sano guards were dragging them away from each other. One of them was crying, yelling the other's name.

"Be strong, they can't break us!" The other one called across the hall.

Zo never saw either of them again, and he had looked for them every day.

Iden put a hand on Zo's cheek. "Hey, you alright?"

Zo didn't say anything, just pulled Iden to him and kissed him long and hard.

Iden wrapped his arms around, and crushed Zo to him, telling Zo that despite Iden's cool, outer calm, he was just as worried as Zo was. When the fire of the kiss slowed down, Iden pressed his forehead to Zo's.

"Let's go see Mom," Iden said.

Zo nodded.

* * *

"Who in their right mind evokes that antiquated law on a seventeen-year-old?" Iden's mother had stood to pace behind her desk in her Library office.

"My mother, apparently," Zo said.

"Is there anything we can do? Any precedent to get the law or paperwork thrown out in Zo's case?" Iden asked.

Iden's mother, stopped, sat behind her desk and pulled out pen and paper.

"I'm not familiar with this law. Like I said, it's old and I haven't heard it used except in custody battles over small children. I will have to do some research." She scribbled some notes on the paper.

"We don't have much time. My mother thinks she can get my contract with the Library canceled and have me on a boat to Eileansano in two days."

Iden's mother scoffed at that. "I have no doubt a member of the Healing Council can get your contract torn up, but I can't see that happening in two days. Plus, the spectacle of dragging you off to House Sano. I doubt the curator would allow such a thing."

"Except the curator is gone," Zo said.

Iden's eyes narrowed. "Your mother seems to have impeccable timing."

Zo's head shot up. "Who's been left in charge with the curator gone?"

"That weaselly inspector," Iden's mother said.

"What better way to get rid of the one person who is in touch with the Protector of the Library, and who knows by what means the Library is being harmed?" Iden said.

Iden's mother stopped writing, her eyes fixed on Zo. She turned pale. "I'll get right on this."

She stood, and taking her notes with her, hurried out into the Library.

"This isn't good," Zo said.

Iden nodded. "This is not good."

Chapter Twenty-One

Journal ???

I missed her! I haven't used my Travel magic since...the sword. I don't remember how I got out of the Origin. Someone must have brought me home. And then...the basement. That awful place they locked me with the rest of their failures. If she fails, they will put her there. I'm sweating all over just thinking about it. I have to leave him here. I can't take him with me. Ships...ships are too slow. I have to. I HAVE TO TRAVEL. No choice.

— From the Journals of Schiz

The morning was calm and chilly. There were mists upon the waters as a small island slid past the ship. Ryn wondered what it would be like to live on that small island. Would it be lonely? Could she spend all her time curled up with books reading? How would she get food? How would she find shelter in bad weather? Still, the little island filled with cedars looked appealing. It would be a place where it wouldn't matter who she was and if she had magic. Although having Zo's fire magic would be useful.

"Looks lonely," Yll's voice was next to Ryn.

"Looks peaceful," Ryn countered.

"Looks like Exile to me."

"Can't be, Exile is full of criminals," Ryn said.

Yll put her hand on Ryn's.

Regg approached them from the other side of the ship. "They said we'll make landfall on Viatoro soon—we need to gather our things and secure them."

Ryn's eyes fixed on Yll's hand. It was somehow warm, despite the frosty fog. Ryn's hands were freezing resting on the railing of the ship. Maybe it wasn't the wintery morning that made them so cold, but the thoughts of what was coming. Ryn had never met her grandmother, and the things her mother said about her didn't help Ryn's nerves. The idea of going to a real Ancestral island had been so appealing, but now that they were almost there, her mother's worries and concerns danced around inside of Ryn. What if her grandmother did wish her harm as her mother feared, or didn't care who she was? Certainly, an Ordinary granddaughter would be a disgrace to the Matriarch of Viator. Something inside her wished she was House Viator, even with all the dangers that could bring. At least she would be someone. Ryn swallowed hard against the lump that threatened to harden in her throat. Yll pulled her away to their cabin where Ryn was already packed. She probably needed to warm up. It was going to be a long day.

* * *

The sea spray flashed in the sun as the dolphins jumped and played at the front of the ship. Viatoro was just ahead. The captain was giving orders to furl the sails as they approached the island. Ships were docked and coming and going from the local village, but their ship was headed for a different dock, partway around the island. As they got closer, Ryn could see a contingent of people and carriages waiting to greet them. Her stomach flip flopped as she thought of her grandmother being with the greeting party. She didn't know what she was going to say—"Hello, I'm your granddaughter from your long-lost daughter, but I'm not really your granddaughter, but I am, but I'm not." She had spent the last two days of the trip trying to come up with the perfect greeting, but everything sounded dumb.

They pulled in next to the docks, and the ship's crew along with the dock crew began to secure the ship. A plank was lowered for exiting the ship, but no one was allowed off yet. Ryn searched the waiting crowd to see if anyone looked old enough to be her grandmother.

Uncle Mik came to stand next to Ryn. "You look white as a sheet, are you nervous?"

Ryn turned to him. His red hair shimmered with blond highlights in the sunshine. His face was serious, but his eyes danced with humor. Ryn shifted her weight from one leg to the other. She still had a hard time sharing with this stranger-turned-family.

"I've never been this far from home," she said. It was a good compromise. She was being honest, but not sharing how she felt about meeting the family.

Uncle Mik put a reassuring hand on her shoulder. "I promise, everything to come is going to be fantastic."

Ryn nodded. As she watched, Viatoro officials boarded the ship, and paperwork was signed, the all clear was given to begin the disembarking. Of course the high ranking officials went first, including Ryn's uncle and the accompanying Library Regents. Ryn was a bit miffed they didn't take Clayr until the second wave. Yll agreed it seemed disrespectful.

When at last it was their turn, Ryn's knees almost buckled when her feet hit the solid dock. Her legs and body still wanted to rock and roll with the waves. These docks were just as chaotic as the one they left, with people going one way, trunks going another way. Ryn, Yll, and Regg got shoved into a carriage with people they didn't know, plus Prym, who was trying to look like she was in charge, but her eyes gave away her confusion like the rest of them. Despite Prym coming from a powerful family, she looked as if this was her first time away from home.

Prym shifted in her seat, then opened a fan to cool herself. The sun on the windows and the amount of people in the carriage was making it hot. Prym turned from a shade of white to a light green. Ryn hoped she wasn't going to be sick in the carriage.

Out the window, fields of lavender captured Ryn's imagination. She could see it full of purple flowers in the summer. She was so focused she didn't notice they had pulled up to what appeared to be the largest log cabin she had ever seen, made from logs as big around as the carriage. She gasped as the door opened and everyone started to exit. Prym held Ryn back.

"I need to talk to you," Prym whispered.

Ryn's heart rate picked up and she started to sweat like when they were kids. After all these years her body still reacted to the bullying that always came after Prym singled Ryn out. Ryn fought to calm herself.

"What is it?" Ryn asked.

Prym looked out the window. "That man there. The one in black and gold." She pointed to Zmej talking with Jeris. "I don't trust him."

Ryn's gaze darted to Prym's face. "Why are you telling me this?"

"Because papa won't listen to me. Berty says he is presenting himself as a neutral party in the delegation, but he thinks he's got his own agenda."

Papa—that would be Jeris, but Berty? "You mean Master Ubert?"

"Of course, who else?"

Weird, Ryn thought.

"I still don't understand why you, of all people, are warning me about Zmej." Ryn felt cold now.

"Because I know your mother trusts him, and that you will be in his protection, and you will be in the best position to keep an eye on him. Berty thinks he's got something planned for this delegation, but he doesn't know what." Prym smoothed her skirts. "Now if you'll excuse me."

Prym stepped out with all the regalness she had at her command, as if she was the Matriarch of House Vivus. Ryn reached out, but instead of a footman helping her, Lar was there to take her hand. She smiled at him, her heart warming at his presence in this foreign place. As soon as her boots crunched on the gravel drive, she was surprised to find a teenage girl, about Ryn's age in a lily-white smock, who curtsied before her.

"I'm Lucy. I will be helping you during your stay. Please let me show you to your room."

Ryn looked back at Regg chatting with Yll next to the carriage.

"I can take both of you," the girl said. "The curator requested adjoining rooms for you."

Ryn turned back and smiled at the girl. "Sounds great."

Lar put his hand on Ryn's back and bent to whisper in her ear. "The sharks are circling. I'm going to stay with Clayr for a bit. You stick with Regg till I get back."

Ryn nodded, and followed Lucy up the steps to the guest house. At the top, before they entered the doors, Ryn thought to look for her trunk. She hoped she saw it come off the ship. She couldn't afford to lose the orphanage book.

"Something wrong?" Lucy asked.

"I'm just worried about my trunk. I have some important documents in it."

Lucy put her hand on Ryn's arm. "I'll make sure it's brought to your room as soon as it's unloaded."

Ryn gave Yll a worried look, but Yll squeezed her hand and they let Lucy usher them inside.

The foyer almost rivaled the Library's grand entrance. The tiles on the floor were marbled and polished to a high shine. A chandelier hung in the center of the room with hundreds of glass shapes which bounced the light from candles in small rainbows around the room. There were two grand staircases, one on each side of the hall.

"This entrance is big enough to hold a party," Yll said.

Lucy smiled. "We do hold balls here for our guests, but not for your visit. Tomorrow night there will be a grand dinner and ball at House Viator. They have been planning it for at least a moon. The Matriarch hasn't thrown such a party in years—you are quite the special guests."

Ryn followed Lucy to the staircase at the left of the foyer, her eyes taking in the high ceiling, paintings, and the ever-glittering light. She almost tripped on the stairs because her focus was up instead of on her feet.

When they reached the top of the stairs, Ryn joined Yll and Regg at the banister, looking down over the foyer and the Library delegates, including Clayr, Jeris, Regent Jordan, the Collections Manager, and the Research Manager, mingling with those sent from House Viator to greet them. Ryn knew she should be paying closer attention to who was grouped together with whom, but she was too dazzled by the spectacle of the place to focus.

"This way to your rooms," Lucy said.

She led them down the hallway, left of the grand entrance, to the second to last door on the right. She pushed the doors open to reveal the fanciest room Ryn had ever seen. There was a huge four poster bed, each pillar carved in a spiral, with a canopy over the bed. After the bed was a sitting area with a fireplace and chairs that looked out over cliffs that ran down to the ocean, sea spray crashing on the rocks below.

Ryn gasped as she approached the windows.

"It's magnificent!" Yll exclaimed.

"This is the curator and the lady Yll's room, yours is just next door." Lucy pulled Ryn toward the door.

Ryn's room was the last door. The room was slightly smaller than Yll's but just as grand, and the view out over the ocean was just as fantastic.

"I think I could sit here forever and take in this view," Ryn said.

"There is a door adjoining the two rooms," Lucy said, opening a door midway down the wall.

Yll and Regg came in to stand next to Ryn looking out over the crashing waves and the sea beyond.

"Dinner is at sunset in the dining room. I will return before then to help you dress. If you need anything, just pull this cord." Lucy put her hand on a huge, braided pull next to Ryn's bed.

"Thank you," Ryn said, barely registering Lucy leaving while still captivated by the ocean view.

Regg found a tray with a pitcher of water and crackers on it. He was happily munching away.

"What was that with Prym in the carriage?" Yll asked.

Ryn rubbed her forehead. "She wanted to warn me about Zmej. She said her and 'Berty' didn't trust him."

Regg choked on his cracker. "*Berty*?"

"That's what she called Master Ubert."

Yll's brow furrowed. "Why would she tell you that?"

"I don't know. She's never liked me, why would she do me any favors?" Ryn said.

"Sounds suspicious to me. Maybe her and 'Berty' want you to distrust Zmej for some reason." Regg munched another cracker.

"Yes, it does." Ryn stared out the window at the waves crashing on the rocks far below.

"Let's go explore," Yll suggested.

"Yes, a walk about the grounds might help clear my mind," Ryn agreed.

Ryn found she was still in her coat, so she made a mental note to talk to Lucy about starting a fire in the fireplace when she got back.

Dodging men with trunks entering and leaving, Ryn, Yll, and Regg slipped out the front door. The walk through the gardens was interesting, but a bit boring in the winter. What Ryn really wanted to see came into view as the gardens wrapped around the house. There was a short lawn before the cliff drop off, but the view of the ocean was just as spectacular from there. The edge dropped straight down to the jagged rocks below. The cliffs were at least twice as tall as the house, yet there was only a short stone wall as a barrier.

Regg leaned over the edge. "Do you think they get rid of unwanted guests this way?"

"Shhh, stop!" Yll pulled him back away from the edge.

Ryn noticed how easy it would be to fall from that wall, maybe even trip over it. A gust of cold wind made her shudder.

"Let's go back inside and have some tea by the fire," Ryn suggested.

As they entered the foyer, Lar strode up to Ryn. It seemed the reception had broken up.

"Can I have a word with you?" Lar asked Ryn.

"Sure." Ryn turned to Yll and Regg. "I'll meet you upstairs, can you have them get the fire going in my room?"

"Of course." Yll squeezed Ryn's arm then took Regg's as they went upstairs.

"We have a meeting with someone. I'm not sure what he's going to say, but I can tell you that whatever it is, I'm on your side," Lar whispered to her as they crossed the marbled floor to a small room to the left of the foyer. It was some sort of office with a desk and a small bookcase.

Zmej stood leaning on the desk staring out the window at the drive, observing the continued activity out there. When he turned to Ryn, something crackled in the air. His gray eyes were also brown, or maybe black. They made her think of fire and smoke. His gaze sent shivers up and down her spine. His hair was a deep, unnatural black so dark it bordered on purple in its sheen. His face was all angles, but in a way that made Ryn long for its perfection. His finely tailored black suit had gold threading with a subtle design of a small thistle, the symbol of House Viator. She had seen him in Clayr's office, but had been too distracted by meeting her uncle to pay attention to him. Now, with Prym's warning, she was paying close attention. She was surprised when her heart skipped a beat as he smiled at her. Somehow, she became an instant bundle of nerves.

"Ryn, it's so good to finally meet you in person. Your mother talks so much about you," Zmej said, holding out his hand.

"Nice to meet you." Ryn tried to keep her hand from trembling.

Zmej gestured to the chair in front of the desk, then sat opposite her.

"Your mother has asked me to watch over you while you are here, as an added precaution." Zmej glanced at Lar. "The more eyes looking for danger the better, but we need to set out some ground rules."

Ryn didn't like the sound of that.

"You must inform Lar or I of your whereabouts at all times. Do not wander anywhere alone. If you ask one of the servers for a cup of rosehip tea I will come immediately to your aid."

Zmej reached inside his jacket pocket and pulled out a velvety cloth. He opened it on the desk in front of Ryn. It was a necklace with a pink gold pendant shaped like a rose.

"You must wear this at all times. It has a bit of magic that will help me track where you are."

Ryn guessed her movements would be monitored, but to be tracked—that felt creepy. This man she barely knew was going to know where she was at all times. Ryn's eyes met Lar's. How well did her mother know this Zmej, and how much did she really trust him? Lar looked to be trying to keep his face neutral, but she could see by the downturn of his mouth that he wasn't happy with this arrangement. Ryn paused.

"Do not worry, this is for your safety only. If your grandmother should try to separate you from the rest of the group, that necklace will tell us where to find you." Zmej looked grim, pushing the cloth with the necklace closer to Ryn.

Ryn swallowed hard. Her hand closed around the cloth and the necklace. She tried to say thank you, but it caught in her throat.

Lar put his hand over Ryn's. "I don't think this is necessary. I am perfectly capable of watching over Ryn. My Earth magic would track her down if needed, and I have fire to protect her."

Fire seemed to flash in Zmej's eyes. "You have fire, do you?" He said with a smirk.

"I really don't think we need your assistance. We shall be going." Lar reached down to help Ryn to her feet.

"Do you really want to face Ryette if something happens to her only daughter?" Zmej frowned.

Lar put himself between Ryn and Zmej. "I'm certain that I can..."

"Like you kept track of her with Master Wes?" Zmej raised an eyebrow.

Lar's fists tightened.

Zmej stepped just inches from Lar. "Do you think Jayne will not take her granddaughter aside in House Viator? Because I am certain she will. I will give you full access to the magic of the pendant. We will both know where she is at all times. That will help put you and Ryette's minds at ease."

Lar let out a long breath. He rubbed the back of his neck as he moved to the side.

"Here, let me help you." Zmej held out his hand for the necklace.

He took the necklace from Ryn's trembling hand then secured it to her throat.

"There." He put his hands on Ryn's shoulders. "Don't worry, Lar and I will be able to locate you should you find yourself in trouble."

Ryn fingered the pendant. She felt like a cat with a bell on its collar to keep track of it, and to scare off the birds.

"Now, go out there and charm House Viator. Avoid being alone with anyone who's not of the Library delegation, and stay where you're told. I would hate to have to tell the staff to keep you locked in your rooms during your stay."

Ryn clamped her mouth shut to keep her jaw from dropping. Zmej might be butterflies-in-the-stomach handsome, but she did not like him at all.

Zmej resumed his spot on the corner of the desk watching out the window.

"You may go now. Remember I'm watching you."

Ryn couldn't flee from his presence fast enough, but her fingers pressed the pendant, knowing she couldn't really get away from him.

Chapter Twenty-Two

The underbelly of the Library was quiet, and for once, the blanket of magic suppression was a welcomed relief. Zo needed it. He was working hard to empty his mind of the mess his mother was attempting to make of his life. Usually, the quiet tedium of taking the Library's temperature was hard for Zo, but today he welcomed the dark. It made him feel like he could hide here forever.

He had finished his job on the third floor, northeast corner shaft and was on his way down the ladder with the thermoscope strapped to his back. His mind drifted to Ryn. He really hoped she would be alright. He'd tried to send a message to his dad, but he couldn't find Ryette, and he couldn't afford a Viator messenger. He'd sent one via a shapeshifter bird messenger, but that would take longer. They still had to fly like a bird. He had to trust that his dad, his brother, and Ryn would be fine. His dad was really good with fire, the best Zo had ever seen, and Regg wouldn't let Yll out of his sight, so hopefully that would include Ryn. Sometimes his brother didn't always pay attention to what was going on around him.

Zo reached the bottom of the ladder and jumped to the ground, careful not to bang the glass thermoscope on anything. He set off toward the north shaft when he heard shuffling feet and whispered voices. Zo tensed. The Protector of the Library neither talked, nor made noise when it moved.

If it was Nix looking for him, he would be calling his name. The possibility of his mother's guards coming for him made Zo tense, ready to run the other way, but there was another option—that someone, possibly the saboteurs, were down here planning something awful. Now Zo was torn between running and hiding, or confronting whomever was coming down the tunnel. He decided on a compromise.

He headed for a nook in the tunnel not too far away. He doused his lantern, and squeezed as far back into the nook's shadow as he could get. It was risky putting out his lantern. It meant he might have to find his way out in the dark, but he knew the tunnels well enough. He slowed his breathing and waited for whoever it was to pass. If it was his mother's guards, he would stay in the shadows, then make his way out in the dark. If it was someone else, he would knock them out with the thermoscope, then go for help. It would probably break the thermoscope, but catching the saboteurs would be worth it.

He took the thermoscope pack off his back. It was long and heavy and would have to make do as a club. Nix would want to kill him for breaking it, but he would understand. Hopefully. Light was coming down the tunnel. He held himself as still as he could get, melting further into the shadows, fleeing from the approaching lantern light.

The whispered voices drew closer. The light was almost upon him. Zo tightened his grip on the thermoscope. He held his breath as the shuffling feet drew next to him.

The first person holding the lantern appeared, their shadowed dress filling the tunnel wall, followed by two more coattailed shadows.

Zo swore. "What do you think you are doing?"

Brynd yelled and jumped back.

Zo emerged from the shadows of the nook.

"Zo, you scared the crap out of me!" Brynd had her hand pressed to her chest, breathing hard.

"How is it you're down here with these two?" Zo pointed to Jak and Dan. "And how did you all get through the Boiler Room without being seen?"

Jak flashed him a grin. "Secret entrance."

There was a hidden entrance to the Library underground. It was through the water tunnels, the source of the water that heated the Library. Zo noted the bottoms of the teen's pants were wet, as was Brynd's skirt.

Zo folded his arms. "You all better start talking about why you're sneaking around in the Library tunnels before I call Errol down here."

Brynd's face dropped and lost all color. "No Zo, I promise we are here for a good reason."

Dan held up his hands and stepped closer to Zo. "There is a legend among the Ordinaries in Waatch that there is writing explaining about the tree and the roots of the Library. We're looking for the answer to the cryptic "Kill the Roots" message."

"Were you planning to use the shafts to sneak into the Library? It's daylight and the Library is full of workers. Trust me when I tell you even in the dead of night it's hard to sneak around the Library," Zo said.

Jak held up his hands. "No man, we did some digging into local legend and we think we can find this writing somewhere down here."

Zo frowned. "There's no writing down here anywhere."

"Are you sure? Have you looked?" Jak flashed him that smile that made Zo want to punch his face.

Brynd stepped between them. "We're here. Let's just have a look around. Maybe you've missed something."

Zo wanted nothing more than to throw these three out of this protected space—right through the Boiler Room where they would most certainly get in the most trouble, but Brynd was Ryn's friend, and Ryn was dating Dan. She might not take kindly to coming home and finding Zo had gotten them all in trouble.

Jak rubbed at his neck. "Look, help us out here, and Dan and I can find a nice hiding place for you from your mother."

"How do you know about my mother?"

Jak laughed. "You two put on a very public display in the Dining Room. Everyone knows about your mother."

Zo replaced the thermoscope on his back and relit his lantern using theirs.

"If you know where this writing is, lead on." Zo gestured with his hand for them to continue.

"Right, you know the underground better than us, are there any tunnels that run through the center?" Jak asked.

"Only the ones that give access to the heating ductwork."

"Show us," Jak said.

Zo didn't like his demanding tone. The idea of showing secret passages to Jak made Zo's skin crawl, but if there was a possibility that what he said was true, it could help protect the Library. And if it wasn't true, showing them that there was nothing there would hopefully get them to leave.

"This way."

In the process of fixing the water leak in the heating duct, Nix had shown Zo a few of the hidden doors that led under the center of the Library. Zo took them to the one in the north tunnel. He pushed on the hidden panel and the wall opened. He didn't like the way Jak and Dan's faces lit up when they saw it. They stepped inside.

"Be careful of the piping, it will burn you," Zo said, taking the lead.

The tunnel followed the pipes of water underneath the flooring of the Library.

At the center of the underground there were four walls that formed a box. It could have been a room, but there were no doors.

"That's it, the heart," Jak said.

"The heart? I've never heard it called that." Zo held up his lantern. "Stay back. I will look." Zo held up his hand to keep them back.

He circled the walls, holding the lantern close.

"See, no writing," Zo said.

"Are you sure? Let us look. You don't know what you're looking for," Jak said.

Zo stood in front of the center of the Library, apparently called the Heart. He was regretting leading them here. "There is nothing. It's time to go."

When they were safely back in the tunnel, Dan took Zo's hand and shook it. "Thank you for letting us look. You're a good man. I can see why Ryn thinks so highly of you."

Zo wondered for a moment at the reach of Jak's information. "I'm worried about Ryn."

"I am too," Dan frowned.

"Can you do something? I sent her a message that the delegation is in danger, but it will take time to reach her."

Dan shook his head. "Viatoro is beyond our reach. We'll all just have to wait and see how that plays out."

Zo's face darkened. "And what if something happens to Ryn while we sit here and wait?"

Dan put a hand on Zo's shoulder. Zo didn't appreciate his touch.

"I'm just as worried as you are, but there's nothing we can do from here but pray to the Ancestors everything works out," Dan said.

"I don't pray to the Ancestors," Zo said.

"Neither do I, but in this case, it's all we have."

Zo bid them to leave quickly. As soon as they moved off back toward the water tunnels, Zo adjusted the thermoscope and turned to head to the last shaft he needed to visit to finish his shift. He took one step before the Protector of the Library coalesced out of the darkness.

Once in human shape it pointed down the tunnel in the direction the other three had gone.

"What about them?" Zo asked.

The Protector shook its head.

"They said they had a clue about what the saboteurs may be after," Zo said.

The Protector was shaking its head again.

"Well, why didn't you stop us?"

The Protector pointed a black inky hand at Zo.

"How is this my fault? I thought you were the 'Protector.'"

The Protector pointed to itself, then to Zo, then back and forth between them.

"We're both protectors?"

The Protector nodded.

"I'm sorry, I've been to the center to repair the damage, and I never saw the writing they were looking for. I only wanted to prove to them they were wrong so they would leave."

The Protector hung its head. The feeling of utter defeat slammed into Zo. He had miscalculated. He had just let something bad happen.

The Protector beckoned him to follow, then walked through the wall. Zo opened the hidden door and followed. Once at the center or Heart, the Protector waved its hand over the wall. In Zo's mind he saw an image of a door. On the door glowed some kind of writing. It looked like the runes on the beads of bone, but they weren't any runes he recognized. The Protector waved its hand again and the door disappeared.

"Don't worry, I'll make sure no one gets in again," Zo said.

The Protector gave a sad nod, then disappeared through the wall.

* * *

"All I can tell you, Nix, is that the Protector is worried, and we need to increase guard on all supposedly secret entrances to the underground." Zo was facing down Nix across his office desk.

"I still think you're hiding something from me. This is way too specific a request to have come from the Protector. And you will address me as Master in the Boiler Room." Nix sat, arms folded across his enormous chest.

Zo cracked his knuckles on Nix's desk.

"Who are you protecting?" Nix asked.

"The Library. I'm worried Errol doesn't have enough guard coverage on all the entrances. Now is not the time to be trusting of anyone," Zo said.

"Looks to me like you need to take your own advice," Nix grunted.

Zo stared him in the eyes, then shook his hand out.

Nix sighed. "Fine. It won't hurt to have extra eyes down here, but the guard is already spread thin with these attacks. I advise you to come forward if you can name specific names."

"At the moment all I have are rumors and tips from concerned parties. When I get something solid, I will go directly to Errol," Zo said.

Nix nodded. "So be it."

Zo turned to go.

"Are you heading to your lessons at the Healing House?"

Zo fought to keep his anger under control. "No. I'm avoiding the place till my mother leaves."

Nix picked up a stack of papers on his desk. "Your mother is demanding I let you out of your contract. She's invoking the right of parental guardianship."

Zo's eyes flashed at Nix. "I'm not a child."

"I've been told the law says you are until you reach the age when the Ancestors will no longer teach you the magic. You are not yet of that age, as you still have a couple months till you're eighteen."

"It's unfortunately not close enough." Zo leaned on Nix's desk. "You've got to do something. Library law is stronger than parental law. You have my blood!"

Nix's eyes shifted to the paperwork in his hands. He seemed to be wrestling thoughts in his mind.

"I will fight to get this thrown out, but that idiot inspector thinks I'm no better than a grunt worker. Without the curator here I don't have much sway or power."

Nix looked at him apologetically. His eyes becoming glassy.

"Wilmar pinned all his hopes on you for our retirement. He's hoping you'll be the next physician for Waatch."

Nix looked down at the papers again, using a finger to wipe at his eye. When he looked back up at Zo it was with a new determined face.

"I will fight for you to the last. No one takes one of my grunts away from me!"

"Hey! I'm not..."

Nix stood, using one hand to wipe his other eye, and the other to push Zo out his office door.

"Now shoo. And don't you say anything to Wilmar about me getting all emotional over a grunt."

Zo punched Nix in the arm. "Nix, I'm not a grunt."

"That's Master Nix to you!"

"Ha!"

With that, Nix shut his office door on Zo.

The smile on Zo's face faded quickly. He put his hand on Nix's door. He remembered his first day in the Boiler Room and how Nix had nearly killed him, but now he couldn't bear the thought of being without him and Wilmar. He had to find a way to thwart his mother's attempts to drag him home. He decided it was time to visit Iden's mother to see if she had found any loopholes in the law.

Chapter Twenty-Three

Jak,

I'm looking forward to our dinner this evening at your place. I trust you've reserved my special table. I have other business I'm attending to, so wait for me if I'm late.

The discussion around the dinner table in the guest house went late into the night. The back and forth about the pros and cons of moving the Library was exciting at first, but became circular and boring. Ryn's head was spinning trying to follow it all.

Jeris was in the middle of a long recounting of the Library's history of growth and expansion that was interesting, but made no mention of the history Ryn really wanted to hear—the history of how the Library was founded. She felt her eyes drooping at the lecture.

Uncle Mik, who was seated next to her, leaned in to whisper to Ryn over Jeris' droning. "Why don't you head off to bed. Nothing critical is going to be decided tonight."

Ryn narrowed her eyes at him.

Her uncle held up his hands. "What? I'm serious. This is all just posturing."

"Excuse me?" Jeris stopped his lecture. "Who's posturing?"

"Look, Regent Jeris, it's late, and we've had a long trip here. Why don't we start on this fresh in the morning?" Uncle Mik said.

"I will agree with that," Clayr said, pushing her chair back from the table.

Regg stood, and put out his hand for Yll to take. She blushed as he helped her stand. Uncle Mik stood and did the same for Ryn, but Lar intervened.

"I'll take care of Ryn," Lar said.

Uncle Mik's lips flattened. "As you wish."

Lar whisked her away before anything else could be said.

Lar and Regg escorted them to their rooms. Once inside Ryn fumbled around undoing her dress, then she opened her trunk and pulled out a nightgown. The Orphanage book caught her eye, and she held it to her as she climbed into bed. The fire crackled while Ryn turned to the page that held the entry about her. It was a strange thing, but she felt that the dream she had with her father and the white-haired man confirmed it was her. She shook her head at the thought that her dreams could be real. How could that possibly work? She didn't have magic. She was running her hands over the ink when Regg came into the room through the shared door.

"Yll's already asleep. I'm just going to be here on the sofa till Clayr comes in," he said.

"Where's Clayr?" Ryn asked.

"She's still talking to that Zmej guy. My dad went to be with her. He doesn't trust Zmej." Regg said.

Ryn nodded, closing the book, she snuggled down into the bed, one hand stretched out on the cover. She fell instantly asleep.

* * *

Sometime in the middle of the night, she woke. The winds blew hard against the windows and the waves crashed on the rocks below. The fire had burned down to a soft glow. Regg was gone, but the connecting door was still open. Ryn could hear Yll and Clayr's soft snoring. She knew that sound well. Ryn moved the orphanage book to the nightstand so she could pull the covers up around her. She closed her eyes, but the wind made the house creak in unfamiliar ways. She felt very alone in that big bed in the giant room. She shivered. She wanted to go crawl in bed with Yll. They had slept in the same bed many times growing up. Even though these beds were large, she knew there was no space for her between Yll and Clayr. She wished Regg hadn't left. She would have felt better with him there.

She tossed and turned, but the wind continued to howl. Lucy had mentioned there was a small library here in the guest house. She decided to see if it held any books about the Library or the history of House Viator. She grabbed the blanket from the end of the bed and wrapped it around her shoulders. Her bare feet hit the cold wood floor. Opening her door a crack, there was only one lantern turned down low at the end of the hallway next to the stairs. She started toward the sitting room, but didn't recall seeing any books in that room. Instead, she continued down the stairs, trying to tiptoe. The great wood stairs occasionally gave a slight creak. Making her way across the foyer, her hand was on the latch to the downstairs sitting room when she noticed a light coming from the end of the hallway to her left. It seemed the room was fully lit in the dead of night. Curious, she made her way down the hall. The sight that greeted her made her gasp.

This is the room!

It was the exact room she had seen in her dreams. Her first dream of her father when he showed her the orphanage book, and encouraged her to find it. The one where they had sat by the window and talked about disobeying her mother to study in the Library. Everything was there, the walls of books, the draperies, the long table, and the potted plant. It was like she had been here before with her father. She stepped into the room, running her hands over the spot on the table where he laid the orphanage book. How could she know this room so well when she only dreamed about it?

She could almost see her father standing there, excited to share the orphanage book with her. She wanted to be with him right then. If he was here, he would make everything alright.

A gasp at the door startled Ryn from her memories.

"Mistress, you should not be wandering the house at night." A servant stood in the doorway.

"Sorry, I couldn't sleep. I just came down to borrow a book from the library."

Ryn reached out and grabbed the closest book that came to hand on the shelf.

"It is not safe to be out of your room at night. Didn't Master Zmej tell you that? The Matriarch has appointed him master over this guest house while you are here."

Ryn had honestly tried to forget her encounter with Zmej earlier that day.

"I'm so groggy with sleep. I guess I forgot," she said.

"Let me take you back to your room. Please do not leave again. The master will be very upset." He held out his arm to beckon to her, then herded her out.

Ryn didn't care if Zmej was upset. She must have been hanging out with Zo too much. The thought made her smile, but then she immediately missed him. She hoped he was alright by himself protecting the Library.

Once back in her room, she crawled into bed with the book she'd managed to grab. She really hoped it would be something that would be something interesting. She hadn't even gotten a chance to check any of the titles of the books there. She would have to take a closer look in the daylight. The fact that someone stopped her from looking made her think there might be something to be found. She opened the book.

Principles of Library Collection Management. "That's an interesting title for a book in a guest house library," she whispered.

Despite its potential to be interesting, the first few pages were the author's thoughts on how they determined which collection management principles were worthy of discussing in the book. Her eyes dropped and she drifted off to sleep with the book in her hands.

* * *

The morning dawned clear and the sun was just lightening the sky when movement in Ryn's room brought awareness back to her. Without opening her eyes, she listened to quiet feet and the swish of skirts as they made their way across the room to her. She cracked an eye open, but didn't move, hoping the person wouldn't know she was awake till she could determine who it was. If she remained still, she couldn't see the person till they came around the bed.

A hand rested on Ryn's arm. Even though she knew someone was there, she still jumped.

"Sorry, sweetheart, I didn't mean to startle you," Ryn's mother's voice was a whisper.

"What are you doing here?" Ryn sat up rubbing her eyes.

"I need to check on you. Hop up and slip on a dress, we need to talk."

"Can't we talk in my nightdress?" Ryn yawned.

"No, I'm taking you someplace."

Ryn frowned at her mother. "We haven't finished what we came to do. I need to be here."

"Not for long, I promise."

Ryn crawled out of bed and pulled on her researcher's dress, but before she could brush out her wildly sticking up hair, her mother pulled her close and she felt the spinning of travel magic.

When the air and the spinning stopped Ryn instantly regretted choosing the long-sleeved black researcher dress. The sun, not having any mountains to rise over, was shining on yellow sand. She already felt very warm. There were no rocks or logs in sight, and the waves crashing on the sand were the biggest she'd ever seen on a non-stormy day. She marveled as the waves broke and rushed up the shore. When the water retreated little bubbling holes appeared in the sand.

"Where are we? I've never heard of a beach with so much sand, and such a warm sun," Ryn asked.

"It is far from where we live. My uncle used to bring me here when things were tense at home. I don't know how he knew of it, but he showed it to me so I could find it myself when I needed to get away. I've never encountered any other people here. I'm grateful to have it in my head so I can come here." Her mother sat in the sand.

"Strange place."

Ryn sat next to her mother. She couldn't resist taking off her shoes and pushing her toes into the warm sand. She hoped to just stay in this moment, sun on her back, waves crashing against the shore.

"I received an official request from House Viator that you and Jett be allowed to take your rightful places in the House hierarchy. It was less of a request and more of a demand. I fear if you set foot inside the Manor House my mother will never let you leave."

Her mother paused, before she turned to Ryn.

"I want you to come home," her mother said.

Ryn didn't respond. She didn't want to argue with her mother again.

"And what happens when she finds out I'm Ordinary?"

Her mother's eyes found Ryn's. "That's what I'm afraid of."

Ryn couldn't dispel her mother's fears. Ever since arriving on the island Ryn had felt a growing sense of wrongness, but she knew the key to finding out who was behind the Library attacks was probably there on Viatoro, plus she couldn't leave till she showed the Orphanage book to the book binder.

"You have not only Lar and Regg watching me, but also this creepy Zmej guy. Who is he anyway? Why do you trust him?"

Her mother sighed, running her fingers through the warm sand. "He was a friend of mine when I was younger. He would come to the House to bring news from other islands. He warned me not to marry Aln, Jett's father. I was too dreamy eyed to listen." Her mother turned red. "Aln had a sweet smile, and the kindest eyes. I had only met him a few times, but I was surely smitten with him. Zmej's the one who told me what my family was planning. He helped me escape. I haven't seen him in a while, but when I saw him with the delegation I asked for his help."

Ryn tried to reconcile the story of the nice man who helped his mother with the one she'd met in the office yesterday. They didn't seem to be the same person. "Well, he put a tracking pendant around my neck." Ryn held up the rose pendant. "Which I can't seem to take off by the way."

Her mother frowned at the pendant. Something was passing through her mind. Ryn could see it in her eyes.

"It was a mistake that I let you come, but I can see it's too late to pull you out. I need to get you back before Zmej tracks you here. I didn't intend for him to put a tracker on you. I wish this place to remain our secret."

"How come you've never brought me here before?" Ryn asked as she brushed the sand off her feet to put her boots back on.

"I didn't want to share it with anyone. It's been my private place to come to think, but anywhere I take you at home, there will be people watching and listening. Come on, let me get you back."

Ryn tied her boots and stood. Sand pelted her face as the travel magic spun. When they were back in Ryn's room at the guest house, her mother hugged her tight. Kissing her on the head, she whispered, "Be safe, and don't accept any offers from House Viator."

"Don't worry, I'm pretty sure when they find out I really am adopted they will change their minds about me."

Her mother kissed her again, then she was gone in a swirl of air.

Ryn realized she didn't ask her mother about Uncle Mik. She always talked about Ryn's grandmother being the problem, but had never mentioned her brother. Uncle Mik seemed to genuinely care about Ryn, and she was starting to enjoy his company.

A light knock came at the door to the hallway.

It was early, and the house was still quiet. Ryn wondered if it was safe to let someone in. She went to the door and cracked it open.

"I have mail and breakfast," Lucy said.

Ryn opened the door wide to let Lucy and her tray inside.

"How did you know I was up?" Ryn yawned.

"I didn't. I was sent by the Patriarch in Waiting to get you ready for the day."

Lucy handed her a note.

My dearest niece,

Please join me today for a tour of Viatoro. I will be round to pick you up after breakfast.

Your loving Uncle Mik

Ryn's heartbeat quickened. She was torn between wanting to spend more time getting to know her Uncle and her mother's constant warnings about her family. Were they really that bad?

"Wait," she told Lucy.

She went into the other room to find Clayr awake and on the couch overlooking the cliffs. Ryn handed her the note and began to pace while Clayr read.

"This is bold. Do they want you as part of the delegation or not? We are to meet here with the House Viator Moving Team today. You are supposed to be in those meetings," Clayr said.

"Not to mention everyone, and I do mean everyone, has told me not to go off alone with these people," Ryn said, but in her mind she wanted to go.

Lucy brought in a cup of chamomile tea. Clayr took the cup in her hands and stared out over the rim at the ocean.

"I do need to visit the village today. Thax the tailor gave me a dress to wear tonight, but it needs to be hemmed," Ryn said.

Clayr nodded. "Good. I was worried you wouldn't have anything but your researcher's dress to wear tonight."

Clayr tapped her finger on the cup, then took a sip.

"Go with Mik. Take Yll and Regg with you. I will make sure you are watched," Clayr frowned.

She looked worried. So was Ryn. It was pretty certain that "making sure she was watched" involved Zmej, which Ryn really didn't like, but if it got her out of the house and to the village where she could get the Orphanage book looked at, it would be worth it.

Ryn woke Yll up, then hurried back to her room to get ready. When she grabbed a piece of toast off the breakfast tray she noticed a stack of letters.

The first was a formal invitation to the feast and ball at House Viator that night. It said they would be introducing long lost heirs to the world. Ryn didn't like the sound of that, but maybe she would see Jett again.

The second was a letter from Dan:

My Darling Ryn,

Guess who it is? It's me! Are you missing me? Because I'm missing you like crazy! I wanted to get on the next boat after you left for Viatoro, but Jak said no. Sigh. He's so practical sometimes. I mean, it would probably be trouble to be caught hanging out with the delegation, but who cares, right? It would be so worth it to be with you right now. Life in Waatch has become lonely without you. Especially because I have to watch Jak and Brynd all the time. You know how that is. That kiss we shared before you left was so special. I can't wait till you get back. Maybe we could go for another walk then, yes?

I cannot go into detail here in this letter, because who knows what eyes might see it, but Brynd helped Jak do that research we discussed and it looks promising. Hopefully we can get you the answers you need by the time you return. Don't worry. We are on track—I promise!

Jak and Brynd came in and the noise they are making is annoying. I'm going to move to a different room. I miss you so much—you're coming home soon right? Aaaand now Maus is using the desk like a drum...I need to find someplace quiet! Ahhhhh—finally locked myself in the toilet to get some peace. Anyway, I guess all I really want to say is that I can't wait till you get back.

You are something really special. I hope to see you soon!

Love,
Dan

Ryn was blushing furiously when she put the letter down. She was not sure how it made her feel. In truth she hadn't thought much about Dan since she left. She certainly had a lot on her mind. Really she had too much on her plate to indulge herself in thinking about a boy—right? She couldn't help but feel a little guilty though. Dan was certainly sweet, but.... She sighed and picked up the next letter.

It was from Zo:

Parva Soror,

I tried to catch you before you left. Something bad happened last night. We had another stabbing victim at Wilmar's. That's the third. The first was the man I failed to save, the second was the man you found. This one was a woman, and Wilmar and I managed to save her. When she woke, she said the Library Delegation was in danger. She indicated that someone in the delegation would die. I ran as fast as I could to the docks, but my mother's thugs stopped me. Yes, my mother is here. She's trying to take me home to House Sano.
Anyway, I'm worried about you. If you can find a way to come home, we need you here. Everyone is worried about Master Ubert being in charge.

Love,
Zo

All of Zo's favorite swear words passed through Ryn's mind. She couldn't believe Zo's mother was in Waatch. And she wanted to take him home? Maybe she should go back. It sounded like Zo could really use some help with his mother.

Maybe she could find a loophole in the law his mother was using. She knew there was no way anyone would let her leave now. Still, she would need to let Lar know what was happening.

Yll came into Ryn's room with a piece of toast hanging out of her mouth while she pulled on her coat.

"Did anyone wake up Regg?" Ryn asked.

Yll nodded. "I sent Lucy to do that. He should be ready."

Ryn tucked the letters into her pockets, grabbed the boxed dress and the Orphanage book and headed for the door.

"Let's go see what my uncle has planned for us."

Yll grimaced, then followed Ryn out the door.

Chapter Twenty-Four

Ryette de Viator, Matriarch in Waiting

You are cordially invited to attend the formal introduction of House Viator's long lost heirs. The Introductions and feast will begin at six, there will be a bead ceremony to follow. We look forward to your attendance at this happy occasion for House Viator.

(Added in personal script at the bottom: *Please attend!*)

The sun was up, and since Zo was staying away from the Healing House, he found himself with the morning off. It was a shame really, he'd only had one day of classes before his mother showed up. Mess hall food didn't sound appealing. After knocking several times on Iden's door, Zo remembered Iden had an early shift in the Library, so he headed off to restaurant row in Waatch. The clear, but crisp morning was helping to clear Zo's mind of all the ugly thoughts he was having. He had visited Iden's mother the night before, but she didn't have any answers for him yet. There had to be something, some precedent that could get him out from under his mother's thumb.

As he exited the Library gates and crossed the street, his mother's guards began to follow him. He was tempted to turn and blast them with fire, but it was too early and he was hungry, so he kept walking and ignored his tail. They could report to his mother everything he ate. He really didn't care.

At the breakfast place he ordered his usual, the tiny pasta and cheese patties with eggs on top, smoked salmon, and gravy. The server knew him and brought him extra bacon.

He was happily munching his bacon, attempting to ignore his mother's thugs at a table in the corner, when a shadow fell across the table.

Zo looked up, dropping bacon at the sight of Keir.

Keir smiled. "It's good to see you."

Zo recovered from his surprise and gestured for Keir to sit. "How did you escape from that horrible place?"

"You mean—why am I not in class?" Keir snatched a piece of bacon off Zo's plate.

Zo waved the server over. He liked Keir, but not enough to share his bacon.

Keir ordered a couple eggs with bacon.

"Well?" Zo asked when she left.

Keir shrugged. "Things are a bit disrupted with your mother around. She seems to feel that since she's in town she should do a full audit of the Waatch Healing House and its classes. She's been attending every class. Stopping the teachers several times. Asking questions. I think the Headmaster is ready to explode, and she's only been here a couple days."

Zo grunted. "Sounds familiar." He attacked his eggs.

Keir leaned in toward Zo. "I was actually hoping to find you. I'm wondering if you've given the notebook any more thought."

Zo eyed his mother's guards in the corner. "Maybe."

Keir didn't turn around to follow Zo's gaze, as he seemed to be following his thoughts. "This could be the answer to your problems."

Zo shook himself. "I'm not killing anyone to get away from my mother."

Keir sat back. "Of course not, of course not."

Zo continued his assault on his breakfast. Something rubbed the inside of his ankle, snaking its way up inside his pant leg. Before Zo could jump back to see what was crawling up his leg, he felt the touch of Keir's healing magic. Zo glanced under the table. Keir had removed his shoe, and his stockinged toes were rubbing up against Zo's leg. Zo's immediate reaction was to pull his leg back, but as always, Keir's Healing magic was overwhelming. Zo felt his muscles unknot, and his body relax. A sigh escaped his lips at the sudden release of tension. Warmth spread through his body as a tingling sensation started at the spot where Keir's toe touched him, and slowly traveled up Zo's calf. In the back of his mind Zo was trying to puzzle out how powerful Keir's magic would need to be to use his Healing magic through the thickness of his stockinged foot. Zo shifted his focus to his food to keep from behaving like a fool in public.

Keir leaned forward, and managed to push his foot higher up Zo's leg, causing his back to arch.

"We have a meeting tonight," Keir whispered. "Join us."

Keir's toe brought the tingling up past Zo's knee.

Zo's heart was pounding. He struggled to find his voice.

"Us?" Zo's voice cracked like he was a young teen again.

"Yes, I have gathered quite the group to my cause," Keir smiled.

Zo cleared his throat, trying to concentrate on asking the questions he had, but his groin was throbbing. "What meeting?"

"I promise it will be nothing like you've ever experienced before." Keir pressed his foot even higher.

Zo inhaled so sharp, the couple next to them looked over. Keir slid his foot back till only his toe was touching Zo's ankle.

"You promised me the other night when you stood me up you would go with me." Keir's voice was low and gravely.

Zo vaguely remembered agreeing to that when Keir showed up with a basket of dinner at Wilmar's. He had agreed to the dinner only to get Keir out of his way at the Healing House, and he promised to go out with him to get him out of Wimar's doorway. Zo's stomach twisted, but he was already shuddering with pleasure and biting his tongue to keep from making embarrassing noises.

"Fine," he managed to gasp out.

Keir's foot withdrew, and Zo slumped forward.

"I'll pick you up from the west Library gate at moonrise." Keir stood.

Zo quivered. "At moonrise."

* * *

Just before moonrise, Zo was chatting with Fergus at the west gate. Fergus was on guard for the night, and Zo had arrived early, unable to wait in his room any longer. His nerves had him on edge. He didn't want to go, and yet he was intrigued by what Keir wanted to show him. At the very least Zo wanted to find reasons to talk Keir out of what he was pursuing.

Fergus' voice turned low and serious. "They found book worms in a few books today. The books are all from different parts of the Library, so they have no idea how they got there or how widespread the infestation might be."

"But we took the stone away," Zo said, confused.

"Didn't the Protector…"

"Show me more than the stone." Of course, there was the branch and the sword. "Do you think they all work the same, though?"

Fergus shrugged. "Who knows, but Master Ubert was livid. He's trying to fire everyone in acquisitions, but with the curator and several board members gone he can't get the action ratified."

"I doubt it was someone in acquisitions."

Zo felt bad. He had all but forgotten there were three objects mentioned by the Protector. What kind of branch could it be, and a sword? Who could bring a sword in the Library without anyone noticing? The rock was easy to conceal in a pocket, but a tree branch and a sword? It didn't make any sense.

"I hope they get back from Viatoro soon." Zo was still worried. The longer they were gone, the more worried he became.

"I don't know why they went. The Board seems to have already made up its mind to move the Library."

Zo shushed Fergus. "Let's not give up yet. I'm trusting Clayr to have a few tricks left to play."

As the moon crested the hills, Keir seemed to melt out of the dark.

Startled, Zo jumped.

"Scared me almost to death."

"Ready?" Keir asked.

"Sure," Zo said, then turned to Fergus. "Let me know if there's anything I can help with. I'm worried the book worms are a sign the negotiations are heating up."

Fergus snorted. "That's a given."

Zo let Keir lead him down the darkened streets. The occasional light from a window or the moon flashed off Keir's silver ringed fingers.

"I'm so glad you decided to join us," Keir's voice almost purred.

Zo held up his hands. "I didn't say anything about joining, but I'm coming along to see how I feel."

Keir nodded slowly, like he was a bit disappointed, but he said, "That seems fair."

They walked down several streets and alleyways, turning often, and at one point climbing over several fences to pass between houses. Zo looked back, to see if they had lost his mother's thugs, but the path had also lost Zo. He had no idea where in Waatch they were when Keir pulled out a key and unlocked a back door to a storage house. The storage was filled with sacks of oats and other grains. In the far corner an overhead lantern was lit. Once they wound their way through the stacks, Zo found a table surrounded by other Healing House students Zo had seen, but hadn't really met.

"Took you long enough," one of them said to Keir.

"Sorry, I had to bring along our new recruit," Keir smiled.

Someone gave a long, low whistle. "Won't his mama be proud?"

There were a couple grunts and a few laughs at that. Zo was ready to leave, but Keir grabbed his hand and wouldn't let go.

"I am pleased you all have come. Tonight we test what we have learned." With a flare Keir uncovered a metal bucket filled with mice struggling to climb the slick sides.

"Yes!" One of the other students exclaimed. "You told us it feels better than killing bugs, how much better?"

Keir grinned. "You won't be disappointed."

"How does it work?" Someone else said while staring down into the bucket of scrambling mice.

"The same as before. Use your Healing magic. Reach in. Stop their hearts. It's that simple," Keir said.

To demonstrate, Keir grabbed a mouse.

Zo took a long step back, attempting to break Keir's hold on his hand, but Keir only tightened his grip. Before he could put up a stronger fight, Keir used his connection to Zo to allow his healing magic to flow between the two of them. Then Zo felt it shift its focus to the mouse. Keir didn't pull Zo's mind along with his into the mouse, but Zo knew the moment the mouse died. Keir let the power of it flow into Zo. He gasped, and his knees buckled, but his hand clung to Keir's. It felt good. It felt really good. It was better than that first glass of wine. Better than some of the more potent herbs Wilmar kept—and Zo had accidentally ingested a few of them. Zo was gasping for breath, as he rode the wave of pure exhilaration.

"As you can see, my friend here didn't even do the killing himself, but he's overwhelmed." Keir's voice sounded strained, as Zo imagined his would be if he tried to talk right now.

It was the most horrific thing Zo had encountered. It must go against nature itself. It seemed to speak to the fact that Ancestor magic and Healing had come with the Dragon Slayer from a different world. How else could he explain how using Healing magic to kill could possibly be a pleasure inducing experience?

Everyone around the table eagerly dove for mice in the bucket. Zo was barely aware of what was happening.

"There is no downside to this killing magic. It can take care of pests, enemies, unwanted relatives"—there was chuckling all around at that—"while providing us with such a high as no one has ever felt before," Keir said.

Some of the other students were already gasping in pleasure.

Keir pulled Zo to his feet. "Take a mouse, do it yourself."

Zo looked into the bucket at the tiny furry creature trembling in the bottom.

"Go on, I promise it's even better when you do it yourself," Keir said.

Zo picked up the mouse and held it in his hand. The beady eyes held his, while its whiskers trembled.

Someone opened a side door.

Keir waved to them. "So glad you could join us."

Keir moved off to greet the new person. Everyone else had their eyes closed in the throes of whatever it was they were feeling.

Zo put the mouse into his coat pocket, then made his way back through the stacks of grain to the door they had entered earlier. He lifted the latch as quietly as he could, then slipped out, back into the night. He wandered the streets until he got his bearings, then headed for the north gate to Waatch. The large gates were closed at this late hour, but the small door off to the side was open. The guards let him pass out of Waatch without question.

Zo wandered his way down to the beach. He walked along the shore, watching the last quarter moonlight shimmer on the water. It was all too much to take in. Between the Library sabotage, the proposed move of the Library, his mother trying to drag him home and marry him off to some girl he never met, and Keir running around promoting killing with magic, Zo's mind was ready to explode.

He kicked a rock at the sand's edge. Tonight had confirmed Keir was up to something horrific. What exactly was he planning to do with this Killing magic? Was it only for pleasure, or was he really wanting to join in combat with it? Zo wondered what Keir's parents would think. A couple who inbred for power, and didn't care if their Ancestral descendant son didn't produce children seemed like the type who would encourage that behavior. Zo shuddered.

When his feet took him close to the forest's edge, Zo reached into his pocket and pulled out the mouse, who was still trembling at Zo's touch.

"Off you go little one, I'm a healer, not a killer." Zo put the mouse down.

It watched him for a few moments more, then scurried off into the undergrowth.

A branch cracked next to him, and Zo jumped to his feet.

"Shhhhh...Don't...Don't worry." The wild man said. He was the one with twigs sticking out of his hair that Zo had met in the forest with Ryn.

He held up a hand as if to forestall any reaction from Zo.

"What do you want?" Zo took a step backward, startled by his sudden appearance.

"I...I need word...The lady Ryn...I haven't seen her."

Creepy, Zo thought, but decided not to say it. The man appeared to need some mind healing.

"Please...I have...someone said she left on a boat...Did she leave on a boat?"

Zo didn't say anything. The man's name came back to Zo: Schiz. He stepped forward and took Zo by the arm. This alarmed Zo until Schiz lifted his head and the moonlight shimmered on the tears flowing down his cheeks.

"Please tell me," Schiz pleaded.

Something tugged at Zo's heart. After all the unkindness he'd seen lately, he felt compassion for this man.

"She left with the Library delegation to Viatoro."

"No!" Schiz put his hands in his hair. "Didn't I tell her? Didn't I warn her to stay away?"

"We all did, but she's bound to the Library and must go where she's assigned."

Schiz nodded. "I must go to her immediately. I'm the only one who can save her."

He grabbed the front of Zo's coat. "Don't tell anyone where I've gone. If they catch me there it will mean my death."

"Sure," Zo said, thinking he didn't know anyone who would believe he'd talked to this man, let alone care where he went.

Schiz turned to go. Zo grabbed his arm.

"Hey, I'm really worried about Ryn. If you can make sure she stays safe, I'll do anything you ask of me."

"I am sworn to protect her."

And with that, he ran off into the woods.

Zo didn't see how the man could even get to Viatoro before the delegation left to come home, but somehow expressing his worry to this stranger had released tension.

Because Zo desperately wanted to believe there was something like hope.

Chapter Twenty-Five

It's lonely here and I miss him. It's been years since he passed, but I've finally finished my epic for him. I'm sending it to the Library for safe keeping. It needs to be there in case another dragon comes. Praedo was certain they would come, and uncertain if another Dragon Slayer would be sent. He gave us his magic so we could be prepared. I fear the power is going to their heads. They have engaged in the silliest squabbles.

— From Luc's Journals

Ryn, Regg, and Yll sat on the bench facing forward in the carriage, while Uncle Mik sat opposite them. His red hair reflected the light, while his eyes sparkled with excitement. Ryn had sandwiched herself between Regg and the window, preferring to be squished than sit next to an uncle she barely knew. Regg sat in the middle between the two girls with his arms crossed, his face almost daring Ryn's uncle to try something. Meanwhile Uncle Mik was happily giving them the history and background of the places they were passing on the road.

"Lavender grows well on the island. You'll find more than one field of it. In the summertime the smell is intoxicating. Did you know you can drink lavender in your tea like chamomile? It tastes wonderful, especially when mixed with other herbs."

"Yes, I love it," Yll said.

Ryn was barely listening to her uncle. She was worried about where he was taking them, and what could happen. Ryn understood that this was her family, but now Regg and Yll were along for the ride. Ryn worried she had brought them into her trouble, and now they might be in danger as well. She hoped not. She hoped everyone was wrong about her family. Uncle Mik had been agreeable enough to take her to the village. He told them he just wanted to stop one place first.

"Your mother loved to run and play in the lavender fields when she was little. She would come home so fragrant her nanny, who was allergic to flowers, would be sneezing the rest of the day." Uncle Mik chuckled at the memory.

Ryn watched the last of the tufts of lavender plants move past the window. She could almost see her mother as a little girl running and laughing.

They entered a tunnel of overhanging trees. Ryn had to admit they were fascinating. The cloudy sky darkened as the pine branches overhead became thick. At the end of the tunnel the road turned and Ryn gasped. The building they were driving to was twice as big as the Library, with a huge thick wall around it. The building was made of stone, but was newly cut and smooth. The whiteness of the stone shone bright even on the cloudy day. The roof at the front was made of something other than wood, that gave the building a sleek look.

Uncle Mik laughed. "That's the new building for the Library. Do you like it?"

Ryn checked herself before she said "yes" too eagerly. She didn't want to seem impressed.

There were House Viator guards at the gate and on the walls. They stopped the carriage, but waved them on when they saw Ryn's uncle. The building was surrounded by the largest, most elaborate garden Ryn had ever seen. Even in the winter there was color everywhere. There were statues and fountains, a feast for the eye that would be a welcome relief to walk among while puzzling out a particularly difficult research problem.

They pulled into a circular drive and the carriage stopped at the bottom of the stairs to the main entrance.

"Do you want to see inside?" Uncle Mik asked.

"Yes!" Ryn and Yll both squealed at the same time, Ryn clapping her hand over her mouth.

"Jinx, you owe her," Regg said.

"Which one of us owes who?" Yll asked.

Regg shrugged, then grinned at them. "Whoever gets something first."

Uncle Mik bounded out of the carriage and helped Ryn down. As he led her up the steps, she glanced back to see Regg and Yll following.

At the top of the stairs, they entered a grand doorway elaborately carved with scenes of Praedo slaying the dragon. The doors swung open to reveal a soaring ceiling. Windows rose all the way to the top letting light cascade down onto a giant fountain which was a marble statue of Praedo's last struggle with the dragon. Water cascaded from the dragon's mouth into a large pool ringed by a low wall. The bottom of the pool was an elaborate mosaic with tiles swirling in bright colors that reflected the conflict happening at the fountain's center. The entirety of the wall behind the statue was also a mosaic depicting Praedo's bestowal of his magic upon the ancestors. The entry was circular like the Library, but instead of being ringed by statues of the ancestors, the walls had four quotes, one on each wall at the points of the compass. Each quote was something attributed to Praedo.

The most spectacular feature was the ceiling made entirely of glass. Between the tall windows and the glass ceiling, even on the darkest day, the entry would be full of light.

Ryn clamped her jaw shut so she wouldn't stand their staring with her mouth hanging open. The grandness and splendor of it surpassed anything she had ever seen—even drawings in books. She didn't think there was anywhere else in this world as spectacular as this entryway.

As much as she loved the mosaic ceiling in the Library, the one on the wall here certainly rivaled, if not surpassed it. The windows and glass ceiling were designed to illuminate the scene perfectly. Ryn stared into Praedo's eyes and thought of the voice she had heard during the Ghost Festival. *Look no further than to who you already are.* It came back to her clearly. She had forgotten much of what happened that evening at the Ghost Festival, because of the Spirit magic. Now as she looked upon Praedo holding the beads in his hands to give to his companions, it echoed in her head.

Uncle Mik cleared his throat. Ryn tore her eyes away to look at him. On his face was a huge grin.

"Come this way, I have something to show you," he said.

They followed him to the right and down the hall. One side of the hall was all windows, and the other was a wall, hung with portraits. Uncle Mik pointed to one of the portraits.

"These are all former Patriarchs of House Viator. What do you think—do I look like my great grandfather?" Uncle Mik stood next to the portrait and posed like the man in the painting.

Yll giggled.

Ryn looked between the two. "I think you do."

"Great, I shall make a distinguished Patriarch as soon as my uncle dies."

Ryn smiled.

"Beautiful smile! This way." Uncle Mik pulled open a door next to the portrait and ushered them inside.

Ryn couldn't help but think it was awfully bold of House Viator to hang pictures of themselves in the potential new "Library."

Inside there were rows upon rows of empty shelves waiting for books and other Library materials. It had all the beauty of clean organization, and none of the haphazard delight of her Library. Uncle Mik led them down the side to the far end, where they found shelves occupied with books.

"Are these from the House Viator library?" Ryn asked.

"No. Actually, these are from the Library, brought over as a good will trust by the delegation."

Ryn shut her mouth tight on the outraged exclamation she wanted to make. Yll, however, made a strangled noise in her throat.

Who in the Library thought bringing materials here was a good idea? Ryn thought.

Uncle Mik had a frozen smile on his face. "Come this way, let me show you something wondrous."

On a table were set a reference book and a few other books.

Uncle Mik moved to the other side of the table. "We have put the very best researcher minds to the task of finding a better system to organize materials in the Library. In the current system, Library materials are organized by type and in order of acquisition." He wrote a few types of materials on a piece of paper—books, bound documents, loose documents. "Then they are carefully added to the reference books." He continued by writing numbers on the paper. "The new system will group materials by subject, and each material will be assigned a number within that subject." Next to the number 100 he wrote "birth records," 200 was "marriage records" and so on. 900 was books on topics such as nature or philosophy. "With everything grouped together it will be easy, for example, to simply go to a certain section of the Library to search birth records."

"But books are already grouped by subject in the Library," Ryn said.

Uncle Mik pointed at her. "Yes, but are they in some sort of order?"

"Well, I mean, the books on plants and animals are on the same floor."

Yll pointed to the paper. "This would be a huge mess. It would take years to reorganize the Library in such a manner. In the process of rearranging shelves, materials would be lost."

"We recognize the trouble of implementing such a system in the current Library. The Library is already overstuffed to capacity with scarcely the space for its new acquisitions. Having the room to rearrange the shelves in this manner would be difficult, and you are correct, materials could get misplaced." He paused, his twinkling eyes. "However, if we move the Library here, to this facility, built to accommodate all the material in the Library and more, we could organize it into this system as we shelve it.

"Ryn, tell me, what is your typical process to find the birth record for a progenitor?"

She cleared her throat. "Well, that would depend upon where the person was from."

"Pretend for me you have only a name and a date." Uncle Mik's eyes danced. She sensed a trap in this no matter how she answered.

"Well, I would begin in the reference books for that date. That would lead me to special collections, the documents archive, as well as the basic collections."

"So you would be all over the Library, up and down the stairs just to track down a birth record."

"Yes, but..."

"You see the beauty of the new system already. With this all of the birth records—no matter their type—would be in one place in the Library. If you needed to research birth records, the birth record section is where you would be—not up and down stairs, pulling them from all over, bringing them back to your desk, without the potential of the materials getting lost in the process, or misshelved, wasting time, and wasting energy."

Uncle Mik handed them a piece of paper, its subjects divided by certain numbers. "Now, look here, what is the number for books about birds?"

"It looks like we would find birds in the 940s," Yll said, reading over Ryn's shoulder.

Uncle Mik gestured to the shelves with the books on them. "Go find it for me."

The shelves started in the 100s so they quickly moved to the last row. Partway down the row they found the books on birds.

"This is incredible!" Yll exclaimed, then quickly covered her mouth.

"Yes," Ryn's whisper hissed out. "It is."

* * *

Ryn found she was reluctant to leave the building. The fact that the books and materials were kept in the middle, inside walls to protect them from the light, but the halls were lined with floor to ceiling windows lifted Ryn's heart. It was the perfect setting, The books stayed safe, but researchers could work in the light. She hated to even think it, but the new system of cataloging, plus the building and grounds, were ideal. There couldn't be a better place for the Library's materials. Yet it lacked the heart and soul of the Library. The character that the multiple rooms and hidden passages gave it. There was no magic. This new facility was a researcher's dream, but the old Library was Ryn's heart.

"There is one thing that is a problem," Ryn said as they rode over the grassy hills. "What about protection for the Library. You didn't say anything about a protective magic for the Library and its materials."

Uncle Mik shrugged. "I think the protective magic has been a crutch really. You have a quarantine for new materials, but no one takes it seriously or that new docent would have never have been able to shelve unquarantined materials. And as we have seen over the past moon, the magic can clearly be circumvented. I do believe starting with a clean slate, with a new facility that has all the updated conveniences is all that the Library needs. The Wild magic is full of ancient superstitions. It's best we break from that and rely on the Ancestors to protect the Library."

That was really the heart of it to Ryn. The new building felt soulless. Her Library beat to the heart of knowledge and family. The new building was wondrous, but her Library was home.

The carriage came to a stop, and Ryn shook her head and realized they were already in the village.

"Here we are, Viatoro's only tailor," Uncle Mik said as he opened the carriage door.

He helped Ryn down, then Yll passed Ryn's dress box to her. Ryn clutched the box trying to think of a way to lose her uncle for a while.

"Ummm...It would be nice if we could stretch our legs a bit and wander around the village. Do you mind giving us some time? Maybe pick us up after lunch?" Ryn asked.

Uncle Mik frowned, and Ryn shrank down.

"I had hoped to bring you up to the House for lunch." Uncle Mik surveyed the village. "But I suppose you should get to know the village. This is your home, you should experience it to the fullest. I'll return after noon."

Uncle Mik bent and kissed Ryn on the cheek. Then he climbed back into the carriage, knocked on the roof and the driver pulled away.

"Yes! We have the rest of the morning to explore." Regg grinned.

They headed into the shop and Ryn immediately missed Thax.

"I'll wait outside," Regg said, leaning against the wall.

The shop was small and cramped. The clothes on display definitely lacked Thax's flair.

"Can I help you?" asked a small man, hardly taller than Ryn. He had a measuring tape around his neck and scissors in his hands.

"Yes," Ryn put the dress box on the counter. "I have this dress, but it needs some minor alterations. I have a formal dinner party to attend this evening. Is it possible to get it altered before then?"

Ryn lifted the lid to the box and the tailor gasped. "Is this Master Thax's work?" His eyes were bulging. "We have been wondering what the latest fashion of the season from his shop would be." He eyed Ryn and Yll. "He's been very secretive about his new collection."

Ryn raised her eyebrow and gave Yll a puzzled look. She shrugged. "Well, his assistant brought it to me before I left, said it was a gift from him."

The tailor turned red. "That scoundrel! He knew you would bring it to me to alter. He wants to torment me with a glimpse of his latest work." He pulled the dress from the box and held it up, muttering to himself as he examined its construction and decoration. Eventually he handed it to Ryn. "Well, put it on so we can see what needs to be done. I have several things that need finishing for that Library delegation reception at House Viator tonight, but I will try to squeeze yours in."

"This is also for the dinner at House Viator," Yll said.

The tailor lifted an eyebrow, then his eyes drifted up and down the girls sizing them up. "A dress the color of wine, eh?" He sniffed. "Well then, I shall make sure it is done and delivered in plenty of time to dress for the reception."

"Thank you so much." Ryn clutched the dress to her. "I really appreciate it."

He waved his hand. "Behind that curtain, hurry up, I have a lot of work to do today!"

Yll had retrieved the orphanage book from the box while the tailor was pinning Ryn's dress for the changes it needed. It really only needed to be hemmed, the rest fit her perfectly. Ryn wondered how much it really was something Thax had lying around or if he had intentionally made it to her measurements needing to be hemmed only. He knew she would end up here showing off his latest work. He really was sly.

The girls left the tailor's shop giggling, as Regg rejoined them. They had left the tailor muttering while he put the dress on a dress form. They turned right and headed up the street as per the tailor's instructions to get to the master book binder's shop. The morning clouds had dissipated, and the sun was glorious in a bright sparkling sky and warm on their backs. The town bustled with people.

"Shouldn't we be seeing more people transporting themselves, like suddenly appearing and disappearing," Yll asked. "I mean, this is Viatoro—most people here have travel magic."

Ryn shook her head. "Probably not in the middle of town, it can get breezy when you travel with magic." Ryn looked at the people around her.

"Or they're just too snooty to use it," Regg said.

"Or you've been listening to your brother too much," Yll said.

"Look." Regg pointed as they passed a jewelry maker. There were promise necklaces in the window.

Yll pointed to one of the necklaces which had purple stones held within a swirling cage of silver. The scroll work was intricate and unique.

"Oh, it's so beautiful!" Yll exclaimed.

Regg nodded. "Purple, like lavender."

Ryn shook her head, and pulled on Yll's arm. "Come on, we don't have all day."

"Yeah, whatever." Yll waved her hand at Ryn. "Let's find this book binder."

* * *

Ryn's hand shook as she placed it on the latch to the shop. This was it, the moment she had been waiting for, the moment when she would discover where she needed to go to find her birth parents. It was a strange feeling. She only knew her mother and her father. Somewhere out there was a family she had never met, but was related to. Somewhere there were people who looked like her. They were strangers, but she was connected to them. She wanted to find them. She needed to find them.

"Hello?" Ryn called.

A cat jumped into the chair next to the fireplace. Yll knelt in from of it.

"Hello Master Clark. Master Maurice send us to you..."

An old man, bent with age with long silver hair tied into a ponytail shuffled into the room from the back.

"That's my cat Lester, he's not me," the old man said.

"Oh!" Yll turned bright red and stood. "Sorry, Master Maurice is..."

"And he's not me is he?" Master Clark shuffled over to his chair, scooted Lester over, and sat.

Ryn clutched the orphanage book to her chest and knelt before him.

"Master Clark, we were told the binding on this book is your work. I am in desperate need of tracking down its former owner. Could you possibly help us locate them?" She fought to keep the sudden tears from her eyes, but couldn't help the swelling of emotion.

Master Clark gave her a troubled look, then he sighed. "Let me see it."

She placed the book gently on his lap. He barely glanced at it.

"This is my work, but as you can see, I make dozens of these." He gestured to the walls.

Ryn noticed them for the first time. They were lined with bookshelves packed with books. Every table and surface in the shop seemed to be piled high with books. Many of those books looked identical to her orphanage book. Ryn's heart sank.

Yll put a hand on Master Clark's shoulder. "Can you help my friend at all? She came all the way from Waatch, to find you. This book is the only clue she has to finding her family."

His eyes shifted to Yll, then back to Ryn. His hands left the book and it almost slid off his lap. "So it's power you crave." His mouth twisted into a sneer.

Was it? Was this all about magic and gaining power? Was this all about fitting in with the rest of the world? Or was there something more? Ryn shook her head. "No. I just want to know who I am and where I came from. Please."

He looked long and hard into her eyes. He seemed to find what he wanted, because his eyes shifted to the book and he opened the cover. He gasped when he saw the missing pages and tutted over them. He flipped through the book for a bit then closed it. "House Viator often buys my journal entry type books to donate to charities. Being an orphanage book, this was most likely donated. I would inquire at the Manor House for records, it's possible they could tell you what orphanage this was donated to." He struggled to hand the book back to Ryn, but his arms lacked the strength, so she collected it from his lap. "If you'll excuse me, I'm overdue for my morning nap." With that he leaned back and closed his eyes. Lester moved from his side onto his now free lap.

She stood. "Thank you, Master Clark, we appreciate your time."

Ryn had been through this disappointment before. She was trying to get used to it, and not feel it so keenly, but the sun had come out and the bright sunny sky and cold crisp air made her eyes water. At least that is what she would tell Yll if she asked.

Yll knew though. She put her arm through Ryn's and pulled her closer to her. "We still have some time before noon—let's see if we can find a tea shop. I'm craving some salmon salad sandwiches!"

They found a little place with a table that overlooked the water of a large bay. This harbor was where the majority of sea traffic came to the island. The cove they had landed in was for private guests of House Viator only. Ryn watched the people on the docks come and go, loading and unloading ships. The sun sparkled on the water making it almost too bright to look at directly. Yll nibbled her sandwich as Ryn sipped her tea.

"It's not over yet," Yll said, eyeing Ryn.

She sighed. "I know, it's just that I get the feeling sneaking a look at House Viator's records is going to be a challenge."

"Why sneak? Just ask," Regg said, ever practical like his brother.

Ryn shrugged. "I don't know. I'm worried. They are powerful people. Will I even have an opportunity to ask?"

Yll looked out over the water for a while. "Well, we'll figure something out. Until then"—she held up another sandwich and grinned—"salmon salad!"

* * *

They were headed back down the street to where they were to meet their carriage when a hand shot out of an alley and pulled Ryn into it. She started to scream, but a hand clamped over her mouth.

"SHHHHH!" A familiar voice whispered. "It's me."

Ryn looked up into Schiz's face. "Schiz...how are you here?"

He released her. His eyes were wet with tears, and frantic at the same time. "I had to come...Even though this place is not safe for me."

She pulled back. "What's going on?"

Schiz peeked around the corner then drew back to face Ryn. "No time to...explain." His brow furrowed like he was trying to focus hard. His hand drifted to his temple and tapped. "I was...sent to be here with you."

Anger flared inside her. She was starting to really hate having so many minders. "By who? No, never mind, I don't want to know. I have a job to do, and I'm going to do it." She held the orphanage book up. "I am so close to finding the answers I can taste it." She took a deep breath so her voice would carry as much force as she could muster. "I need to stay."

Schiz's eyes were fixed on the orphanage book. "Where did you find that?"

"In the Library. Long story, but I'm pretty sure it will show me where to go to find my family."

Schiz nodded. "So be it."

Ryn studied Schiz. "You were one of my grandmother's experiments, weren't you?"

Schiz went still. She'd never seen him this still. His head dropped.

"What did they do?"

Schiz peaked around the alley corner. "It's not safe to talk about."

"I need to know. I think they used my brother Jett."

Schiz's cheeks turned red. "I...was once much favored of the House...and I did try it."

"What happened?" Ryn asked, trying to keep her patience, knowing Uncle Mik could be back any minute.

"I traveled there...to the Origin...the place where Praedo slayed the dragon...it is a terrible place." Schiz paced back down the alley, his fingers tapping at his temple. He turned back. "My Water magic...we thought it would dissipate the sword's power...We were wrong."

"What does the sword do?"

Schiz's eyes lit up like they were on fire. "Power! Such terrible power! No way to control it. It crushes you to dust inside."

Ryn's brow furrowed. Nothing he was saying made sense.

"If your brother has gone there, he is gone." Schiz's chin trembled, and his eyes were wet. "And I am here to keep you from going."

A carriage drove by the alley startling Ryn. When it had passed, Schiz was gone.

Chapter Twenty-Six

Journal ???

I tried, but I just look like some kind of strange person. I'm sure she's afraid of me. How could she possibly trust me? And yet I know everything. I hold all the answers, if only my stupid brain could connect properly to my mouth! Well, I will hide outside in the woods, and pray to the Ancestors for some sign if I'm needed to keep them from taking her to the Origin.

— From the Journals of Schiz

Nix stopped Zo on his way into the Boiler Room.

"You need to go help Wilmar. The flu going around this winter has been particularly bad the past few says, and he's exhausted and overwhelmed," Nix said.

"But I have a temperature shift, and I'm avoiding that part of town right now. I don't want to run into my mother."

"I'll take your shift. Go to Wilmar's through the back garden...Please."

Zo was taken aback. He'd never seen Nix this concerned.

"Sure. I'll go."

Relief flooded Nix's face. "Thank you."

Zo changed direction toward the Library west gate. It was a hard turn for him to switch his mind from Library work to physician's work, but he figured he had the walk across town to get his mind into it.

As soon as he crossed the street from the Library, his mother's thugs approached him.

"Your mother wants to meet with you," Thug number one said. His muscles were bursting out of his uniform.

"I don't want to see her." Zo turned and continued on his way.

Thug number two reached out and grabbed Zo's arm. Zo shrugged him off.

"I won't be manhandled again. See that Library guard standing by the gate?" Zo pointed.

The thugs turned to the west gate. Fergus waved at them.

"Try anything funny again and my friend Fergus there will bring down the Library guard on you." Zo paused. "Hard."

Thug number two removed his hand from Zo and stepped back. Muscle Thug put his hands up which made his chest muscles stand out.

They let him walk away, so Zo tried taking the most confusing path to Wilmar's he could find. He used Keir's technique of hopping a few fences. He wasn't sure how well that worked in the daylight, but he hoped he lost them. The last thing he needed was for his mother to know he was across the street from the Healing House.

When he finally walked through the back door from Wilmar's garden, he entered into utter chaos. The room was filled with patients coughing and sneezing. The door to the street was open and patients were lined up out into the street. Wilmar looked up from examining someone's tonsils and sighed in relief.

"Zo, thank goodness. Grab an apron and some gloves and start looking at patients. If you can send them on their way with some medicine, do so. If they need to be seen by me, have them sit on the recovery bed."

Wilmar was pale, and his eyes had dark circles under them. Zo hadn't been gone that long, only since his mother had shown up, and Zo couldn't risk being seen across from the Healing House. He was instantly worried about Wilmar and set about getting rid of the line of patients so Wilmar could get some rest.

He saw patient after patient, giving them ointments and syrups to clear up coughs and runny noses. He was beginning to see why Wilmar had him constantly crushing herbs over the past couple moons adding to the wall of medicines. Even still, Wilmar's supply seemed to be getting low. Someone puked in the mop bucket. Zo got them cleaned up and sent on their way with something to soothe their stomach, but the line didn't stop. It wasn't getting any shorter. Frustrated, Zo started using a bit of his healing magic while he examined the patients. He was trying to identify the illness affecting them all so maybe he could stop the spread. It wasn't one of the lessons he'd had yet from Madame Sano, nor from the Healing House, but he felt he could figure it out on his own. Couldn't be that hard to find diseased cells and get rid of them.

He eventually thought he identified what he was looking for. Most of the patients who were coughing and sneezing had the same illness. Some of them did not. He did what he could to get rid of it.

He was working on a girl who had, for a change from what he'd been seeing, had some severe burns on her arm. She was already shivering with fever from infection. Her father hovered over her, wringing his hat in his hands. Zo pulled his pantleg up a little so he could press his ankle to her bare ankle and use his Healing magic to kill the infection. He would have to thank Keir for teaching him that trick later. He was putting burn ointment on her arm, and wrapping it in ice when his Healing bead started to burn.

He looked down at his collar and said, "Now?"

Wilmar sensed something was up. "What's going on?"

"Madame Sano wants to give me a lesson *right now*."

Wilmar looked up at the line that was still out the door and sighed. "Well, you don't have a choice. Go find out what the old bat wants."

Zo laughed.

Wilmar's brow furrowed and he whispered to Zo, "Don't tell her I called her that." As if Madame Sano could hear him. Maybe she could.

Zo pushed past the curtain into Wilmar's private quarters. He sat down on Wilmar's bed, pulled his long legs cross legged onto the bed and leaned back against the wall. Closing his eyes, he waited.

Zo of Ingis, I swear on this green earth I don't know what to do with you.

Madame Sano's voice came faster than Zo thought it would. He had hoped he might get to doze off for a few.

"Yes, Madame Sano."

Don't Madame Sano me, I know you're over there thinking about the fastest way to get rid of me.

Actually, Zo had decided to just go along with whatever so he could get rid of her faster. Since he'd returned to studying Healing, his lessons with her had increased. He'd learned the more he fought, the longer his lessons took.

"Yes Madame."

Ugh. Hopeless child. I've come because you've been naughty.

"That seems pretty normal."

Worse than usual. This is serious. You have the taint of Killing magic on you.

Zo startled and sat up. "What?"

Don't "what" me. You've been in proximity to Killing magic, and since you haven't finished your lessons yet, or taken your oath I'm here to give you a portion of that final lesson you will get when you are finished studying Healing.

Zo relaxed back, his head on the wall, trying to calm himself. He thought no one would know about his little encounter with Keir. "So let's hear it."

Insolent child. You have no idea what you are messing with. In all magics there is a reverse. In every one, the inverse of the magic is forbidden. You are not meant to hear this until your final lesson. It is a highly guarded secret.

"Why? Doesn't secrecy breed exploration? You should be upfront with this knowledge."

We don't tell students till they are ready to take their oaths, oaths that prevent them from using the inverse of the magic. We don't teach it so there is no curiosity.

"This is not preventing students from exploring."

Any who do will be punished by the Healing Council. I'm here to warn you—use Healing magic to kill and there will be severe consequences, the least of which will be the termination of your lessons at once. I cannot abide in someone who wishes harm, rather than help.

Zo nodded. "I understand."

Madame Sano grunted like she didn't believe him.

"Could you possibly show me how to track down and identify a disease to eliminate it?"

Madame Sano was silent. Zo imagined her with her jaw dropped. *Uh, I mean, yes, I think you are ready for that.*

"Good."

And his lesson began.

* * *

The sunlight was fading fast. Zo finished up the last couple patients, fed Wilmar some leftover chicken he found, and put him to bed. He locked the exam room door, so no one would disturb Wilmar till he woke, then he headed out the back door.

A dark figure emerged from behind one of the bushes. Zo snapped his figures and brought fire to his hands.

"Whoa, whoa, it's just me."

Zo held up the fire to Keir's face. He shook out his hands.

"What are you doing in Wilmar's garden?"

"Waiting for you. I saw you through the door seeing patients today, so I came over when you closed up."

Great, Zo thought, *I hope my mother didn't see me.*

"I'm really tired, what is it you need?" Zo headed to the back fence.

As they were passing a bench under the bare branched cherry tree, Keir took Zo's hand and pulled him down to sit next to him.

"You disappeared the other night. I wanted to ask what you thought," Keir said.

All of Madame Sano's warnings were spinning through Zo's head.

"Have you had any lessons from Madame Sano lately?" Zo asked.

Keir scoffed. "I don't need her. I know everything I need to know. I'm the most powerful Healer at the Healing House. Having double the magic from my father and my mother makes me strong."

"I have felt your Healing power, it is great."

Zo pushed aside Keir's, for once, unfashionably high collar. Keir's bead necklace was gone, and there were no bead scars to indicate he'd finished his lessons. It looked like what Madame Sano said was right, if you did Killing magic, your lessons ceased. The idea of getting rid of Madame Sano had its appeal, but helping people was much more appealing.

Keir's many ringed fingers caught Zo's hand and pulled him closer. "You're the most talented, powerful Healing student in Waatch, and you like to buck the rules. I like that. You're like me. We fit together."

He leaned in and kissed Zo. It was slow and sweet at first, his lips barely brushing Zo's like gentle feathers. It grew in intensity and need, till Keir consumed Zo's whole mouth, for once setting Zo's body on fire without the aid of his Healing magic. Zo fell into it hard. Keir's mouth was pure pleasure, and his questing fingers left Zo breathless. His mind went blank with need. He wanted more. So much more.

Keir pulled his mouth away and whispered in Zo's ear. "Come with me. There's another meeting tonight. I have a place for us afterward where we can bask in the glory of each other."

Keir nibbled on Zo's ear which elicited an involuntary moan. Keir was so intoxicating. Every part of Zo's body remembered the breakfast, and Keir's toe snaking up his leg. Zo quiver in anticipation. His body was ready to do anything Keir wanted.

Mess around but chose me. Zo could hear Iden's voice. In the heat of the moment, he took it as permission. He brought Keir's mouth back to his and kissed him harder and deeper than he'd ever kissed anyone. His hands roamed over Keir's fit chest. It lacked the muscles Zo preferred, but he was still cut. Zo's tongue found a particular spot and this time Keir broke away gasping.

"This is going to be the best night of my life," Keir said.

Zo couldn't agree more. He went in for another kiss, but a small, tiny mew grabbed his attention. Keir noticed it too.

The mew came again louder, and two eyes shone in the dark inside the bush next to the bench. Zo took a deep breath, and shook himself. He reached out his hand. A tiny gray kitten hissed at him, then sniffed his fingers and rubbed its soft head against his hand. Zo reached down and scooped the kitten up. Holding it close to his chest, it started to purr.

"Kitten! Perfect, bring it with us, we'll go to my loft, and we can enjoy a kill *and* each other before the meeting starts." Keir leaned in and began nibbling on Zo's ear again.

Zo held the kitten close and stood.

Keir smiled and got to his feet next to Zo. "I like eagerness." He slipped his arm around Zo's waist.

Zo jerked away.

"Something wrong?" Keir asked.

Zo gently stroked the kitten's head. It mewed.

"This is going to feel fantastic, I promise." Keir reached out a hand to the kitten.

"No."

Keir's eyes snapped to Zo's. "What do you mean no? I know you're into it, and me. Don't deny it. I could feel your passion in your kiss."

"*No.* I'm not into it. I'm not killing a tiny kitten. That's not who I am. I'm tired. It's been a long day of patients. I'm heading home." Zo cradled the kitten against him with one hand, and hopped the fence into the next yard with the other.

Keir landed next to him. "Another night then."

Keir reached for Zo, but Zo moved out of reach. Keir took his hand back.

"I don't think so," Zo said.

"You're going to regret this choice," Keir spat.

Zo let out a long cleansing breath. "I don't think so."

Frowning, Keir turned and walked away.

Zo lifted the kitten to his face. "Looks like I made my choice, and it's Iden." he told the kitten.

The kitten mewed. Zo took long strides toward his Library home. He would have left the kitten with Wilmar—he needed a good mouser for the winter—but Zo didn't want anything to disturb Wilmar's rest. Maybe he would bring the kitten back later.

With that thought, Zo put as much distance between himself and what happened in the garden as he could.

* * *

Zo opened his dorm room door to find Iden waiting for him. A flood of relief swept over Zo, and tears threatened his eyes. Relief that he hadn't gone with Keir. Relief that Iden was here when Zo didn't deserve it. Iden stood and wrapped his arms around Zo.

Iden frowned. "Rough day?"

"Something like that."

Iden went to tighten his hug, but Zo stopped him, pulling back. Iden gave him a curious look until Zo pulled the kitten out from inside his coat.

"Oh my goodness! Where did you find him? He's adorable!"

Iden took the little kitten from Zo and started cooing and talking to the kitten who mewed back at him. They were having their own little conversion.

Zo stood back and wiped tears from his eyes. He laughed as Iden went to Zo's cupboard and found a bit of cheese to give the kitten.

"Zo doesn't drink milk, we'll have to find you some," Iden told the kitten.

Zo smiled. This was everything. This was home. He wanted nothing else, but to shut away the world, and stay here.

Iden looked to Zo. "Are you hungry? I have a restaurant in mind for dinner."

Zo nodded. "I would love that."

* * *

Iden took him to this place that specialized in food from Oydico, the home of Iden's Ancestral House. It lacked the usual emphasis on fish, but had lots of cheeses, and was heavy on the vegetables and winter squashes. The blended butternut soup, with carrots and a hint of ginger was exceptional. The cheese grated on top made it a reason to return frequently to the restaurant.

At the end of the meal Iden smiled at Zo contentedly, rubbing his stomach.

Zo turned thoughtful. "You once said you wished to live on Oydico, and learn to live in a community without verbal communication."

Iden became quiet, examining his hands. "I did once dream of that, but it was only because I wished to escape a pending arranged marriage."

His eyes lifted to Zo's, the candlelight reflected in them was a sparkle and a twinkle. He held a hand out to Zo.

"Come. I have something to show you."

Iden led Zo over a few streets then down one of Waatch wheel spoke streets. He stopped in front of a shop that had clothes displayed in the window.

"It's late. That shop is closed," Zo said.

Iden just grinned and knocked on the door.

After a few minutes, a man in a robe opened it to them.

"Zo, I don't believe you've met the Waatch tailor, Thax," Iden said.

"I've heard so much about you," Thax said, greeting them with kisses on both cheeks and fussing over what they were wearing.

"Come in, Tory is waiting," Thax said.

Iden led Zo through the shop to the back where two dress forms stood with two suits on them. One had a navy-blue coat and waistcoat with gray slacks and the other had navy-blue slacks with a gray waistcoat and coat. Both were embroidered with the same design of flowers in oranges, browns, and golds. The gold thread caught the light, and made the embroidery shimmer.

"These are gorgeous, Thax," Zo said.

"I'm glad you like them," Iden said, then he took Zo's hands, his eyes drifting down to them, his thumb absently rubbing the back of Zo's hand.

When Iden's eyes lifted to Zo's they were full of earnestness and maybe a little fear. "I had Thax make these suits for us. Will you attend the Winter Solstice Ball with me?"

Zo's heart leapt. There was nothing more that Zo wanted than to spend time dancing the night away with Iden, but as he opened his mouth to say 'yes' the reality of what Iden was asking hit him.

Everybody who was anybody would be at that ball, that included Library staff, Healing House staff and students, and Waatch's wealthy merchants. It would be the equivalent of declaring to all the world who and what he was. It was terrifying. Ancestor Houses had strict rules and penalties against dating someone of the same sex. If he lived on Eileansano the Healing Council could send him to Exile for being in a same sex relationship. Yet another reason he needed to get away from his mother.

On the other hand, he lived in Waatch where those laws were unenforceable.

And there was a possibility his mother might attend the ball, if she's still in town by then. Zo had flinched at telling her who Iden was before.

Zo's eyes drifted to the two suits. They were the finest Zo had seen, the hand embroidery taking hundreds of hours to create. Zo imagined him and Iden entering the ball arm and arm. Zo's eyes shifted back to Iden's anxious ones.

"Yes, Iden de Dico, I will go to the ball with you."

Iden whooped, and Thax popped a cork out of a wine bottle.

"Let's celebrate!" Thax said, as Tory brought glasses and he poured the wine.

My Wildfire. Zo heard Iden's voice in his head as Iden came in to kiss Zo.

Zo's eyes bulged and his jaw dropped.

Iden stopped, his eyes searching Zo's face. "What is it?"

"I just heard you call me 'Wildfire' in my head."

Tears came to Iden's eyes. "You chose me. Our connection is solidified."

A dark shadow passed over Zo and his vision dimmed. He stumbled, and Iden reached out, grabbing Zo to support him. Thax pulled up a chair and put it under Zo while Iden lowered him onto it. Everything went dark.

A voice rang inside Zo's head, *Help! Someone is breaking into the Library's heart!*

Although he'd never heard the voice, he somehow knew it was the Protector of the Library.

Chapter Twenty-Seven

Zmej,

This has been a horrendous embarrassment for House Viator. I expect you to deal with the problem with your usual efficiency.

Silas de Viator, Patriarch of House Viator

House Viator was so lit up with torches and lanterns the face of it glowed in the twilight of the setting sun. Red carpet spilled from the front door and down the steps. Servants of House Viator stood ready, but the guests had not yet begun to arrive. The carriage Ryn rode in with the core of the Library delegation was the only one approaching the house down the long drive. House Viator gave the appearance of stately age and wealth. It was easily almost as large as the Library.

"House Muto isn't this big!" Yll whispered.

"Everyone be on your toes tonight. Who knows what House Viator will be up to," Lar said.

Clayr sighed. "Their surprising hospitality and lack of menace since we arrived has me on edge. I keep waiting for them to drop whatever it is that they're going to drop on us."

Regg put his arm around Yll and pulled her protectively closer to him.

Clayr frowned at that.

When the carriage pulled to a stop at the bottom of the stairs, Uncle Mik was standing there to greet them as they exited the carriage.

Ryn stepped out in her wine-colored gown. The bodice was embroidered in swirling gold threading. The embroidery began at her, thankfully, high collar and traveled down the front to circle her waist. Her long sleeves were tight to her arms, making it hard for her to lift them as she reached for Uncle Mik's hand. Her skirt barely brushed the top of her shoes as she landed on the carpet—the perfect length. The Viatoro tailor did a fine job.

"So glad you all could make it here early. There is much to discuss," he said, as he put Ryn's hand on his arm and led her up the red carpeted stairs.

Lar was scarcely a pace behind Ryn. She was glad he had her back, because the moment she stepped from the carriage, her stomach had filled with butterflies. Here she was, a simple girl who grew up in a cottage in the woods, suddenly being treated as the daughter of the Matriarch in Waiting for one of the most powerful Ancestral Houses. It was unbelievable. Despite her misgivings, and all the warnings she'd been given, she suddenly longed for it all to be true—even though she knew she didn't fit in here.

The entrance to House Viator had soaring ceilings and gilded scrollwork that made the guest house seem like a quaint cabin in the woods. To one side was a floor to ceiling painting of an elderly woman, and on the other side was a portrait of a man. Their facial features were similar and somehow familiar.

"That's your grandmother and your great uncle," Uncle Mik said.

What stopped Ryn mid stride though was the portrait next to her grandmother's.

It was a painting of Ryn's mother when she was about Ryn's age. Her strawberry blond hair was pulled back from her face and cascaded down her shoulder in ringlet curls. She wore a dress in a deep color of wine that flowed over the edge of the velvety sofa she was seated upon. Her hands rested on an open book as if she had just glanced up from reading. It was perfectly her mother, and yet to see this giant portrait of her at the entrance to this magnificent house felt wrong to Ryn.

"My sister is a stunning beauty," Uncle Mik said.

Ryn felt him move away, only to find him standing in the same position as his own portrait on the opposite wall. He had an exaggerated frown, with his nose held high in a mockery of the serious face on his own portrait. Ryn giggled.

They passed between the portraits into a large hall.

"This is where the bead ceremonies take place for House Viator. We shall return here later," Uncle Mik said.

Just then a man stepped through a side door into the room. He looked like the portrait of Ryn's great uncle, but much younger, dressed in full House Viator colors, a rich deep wine color with gold embroidery. She had to admit it was a handsome combination. He smiled and gave her an awkward wave—and Ryn realized it was her brother Jett.

Jett crossed the hall to her, and held out his arm. She was so stunned she could hardly register what he was doing.

He leaned down and whispered to her, "Take my arm. I'll show you to the library."

Tentatively, Ryn put her hand on his arm. He led her out of the hall and down a passageway. When she recovered from her shock, she looked back and realized no one else was with them. She swallowed hard.

"It's good to see you," Jett said, his free hand tapped at his temple.

"Mother said you were here. I kind of didn't believe her," Ryn said.

"She knows I'm here, and yet she doesn't say anything to me? She's taken this feud with grandmother too far, really."

"She doesn't want to be used and manipulated."

"She's been in hiding for almost eighteen years for nothing. I did it. I used my magics, I went to the origin. I put my hand on the sword. There was a strong burst of power, but I'm fine." Jett lifted his hand to his temple and brushed back a stray hair.

Ryn narrowed her eyes at him. "So what powers did you add to yourself?"

Jett waved his hand. "It didn't work. All these years of scheming for this particular combination of magic, and it still didn't work. Grandmother and Grand Uncle are disappointed. It's not the outcome they were hoping for, and at a great cost. The biggest is Mother's betrayal of her House."

"If she's seen as a traitor, then why does her portrait still hang in the hall entry?"

"She is the closest in bloodline. Grandmother is still hoping Mother will change her mind and come back."

Ryn scoffed at that, but Jett stopped at a door. A servant, or maybe it was a guard, opened the door for them. Jett swept Ryn inside and the person closed the door behind them. Ryn's stomach dropped.

"What are we doing here?" Ryn asked.

"Waiting for Grandmother."

Ryn scanned the walls of books that went from the floor all the way up to the ceiling. At the top was another ceiling of glass. There was a study area at the top of a set of stairs, and a fireplace with cozy chairs underneath. It was the grandest home library Ryn had ever seen, though she could admit she hadn't seen many. Ryn would have been delighted if she didn't feel trapped.

"Why didn't you come to the guest house to see me if you knew I was here?" Ryn asked.

"Grandmother wanted it to be a surprise," Jett said.

It seemed more like her grandmother was hiding things. Ryn stood next to her brother, not knowing what to say. There had always been distance between them, but now it seemed greater. To distract herself, she focused on the room and its many shelves and books. As her gaze shifted from one shelf to another, a thought occurred to her.

"Do you know where they keep records of their donations? Specifically books?"

Jett's hand drifted to his temple and tapped at it. "I don't know, somewhere in this room probably."

Ryn couldn't find any reference books, but she noticed the sections were divided by numbers. Uncle Mik hadn't mentioned all the categories for the number system, but Ryn did find birth records in the 100s. She looked around, but it would take too much time to examine each section separately. She started opening drawers.

"What are you doing?" Jett's whisper was harsh.

"They keep telling me I'm part of this House, so I'm going to access it."

In a long flat drawer was a diagram that told what subject was in each numbered group. Charity and donation records were in the 500s, on the second tier.

Acutely aware she was rapidly running out of time, she lifted her skirts and raced up the stairs.

"I don't think that's wise. You shouldn't snoop through house records. Grandmother will be angry." Jett said.

Ryn scanned the spines of the books. Most of them looked like Master Clark's binding.

There! A book on charitable donations to orphanages.

Ryn opened it and began to scan it. It was a ledger with rows upon rows of donations to different orphanages on Viatoro as well as on the mainland. Some of them clearly didn't specify where the orphanage was located. There was money donated as well as cast off clothes, furnishings, and other items. There was mention of books, but no note as to what those books were.

She closed the book and fought the crushing weight of frustration on her chest.

"Shhhhhh, they are coming!" Jett hissed up at her.

Ryn agreed with Jett that it would be bad form to have them find her snooping through Viator records. She returned the book to the shelf, and descended the stairs as quickly as she dared in slippery dress shoes and long skirts.

She reached the bottom next to Jett just as the door opened and a tall, thin woman with graying hair pulled up into a tight roll on her head swept the room. Her dress was of a shimmering wine velvet that flowed around her feet as she walked. She was the most elegant woman Ryn had ever seen.

"Ah, there you are," she said, as if they had been lost.

Jett pulled Ryn forward. "Grandmother, this is my sister Ryn."

Ryn wasn't sure what was expected. Was she supposed to shake her hand, or give her a hug? Ryn opted for dropping into a curtsey.

"Well, at least your mother taught you manners out in the wild," her grandmother said, gesturing with one hand. "Come give your grandmama a hug."

Ryn walked forward till her grandmother could reach her. They barely touched. It definitely wasn't a "long-lost granddaughter, I'm so glad to meet you," hug.

"Now come, have a seat. I want to know my granddaughter."

Her grandmother sat in a chair by the fire and Ryn took the other.

"Tell me about yourself." her grandmother waved to someone by the door and a tea tray was brought in.

"Well, I work in the Library."

"Assistant Researcher, I've heard." her grandmother poured some tea for herself and for Ryn.

"Yes, well, I'm still learning so they haven't given me any research projects yet."

Her grandmother clicked her tongue. "That's a shame. Such a bright girl like you."

Ryn was sitting there wondering how her grandmother could know anything about how bright she was.

Her grandmother stirred her tea with a teaspoon. "Such a high collar for a descendant of House Viator. No beads?" Her grandmother sipped her tea.

"No." Ryn took a deep breath and swallowed hard. "I'm adopted."

"Nonsense. Tales your mother told you to keep you away from your family." Her grandmother waved a dismissive hand.

Ryn looked across the room to where Jett was standing watching. "You were there, tell her what you told me when I wanted to search for my birth family."

Jett cleared his throat and moved closer. "I'm only two years older than you, Ryn. I don't remember. All I remember is what Mother told me, and she could have told me anything. She already proved she could lie to us by hiding the fact that she came from House Viator."

Ryn's jaw dropped. She was glad she hadn't sipped any of the tea because she would be choking on it right now.

Her grandmother reached over and patted Ryn's hand. "We shall right this wrong my daughter has caused. You shall take your rightful place as the next in line after your mother."

"No, my mother couldn't have any more children, but she really wanted a daughter. She was distraught. My father found me in an orphanage, and brought me home to her. That's what *you* told me, Jett."

Jett's eyes dropped to the floor, his cheeks turned red. His right hand went to his temple again.

Ryn frowned at the gesture. *'The experiment didn't affect me', my foot.*

Her grandmother tapped her spoon on her teacup. "Yes, well, I'm sure your mother is full of tales, but we shall right everything tonight. Now I've heard you've been involved in some interesting research. Tell me about it." Her grandmother sipped at her tea.

"I really haven't done much, except catalog books in reference books then shelve them." Ryn took a drink of her tea as an effort to try and hide her half-truth.

"I've heard you've held one of Luc's lost journals in your hand." Her grandmother smiled behind her teacup.

Ryn took another sip. No one was supposed to know that. No one outside a small group of people loyal to Clayr anyway. Ryn's eyes narrowed as she thought of Jeris. He was awfully chummy with House Viator.

"I read it. All it contains is Luc's tales about Praedo and their adventures together, just like in the story books." Ryn looked her grandmother in the eye so she would know she told the truth.

Her grandmother absently nodded.

Ryn was suddenly relieved Yll hadn't written anything down from the journals yet. It was all still in Yll's head. Ryn hoped her grandmother didn't find out about that.

Someone knocked at the door.

"Come," her grandmother said.

"Guests are arriving."

"Then let us join them." Her grandmother rose in her House Viator colored dress, with gold embroidery around a collar Ryn felt was cut a bit low for a grandmother, sleeve cuffs, and the hem of her skirt.

Ryn's dress almost matched the color, and the design of the embroidery caught her eye for the first time. It was tiny thistles. Her grandmother's embroidery was larger thistles. Ryn's dress matched the scrolling stitches. Thax was clever indeed.

Jett came to Ryn's side, and she realized they were meant to be presented together to the guests. Uncle Mik appeared, and Ryn's grandmother took his arm. Jett explained that their great uncle was too frail for such a large event. Ryn puzzled over how large of an event it could be when they re-entered the Ceremony Hall and it was packed with guests. Somehow the crowd instinctively parted and her grandmother and Uncle Mik led the way to a raised platform at the back of the hall.

"Welcome esteemed guests. We are honored tonight by the presence of the Library Board regents, as well as the Library curator, and other dignitaries from Waatch. They have examined the new facility Viatoro has worked so hard to build, and have found it more than satisfactory."

There was applause throughout the audience.

"And now to a more personal matter for House Viator, I would like to introduce to all of you our long-lost heirs, my grandson, Jett de Pentral, and my granddaughter Ryn de Viator."

During the applause that followed, Ryn felt like she must be in some kind of dream. None of it felt real. She was in someone else's body, living someone else's life. The number of times she had dreamed of someone calling her Ryn de *something*. At the same time, no matter how much her grandmother protested, Ryn knew it wasn't true. She knew she didn't belong here.

Her grandmother held her head high. "Let us feast, then we shall reconvene here to make it all official, and after that we shall spend the rest of the evening celebrating our victory."

There was a cheer, then everyone started milling about and moving off through the doors down that lead away from the hallway to the library.

Yll and Regg were waiting at the bottom of the stairs to the platform.

"I can't believe you're going to be officially House Viator." Yll threw her arms around Ryn, giving her a hug. "Your grandmother's alright with you being adopted?"

Ryn didn't answer, her gaze was fixed on the crowd, chatting and celebrating.

"We were worried when they took you away without us," Regg said.

"I don't know what everyone was fussing about. They seem to be very welcoming," Yll said, releasing Ryn.

Ryn watched her grandmother greet people in the crowd. Ryn's brow furrowed. "Yes, they do."

Dinner was at the longest table Ryn had ever seen. Her grandmother was seated at the head of the table, with Uncle Mik next to her on one side, and Ryn on the other. The rest of the Library delegation was seated close to them. Ryn was appalled to find they seated Jeris next to her, and Yll and Regg were seated further down the table. She felt trapped in an ocean of awkwardness.

Ryn shifted in her chair. Servants brought the first course. There was a confusing array of silverware and glasses in front of her, more confusing than the Dining Room in Waatch. She decided to follow Uncle Mik exactly in everything that he did. Hopefully that would keep her from completely embarrassing herself in front of everyone. She also didn't want to mess this up and embarrass her mother.

Uncle Mik engaged Jeris in a conversation about how long it would take to get the Board of Regents to officially vote for the move. Prym was seated next to Jett, and was flirting with him shamelessly. Ryn realized Jett seemed to have lost his House Viator girlfriend. Probably because grandmama didn't want any inbreeding. Jett did start dating Thalya before they found out their mother was House Viator.

Uncle Mik's attention shifted to Ryn. "Your mother was happy here, once. We managed to get ourselves into loads of trouble." He winked at her. "There was that one time, when the Matriarch of House Pentral was visiting. Your mother started a food fight." He chuckled.

"As I recall"—Ryn's grandmother's eyes danced like Uncle Mik's—"you shot the first pea across the table."

Uncle Mik waved his hand. "Nonsense, I would never do that."

Ryn laughed as she thought of the trouble she and Zo had gotten into together. The thought of him lifted her heart.

"You could be happy here too," her uncle said. "When the Library moves here, you will be welcome at House Viator." He twisted the glass in his hand by the stem. "I'm certain by the time the move is done you could easily become a full researcher in the Library." He looked her in the eyes. "You would like that wouldn't you?"

Ryn had started dreaming of being a researcher at her first meeting with Master Wes, but she wanted to earn it, not be handed it to her by her family. What if she was actually a disaster as a researcher? She would end up as one of "those" researchers that everyone whispered about behind their back. Of course, everyone probably did that already. She was pretty sure Prym made sure of it.

"I do hope to be a full researcher someday, but it requires many hours of hard work to earn it, or a spectacular feat of researching skill." She glanced at her grandmother. "I prefer to prove that I am worthy."

Uncle Mik held up his hands. "Certainly, I have no intention to suggest otherwise, I have heard that you are already quite skilled."

Her eyes narrowed at him. "From who?"

"Oh, don't be so surprised, 'Youngest to be promoted from student to assistant in centuries. You have been quite the topic of discussion in research circles." Her uncle sat back so the servant could put a plate of food in front of him.

Ryn followed as a plate of salad was placed in front of her. She watched her uncle pick up a small fork and she copied him. "And those same circles have said that I only got the position because of my friendship with Madame Curator's daughter. I know what people say about me, Uncle. They don't tend to hide it well."

He waved his fork in the air. "But you are of House Viator. You can have anything you want." He stabbed his salad and took a bite. When he swallowed, he leaned in closer to Ryn. "I don't know what your mother has told you about us, but I can assure you we do not bite."

Jeris' face looked like he was holding his nose against a bad smell.

On the one hand, Ryn didn't like the way her family was trying to bribe her to their side. On the other hand, the look on Jeris' face was almost worth it.

A servant handed Jeris a note. He opened it and Ryn snuck a glance at it. She caught a glimpse of a wolf head and words that said something about the problem would be taken care of. Ryn's pulse quickened. Did she really see a wolf's head on that paper? Could Jeris have something to do with Evalesco? She would need to tell Regg and Yll.

* * *

After dessert everyone was invited back into the Ceremony Hall.

They put a long cape of gold on Ryn and had her kneel at the foot of the stairs.

Her grandmother stood on the platform between the two casks of beads, one on the right for the father's side, one on the left for the mother's. Her grandmother held cording for the bead necklace in her hands.

"Ryn de Viator, we welcome you as a descendant of House Viator for your testing of the beads."

Ryn's stomach churned. She needed to protest. As much as she wanted to belong, she wasn't one of them and she knew it.

"Who here vouches for this girl's Ancestral line?" her grandmother asked.

"I do." Jett stepped up next to Ryn.

"Then come forth and claim your Ancestors!" Her grandmother's voice boomed throughout the room.

Ryn took hesitant steps up the stairs. Part of her wanted it all to be true. That she really was her mother's daughter, that she really had been hiding her, and that she really was an Ancestor descendant. For a moment while she climbed the stairs, she almost believed it, but the knot in the pit of her stomach was growing into full on nausea the closer she got to the bead casks.

"You may approach the bones of your Ancestors." her grandmother held out her right hand to indicate the cask to the left.

Ryn reached out a hand to the cask with the beads of House Viator. As she did, her stomach roiled and she barely kept from being sick.

She opened the cask. All the beads lay there inside. What was she supposed to do? Pick one? She needed this to be over, because she was very soon going to make a spectacle of herself in front of all these people.

Ryn's grandmother frowned at her. Her Uncle Mik stepped forward and took her hand and placed it on the cask for House Dico, her father's house that Viator must keep for bead ceremonies. The sudden motion made Ryn's head spin.

"I don't understand." She heard her grandmother say right before she couldn't hold it in any longer, and spewed forth her dinner all over the red carpeting.

Ryn collapsed to the ground, her stomach continuing to heave, and heave, and heave.

"What is happening?" Jett asked.

"I don't know. This has never happened before." Uncle Mik' cold eyes were glaring at her.

The crowd was screaming

"Not even if you're Ordinary?" Jett asked.

"An Ordinary couldn't set foot on these stairs," Ryn's grandmother snapped.

Clayr and Lar came to Ryn's side. Clayr was stroking Ryn's back saying soothing words. Someone brought a bucket. When Ryn finally stopped, Lar scooped her up.

"Where can we take her?" Lar asked.

"Back to the guest house." Ryn's grandmother's voice came icy cold.

Ryn didn't remember much of the carriage ride back except for it being terribly uncomfortable on a nauseated stomach. Once in her room, Lucy helped Ryn undress and get cleaned up, then put her to bed.

As Ryn drifted off to sleep, she remembered she had felt that same nausea in the Spirit teller's tent at the ghost festival.

* * *

Ryn found her toes in the warm sand on the beach where her mother had brought her. She sat heaping the sand on her feet. The waves crashed onto the shore then rushed up the beach. She closed her eyes and listened to the rhythm of the roar and splash of it. The breeze tickled her face, smelling of salt and seaweed. A shadow cooled the sun's rays, and someone kicked sand on her hand. Shading her eyes, she looked up to find, not her mother, but Zo standing next to her.

"How did you find this place?" he asked as he sat in the sand beside her.

"My mother brought me here. How are you here?"

"I'm dreaming," he said.

"So am I."

Zo said nothing, just stared out at the ocean.

"Well, I'm glad to see you. It's been awful. I'm sorry I didn't come home right away like you said I should," Ryn said.

Zo's gaze shifted to her slowly, like he wasn't quite all the way there. "You'll be coming home tonight. Someone has broken into the Library. I have to go."

With that, he disappeared, and Ryn woke with an urgent feeling she needed to get out of the house.

Ryn shook her head. How could she be talking to Zo, in what seemed like real time? She climbed out of bed. The door to her room was open a crack, so she slipped out into the hallway. The house was quiet, no one must be home from the ball yet. Ryn made her way to the top of the stairs and descended them like a ghost. She passed through the ground floor sitting room and found the door outside open. Zmej was at the doorway.

"Come quickly, Ryn. Your mother has been injured, and I need to take you to her."

Ryn's foot hovered over the threshold. The urgency in Zmej's voice compelled her to obey.

"Come on, take that step. Once you do, I will take you away from here."

Still Ryn's foot hovered.

"It's just one step."

Ryn forced her foot down. She needed to go. She needed to be with her mother.

* * *

Somewhere in her mind she heard people screaming her name.

"*Ryn!*" Regg's voice was in her ear.

Arms went around her waist and held her tight.

She awoke to find herself standing on the low wall barrier overlooking the cliffs, with the rocky beach far below. Her foot was hovering over the edge.

Regg pulled her down off the wall.

"What were you doing?"

Ryn started trembling uncontrollably.

"Get her inside," Clayr's voice came.

Yll wrapped a blanket around Ryn, and Regg picked her up and carried her inside.

Once she was safely tucked back into her room by the fireplace, Lucy gave her a cup of hot chamomile tea and Ryn used the warmth to try and get control of her shaking.

"What happened?" Clayr asked.

"I don't know. I was dreaming, then I thought I was awake, and that Zmej was calling me to come with him to see my mother, and then I suddenly found myself on the edge of the cliff ready to step off." Ryn's teeth chattered.

"You've never slept walked before," Clayr said.

Ryn's fingers found the pendant Zmej had given her around her throat. She slid the chain around, but couldn't find a clasp. Her hands shook, as she wrapped her hands around the pendant and yanked as hard as she could. The chain was made of almost tissue-thin gold, but it did not break. She pulled and pulled, until the chain started to cut into her neck, but it would not come off.

She sighed and relaxed back into her pillow. Maybe Lar or Regg could melt it off. Until then, there was something else on her mind.

Ryn looked into Clayr's eyes. "I don't understand what happened at the bead ceremony."

The door to Ryn's room flew open and Errol stormed into the room. Ryn took a double take. Someone must have Travel magicked him here.

Clayr came to her feet. "What's wrong?"

"Two young men have broken into the heart of the Library. We need you home now."

Chapter Twenty-Eight

Jak,

I have done as I said I would. I have taken something of yours. In return you will do what I asked.

When the darkness left and the sound of waves faded, Zo opened his eyes to the anxious faces of Iden and Thax hovering over him.

"Are you alright?" Iden asked.

"Of course the boy's not alright, we need to get him to Wilmar's right away," Thax said.

Zo sat up gingerly. "I'm fine. I got a message from…"

Zo rubbed his forehead, struggling to remember what happened.

He jumped to his feet as it came back to him in a rush.

"The Protector of the Library!" Zo strode toward the exit.

"Zo!" Iden called after him.

Zo turned around. "Thank you, Thax."

Then he was out the door.

Iden chased him down the street. Fortunately, Thax's shop wasn't far from the Library. Zo ran faster than he'd run in a long time. He was out of breath by the time he got to Fergus at the west gate.

"What's wrong?" Fergus asked.

Zo bent to catch his breath as Iden caught up to him.

"Grab as many guards as you can." Zo finally got out. "Someone is breaking into the heart of the Library."

Fergus, to his credit, didn't even question how Zo could possibly know such a thing. They all ran for the guard house to sound the alarm, then tore off toward the Boiler Room, Zo shouting at Nix as they passed. Within a few heartbeats there were guards pouring into the tunnels and Boiler workers following, holding their hands aloft with flames like torches.

Nix came from behind and pushed Zo and Fergus out of the way so he could take the lead. He opened the secret panel leading to the Heart with Zo and Fergus right on his heels.

When they got to the Heart they found Jak and Dan holding lanterns, circling the Heart, and examining the walls. Nix moved faster than Zo thought his bulk would ever allow. He was on Jak and Dan so fast they could barely react to his presence. As Nix pinned them both to the wall, the guards swarmed in and took over. Before Zo could say anything to them, the guards had them tied up and were hauling them away.

"Isn't that..." Iden started.

Zo nudged him hard in the ribs.

"Let's go. I need to see where they take them. I want to be there when they're questioned," Zo said.

"They'll take them to the Board of Regents building," Fergus said.

"Right." Zo turned to follow, when he saw the Protector off in a dark corner.

The Protector looked relieved to see Zo, but its hands were also all over the place trying to say something. Zo moved in front of the Protector and tried to grab its ethereal hands.

"Slow down. What's happening?" Zo looked deep into the pools of black that were the Protector's eyes.

The Protector made signs with its hands in rows.

Zo shook his head. "I'm not sure what you're saying."

"Looks like books," Fergus said.

Zo was startled to see Fergus had followed him.

The Protector nodded, then made its hands cupped with a mast.

Zo nodded. "A boat."

The Protector repeated the two hand shapes.

"Books, boat." Zo said.

"Some Library materials were taken to House Viator with the delegation," Nix said as he approached from behind Zo.

The Protector shied back into the shadows but nodded. It then made crawling finger movements.

"The pests! The book worms came after the materials were moved," Fergus said.

"It wasn't the sword or the branch, The removal of Library materials has weakened the Library's magic." It all clicked in Zo's head.

The Protector was nodding vigorously.

"Let's get to the Regent's House. We need answers from those two."

The Protector swirled away into the dark.

* * *

When Zo, Fergus, Iden, and Nix finally found the room where they were holding Jak and Dan, the guards stopped them from entering. Nix started to protest when Ryn came around the corner, followed swiftly by Clayr, Lar, Yll, and Regg. Someone in House Viator colors trailed behind them. Probably the person who helped Travel magic them home.

The guards immediately moved aside, and Zo and the rest followed Clayr through the door. At the sight of Jak and Dan tied up in chairs Ryn gasped. Jak and Dan had a few cuts and bruises. It looked like the guards had already been a little rough with them. Zo went to Ryn and put his arm around her.

"I don't understand. How did these two get all the way to the Heart?" Clayr asked.

Norm stepped forward. "We've been trying to get answers out of them, but they aren't talking."

"Make them talk," Errol said.

Ryn buried her face in Zo's chest. He was torn between taking her out and staying to hear what they had to say. Fortunately, someone else stepped up.

Brynd rushed past Zo and kneeled before Clayr. He hadn't even seen her enter the room,

"Madame Curator, if you please, it is my fault. These two led me to believe there were clues beneath the Library to why the protective magic was failing. I believed them and let them into the tunnels. We didn't find anything, so we left. I'm sorry, I was fooled into believing I was helping." Brynd was crying.

"Foolish child, there will be consequences." Clayr said.

Zo cleared his throat. All eyes turned to him. "It's true. I found them there. I agreed to show them the center of the Library, or the Heart, but only so I could prove to them there was no inscription saying anything about the protective magic of the Library. I showed them out and had guards placed at all the entrances to the underground."

"You should have told us," Nix said.

Clayr turned her vehemence on Jak and Dan. "Call the Waatch prison guard. They were caught in the act. There is no need for a trial." She turned to go.

"Wait!" Jak said.

Clayr stopped.

"We were hired by someone to break in. It was just a job," Jak said.

Clayr folded her arms. "Who?"

Jak and Dan exchanged a look.

"He didn't give us a name, and we've never seen him in Waatch before," Dan said, his split lip starting to swell.

"Right. Take them away," Clayr said.

Norm and Ed moved in.

Dan looked directly at Ryn with his one swollen eye. "He's taken Maus. We had no choice."

Ryn gasped and covered her mouth.

"What?" Brynd grabbed Clayr's sleeve. "Someone's kidnapped Maus."

Clayr's brow furrowed. "How can someone kidnap a mouse?"

"Not a rodent mouse, a person Maus. They're our responsibility," Dan said.

Jak hung his head. "We would have never have gone back after we went with Zo. We told our employer that there was no writing on the Heart, and that we were done with the whole business. He told us he would not pay us unless we went back. We told him we didn't need his money, and walked away. A few hours later Maus was missing and we received a note instructing us to finish the job or we would never see Maus again."

In her mind Ryn imagined Maus' shy smile. She reached out and took Brynd's hand.

Clayr's fingers rubbed her forehead. "I'm sorry to hear about your loss. I will alert the Waatch guard to your friend's potential kidnapping, but there's nothing I can do. You broke into the Library." She turned to Norm and Ed. "Take them away."

"Wait! We could help you find our employer!" Jak said.

"How?" Lar asked.

"We've seen him. We can identify him," Dan said.

"We can't let you roam the streets of Waatch trying to find this non-existent person," Errol said.

"The Winter Solstice Ball," Iden said.

Clayr frowned.

Jak's eyes lit up. "Yes. Everyone from the Healing House, dignitaries, plus the majority of the Library staff will be at the ball."

Ryn let go of Zo. "Including most of the guard?"

Clayr nodded. "It is tradition to give the staff time off to celebrate the end of the dark and the return of the sun."

Zo stepped forward. "The Protector just told me the transfer of Library materials to Viatoro has weakened the Library's defenses. That is how the book worms got in. The Library is vulnerable. It will be doubly so the night of the ball."

"The perfect opportunity to trap our employer." Jak smirked. "Let us help."

Clayr raised an eyebrow. "In exchange for?"

"Our freedom and a promise to never set foot on Library grounds," Jak said.

"You were already banned from Library grounds, but that didn't stop you," said Errol.

"We are a force in Waatch. A force that keeps many things in balance. Plus, we will put ourselves at your disposal for future information gathering," Jak said.

"I don't like it," Norm said.

"Mama, this could be our only chance to catch who's been doing this to the Library," Yll said.

"They do have an impressive knowledge of the Waatch underground," Brynd added.

"Your employer will know you have been caught. You will spend your time in prison until the ball. After that, we'll negotiate," Clayr said.

"It's the perfect set up. Our employer will not be expecting us to be at the ball, because...uh, we try to avoid most of the people who will be there." Dan added.

"Yes, I bet you do," Norm said.

Clayr gazed around the room. "Alright. No one outside of this room is to know about this. I need a vow from each of you that everything said here will not leave your lips outside this room. Not even to talk amongst yourselves."

They went around the room, each of them giving their vow.

"Alright, let's get planning. After tonight you will all act out your parts without discussion," Clayr said.

Zo sighed. It had been a long day, and it was going to be an even longer night.

* * *

Zo buttoned his waistcoat and fiddled with his cufflinks. He looked at himself in the mirror over his washbasin and examined his reflection. The deep browns and oranges of the embroidered flowers crawled up the waistcoat, drawing the eye to Zo's neckline and face. It had been a harrowing couple of days of preparation and dodging his mother. Zo was afraid it showed. Clayr had promised to do what she could to block his mother's request, but it still hung over his head. He couldn't think about that now.

A knock at the door and a mew from the little gray fluffball brought a smile to Zo's face. He scooped up the tiny kitten as it bounded toward the door, then opened it to a huge spray of cedar and red elderberry.

Zo laughed. "Is there a boyfriend in there somewhere?"

Iden let the bouquet drop, giving that mischievous grin Zo loved so much.

Iden sucked in his breath. *Wildfire.*

And Zo was in his arms. Their mouths came together. Their tongues questing, seeking the joy of being together. All too soon it slowed to a few quick kisses.

"Do you have some twine?" Iden asked, out of breath.

Zo realized Iden was still holding the heavy bouquet in one hand.

"Oh yeah, I think I do." Zo dug around in a drawer till he found a small ball of it in the back.

Iden tied the spray upside down next to Zo's door. "There. Now you'll have good luck all year."

Zo didn't put much stock in that sort of tradition, but this year he needed the luck.

Iden finished tying it to the hook by the door, then entered Zo's room, giving him a long deep kiss that made Zo suddenly overheated in his formal attire. Iden brought the kiss to a slow conclusion.

"You're not ready," Iden whispered.

"Just need my coat." Zo pulled away reluctantly to grab his coat from where it was hanging. He put it on, pulling at his sleeves, and shaking his shoulders to settle it.

"Thax was right, the dark blue looks fantastic on you." Iden's eyes twinkled.

Zo looked at himself in the mirror. The coat was expertly tailored, it hung right, plus it gave him the perfect shape, it even showed off some of the muscle he'd developed from climbing ladders in the underbelly of the Library.

In the mirror Zo noticed Iden's jacket fit him just as well, but was tailored to his physique. Iden stepped up next to Zo both reflected in the mirror.

"Maybe we should just stay home," Zo grinned.

Iden laughed. "If only there wasn't so much resting on your shoulders this evening."

Zo's stomach fluttered. A lot of the plans for this evening hinged on his strange connection with the Protector of the Library. He cracked his knuckles on the table. If it worked the way they hoped.

"Plus, I wouldn't miss tonight for the world," Iden whispered.

Zo shivered. "Let's go before I change my mind and we spend the rest of the night with the fluffball."

Iden laughed and held out his arm to Zo, who inhaled deeply the smell of cedar on Iden, then took his arm and let him lead him out the door.

* * *

When their carriage pulled up to the Dining Room, it swung into the long line of carriages to drop off ball goers.

Zo cracked his knuckles on his thigh. "Let's walk the rest of the way," Zo said, opening the door.

Iden followed him out, paid the driver then started down the street after Zo, who was too nervous to wait that long for Iden.

"Slow down." Iden took Zo's arm. "It's not a race."

Zo's eyes were fixed on who was exiting the carriages ahead of them. Who was there, and who was not could tell them a lot. Their saboteur could be here, or they could be on their way to the Library. They were prepared in both cases, but Zo wanted to keep track of everyone here tonight. He watched his father exit a carriage, then help Ryette out. Next was Prym's father and mother, then Master Ubert alone by himself. Iden had to tug on Zo to slow him down when Zo saw Jett and Prym arrive together.

"Seems the whole delegation has returned from Viatoro," Zo said.

Iden squeezed Zo's arm. "I can feel you tensing. It's not worth it this early in the evening."

Zo wanted to watch everyone arriving, but Iden dragged him up the stairs to the Dining Room.

The doormen opened the doors and Zo took a deep breath. This was it—the moment of no return. Iden took Zo's arm and they stepped into the entry. Zo expected some kind of reaction from the room—a collective gasp, or maybe a scream, but on that point he was disappointed. He did notice that for the guests who were recognizable Ancestor descendants, there were halts in conversation, and more than a few stares. The rest of the party goers scarcely glanced their way. Zo let out the breath he was holding, slow and steady.

"We've got this, Wildfire," Iden whispered in his ear.

Zo nodded and let Iden pull him forward.

All the tables in the Dining Room had been pushed to the sides to make way for the dance floor. Many guests had already arrived, including Ryn and Dan, and Brynd and Jak. The boys were wearing masks as if it were a masquerade ball. Dan was doing some kind of silly dance that had Jak laughing. Ryn's arms were folded, but one corner of her mouth was raised in a half smile. Zo didn't find it amusing. Iden's hand was on Zo's arm and as soon as Zo tried to take a step toward Jak and Dan, Iden swung him around in the opposite direction. Zo tried to protest. He did not like the fact that Ryn was with those two. He knew they needed to be close to Jak and Dan to supposedly find the Library saboteur, but Zo wasn't happy about it. If he could punch those two for using Ryn and Brynd he would, even if their young friend was still missing.

As Zo and Iden moved deeper into the room, Zo's steps faltered. There was his mother, sitting at a table with the Healing House Headmaster, as well as Keir's parents, and a couple Library Regents. His mother was staring at him, eyes narrowed, her face turning red. Zo forced himself to hold his head higher, and walk with Iden to where Yll and Regg were standing with Nix and Wilmar. It seemed Zo and Iden weren't the only ones being bold tonight. Zo was aware of his mother's eyes on him all the way across the room.

"Zo my boy, thanks for the save the other night," Wilmar said.

"Of course. I regret I haven't been able to study with you so much lately."

"It's alright, I understand the difficulties you've been facing." Wilmar's eyes were staring past Zo to where Zo's mother was seated.

"Tell me who we are keeping an eye on this evening," Wilmar said.

Yll subtly pointed with her glass of punch. "That man there, standing by the potted plant with Prym and..." Yll choked. "Ryn's brother, that's Master Ubert. The Library hired him to investigate the problems in the Library. I'm pretty certain he is our man."

"How's that?" Wilmar asked.

"He seems determined to undermine Clayr, and prove the Library is unfit. We think he's working for House Viator," Regg said.

"I happen to agree. Him or Jeris," Nix said.

"As much as I don't like the Library Regent, it's hard to believe a Jeris would betray the Library like that. Ubert, however, is an outsider, and I'm certain he hates my mother——probably for being a powerful Ordinary." Yll said.

"I think Jeris would. He hates Ordinaries just as much, and he seems to put his own interests before the Library," Iden said.

"Have Jak and Dan seen Ubert yet?" Zo asked.

Yll shook her head. "I don't think so. We should take them over and introduce them."

"Who else?" Wilmar asked.

Iden gave a slight nod. "I still say we need to watch Jeris there next to Zo's mother. He's in deep with House Viator. He's a huge proponent of moving the Library to Viatoro. I wouldn't put it past him to hire someone to sabotage the Library, in order to make the move look good."

"And it is an amazing move. I've seen the facility, it's gorgeous. So hard to argue against," Yll said.

Wilmar nodded toward Ryn. "I'm sure Jak and Dan are up to no good. I know them too well, if there's something underhanded going on, they would be a part of it."

"Yes, keep your eyes on those two as well," Zo said.

Zo chanced a glance back at his mother and saw Keir approaching with Ayn, the Mind Healing student, on his arm. Zo cracked his knuckles on his thigh. Iden slid his hand to the middle of Zo's back in a possessive way.

"Well don't you two look dashing this evening," Keir said. He made a show of looking around the room. "I'm sure you'll be the talk of the ball." He winked at them.

Iden frowned.

"Anyway, your mother wishes a word with you," Keir said.

"My mother wishes a lot of things," Zo said, turning away.

"This is a ball. I think it's time for a dance." Iden held out his arm to Zo.

Zo's eyes watched Keir frown, then shifted to his mother's expectant face further across the room.

"I think you're right," Zo said, taking Iden's arm.

Iden led him to the dance floor just as the musicians began a slow song about love found, and love lost. Instead of taking up the traditional steps of the dance, Iden just put his arms around Zo's waist and pressed his forehead to Zo's, swaying back and forth sweetly to the music. It was pure bliss. The other dancers, the Dining Hall, in fact the whole party fell away and it was just them. Zo closed his eyes and shifted so they were cheek to cheek. Nothing else mattered in the world, except being there, moving in sync with Iden.

"I'm sorry," Zo whispered in Iden's ear.

Iden's arms tightened around Zo's waist. They danced on.

"Zo," Iden said.

"Hmmmm?"

Iden pulled back a little so he could look into Zo's face. "I've been meaning to ask you something..."

But Zo never found out what Iden was going to ask. His mother broke into their little love cave, grabbed Zo's arm, and tried to drag him away. Several people around them gasped.

His mother plastered a fake smile on her face, but her hand was shaking on his arm. "Nothing to worry about, just need to speak to my son."

Dancers were moving away from them.

Zo yanked his arm from his mother's grip, but one of her thugs, the muscly one, grabbed him and pushed him forward. Several couples on the dance floor moved out of the way, their faces looking scandalized.

"No need to worry, just need a few minutes to talk," Muscle Thug said.

Fergus appeared in front of them, he was a bit shorter than Muscle Thug, but he had all the bearing and authority of a Library guard. "I'm sorry, but the directors of the ball are asking that you to stop causing a scene."

"No scene, just helping the lady's son find the restroom." Muscle Thug gave a sneery smile and pulled Zo past Fergus.

Fergus put his hand to his sword, but Zo waved him down. It was best to just deal with his mother and get it over with. He knew going into this night that she was going to be a problem.

Zo caught a glimpse of Nix holding back a red-faced Wilmar. Zo almost smiled at that. The gruff Nix holding back sweet-tempered Wilmar. He shook his head at them, hoping they wouldn't make this scene worse. The thugs dragged him into the men's restroom following Fyri inside. Muscle Thug shoved the one ball goer who was there out, and locked the door.

"Zo de Ingis, I...I can*not*...I..." his mother started hyperventilating.

"Mother, slow down. You're going to pass out, then you'll never get to yell at me properly."

His mother slapped him.

Zo's heart stopped. He took a step back. His hand pressed to his stinging cheek that only minutes before had been pressed warmly against Iden's.

She had done a lot of despicable things, but she'd never hit him before. The sudden violence of it caught him completely off guard.

"What in all the name of the Ancestors which saved us from the dragon do you think you are doing?" His mother's voice was low and menacing.

She grabbed the front of his shirt. "Do you know what the Healing Council will do to you if they find out about this?"

Zo's anger rose. "I live in Waatch."

She started to pace, wringing her hands. "They'll send you to Exile. We have to make sure this doesn't get back to

Eileansano. I'll just need to bribe a few people, but it can be salvaged. If I get you home and under contract for marriage all of this will fade. Yes. It will just be a vicious rumor people have spread. It can be dismissed as vicious gossip. I can make it disappear."

"Like you tried to make my fire disappear?" Zo asked.

"If I had only known then that Fire magic was the least of my worries with you." She stopped. "We need to break your contract with the Library now. Yes. You must be married by the next quarter moon. It can no longer wait. I'll call in the whole Board of Library Regents tonight if I have to."

"Go to the grave with the Ancestors."

Zo strode past her to the door and flung it open.

Screams were coming down the hall from the ballroom, and Regg was racing toward him.

"Zo! Come quick!" Regg shouted.

Zo broke into a run.

"Oh, hello Mother." Regg waved at her.

"And you..." Zo heard his mother yell at Regg down the hallway.

Zo caught up to Regg, who slid to a stop, spun around and followed Zo back to the ballroom.

When they entered the main room, everything was in an uproar. People were talking, and a couple ladies had gotten sick. The doors to the Dining Room had been shut and members of the Library guard, along with Waatch guards, were blocking them, not allowing anyone to leave. Zo caught sight of Ryn waving him over.

When he got to her, she was pale and looking like she wanted to throw her arms around him, but instead she clutched his arm like she was holding on for her life.

"It's Master Ubert. He's hurt." she said.

"Where?"

She pulled him forward to a table in the corner. His bald head was tipped back in the chair. A knife was sticking out of him. It was buried to the hilt in his chest. Wilmar was there checking for a pulse and examining the wound. He glanced up and shook his head when Zo reached him.

Zo put his hand on Master Ubert's neck and checked for himself. He was definitely dead.

"Look at the shape of this blade," Wilmar said.

He tried to pull the blade out to examine it, but it was stuck, possibly caught in his rib or spine. Zo yanked harder, it was still stuck. "This must be why it's still in him."

Nix came over and finally managed to remove the blade. They examined it closely. It had that strange four-pointed star shape. It was clearly the weapon that had been used in the other stabbings they had seen. The handle of the dagger ended in what looked like a wolf's head.

"Evelesco," Zo whispered.

Ryn pulled Zo aside. "What do we do? Someone was willing to kill Master Ubert. What do you think his investigation found?" she asked.

Zo looked back at the body, trying to puzzle it out.

"Yll said Master Ubert was a suspect. Did Jak and Dan identify him?" Zo asked.

Ryn nodded. "He didn't hire them. I don't think Master Ubert liked Clayr, but I think he was just doing his job."

"Who does that leave?" Zo asked.

"Jeris. I'm sure of it. I saw him get a note with a wolf head on it at dinner in House Viator. If they can make the Library look like it's falling apart, that the magic is failing, and that Clayr is incompetent, the Board of Regents will vote to move the Library for sure."

Zo looked over to where Jeris was in conversation with Nix and Clayr.

"He doesn't seem to have blood on his hands," Zo said.

"Well then, he hired someone."

"Did Jak and Dan recognize him?"

"Who else would it be?" Ryn threw her hands up in exasperation.

"I don't know, your family maybe? Where are they?"

Ryn pointed to a red-haired man talking with Ryette. "My uncle is here."

"Let's go see what he has to say." Zo put his arm around Ryn's shoulders and guided her to her mother, his father, and her uncle.

They were standing to one side of the doors that led to the garden. An elderly lady Zo didn't recognize approached, fanning herself. One of the men with her spoke to Fergus, who was guarding the door. A heated argument began between the two.

Ryn gasped, "Grandmother! How is she here?"

The man with Ryn's grandmother stepped around Fergus and flung open the doors.

"Oh, thank goodness," Ryn's grandmother said, putting away her fan and moving to join Ryette and Lar.

Ryn slowed their trek toward her mother.

"Oh boy," she said, taking a deep breath. "This can't be good. Sparks are going to fly now."

"Maybe we should find Jak and Dan," Zo said, eyes searching the room for them.

"No, I can deal with my family."

Ryn started forward. As soon as they were in front of the open doors, Zo felt a chill breeze that made him shiver.

Then it came. The start of blackness at the edge of his vision, and he heard the Protector's voice.

Help!

It was the signal they had been waiting for. Someone had taken the bait and was breaking into the Library. Zo turned to Ryn, but before he could say anything a low growl came from the dark garden.

"What was that?" Ryn said.

Zo didn't want to find out. Just as he reached for Ryn's arm to pull her out of the doorway, something bigger than a wild cat came at them out of the dark.

Zo shoved Ryn behind him, and got his arm up just in time to take the full force of this thing with a long snout full of teeth. I was a blur of gray hair and was making noise like when animals fight. The thing knocked Zo to the floor. Ryn somehow managed to get out of the way, because he didn't land on top of her. The thing had clamped its teeth down on

Zo's arm and was shaking its head back and forth. Zo tried to pull its jaw off with his free hand.

There was screaming behind Zo. The hairy thing's eyes shifted to the screams. It let go of Zo's arm, and faster than he could get his hands on its head to knock it away, the thing had its teeth on his neck. His hands pulled at its jaw, but it was strong like a steel trap. The teeth began digging into Zo's neck. He got a brief glimpse of Fergus swinging at the thing with his sword. The blow didn't stop it, the teeth sank deeper. Zo was struggling to breathe. Any second now this thing was going to rip out his throat.

Without thinking, he reached out his hand and put it on the thing's throat. Just as his airway began to close off, Zo shot his Healing magic straight to the heart of the thing.

And killed it.

Chapter Twenty-Nine

*One of the most marvelous things about the Tree is its love of family
and family history. It is, after all, a Family Tree.*

— From Luc's Journals

Everything seemed to slow. Ryn considered the horror
unfolding in front of her like it was some sort of play on a
stage. The creature on top of Zo had a grip on his throat.
People around her were shouting "Wolf!" Ryn had only seen
a wolf in books about myths, but there was one, in real life,
attempting to end her brother. She screamed Zo's name, but
it just sounded like a scream. Dan jumped in front of her,
shielding her from the wolf, but also her view of what was
happening. Still upset with the way he had used her, she
wanted to shove him out of the way. Instead, she managed
to duck around him just as Fergus and Iden pulled the wolf
off Zo, who was convulsing on the ground.

Ryn ran to him, putting her hands on his throat,
screaming for Regg. Zo's eyes rolled back into his head just
as Regg got there followed by Wilmar. Fergus pulled Ryn
back. Her hands were covered in blood and shaking. Keir
joined Regg to help, grabbed Zo's hand, and immediately
collapsed. A scream of pain escaped Keir before he gasped
for air, dropped Zo's hand, and rolled away from him.
Wilmar was asking for napkins and applying pressure to Zo's
neck. Zo's convulsions stopped. His eyes opened and he
began coughing. Iden put one hand on Lar's shoulder.

"I'm alright, I'm alright." Zo's voice was rough from the
pressure on his neck. He pushed Wilmar's hand away and
struggled to sit up. His neck was still bleeding, but he pulled
on Lar and Regg's hands to sit up.

"Lie back down," Wilmar said.

"Can't. Just before the attack I got a message from the
Protector." Zo turned till he found Clayr. "They took the bait,
the attack is underway."

Clayr paled. "We need to go now. Where's House Viator?"

Ryn scanned the room. The only person left from House Viator was her mother, who had quietly slipped up beside Ryn and was rubbing her back.

"Seems our help has abandoned us. Almost as if they intended to do that," Clayr said.

Ryn's mother nodded. "Let's go, we're all the Library's got."

"Take me with you," Ryn and Fergus said at the same time.

"Jinx, you owe her," Regg said, his voice sounding like all the life had been sucked out of it.

"No. I can't take everyone," Ryn's mother said.

Clayr turned to Fergus. "Bring the rest of the guard to the Library as fast as you can." She scanned everyone else. "The rest of you stay here with the Waatch guard."

Ryn's mother kissed Ryn on the cheek, holding her tight. Then she moved to surround Clayr and Lar with her arms and they were gone in a swirl of wind.

Fergus and the rest of the Library guards took off after them.

Iden helped Zo to his feet, pulling him into a hug as tears glistened his cheeks.

"We can't just stay here and do nothing," Yll said.

"People are leaving and taking all the carriages," Regg said.

Jak stepped into the middle of everyone. "I know I don't deserve any trust, but I know most of the carriage drivers. I can get them to drive us instead. Let me help you."

Ryn looked to Zo. She hated the thought of needing Jak, but even if they ran all the way to the Library they'd ever get there in time.

Zo rolled his eyes, but gave her a reluctant nod.

"Let's go!" Ryn said.

Despite Jak and Dan quickly helping to acquire carriages, many had left already, so Ryn was smashed into the carriage with Yll, Regg, Brynd, Jak, Dan, Iden, and Zo. Ryn wouldn't let Zo out of her sight, and Zo wouldn't let Jak and Dan out of his. She could tell he still didn't trust them. She understood. Zo hadn't met Maus. He wouldn't know how important Maus was to Jak and Dan. It was a tight fit in the carriage, and Ryn, being the tiniest, couldn't hardly breathe, but at least being wedged in meant she didn't bounce all over when the carriage hit a bump. The bite on Zo's neck was bleeding again. Ryn grabbed a handkerchief sticking out of Iden's pocket and pressed it to Zo's neck.

"So you were playing my sister this whole time." Zo glared at Dan. He took the handkerchief from Ryn and applied pressure himself.

Dan held up his hands. "Ryn and Brynd were a great way to get access to the Library, but once I met Ryn, I..." Dan flushed. "I admit I like her very much, and I'm hoping tonight makes up for the mistake in taking that job."

Jak winced. "We knew our employer was mysterious, and most likely dangerous, but the task seemed harmless—find out if there were symbols or markings on the walls to the heart of the Library, and report back what they were. Getting into the Library underground presented a challenge. We like a challenge, so we accepted."

Dan nodded. "We were hoping working with them might help us find the saboteur."

"And to impress my sister so she'll forgive you for lying to her?" Zo raised one eyebrow.

Dan swallowed visibly, looking down at his hands in his lap, because his shoulders were pressed in from being sandwiched between Jak and Regg. "Maybe."

Ryn watched him looking miserable, but she couldn't think of a way she could trust him again. He had used her to get what he needed. Ryn's gaze shifted to Yll. She had used Ryn as well, yet Ryn had let her try to heal things between them. Both betrayals had been awful, so why was she letting Yll back in, but wouldn't even consider it with Dan? Probably because Yll had been her best friend since they were both toddlers. Ryn barely knew Dan.

The carriage driver knocked on the top of the roof, and Jak stuck his head out the window. "We're approaching the Library."

"Stop at the gate and we'll talk to whoever's on guard," Zo said.

Herb was at the gate, and Ryn stuck her head out. "It's us. Let us through—the Protector has called for help."

Herb scanned the faces, frowning at Jak and Dan, but lingering on Zo. "Fergus was just here. I suppose we need all the help we can get." He waved them through.

They told the driver to stop in front of the Boiler Room and they all piled out. Ryn thought about how ridiculous they must all look wearing formal clothing, hiking up their dresses so they could run full tilt through the Boiler Room and into the tunnels. Ryn was so focused on getting to the Heart, she scarcely recognized how hot the pipes had become as the weather turned colder.

By the time they entered a secret door Ryn had never seen before, and made their way around the heating ducting that hung from the ceiling to the Heart they, were all breathing hard, but no one was there.

"Where's Clayr and everyone?" Iden asked.

Ryn shook her head, confused. "But this is the Heart—right? Isn't this where the Protector called from?"

Zo's eyes were fixed in a dark corner. Ryn looked and saw what he did, the Protector. It used its hands to describe something. It repeated the motions over and over till Ryn got it.

"The Heart travels up through the Library, all the way to the top," Zo said.

"I wonder..." Ryn started.

She approached the Heart. She had never been in this area before. She had only traveled the tunnels with Zo. Now that she was looking at the walls there was something about them that seemed familiar.

"Do you see this?" Ryn asked, pointing to a writing that was neither Ancestral, nor the common language they used.

They all moved closer. "I don't see anything," Regg said.

Yll put her hand on the wall and brushed away dust. "I think maybe there's something very faint." She squinted at the wall.

"I don't see anything either." Iden squinted at the spot Yll had cleared.

"But it's so clear," Ryn said.

Jak put his hand on the wall. "I can feel the lines."

Dan pointed to the pattern of small pictures, or maybe symbols on the walls that Ryn was seeing. "This is what we were looking for."

"Why can't I see it?" Regg asked.

Iden looked around at all of them. "Zo, Regg, and I have full Ancestor magic." Iden inspected Jak and Dan's collars. "The rest of you don't."

"I'm half Ordinary, so the lines are faint," Yll said, running her hands further down the wall.

"I'm Ordinary, so I can see them clearly up close," Dan said.

"Fascinating," Jak said.

To Ryn's mind they jumped out, clear as day. They matched something else she had seen before.

She reached her hand out and traced each symbol with her fingers. "These match the drawings of the tree in those books about the founding of the Library."

Yll gasped. "You're right!"

In these carvings Ryn saw a pattern she hadn't seen before. The leaves and branches swirled into a circle, a heart, that drew her eye to the middle of it. It almost seemed to glow.

"Do you see that?" Ryn asked.

"See what?" Zo said.

"It's glowing." Ryn reached out her hand and pressed her palm to the spot on the wall that was singing to her, calling her.

"Ryn, wait!" Zo lurched forward to grab her, but all she saw was light, and she was gone from the underground.

* * *

Zo was swearing his favorite swear word over and over, his heart pounding. This couldn't be good.

Yll's eyes were huge. "What just happened?"

Dan, a full Ordinary, went to the wall and put his hand on the spot Ryn had touched. Nothing happened.

Zo glanced over at the Protector. Its hand was pointing upstairs. Zo ran his hand over the wall of the heart and swallowed hard. There was no crack, there was no physical door, there was no way in. Ryn needed help, but so did the Library. Reluctantly, he let his hand drop.

"The Protector said Clayr's upstairs. Let's go."

* * *

When the light faded, Ryn was standing next to twisting roots thicker around than a large adult. They flowed down around and beneath her. The air had a shimmering quality to it, almost like she was under water. She could breathe just fine, but the air felt thick. Every once in a while something twinkled in the corner of her eye, but when she turned to look, there was nothing there. She found herself standing on a rounded root, and had to balance carefully so she didn't fall. She chanced a glance behind her, but the wall she had been standing in front of a few heartbeats ago was gone. Balancing carefully, she made her way up the root until she could grab onto others. The roots were growing in such a way that they almost seemed like stairs. She began picking her way up the roots, hand going from one root to another to steady herself. Partway up, the root she grabbed broke off, and crumbled in her hand.

Kill the roots...

She knew this was where that phrase was leading her. The stories about the tree inside the Library seemed fantastical, but in a weird way it all made sense.

When she got to the end of the roots, an enormous trunk of a tree rose before her. Her hand landed on soft grass surrounding the tree. Given that the door from the Heart was in the underground, beneath the Library, it made sense that the roots should be there. With the tree's strange location, they weren't surrounded by dirt, but by some kind of magical water that nourished the roots. Now as she stood on the grass, she realized she must be on the first floor of the Library. She ran her hand over the trunk. It was somewhat rough, like a cedar tree, but it was easily as big around as her cottage in Sooke. Ryn's eyes followed the trunk up, and up, and up. Toward the top there were branches with leaves. One of the branches ended in a cut stump. Sap dripped from it like tears, and made her first instinct to reach out and comfort it. The tree was massive—and somehow growing *inside* the Library.

"How is it you are here?" Ryn asked the tree.

Beyond the tree there were no walls, only light.

"And how do I get out?"

"Easy, you just open the door," A voice came, dark as night.

Ryn startled. Black smoke was curling through the light, weaving its way, this way and that, finally coalescing in front of Ryn. The smoke resolved itself, not into the Protector, like she had hoped, but Zmej.

She stepped away from him, her back pressed against the tree. Thoughts of him in her dream encouraging her to step off the edge, and plunge to her death filled her head.

"I admit, I thought I wouldn't need help to access the Heart, so I'm glad you didn't tumble over the cliffs. I thought you were in my way. Now I see, you were the key." Zmej's fingers closed around the tracking pendant he had given her. Ryn had tried to remove it, but even melting it wouldn't get it off.

"What are you going to do now?" Ryn asked, pulling the necklace out of his fingers.

Zmej pressed his hand to the tree. "The magic native to this planet is powerful. This tree, and others like it, are the focus for that power. They are the reason my predecessor failed. I have destroyed others. This one is particularly strong, because of having the slayer's magic to protect it."

He looked down at her and grinned. "Don't worry, none of your precious Ancestor records will be harmed. I even made sure there was a wonderful alternative to this building."

Zmej put his hand on Ryn's chin. "Unfortunately, you will be a casualty. Nothing in this room will survive."

With that, he stepped back and snapped his fingers, producing blue flames a thousand times hotter than the roaring bonfire on the beach.

Ryn's skirts instantly caught on fire.

* * *

Zo felt like he was running for his life. The puncture wounds at his throat, which were barely crusting over, started to ooze blood again. He put his hand to his throat to casually wipe away a drip of blood, but Iden frowned at him. His throat throbbed. Too late to do anything but press forward, Zo took the stairs to the Library entrance two at a time.

The front door was open, and no one was guarding it. He put more effort into reaching the top faster. At the entrance, Zo held up his hand for everyone to stop.

"Hello?" He said.

He couldn't hear much through all of them breathing hard, so he cautiously waved them all forward.

"Where's this door we're looking for?" Zo asked Yll.

"This way." She led them under the arch and into the dark of the Library.

Yll stopped at a desk to reach for a lantern, but Zo shook his head. It was always dark in the Library, but at night, when not even windows let in light, it was pitch black. All of them were used to moving in the dark, and carrying a light would announce their presence. There were a few lit lanterns at key points the guards used at night. They would have to make their way by what little light those lanterns provided.

Yll led them past the objects room and through some selves, then down an aisle and around a corner.

They all followed, creeping along, listening to the sound of the Library in the dark. A creak here, and groan there, Zo's focus played on his imagination. At one point he could have sworn he heard a growl somewhere.

When they at last approached an aisle that was brightly lit, Zo and Yll peeked around the corner. Zo put his hand over Yll's sharp intake of breath.

Halfway down the aisle, Clayr, Ryette, Lar, and Fergus, along with a few of the Library guards, were standing with their backs to a large wooden door. They all held weapons in their hands, pointed toward three wolves who had them surrounded.

The wolves were growling, baring their teeth, and pacing back and forth like they were just waiting for a signal to pounce.

"Where's everyone else?" Iden asked, after he took a peek.

"What do we do?" Yll asked.

Zo's mind flashed back to the wolf that had nearly ended him less than an hour ago. He could still feel its hot breath and his throat closing. His hands started to shake when he remembered what he did. Killing it hadn't been any sort of pleasure at all, in fact it had hurt every cell in his body, and he still felt broken by it. He wasn't sure if it was Keir perverting the killing magic that made it pleasurable, or if killing something as large as a wolf was a whole different experience. A cold sweat drenched him just thinking about it. There was no way he was repeating that action again. The thought of what he'd done was horrific, even though it had come down to the wolf's life or his. He wouldn't do it again. So how else could they save their parents?

Jak sighed. "I don't suppose any of you thought to bring a weapon?"

Zo had a small utility knife on him. That was it. Regg took another one out of his pocket.

"That's not helpful," Jak said.

Jak and Dan pulled larger dagger-sized knives from various places stashed about their body, pockets, belts, boots, wherever a knife could be concealed.

"Never leave home unprepared," Dan said as he started handing knives out.

Jak handed Zo a dagger. He recognized the wolf head instantly. "Where did you get this? This is the dagger that killed Master Ubert."

"Shhhhhh. I have a feeling the owner didn't mean to leave it in Master Ubert. I was hoping it would give us an advantage over them." Jak grinned that grin Zo didn't like.

Dan handed a dagger to Brynd. "So here's the plan. I will take Iden and Regg with me. We'll attack the wolves and get them to follow us. Zo, you, Jak and the girls will help Fergus and the boys protect the curator."

"What if all the wolves don't follow you?" Zo asked.

"If we get at least one to follow, you'll have less to deal with here," Jak said, completely ignoring Zo's question.

Yll stepped up next to Regg and took his arm. "I'm going with you."

"You can't run fast enough in those heavy ball skirts," Dan said.

Zo thought it through. It didn't seem like a great idea, but he couldn't think of anything better.

"With these daggers we will only be able to engage the wolves in close quarters," Iden said.

"Don't let them get close. These are only if you find yourself in a situation like Zo did earlier this evening," Jak said.

"Iden will help us sneak back around to the other side. Wait till we get the wolves to chase us before moving in," Dan said.

Iden kissed Zo on the cheek, and Zo grabbed his hand and squeezed it. He didn't like sending Iden and Regg off to be bait. Not at all.

When they had gone, Zo sat waiting. The girls were tense, Jak casually twirled his knife, leaning against the bookshelf, as if he did this kind of thing every day.

When Dan and the others appeared at the other end of the aisle and started shouting at the wolves, Jak straightened and waved them to go. They turned the corner of the bookshelf and tore down the aisle to where the parents were. One of the wolves ran after Dan, Iden, and Regg. The wolf on Zo's side of the door turned, nails scraping on the stone floor, and charged Zo and his group. Zo's brain stopped. Jak grabbed him by the coat and yanked him back down the aisle. Zo glanced back and saw Fergus and the rest of the guard attack the remaining wolf in front of them. At least that part of the plan had worked.

Now if only Zo and the others could stay alive.

* * *

Ryn panicked, beating her skirt against the grass. A wave of the shimmering air rose up from the roots and crashed down over her like a wave of water, extinguishing her skirts.

Zmej was busy forming his blue flames into a large fireball, larger than anything Ryn had seen Zo or Lar make. It was getting hotter. The bark under her fingers became hot to the touch. The leaves up above began to wilt. She was powerless to do anything. She threw her arms around the tree and hugged it. The tree seemed to know her—and she knew it. It was everything that embodied the Library, history and family, and connection to the past. She scanned the area around the tree but could find nothing that would save it.

A wind swirling around the tree trunk, shaking the leaves above. It grew in intensity until it was swirling around Ryn threatening to sweep her up in it. Her fingers dug into the bark trying to hang on. All at once, the whirlwind shot out directly at Zmej, knocking him backward. The fireball went straight up. The wind blew it back at Zmej, who waved his arms and dissipated it. The wind faded, and Zmej got back to his feet and began again.

"I can do this all night." Zmej's blue fire began to form a ball again. "All the trees I've fought eventually succumb. Give up now and I will spare the daughter."

The sparkling air from below rose up in a giant wave. Zmej shot a stream of fire at it. The two forces pressed against each other. At one point the life water was above Zmej, pressing down on him. Ryn's heart leapt. The tree was winning, but then the blue fire intensified, blasting the shimmering wave back with a wall of fire. Steam started rising from the tree bark as the wave receded, and the shimmer sank far below the roots.

"You have expended your life water. Now you will die." Zmej raised his fiery hands.

* * *

Zo was tired of running. He banged his shins on the corners of bookshelves, almost tripping over desk legs. He was completely out of breath, and yet the wolf kept coming. He clutched the dagger. It was his only lifeline to saving himself without using Killing magic. Zo's neck was freely bleeding. Yll and Brynd were stumbling over their skirts and breathing hard. Jak was the only one who seemed like he could run forever. He probably did this all the time.

The only thing keeping the wolf from overtaking them was the slippery, clean floors and too narrow aisles.

Jak overturned a cart full of books to be reshelved. The wolf jumped it, sliding across the floor. It struggled for a minute to get its footing, but it was soon after them again.

"We...have to end this," Zo gasped out at Jak.

"Hidden staircase...up ahead." Brynd heaved gulps of breath.

"The wolf...would be free...to get Iden...and the others," Zo managed to get out.

Jak nodded and turned a corner. They were back on the aisle with Clayr and the others. The guards were still fighting the one wolf, but it appeared to be severely injured and struggling.

"Incoming!" Jak yelled, and they all ran behind the Library guard.

"What, you can't take them out by yourselves?" Fergus quipped.

Zo was gasping for air. "Not with this." He held up the dagger.

Fergus scoffed, then grinned. "I'll be happy to dispatch both of these wolves for you."

"Thanks," Zo breathed.

Around the corner down the aisle came Dan, Iden, and Regg, with their wolf hot on their heels. Zo groaned. All they'd managed to do was wear themselves out.

"Great, we're surrounded," Zo said.

Just as Dan and the others reached them, Ryn's uncle, Jeris and a bunch of House Viator guards came storming down the aisle toward the wolf following Dan's group. They began attacking that wolf from behind. The wolf turned on them, yipping and snarling.

Yll and Brynd collapsed to the floor. Zo wanted to join them, but opted for leaning against the carved door. With his head pressed against it, he thought he heard a scream...

Ryette's anxious face joined him. "Was that Ryn?"

"I don't know. Shhhh," he said, pressing his ear against the door.

There was rumbling and shouting, but it was hard to hear over the sound of the others fighting the wolves.

"How do you get in?" Zo examined the door, but there was no handle.

"I don't know," Clayr said.

"What do you mean, it's your Library!" Zo wanted to shake her.

"No one enters, not even the curator," Clayr said.

Just then the Protector appeared beside Zo. Turning into white vaporous smoke, it swirled in the air then coalesced around Zo's hand. He held up his hand and watched the Protector swirl around it. In his mind he felt the impression to press his hand to the center of the swirled carvings on the door.

As soon as his palm touched the wood everything fell away, and became nothing but light.

* * *

Zmej's hands of fire were no longer trying for just a fireball, he was creating a wall of fire. It was spreading out to surround the tree and rose up to the top.

Ryn's nose and throat were dry. Her skin was hot. She was getting dizzy and sick in the heat. She regretted every unkind thing she'd ever said to anyone, especially to those she loved. She wanted a chance to say she was sorry. She pressed her cheek to the tree.

"I'm sorry," she whispered. "This is all my fault."

Then she closed her eyes and waited for her fate.

A blast of yellow fire slammed against Zmej's wall of blue.

It wasn't nearly as strong, but Zmej was taken by surprise, and faltered.

Zmej swore. "My wolf was supposed to get rid of you. Your connection to the Protector is too convenient." He regathered his fire. "That's alright, I will take care of you now."

"Not if I can help it."

At the sound of his voice, Ryn turned to see Zo, shooting fire at Zmej with more power than she'd ever seen him use before.

"No, Zo. The heat—it will burn the tree," she yelled.

Zo looked up at the branches, but drove his fire forward, forcing Zmej back.

The shimmering life water rose up from the roots again. Somehow Ryn knew that it was the last of it. If they didn't defeat Zmej now the tree would die.

Zo glanced to the side and nodded. "Grab the dagger in my belt."

Ryn saw it, the dagger that had stuck out of the chest of Master Uber. The wolf's head on the pommel, and now Ryn noticed, the buttons on Zmej's coat. He was the one. He had been behind everything.

She pulled the dagger out of Zo's belt, not sure if she even knew what she would do with it, but she pointed it at Zmej. When the wave hit, she let her mind completely forget what she was doing and leapt. She wasn't going to let this man kill the Tree, the Library, or Zo. She drove the dagger straight toward Zmej's chest. He stumbled backward as she crashed into him.

As Zmej hit the ground, the dagger came down.

And Zmej and the dagger disappeared.

Chapter Thirty

Moult,

It seems there really is a tree of Wild magic growing inside of the Library. Zmej, whom I've trusted for many years, is a part, if not the head, of Evelesco. I am on his trail, but it seems with the failure of Jett's imprinting, and Zmej's failure to destroy the tree, everyone is after Praedo's beads. Heads up—it's all headed your way!

Ryette

Zo sat on the top of the steps to the Library entrance. He had one arm around Iden and the other around Ryn. Iden was using his handkerchief to dab at the blood still oozing at Zo's neck. Zo breathed in deep and let it all go slowly. His head sank to Iden's shoulder, while his other arm pulled Ryn in closer. The adrenaline was washing away and Zo's eyes closed. He could still hear people entering and exiting the Library. Apparently, as soon as Ryn had attacked that Zmej guy the wolves had turned and fled. The voices around them were talking in anxious tones, some angry, some yelling. Zo didn't care. They had made it through the night and had stopped the saboteur, that was all that mattered.

"Let me through! That's my son and I'm taking him home!"

Zo heard his mother's voice drifting up from the bottom of the stairs. He was hoping if he kept his eyes closed it would go away, but it didn't. He listened to her protesting, saying she had the right to see her children. Zo felt Iden and Ryn both tense beneath his arms. He sighed deeply and sat up, but didn't have the energy to stand.

His mother came rushing up the steps. "Come now Zo, it's time to go. Enough of this craziness, you will be safe at home."

Zo didn't move a muscle.

Lar came from somewhere behind Zo, rushing down the stairs to intercept her.

"That is enough Fyri! As if what you did to him as a child isn't enough, now you are attempting to kidnap him and take him from his life. Stop now. If you haven't already ruined your relationship with him, you are very close to it," Lar said, shifting to stand between Fyri and Zo.

"His contract with the Library has been canceled. I'm taking him home where he belongs," Zo's mother said.

Zo's stomach twisted, and his arms tightened around Iden and Ryn.

"I approved no such thing." Clayr's voice came from above Zo.

He looked up to find her standing over him. "This man is the only person we have who can communicate with the Protector of the Library, and the Library needs a lot of work to heal from its wounds it was dealt this evening." The fire in her voice almost roused Zo to do something. Almost.

"But he's my son," Fyri shot back.

"And he's my worker. Please leave the Library grounds now." Clayr's voice wasn't quite a shout, but it was full of menace.

"Fergus, will you see Fyri de Sano and her guards make their way out and aren't admitted back?" Clayr said as Fergus started down the stairs.

"Yes, Madame Curator," Fergus said, waving to Ed to help him.

The two took the task maybe a little too eagerly, with Fergus dragging off a protesting Fyri.

Zo nodded his thanks to Clayr, hardly trusting his voice to say something, then let his head sink back onto Iden's shoulder.

* * *

In the morning the clouds had that flat look they got before it snowed. It was cold in Ryn's dorm room, but her many burns on her arms and legs seemed to appreciate it. She hadn't realized till she went to crawl into bed the night before exactly how much Zmej's fire had burned her. She had burns in places she had thought were safe.

On her bedside table she found a note:

Sweetheart,

I stopped by to say goodbye, but you were sleeping so soundly I didn't wish to wake you. I'm off on an errand for the Library, I'll be back soon. Until then, be safe. I love you!

Love,
Mom

Her brain briefly wondered what errand Clayr could have sent her on, before the burning on her arms and legs sent her looking for the ointment Wilmar had left for her. As she was applying ointment liberally, there came a knock at the door. Ryn glanced over at Brynd. She was sprawled in her bed and didn't even stir. Ryn groaned and hobbled over to the door to answer it.

Fergus was there smiling, but his face fell when he got a look at her.

"Hey, are you alright?" he asked, his brows furrowing.

Ryn waved him inside, as it was far too cold out to leave the door open.

"I'm fine." Ryn sat back down next to her ointment, putting her leg up on the chair next to it.

"Clayr would like to see you in her office," Fergus said.

Ryn pulled back her nightdress to expose the burns on her leg.

"Oh, wow, that's a lot of burns."

Ryn looked up at him to see his face and ears had turned as red as her burns. She would have found it adorable, but she was so exhausted.

"Sure," Ryn said, but continued to apply the ointment to her various burns.

Fergus shifted. "Um, she's waiting, and um...hoping you'll come soon?"

Ryn's eyes shifted to him slowly. "Right. I'll get dressed."

Fergus pointed to the door. "I'll just be outside."

Ryn felt like she was walking through mud across the Library grounds. Fortunately, Fergus didn't try to force a conversation. He was just the quiet presence Ryn needed. When they got to Clayr's office door, Ryn took Fergus' hand and pulled him down closer.

"Thank you," she said, and kissed him on the cheek.

He gave her a slow smile that lit up his eyes, then opened the door for her.

Ryn was surprised to find only Clayr in her office. She had come to expect her mother and Lar there.

Clayr looked up from a notebook she was reading. "Ryn, oh good, have a seat."

Ryn's heartbeat quickened as she had flashbacks to the end of the whole Master Wes kidnapping thing. She had been in trouble then. She hoped she wasn't in trouble now.

"What's happening? Last night was kind of a blur," Ryn asked.

"Maintenance is working on putting the Library back together. Nix is stomping around demanding we fortify the Library underground. Hal had to keep him from throttling the few of his fire grunts who admitted they'd seen some suspicious activities, but hadn't said anything to anyone. Prym tried to submit a report to the Board of Regents claiming it was Master Ubert's findings, but with his passing, the Board deemed it invalid. With the real culprit uncovered there is debate on the Board if an inspection is still needed." Clayr gave a not quite amused half smile, then sighed. "Ryette, Lar, and surprisingly, your Uncle Mik went looking for Zmej."

"But Zmej disappeared," Ryn said.

"It seems Zmej has the ability to do some kind of Travel magic, though it's different from what we're used to. At least that's what your uncle reports."

It was kind of a relief to Ryn to know for sure she hadn't killed him. She didn't think she did, but she had pounced on him with a knife aimed straight at his chest. Ryn's stomach clenched. "Should the three of them go after him alone? He's dangerous. The amount of raw power he uses."

Clayr's lips went flat. "That's why I wanted to talk to you first. What happened in that room? You and Zo have been quiet about it. I need to know. It won't leave this room."

"It's true. There's a tree growing inside the Library," Ryn said.

Clayr nodded slowly. "As soon as we returned home from Viatoro, I had Yll start writing down what she saw in the journals, starting with his account of the founding of the Library. It still doesn't clearly state that the ancient Wild magic tree grows inside the Library, but there is no account of it being removed. It also talks about a tree protecting the Library, so it's pretty clear."

Ryn nodded. "It's there. The roots grow past the basement into the underground. The trunk soars up higher than the Library's roof, I'm certain. And...a branch." The image of the cut off branch that seemed to be crying came clearly back to her mind. "It was missing a branch. Do you think it could be the branch the Protector showed us?"

Clayr tapped her chin. "It's possible. I would think that a branch from the Wild magic tree growing inside the Library had the potential to be powerful to do, who knows what, but where is this branch?"

Ryn shrugged. "It wasn't there with the tree. And the sword?"

Clayr sighed. "The only sword I'm aware of with any power is Praedo's buried in stone at the Origin. There's no way that sword's going anywhere, so it's no threat to the Library, or the tree."

Ryn nodded slowly. After seeing a huge tree growing *inside* the Library, she was willing to believe a lot of things that didn't seem possible before.

She shook herself. "Anyway, there's also a kind of shimmering air around the tree roots, like water that nourishes it. Zmej used fire to try to kill it." Ryn held up an ointment covered hand. "I have the burns to prove it."

Clayr inhaled sharply. "And what was his purpose in 'Killing the roots' and destroying the tree?"

Ryn rubbed at her forehead. "Something about there being other such trees in the world, and that he killed them all, and that this one was the last."

"Anything else?"

"Oh yes. He's the one who's behind the Library move. If you take away the Library contents the magic will weaken, and the tree will be vulnerable," Ryn said.

Clayr tipped the notebook in front of her up and began to read. "*In time, the Wild magic of the tree and the Library will become inseparable, dependent upon one another. Praedo's companions have much for which to be grateful to the Wild magic. Their family histories will be safe, but the companion's building keeps the tree safe*—Luc's final journal."

"The Library can't be moved," Ryn said.

"The Library can't be moved," Clayr agreed.

"One more thing." Ryn shifted in her seat.

Clayr set the notebook down and nodded.

"Why did I get sick during the bead ceremony?"

"That is a very good question. You don't get sick when you're around Yll or the other's beads do you?" Clayr asked.

Ryn frowned, thinking back on her experiences. "Not that I know of."

"I'm sorry Ryn, I really don't have any answers, but I do know a fantastic researcher who could possibly find the answers, somewhere in this Library."

A smile spread slowly across Ryn's face. "Researcher?"

Clayr grinned. "Yes, the Board of Regents would like to reward you for saving the Library. You are being promoted to a full researcher, though I doubt Sandy will let you do anything more than shelving new acquisitions for moons."

"But that's what I do now," Ryn frowned.

"Exactly."

A bitter wind blew against Ryn as she crossed from the Library grounds on her way back to her dorm room. Her burns were numb, but Ryn shivered. The wind suddenly stopped and Ryn looked up to see if Iden was there controlling it, but instead she found the mountain that was Nix blocking it.

"You look like a brand-new fire grunt who can't control their magic," Nix grunted.

Ryn gave him a weak smile. "Um. Thanks?"

"I'll wake Zo up and send him round to see you."

Ryn waved her hand. "Don't wake him. I'll be fine." Ryn reluctantly left Nix's windbreak and started off toward her dorm.

"Wait." Nix pulled a piece of paper out of his coat. "I was headed back from Wilmar's and that young man from last night handed me this."

Ryn took it and unfolded it.

Ryn,

I know I messed up, but I need to see you. I'm on the street corner across from the Library west gate and I'm going to stay here all day and night if I have to till you come see me. I might freeze to death if you don't come soon. I understand if you don't want to see me, but if you see a frozen guy on the corner that was me. I'm joking, I'm joking, but...please? I promise I won't bother you again if you say so.

Yours,
Dan

Ryn held the note. She had really enjoyed spending time with him. He was funny and sweet, but she really hadn't felt that spark of romance with him. Then he used her to get close to the Library for his own gain. And how was it that he was across the street and not in jail? She decided to see him, if for no other reason than to tell him to leave her alone. Her hand squeezed the note.

"Thanks Nix. I'll take care of it."

Nix straightened. "You need an escort?" He held up a hand full of fire without even snapping his fingers. "I could roast him for you?"

Ryn blushed and shook her head. "That's alright."

"Maybe just a scalding hot handshake?"

Ryn looked up at his perpetually scowling face. It was tempting. She could have Nix run Dan off. "No, I'll handle it."

Nix shook out his hand and surprised her by giving her a crushing hug that shoved his fur trimmed coat right into her mouth. She patted Nix on the back.

"Thank you Nix," Ryn said, picking fur off her lips.

"Make sure the Library gate guard watches out for you."

"I will."

She set off toward the west gate while Nix watched her leave. Ryn understood why Zo loved his mentor so much.

At the west gate Ryn caught a glimpse of a guy all bundled up in a wool coat, a scarf, a hat, and a cloak. It certainly didn't look like he was going to freeze to death any time soon. She took a deep breath and crossed the street.

"You came!" Dan's eyes lit up.

"Don't get excited, I just came to say..."

Dan held up his hand. "Wait. Please, wait."

Ryn opened her mouth, determined to be done so she could go back to her warm room, but something in his eyes made her stop.

"I'm so sorry about everything, and if I could take it all back and start over I would, but I know I can't. I just wanted you to know that I know I hurt you, and that I hate that I hurt you, and I hope that you'll at least consider me a friend." Dan held her gaze for a long time. "Please?"

Ryn inhaled the cold air. "Have you found Maus?"

Dan's lips pursed. His gaze drifted down to his hands. "No." His voice was rough. When he looked back up at her a tear ran down his cheek.

Ryn felt her own eyes tear up. "But surely you and Jak...with all your resources..."

Dan looked away down the street, rubbing his eyes. "You would think." His laugh was bitter.

Ryn took in the street. She didn't see anyone else. The cold must be keeping everyone indoors today. She shivered.

"How come you aren't in jail, by the way?" Ryn asked.

Dan shrugged. "I guess the Library was grateful for how we helped with the wolves. Not that they'll ever let us set foot on Library grounds again."

Ryn nodded. "Well, let me know if you hear anything about Maus."

Dan tentatively reached out and gave her a hug, and she let him. She would give him that. Then she pulled away and headed back to her Library home, hoping Brynd was up and had made some mint tea.

Epilogue

Ryn was still blurry eyed from spending her days since the attack on the Library trying to put it back together. The door to the Heart hadn't opened to her again, but the books that had been taken to Viatoro were returned, and the magic barrier had restored itself. Zo said the Protector had indicated the tree was healing, but it would take time for it to come back to full strength. Ryn hoped one day she could see the tree again. She didn't know if it was the heat of the moment, or what, but she had felt a strong connection to the tree, and she would like to find out why.

Right now she was on her way to do a task that made her heart heavy.

She descended the stairs into the basement, then knocked on the door at the end of the hall to the Repairs and Restoration room.

"Come!" A voice called from inside.

Ryn opened the door, and approached Walt, the Master Restorer.

"I've come to return this," Ryn said, setting the orphanage book gently on Walt's desk.

Walt's eyes shifted to the book, then up at Ryn. One of his eyes was magnified by the glass he was wearing, making it huge.

"Why?"

Ryn ran her hand over the tree calf cover of the book. "I found that it was made by Master Clark on Viatoro, and I went to see him. He told me that House Viator buys many such ledgers from him, and often donates them to orphanages. I was able to take a peek at House Viator's records, but they donate books and other things to many orphanages, several on the mainland. It's a dead end. I have no way to figure out the provenance of this book for certain."

Master Walt's gaze shifted thoughtfully to the book.

"Did your parents get you from a Waatch orphanage?" he asked.

"I don't think so. My brother said my father was on his way home from the peninsula when he stopped at an orphanage and found me. I suppose it could have been that he stopped somewhere in Waatch."

"Possibly. There are a few different orphanages in Waatch that House Viator donates to, but only one outside Waatch on the mainland."

Ryn looked up sharply into Master Walt's eyes. "How do you know?"

Walt chuckled, and put his hand out to indicate the room full of damaged books. "It's my job to figure out where lost books come from. I know many things that help me figure out the provenance of records."

Ryn's pulse quickened. She could scarcely breathe to ask the question. "Which orphanage outside of Waatch?"

"The orphanage in Lummi. It's on the main road to the peninsula, just a few days walk from here." Master Walt eyed Ryn. "Would you like to keep the book so you can take it there to confirm? It would be a great service if we could return this book to its proper place."

Ryn snatched the book off his desk and clutched it to her chest.

"Yes! Very much so, yes."

Master Walt's grin was incredibly silly with his bulging magnified eye.

* * *

Ryn practically ran up the stairs from the Library basement, and flew out the front doors—to snow falling heavily from the sky. Her nose and fingers quickly got cold, and the absence of her cloak became apparent. Her heart sank. She descended the stairs slowly and walked through the gardens. When she was thoroughly wet and cold she headed for the mess hall, got a hot cup of chamomile, and found a quiet corner to sit. She placed the book on the table in front of her, staring at it over her steaming cup.

"Hey, what's up?"

Ryn looked up to see Zo carrying a tray and moving to sit in front of her. He was pale and the wounds on his neck were still visible.

"Nothing," she told him. He had a lot of worries on his mind now that he had the responsibility to help the Library heal, as well as his other duties. Plus, even though Clayr had kicked his mother out, Fyri still hadn't left Waatch. Ryn knew his mother's presence troubled Zo. She didn't want to burden him with her silly worries.

"Hey little sis, this is me talking to you. Tell me." Zo picked up a roll and dipped it in his gravy.

Ryn eyed him as she sipped her chamomile tea.

"If you don't tell me I'm going to bring the gray monster over to torment Abby."

"You haven't named him yet?" Ryn asked.

Zo shrugged. "Nothing has stuck."

Zo nudged her with his foot.

Ryn gave in, running her hand over the cover of the book again she said, "I found out where the orphanage book came from. I was so excited, but then I walked outside into snowfall. It's full winter now and too cold to travel beyond Sooke, not by walking anyway, and then—where would I stay? I finally know where to go, and now I can't go there."

Zo sat back, picking a baby carrot off his plate and munching it.

"Let's go," he said.

"What?"

He rolled his head cracking his neck. "I need a break from Waatch. Let's go."

"But it's a few days' walk and it's freezing outside."

Zo shrugged. "We'll hitch a ride, or we'll hire a carriage."

"That's more money than either of us have."

"We'll find a way. You've waited so long, it's time you get some answers."

Ryn let her heart hope. "Really? But we'll have to wait till the snow is gone at least."

Zo shook his head. "Naw, it won't stick around, and I really need to get out. Let's leave tomorrow morning. I'll see about finding us a ride."

"Yes!" Ryn stood, and reached across the table, but only managed to kind of hug Zo's head.

Zo chuckled. "We're going to find your birth family or die trying."

* * *

Zo cinched up his pack as the gray ball of terror mewed at his feet, weaving in and out trying to trip him. Zo scooped him up.

"No, you can't come. Daddy Iden's going to take care of you."

He passed his dresser and examined his wolf bite in the mirror. The puncture wounds were healing—naturally. Zo hadn't tried to heal them. Something inside him still felt off. His stomach twisted at the thought of reaching for his Healing magic. He had denied his healing half for so long, and now...he kept his mind from thinking that he had done something to ruin it.

There was a knock at the door, Zo opened it to find not Ryn, but Regg standing there.

"Hey little bro, what's up?" Zo asked.

Regg stamped the snow off his feet and entered Zo's dorm room.

"Three things: Before Dad left he said he's having our neighbor in Sooke, who has been cat sitting, bring you Beardslee, because none of us have been at the cabin enough to take care of him properly, and since you have this rascal now, you get to be the cat man." Regg grinned.

Zo sighed. "That's more like Iden, he's here more than me, but whatever."

Regg scratched the kitten's chin. "Who's a good little kitten? Jinx is a good little kitten," Regg said in a baby talk voice.

"Jinx?" Zo raised an eyebrow at that.

"Yes. He's that much trouble." Regg laughed.

"What else?" Zo said, looking outside, he was expecting Ryn any moment.

Regg shifted.

Zo raised an eyebrow.

Regg blew out his breath. "Mother's getting ready to leave for Eileansano, and I'm afraid she's going to want me to take your place as her hopeful heir."

"Naw, you have second born, baby of the family privileges. I'm sure you'll be fine."

"But...I overheard her talking to the Headmaster. Something about shifting your marriage contract to me!"

Zo choked.

Regg grabbed a fist full of Zo's heavy linen shirt.

"Zo, I was planning to give Yll a promise necklace at the ball." Regg pulled a box from his pocket. "Mother can't do this to me!"

Zo rubbed his forehead in thought. "I seriously doubt she will shift it to you. What you probably overheard was her still scheming to get me somehow. I wouldn't worry about it. Ryn'll be here soon. I told her I would take her to the orphanage to find her birth parents. I can't confirm anything at the moment, but if you're afraid Mother will take you with her, you're welcome to stay here. I don't think Fyri will dare set foot on the Library grounds for a while anyway. I'm sure Clayr won't mind if you stay."

Regg gave him a half grin. "Thanks, I think I'll do that."

Zo held up Jinx and gave him kisses. "You'll just have to put up with this one, and apparently Beardslee."

Another knock came at the door. This time it was Ryn dressed for a snow expedition, she looked all bundled up in coats and a heavy cloak.

"You ready?" She asked.

"Yep." Zo handed the kitten to Regg, then shouldered his pack. "Let's go."

* * *

Ryn had no idea how Zo had managed to arrange a ride in the back of the farmer's wagon on such short notice, but she was grateful for her brother's resourcefulness. The journey down the road was beautiful. She had never been west of Waatch. The trees had snow on the branches, but Zo was right, it didn't stick to the road. They rolled along, occasionally passing orchards or farms. Ryn knew Brynd's family owned an apple orchard out this way somewhere. She should have asked where. They rode all day, neither of them saying much, both of them bone wearily tired. Zo occasionally would rest his head on the top of hers and doze. By the end of the day, they reached a crossroad, and the farmer let them out.

"This is where we part. There's a farmhouse just a bit up the road there. They take in travelers for the night. You might be able to find a ride there for tomorrow."

"Thanks," Zo said, putting his hand out to shake the man's hand.

"No, thank you for healing my daughter from those horrible burns. When she got the chills I was afraid she wasn't going to make it."

"I was happy to help," Zo said, then waved goodbye.

"You healed his daughter?" Ryn asked.

"Yeah, that day I went to help Wilmar because he was overwhelmed with patients." He gave Ryn a side eye, then coughed. "I may have cheated and used a little Healing magic."

Ryn looked up at her brother with new admiration as the farmer drove off. She knew Zo was a healer, but it was inspiring to see its effect on those he helped.

"Let's get out of the cold." Zo hiked up his pack and started down the road.

Ryn scurried after him, working hard to keep up.

The farmhouse was warm inside, and the farmers willingly took them in, and gave them a nice dinner. Zo paid to rent a room for the night. It was tiny with only one bed, but they managed to both squeeze onto it. Ryn was grateful in the middle of the night when the room grew cold, and she could press her back tighter to Zo's. His warmth calmed her troubled heart, and she fell deep asleep.

* * *

The next morning, they were up and off early. A merchant traveling to the outposts on the peninsula had stopped at the farmhouse for breakfast and was willing to drive them the rest of the way to Lummi.

Today they both recovered enough to chat and they spent the day talking, and catching up. Ryn told Zo all about everything that happened on Viatoro, and Zo told her about everything that had gone on while she was gone.

"I asked Clayr why I had such a horrible reaction to the Ancestor beads, but she had no answers," Ryn said.

"It's like when you visited the Spirit magic lady. You got sick then too," he said.

"It felt the same!"

"I wonder if you're somehow allergic to Ancestor magic."

"That seems silly," Ryn said, but it was really the only thing that fit.

It gave her a sinking feeling that she really didn't belong to any Ancestral House. Perhaps she was just an Ordinary child of one of these local farmers. She looked out the window despondent. Maybe she was just some unwanted thing given away to prevent a family feud.

"I almost knew what it felt like to be a part of a family—to really belong. They welcomed me in. Made me feel wanted. They pulled me in then abandoned me as soon as they found out I'm an Ordinary. And I fell for it so easily." Ryn fought back the tears rising up.

Zo put his hand on hers. "You have a family that loves you, and a researcher life you love. I know it's not what you were hoping for, but it's still a good thing." He squeezed her hand.

Ryn nodded slowly. He was right, but it still hurt. She had looked through a window at all the things she had hoped and dreamed of since she was a kid, but now realized it would never be hers. Her chest felt heavy, and her vision blurred.

"I almost messed up everything with Keir." Zo broke into her melancholy thoughts. Her stomach twisted as she took in his lowered head and slumped shoulders. He was already talking really fast, telling Ryn about how he had kissed Keir, how he had let Keir take him to dark places. How he had let his attraction to Keir almost pull him away from Iden. He told her about Killing magic.

Ryn listened, trying to process what he was saying as it came at her in a flood. When Zo finally stopped, she sat quietly. Her stomach was chilled in a way that had nothing to do with the weather. She thought about how the wolf had suddenly stopped attacking Zo. Fergus had stabbed it, but none of the rest of the wolves that night had been stopped so easily. Ryn shook the thought off. She didn't want to think of her Zo, who would put a spider out the door rather than killing it, could have killed the wolf with his magic.

"I glad you chose Iden, he's always been my choice."

He laughed at her reference to how she had grown up with a crush on Iden.

Zo spent the rest of the ride telling funny stories, and making her laugh in an effort to lighten the mood. It worked for the most part, until the merchant pulled over and stopped.

"We're here," he said, climbing down to begin the process of opening up his wagon to sell his goods.

"Thank you so much," Zo said, giving the merchant a coin.

The merchant hefted the coin. "Anytime."

Ryn had planned to pay for the trip, but Zo was purposely making sure she didn't have a chance. She wanted to give him some money, but she had a strong feeling he wouldn't take it. She didn't want to make it awkward, so she just filled her heart with gratitude for him, and hoped that she could repay him in some other way.

As they began to walk down the road into Lummi, Ryn stopped.

Zo paused and looked back at her. "What's wrong?"

"This is it. This is the place in my dream."

"What?" Zo's brow furrowed.

"That dream I had of my father. The one where he showed me a man dropping a baby at an orphanage. This is the place!"

"Ryn, how is it your dreams are real?" He cracked his knuckles on his thigh. "That dream on that warm beach in the sunshine. I told you about the break-in. Where you there? Do you remember it?"

Ryn remembered. It was the dream she was having right before Zmej tried to get her to jump off a cliff.

"I remember. I don't know how they're real," she said.

"We should talk to Iden when we get back. Sounds like something Mind magic could do."

"Well, I'm certainly not House Dico. I had just as horrible a reaction to those beads as I did House Viator's at the bead ceremony," Ryn said.

"Hmmmm...."

"My father is from House Dico. Maybe he's been sending me dreams?"

"Maybe." Zo gazed around at the town. "Let's find this orphanage."

At the end of the town on the west side they found it. Just like in her dream there, was a large tree in the front with a swing, and a short fence surrounding the place.

Zo opened the gate in the fence and held it open for Ryn.

She approached the door, reaching for his hand.

"I need you," she said.

"I'm here."

She raised her hand to knock on the door, then stopped.

"I...I...I don't know if I can." she said, burying her face in her hand. "This could change everything."

"Or nothing," he said. "You still love your parents, right?"

"Of course!"

"Then what changes?"

"I don't know...who I am?"

He crouched in front of her so he could be eye level with her. "If you really want to leave, we can turn around and leave right now, but I don't think you do. Courage, little sister, I will always be your brother."

She turned to the door. Raising a shaking hand again, she knocked.

The sound of a chair scraping on the floor and heavy footsteps came from inside. The door opened to a face every child could love—round and open and friendly.

"Shhhh—it's study time!" She pushed them back down the steps as she came to stand on the porch, closing the door behind her. "What do you young ones need?"

Zo nudged her with his elbow and she came back to herself.

"I have been sent by the Library to find the provenance of a book," Ryn managed to get out.

The lady on the porch looked her up and down. "The Library doesn't send workers out to identify records. Usually someone is summoned to the Library."

Ryn nodded. "Yes, but I am in this record, and I need to know."

The orphanage workers' eyes narrowed. "Come inside...quietly!"

They followed her, tiptoeing past a room full of children working at tables to an office off to the side.

"Sit." the worker gestured to the seats in front of the desk. "I am Yvette, director of this orphanage. And who might you be?"

Sitting in the chairs in front of her desk, Ryn felt every bit the student in trouble with the Headmaster, even though her education had been mostly with tutors. Ryn's stomach flip flopped at the possibilities of what this woman could tell her.

Ryn shook her head, trying to clear it, and her anxiousness. "I'm Ryn, I work for the Library, and this is my brother Zo."

Yvette nodded in acknowledgement. "So, where's this record?" she asked.

Ryn jumped. She dug it out of her bag, placing it reverently on the desk in front of Yvette.

Yvette ran her hand over the cover. "Looks familiar." Opening the cover she stopped at the missing front pages. "I can see why you are having trouble identifying this book. What made you think it's ours?"

"I took it to Master Clark, the book binder on Viatoro. He said House Viator buys from him and donates them. Master Walt in book repairs said you're the only orphanage outside Waatch House Viator donates to."

Yvette nodded, as she turned the pages of the book.

"This certainly looks like my handwriting."

When she got to a certain page Ryn stood and pointed to an entry.

"That's me," she said.

Yvette looked up at her, sharp. Her eyes narrowed. "Yes. That was a strange case, and we get a lot of strange cases." Yvette's eyes went unfocused as she remembered. "A young man showed up pounding on the door just before dawn one summer morning." She glanced at them. "Had nothing on but a cloak. There he stood, clutching a newborn baby and sobbing uncontrollably. I was blurry eyed and tired, so I let him stand there as long as he needed. Poor dear." She shook her head slowly. "He said nothing to me, just placed the baby in my arms and fled, still crying." She heaved a sigh. "Children come to us in many ways. His anguish really struck me."

There was silence for a long moment. Tears welled up in Ryn's eyes, but didn't spill over. Zo took her hand and held it.

"Do you know who he was?" Ryn's voice was rough.

"Sorry love, I do not. He had hair white as snow, but he was young with the purest blue eyes. Quite startling and easy to remember, but no one knew who he was, and I've never seen him again," she said.

Ryn bowed her head.

"Your father was here a fortnight or so later, looking for a baby girl to adopt. He was thrilled to take you home." Yvette smiled. Then she cocked her head in thought. She examined Ryn's record more closely, then stood. "Excuse me for a moment." She left the office.

Zo squeezed her hand. "You alright?"

She gave him a half smile, but said nothing.

The office was still, but the sound of a baby crying somewhere upstairs broke the quiet. Zo fiddled with the ties on the top of his pack. After what seemed like hours, but probably wasn't, Yvette returned with cobwebs in her hair.

"Sorry," she huffed as if she had been exerting herself. "I looked everywhere, but I couldn't find it."

"Find what?" Zo asked.

"Some time after your father adopted you, a man came to the door. He had sort of wild hair and an odd look about him, but he was kind enough. He gave us a large donation and a book—an illustrated story book. He said it was to go to you. I told him you'd been adopted. He seemed a bit shocked, but insisted we keep the book in case you or your parents returned. I've searched our storage thoroughly but it's not there. I don't recall anyone taking it, and no one else does either. I'm sorry, I have no idea what happened to it."

Ryn swayed in her seat. Zo put his arm around her to keep her from falling off her chair.

Silence blanketed the office.

Yvette shook her head sadly. "I'm sorry I couldn't be of more help, but I can confirm that this record is for this orphanage. I'll give you the dates."

"Thank you," Ryn managed to get out.

Yvette took out a sheet of paper and wrote out the missing information. Then she tucked it inside the book and stood.

Ryn and Zo followed her to their feet. Ryn accepted the book from Yvette.

"If I find any other information about the missing book, I will write to you at the Library," Yvette said.

"We are grateful, thank you," Zo said, shaking Yvette's hand.

Shouldering their packs, Zo turned Ryn around and led her to the door. She was in a daze all the way out and down the street.

They walked the main road through the village. Ryn watched the villagers about their business in the cold of the snowy day, but didn't really register what was happening.

"We should find a place to spend the night," Zo said.

Ryn nodded absently. She skirted a large puddle of water which put her in front of Zo.

A carriage was coming down the road toward them in a hurry. Ryn's ankle gave out, and she fell into the path of the oncoming carriage.

Zo grabbed her and pulled her out of the way, but not fast enough.

Something on the carriage hit Ryn in the arm, sending her spinning.

* * *

Zo caught Ryn, pulling her over to the side of the road and leaning her against the picket fence.

"You're supposed to let me walk on the outside," he fretted.

"There was a puddle," she said, dazed.

Zo opened her cloak and pulled off her coat to find a gash on her arm. It was starting to bleed a lot. He swore.

Taking a scarf from his bag, he wrapped it around her arm, putting pressure on it.

Ryn's eyes looked up at him, then drifted down to his neck.

"Can you heal it?" she asked him.

Zo didn't know. He'd felt strange inside ever since he'd killed the wolf. He hadn't tried to heal the puncture wounds on his neck, because he was afraid. Afraid something was terribly wrong, and he didn't want to know it.

He took a deep breath, placed his hand on her neck, closed his eyes...and nothing happened. His mind didn't enter her body. His magic didn't come to him. The broken inside of him screamed at him.

"I can't," he said. Then he turned and threw up on the side of the road.

Appendix I: The Ancestral Houses

House Terr
Earth Magic. House seat located on Daoterr

House Mare
Water Magic. House seat located on Shimamare

House Venti
Air Magic. House seat located on Kohventi

House Ignis
Fire Magic. House seat located on Ignisapan

House Lux
Lightning Magic. House Lux is located on Luxpulau

House Viator
Travel Magic. House Viator is located on Viatoro

House Dico
Mind Magic. House Dico is located on Oydico

House Muto
Shape shifting Magic. House Muto is located on Saarimuto

House Sano
Healing Magic. House Sano is located on Eileansano

House Pentral
Spirit Magic. House Pentral is located on Inispentral

House Vivus
Animation Magic. House Vivus in located on Ynysvivus

House Illusio
Illusion magic. House Illusio is located on Iegillusio

Appendix II: Luc's Poem as recorded in *On the Legend of Luc, Praedo's Scribe*

In shadows deep, where ancient echoes sing,
Shores were cursed by the serpent's wing.
Where the beastly dragon ruled the land,
The most majestic mountains stand.

Citizens cowered, afraid for their life,
When Praedo came to end the strife.
Holding great power he set on the quest,
To conquer the dragon, to vanquish the test.

With twelve companions to fight at his side,
The dragon had nowhere safe to hide.
His fierce evil eyes glowed of embering flame,
Praedo outsmarted the dragon with magical game.

Flashes of lightning and roaring thunder,
The earth moved and rocked asunder.
The dragon fell and crashed in the deep,
Where the waters devoured and his corpse sleeps.

Injured our hero fell to the ground,
To aid his needs his friends gathered round.
Alas it was late, as his dying breath whispered,
They drew near to him to help and they heard.

Take ye my bones and turn them to beads,
My magic will guide and protect your needs.
As long as it's used for the good of the land,
Ye shall hold great power within your hand.

Pass this gift down through each family line,
To guard this place throughout all of time.
So they crafted beads from his magical bones,
And wore them round necks like tiny white stones.

What's left must stay safe and must be hidden,
To fall in the wrong hands is forbidden.
From the start where the mountains rise,
The treasure was hidden neath azure skies.

Seek the glade where whispers of pines,
Guard the secret that time defines.
By rivers winding through emerald lands,
Where the eagle soars, the seeker stands.
Follow the call of the owl at night,
To a secret passage where ye will find light.

Appendix III: Gesta Praediana

Invocation
In the verdant fronds of my solitudes,
My verses flourished with a mountain voice.
I sang the archaic echoes of the earth,
In the growing poppies, and the grassy herbs.
In the streamy waters, I sipped the sweet truths,
That the mountain gives to those who love them.

My lyre was foraging for the perfect cadence,
In the vitreous rhythms of a full, cold rain,
And under the moonlight, between sea and sand,
I searched the sonorous accents of the waves.

But alas! My verses turned into a lament,
Under the bright flashes of the traveling star,
Who would have thought that a radiant sky,
Omen would be of such pain and despair?

Sweet melodic accents dying in the ash,
Great agrestal anthems profaned in the flames,
Fire in the forest, trees becoming blaze,
And a solemn requiem left in the night air.

When the somber fumes invaded the skies,
They spread in fields, through cities and towns,
Becoming the voice, the herald, and sign,
Of pain and calamities, misery, and mourn.

But what was the cause of so much commotion?
What turned all my odes into burial hymns?
What tinted the lights of the day with black shadows?
The old vicious dragon and his conquest thirst.

The burdens of servitude fall on our backs,
Where freedom existed, bondage came to be,
Where joyfulness flourished, bitterness remained,
Where beauty and grace blossomed, only rot was seen.

What will bring joy back to the chants?
Who will deliver from the iron yoke?
What will scourge the draconic lord?
The strong arm of Praedo, his power and sword.

Numeration...

Chant I...II...

...XII

Cantum Sanationis
There was perfect silence, all was calm, at rest,
No thunder, nor lightning, no loud fiery sound,
The clouds, humbly parted, made way all around,
For a pillar golden to descend from west.

And there, midst the column of glory and light,
With breastplate now shattered, his helm split apart,
His face bruised and dirtied, yet joy in his heart,
Praedo, smiling, joyful, came down from the sky

It was all completed, we were fin'lly free,
The songs of great gladness returned to the soul,
Like waters soft flowing, the praises made whole,
Exalting brave Praedo, his courage and deeds.

But alas! The earth, the grove once divine,
The rivers, the meadows, all destroyed, decayed,
And there in the ruins, injured, almost dead,
The thirteen brave warriors whom Praedo assigned.

The hero himself was not free from pain,
His proud chest was bleeding, his strength nearly gone,
Yet weak as he faltered, his will carried on,
And showed the last magic we needed to learn

He asked his companions to come, one by one,
And upon their heads his two hands he laid,
He murmured old verses in a distant tongue,
And with gentle power, he healed every face.

With what life remained in his dying frame,
He knelt on the soil, lifeless, torn, yet dear,
And thinking of us, with death drawing near,
He healed mighty rivers, the woods, and the plains.

The forests returned with their emerald hue,
The rivers shone clear like bright crystal streams,
The meadows adorned in gold, white, and green,
But Praedo's face paled as snow's icy blue.

With the breath so faint that still left his chest,
He called his friends close and gave them command:
"Carve beads from my bones, as fate may demand,
That I may yet teach you from my place of rest."

No more did he speak, as his eyes grew still,
His lips, softly smiling, lay calm as he passed,
His deeds may be finished, but echoes will last,
For his songs of valor the ages will fill.

Epilogue
Much have I spoken of Praedo the brave,
Yet little was told of the friend we knew well,
A brother, beloved, in kindness he dwelled,
A heart full of mercy, gentle, pure and grave.

Praedo's great power lay not in the blade,
Nor armor, nor magic, nor bone's sacred thread,

His strength was the truth that his spirit spread,
The faith and conviction he always displayed.

Twelve were his virtues, twelve powers he bore,
Twelve were the magics Praedo passed on,
All held in secret, though never quite gone,
Within the heart's depths forevermore.

The years have now passed, and in solitude,
I've sought my shelter, far from human crowds,
Among the high mountains and under the clouds,
Within the green woods Praedo once renewed.

And now, I've grown old, in a cavern I stay,
And search with my lyre for perfect refrain,
Till under the echoes of earth's arcane,
A deep song of bones calls my heart to play.

I carry the tale of Praedo with me,
His magic, his legacy, close to my breast,
His spirit I've guarded, his memory blessed,
And now I release it with this, my song, free.

Follow these verses to where they shall end,
Where both our stories shall join and resign,
And may his old bones your strength now refine,
When the dragon rises to battle again.

ACKNOWLEDGEMENTS

This book has been a journey, and I'm so grateful for all those who came along for the ride!

To all those who endured reading the original draft of this novel: Angela Snedaker, Lyn McCarty, Lorenzo Frazier, Tracy Shew, and all the readers on The Seventeenth Shard's Reading Excuses—I'm so sorry! It was rough.

I'm grateful to my alpha readers for this new version of The Traveler's Magic. To Amy Maker for catching some embarrassing continuity errors, and to Lorenzo Frazer for being my inspiration and cheerleader, and for always demanding the next chapter. You're the best!

To my Potted Plant Peeps who generously gave up so much of their time to help shape this novel into what it is: To Michael Roth who, as always, spent a long afternoon helping me plot and plan out the new version. A special thanks to Roselyn James, Kim Aippersbach, and Laura Blegen for beta reading the huge mess of a novel this was before they got their hands on it. I can't tell you how much I appreciate you! And to everyone else in the Plont for keeping me from spiraling into destruction. I love you all so much!

To my family and friends: Hannah Lim, John Lim, Aj Lim, Antonio Lim, Tyler Bland, Emily Lim, Maleah Lim, Sumire Lim, Noreen Hosack, Robert Berardinelli, Lorenzo Fraizer, Pietro Berardinelli, Jennifer White, Nikki Johnson, Melanie Cameron, Bridget Shew, Alisa Jeremica, Angela Snedaker, Celia Nilson, Amy Maker, Morgan Cameron, Ej Lim, Derrick Larsen, Yvonne Hamilton, and Jyll Hembre. They have sat in festival booths with me, worn Slayer's Magic t-shirts, recommended my book, hosted book signings, given my book to friends, taken my book on vacation, and handed out hundreds of bookmarks. I couldn't have done this without your support!

To my husband, Benjamin Lim, for pitching my book to absolutely everyone he meets, and for taking care of me so I can spend my evenings and Saturdays writing. I love and appreciate you so much!

Special thanks again to Lehonti Perez Ovalle for continuing to expand Luc's epic poem. Looking forward to seeing it all come together!

Lastly to my publisher William C. Tracy for continuing to believe in me and my magical Library. I appreciate the time you spend adding hundreds of commas to my manuscript, and for pushing me to make my stories better. Your support gets me through the rough spots. You're amazing!

ABOUT THE AUTHOR

CJ grew up in Southern California loving fantasy and science fiction. She is married to her husband of thirty plus years, has four children, and an ever-growing number of grandchildren. Adopted at eight months old, she recently found her birth parents. She has a Master's Degree in Public History from Southern New Hampshire University, and if she's not writing you can generally find her quilting, costuming, or traveling to spend time with those she loves. She's a wannabe dress historian and has worked with museums on historical dress recreation. *The Slayer's Magic* is her first book in *The Beads of Bone* series. You can find CJ at her website cjhosack.com and on Instagram @cj_hosack

Please take a moment to review this book at your favorite retailer's website, Goodreads, or simply tell your friends!

www.ingramcontent.com/pod-product-compliance
Lightning Source LLC
Chambersburg PA
CBHW061337310726
48974CB00001B/79